Tim lives in France close to Cognac, writing, cooking, gardening and enjoying life with his wife and friends. Before retiring, he worked in child protection in the UK, moving on to teach the subject at university. Understanding perpetrators and victims has driven his non-fiction writing, and now this his first novel.

To Pam, Matt and Chris

Tim Cheverton

South Island Slaughter

Austin Macauley Publishers™
London * Cambridge * New York * Sharjah

This is a work of fiction. Names, characters, businesses, places, events, locales, and incidents are either the products of the author's imagination or used in a fictitious manner. Any resemblance to actual persons, living or dead, or actual events is purely coincidental.

A CIP catalogue record for this title is available from the British Library.

ISBN 9781398496712 (Paperback)
ISBN 9781398496729 (Hardback)
ISBN 9781398496736 (ePub e-book)

www.austinmacauley.com

First Published 2023
Austin Macauley Publishers Ltd®
1 Canada Square
Canary Wharf
London
E14 5AA

Table of Contents

Ten Years Ago

She stops abruptly, feeling a shiver run up her spine, causing her shoulders to pull up into an involuntary shrug. Sucking in a hissing stream of breath, she moves forward. A rotund bald-headed man with a wispy ginger moustache and wearing a blue overcoat lays dead in the hallway. Superintendent Sylvia Greening steps over him and there to her left, on the floor of the lounge, is the body of a young woman staining the white carpet red. Sylvia notices the old-fashioned hat stand holding three coats, a cloche hat and beside it three pairs of walking boots decreasing in size. She hears approaching sirens and flashing blue lights reflect in hallway mirrors engulfing her. She turns swiftly towards the closed door to her right, but hears movement above. Looking up, she is taken by the ornately carved mahogany banister and on the opposite wall a fresco of plump pink cherubs climbing ivy upwards. 'Cully!'

'Here Sylvia.' She hurries up the stairs, slowing halfway to avoid an arm sticking through the landing banister. Catching her breath, she moves on until she is standing on the landing, looking down at a dead man with a *café au lait* complexion. 'In here.'

Feeling uneasy, Sylvia walks slowly into the large bedroom where she finds him kneeling on the floor beside Caitland. He presses a blood-soaked towel against her chest. 'There were four of them,' he mutters, but does not take his eyes from the grey contorted face of his wife. 'Where the fuck are the paramedics?'

'I counted three.' Sylvia, suddenly afraid, adrenaline pumping, looks around. 'Tizard said it was clear.'

'A fool, but he's right. There's one in the bathroom. Caitland got him before…'

'Paramedics are coming,' Sylvia assures him, hearing foot-steps on the stairs. 'You've been hit, Cully. You need help.'

'It's nothing. She mustn't die.'

'She won't.' Paramedics appear and as one eases Cully away the other takes over the task of stemming blood flow. 'Come away,' Sylvia encourages. 'Let them do their job.'

'I'm not leaving Caitland.'

'Let's get your wounds seen to.' She leads him towards the door. 'More help up here. Hurry!'

'This was meant to be a safe house,' Cully mumbles.

'I know.'

'The protection team outside?'

'Both dead,' Sylvia tells him, touched he thinks about them. 'Where is Linda?'

'There.' Cully nods to the wardrobe on the far side of the room, in the door of which are two dark bullet holes. 'Go see please. I can't.'

Sylvia cannot ever remember feeling maternal, but suddenly she dreads opening the wardrobe door as if it's her own child in there. She knows Linda, has done since she was born and cannot rationalise how she feels. Taking a grip on the handle, she hesitates, but taking a deep breath pulls. There is a shrill scream and in the corner of the wardrobe, beneath a row of women's clothes, a thin teenager is curled into a ball.

'Dad?' she asks.

'He's here,' Sylvia smiles thinly.

'Mum?' Some change on Sylvia's face alerts her. 'Mummy!'

Present Time Friday

'Ma'am.'

'I'm going home.' Chief Constable Sylvia Greening knew that her wife would be furious if she misses another of their special Friday nights in, wine, fish and chips in front of a blazing log fire. There used to be sex, but how long since they even tried on the sheepskin rug in front of the smouldering embers of the fire? 'Bloody metaphors!'

'Sorry?'

'Nothing to concern you, Jade,' she sighs. 'Get someone else.'

'It's the Island, Ma'am.'

'Has it been cast adrift and floated into foreign waters? They can bloody have it. Now, excuse me, Jade.'

'No Ma'am, it's still there and this is serious.'

'Fuck! Do you want to hear an Island joke?'

'Ma'am?'

'They don't do high five over there, they do high six and I've got another one.'

'Ma'am, please?'

'You know I used to work there, only for two thankless years.' Sylvia groans. 'What is it?'

'There's been a shooting at a school, at least five dead, maybe more.'

'Shit!' The place always causes problems. 'Who is the senior officer there?'

'Inspector Lisa Lynn.'

'Haven't we got anyone senior?'

'You sacked them all, Ma'am.'

'No,' she remembers, 'it wasn't me, it was a tribunal recommendation that the management team agreed with and the Commissioner supported. He even went on the news and said it was vital we cleanse the force of discriminatory practice.' She shakes her head, for no other reason than she needs a smoke. 'Even the Union rep' didn't object too strongly.'

'Ma'am, we've not replaced the officers that went, or Superintendent Harris,' Jade persists.

'He committed suicide.'

'You remember, Ma'am?'

'Of course, I bloody remember, he only had to retire with full pension, instead of hanging himself and causing me headaches.' She'd personally gone to see him, driven through a bleak landscape where troglodytes worked the soil and one could never escape the smell of pig shit. 'Bloody Island, like Alabama, full of ingrates.' Dropping her case to the floor, Sylvia returns behind her desk and sits, Friday night-in already a memory. 'Jade, I need coffee, probably lots. What school?'

'The private one.'

'That rings a bell.' Sylvia knows she's on the edge, of exactly what she isn't certain, but certainly looking down into blackness. It is affecting her memory. 'Jesus no! That's where Cully was going to his reunion. He didn't want to go, but I encouraged him. Surely to God he's not been shot again. Ring him.'

'It's ringing,' states Jade, holding the phone to her ear. 'Superintendent Cully, are you ok? Good, I've got the Chief Constable for you.'

'Cully, difficult to hear you.'

'I'm,' he hesitates, 'about to catch the ferry. There are some forest gremlins chasing around and reception out west is never good, Ma'am.'

'You Islanders are weird.'

'No weirder than you overners, Ma'am.'

'Perhaps not,' she sighs. 'Did you go to the reunion?'

'I bottled it, like I told you when we had lunch, it was Linda's idea and I was never keen. Too many bad memories. Really enjoy lunch with you and—'

'Stop!'

'You sound a bit…'

'Stressed, you can say it, Cully, and yes I do, enjoy lunch.' Probably enjoy it too much, she thinks, remembering they usually finish a bottle of good red. It's becoming a habit, lunch with him, like an oasis of calm that left her wondering if it was too late to switch to heterosexual or at least bi?

He is still talking. 'I've had a good day though. Did all the other stuff I planned to do.'

'Shut up, Cully.'

'Understood, no more small talk.'

'Sorry, I'm about to ruin your evening, we've got an emergency. You've not heard the news?'

'No.'

An alarm goes off close by followed by running footsteps.

'What's that noise?' she asks.

'Someone's car alarm,' he lies easily. 'How can I help, Ma'am?'

'I'm relieved you're ok and still on South bloody Island. You are now acting SIO until I send someone else. Nothing against you, but I can see the ethical conflicts coming and I don't need more problems. I'll clear it with the Commissioner. I've really got no choice and you are the best.'

'Thanks Ma'am, but in charge of what?'

'The slaughter at your old school. Hurry, Cully, get there.'

++++

There is no rush. Cully is twenty minutes closer to the school than he'd let Sylvia believe.

The emergency in the other room is over and the place is quiet again. Odd, but he likes the hospice. It is peaceful, restful and he can think clearly sitting there. It smells nice, not like a hospital, but like heaven. He thinks they should market the perfume, make a fortune to keep the place running. He contributes, of course he does, but there is a limit to what he can do.

The door opens and a young nurse brings him a mug of leaded tea. If you're dying, the last thing you need is messed with stuff in a small cup. 'Something happen in the next room?'

'Charlie died.' There are no platitudes, nothing about passing away or being at peace. When you die, you die. 'We've been expecting it. His parents were there at the end. Charlie was only ten, poor kid.'

'I'm sorry.'

'Kids are the most difficult to…to care for.' She manages a thin smile. 'But now there's the tragedy at the school,' and she tells him about the shooting. 'It's all over the news. Who'd do that?' she wonders aloud.

'No idea,' Cully shrugs, glancing at the man in the bed. 'Thanks for the tea. I'll be heading off soon.'

'Back to the mainland?'

'If only,' but adds nothing more. 'Is your shift nearly over?'

'I'm half time here. I've got another eight hours at the General, but that's a break from this place.'

She leaves and the door sighs closed.

'Leave Sabrina alone, Cully.'

'I thought you were asleep Jamie.'

'In and out. Morphine is wonderful. I've got shares in the company that makes it.' Acetaminophen, haloperidol, lorazepam, prochlorperazine, and atropine, he'd had them all and many more he'd forgotten about because when you are dying your memory plays tricks. 'The one thing it doesn't do is dull the pain from that bloody school,' he hisses. 'She looks like your daughter, like…'

'Linda,' Cully prompts. 'The nurse?'

'Yes. I'm guessing you weren't looking at her face.'

'We've been friends far too long,' Cully laughs. 'You've been a good Godfather to Linda.'

'Fuck God! You should know I've left most of my money to this place, but Linda will get enough for a descent deposit on a place of her own and she can have the morphine shares. It's time she moved out.'

'You want her to leave me all alone?'

'No, so a woman can move in with you,' he sighs. 'It's been ten years, Cully.'

'The Chief rang,' Cully says softly, ignoring the reference to Caitland. 'She's made me SIO.'

'Of course she has,' Jamie mutters, 'she's predictable, like you, Cully. I'm her accountant and know everything, secrets and lies, about all my clients.'

'You know all my secrets Jamie.'

'And you know mine, every last painful detail.' Jamie coughs, a wet guttural sound. Cully rises, reaches for a glass of water, is careful to avoid the morphine drip and wires running to various monitors, and helps him take sips of water before mopping his chin. 'She shaves me, I rather enjoy it.'

'She?'

'Sabrina, stop being obtuse. You'd make a reasonably good nurse, Cully and…Jesus! Why can't I remember names? Don't help me. Your wife,' he groans. 'Caitland, that's it, she said you were a gentle caring man.'

'But I couldn't protect her.'

'And you can't save me my friend. Shouldn't you be going?'

'No.' The curtains are drawn, the electric light soft, the constant temperature in the room warm. A cocoon Cully had no wish to leave and has to glance at his watch to get what time it is. 'I suppose I'm reluctant to go. I'm guessing, avoidance is what Sophie would call it.'

'Have you seen her?'

'Not for thirty years. What if she's one of the dead?'

'She won't be,' Jamie states with confidence. 'She could move in with you. You were perfect together.'

'My darling daughter Linda,' Cully begins having learned to give clues to whom he is talking about, 'reads her book over and over and comes out with all this psycho-babble stuff. She says I should read it.'

'You should, if only the first chapter, powerful stuff.'

'Linda says I'm too buttoned-up, never grieved properly for Caitland. Emotional repression. It helps to be a white male, apparently. No woman would put up with me for long.' Cully sits back down. 'I see you've got her book,' and lifts it from the side. There is a picture of Sophie on the back, shoulder length light brown hair framing a smiling face. 'She hasn't changed. She's been to see you Jamie?'

'She has. Gives the book to everyone she works with. She'll sort you out, Cully,' he chuckles.

'You're a bad man. I should go,' and Cully forces himself to stand.

'Swing my laptop round will you, there's a film I want to watch?' The shiny new machine is supported on a metal arm and Cully does as he's asked. The password is printed on a sticky next to the mouse pad. 'Amazing, one can manage the world through this thing. Now go. Take the book and be careful my friend.'

'Not to worry Jamie, I'll be fine,' and takes the man's skeletal hand. 'I'll keep you out of it as long as I can.'

Stepping outside the building, Cully looks about. Dusk, a relatively warm evening for March, a week before Easter Bank Holiday, but can feel fingers of a chill breeze reaching in off the sea. Bloody Island! To Cully it is as much a state of mind as a physical place. His grandmother once said, 'You can take the boy out the Island, but not the Island out the boy.' He'd always hoped she was wrong, but knew deep down she wasn't. Apart from an occasional visit he rarely came and certainly not to go near the school. Thirty years had slipped by and yet it's beginning to feel like yesterday.

++++

Fifteen minutes later, with his car parked away from the school, Cully walks back in time.

Phone rings and he instantly recognises the number.

'Ma'am?'

'Are you there yet?'

'Just got here. Walking towards the school now.'

'Took your time.'

'Island roads, Ma'am.'

'Horrendous I remember, all potholes and old people on the wrong side. I didn't mean to snap.'

'Understandable and you're missing Friday night in.'

'Yes.' Had she really told him about that? She relaxes too much during their cosy lunches, when she needs to talk. He was, after all, a friend as much as a bloody good detective. What else has she told him? There would be no more lunches, but who is she kidding? 'Sorry, to drop you in it, Cully, but we've already got the gang shooting and there's something happening up north, don't know what yet, but sounds bad. MIU are on both.'

'Have you told DI Lynn I'm coming? I bet she's pissed.'

'Relieved I think. She's asked for extra officers to be sent over. I'm doing my best, but it won't be until tomorrow or even Sunday. You'll cope. I'm not going home. I'm here for you, Cully, I think it's going to be a busy weekend,' she sighs desperate to get outside for another smoke. 'Take care.'

Cully shows his ID to the bored-looking uniform at the outer cordon and again to another at the school gate. The officer writes his name on a clipboard and lifts the tape for Cully to duck under. It's then the blow hits him, hard in the stomach taking his breath away, forcing him to bend over and clasp his knees.

'You alright Sir?'

'Yes, stitch, I shouldn't eat and run.' Standing upright, Cully takes one cautious step and then another. Linda told him there was a chapter in Sophie's book dealing with rekindled historical stress, something like PTSD. He should read it. He hadn't. A couple of years back he arrested an ex-soldier after he shot and killed four mates at a regimental reunion. The defence psychiatrist remarked that "aging is a chance to face hidden conflicts".

Pausing, Cully cannot deny he is aging and taking a deep breath enters the place he'd sworn never to return to where conflicts were sure to follow.

Walking down the drive, he admires a large modern glass and steel teaching block to his left, a smaller one to his right, and there is the cycle shed. A memory forces its way through and grinning, Cully recalls fumbling there with Sophie, his first feel of naked female thigh, and later something more serious with Jenny.

Emerging into the upper quadrangle he sees the tuck shop has gone, as has the urinal where they used to compete to see who could piss the highest. Ahead is the school hall with playing fields in the distance. Between him and the hall are ambulances, police cars and a fire engine all sparkling in a blue neon haze. Easing between them he catches sight of himself in a wing mirror, forty-eight, fox face, tired with short-cut brown hair where once he'd a mop of curls. Moving on, he comes upon a group of people, one of whom he instantly recognises and for a moment thinks he's going to vomit, but controlling himself steps forward. 'DI Lynn?'

'Ah, Sir, good to have you here.' She means it, there is relief in her voice. 'You found us.'

'Sorry, we meet under these circumstances. It looks like you've got things under control.'

'Organised chaos I think, Sir.'

'Sir?' A man's voice. 'Sergeant Tizard.' Tall, dark haired, dressed for war in black, wearing a bullet-proof vest, a side arm and carrying an automatic rifle. 'We've met.'

'We have,' Cully agrees reasonably, but through teeth gritted hard, remembering the sham board of enquiry that cleared Tizard. 'What are you doing?'

'My men and dog teams are searching the school grounds in case the shooter is still here.'

'Then get back to that while I meet with Inspector Lynn and her team.'

'Sir,' and he retreats.

'Let me introduce Sergeant Tom Whitworth and DC Indah Kasali. I've already sent DC Kerry Harris to the hospital as family liaison, but we'll need more bodies. We're all that's left in CID. They can't fill the vacancies. No one wants to come here after what happened.' Lisa is nervous, babbling. 'You'll know about the sackings?' He nods. 'People are still raw.'

'I'll do my best to tread carefully, but no promises.'

'Understood,' Lisa answers. 'I've called in every uniform, community officer and volunteer I can,' she explains. 'We've secured the hall, no one else to go in until you arrive. We've established an inner and outer perimeter round the school.'

'You sent armed officers to the hospital?'

'Yes, but we've only got eight available.'

'I'll ask for more, but lots happening, on the mainland. I'm sure the Chief Constable will tell me there's a limited budget, even for multiple murder. Incident room?'

'The Vicar from the church opposite has given us the church hall.'

'On the car radio, there was talk of explosions as well as shots. So, we need bomb disposal to check it out before anyone else goes in.'

'Like the City shooting,' begins Indah, large brown eyes bright with intelligence, 'when the gunman shot-up the takeaway, the services went in and a bomb detonated killing paramedics and police.'

'Exactly, we can't be too careful,' Cully smiles at her. 'I'll phone and get them here.'

++++

'Bomb disposal on way,' Cully announces, slipping his phone away. 'Tell me about casualties.'

'Five dead still in the hall and several injured taken to hospital,' answers Tom Whitworth from behind a neat ginger moustache, below glasses and a head of curly red hair. 'The hall was crowded to watch a film before dinner.'

'I should have been there.'

'Sir?'

'It's why I'm on the Island Tom. I went to this school thirty years ago. Imagine I know nothing. Let me have all you've got so far.'

Reading from his notebook Tom explains that at six-thirty one hundred guests gathered for drinks on the lawn in front of School House before going into the hall. There, they were due to see a film the sixth-formers produced followed by a three course dinner for which they each paid one hundred pounds. The event was organised by the Alumni Association to raise funds for a new music room. This was the first of identical events scheduled for future weekends. Five past year groups had been invited this evening. Two tables of ten for each year. Sixth-form pupils were hosting, serving drinks, helping with food. They had caterers in.

'Very clear Tom. I'll say this again later, Lisa, but the team need to put aside the fact I used to attend and was coming tonight.'

'Understood.'

'We'll need to interview the caterers when we can, but make the pupils a priority. Indah you can do that?'

'Certainly,' she nods.

'What about the guests?'

'We've been rounding people up,' answers Tom. 'We've collected them from all over the campus, terrified, hiding and there are a few I think ran home or back to where they are staying.'

'We have to trace those,' Cully states before glancing at his watch, aware how important these first few hours are in any investigation.

'Apart from the ones that ran away we've got them in classrooms ready to be processed, group by group,' Lisa explains, anxious to keep his attention.

'You really don't need me, Lisa, you and your team are good.'

'Thank you, but I think we, I need you Sir,' she says. 'As far as we know we're looking at one gunman with an automatic weapon entering the hall a fraction after seven when the film was about to start. The place was in darkness. I've briefly spoken to a couple of guests. They say he or she had lights.'

'Lights?' Cully thinks. 'Maybe a laser sight to target people,' he suggests.

'It does seem that all the casualties were from two tables on the right as you enter the hall, therefore from the same year.'

'What year?'

'Ninety.'

'Shit, my year, I know these people.' For a moment, he feels faint, but taking several deep breaths recovers his composure. 'Lisa, find us some uniforms able to step up to CID. Pick good ones, rather than random volunteers.'

'Got one here,' she says, pleased to quickly respond. 'Officer White.'

'Ma'am.' Short blond hair, he stands tall, two metres plus with a ramrod back. 'What can I do?'

'You are working with CID now.'

'Ma'am.'

'This is Superintendent Cully; you'll take orders from him.'

'I'm guessing you've a military background Officer White?'

'Petty Officer in the navy, Sir.'

'Good to meet you. What do people call you?'

'Chalky.'

'I had a teacher here called Chalky White.'

'My dad,' he smiles.

'Really?' Cully is surprised how easily memories return. 'You've got a sister.' Chalky nods, grinning, showing rows of perfect white teeth. 'You're twins, I remember. Your dad took us on a school trip and the two of you came along.'

'That's right, to a museum.'

'I remember, because your dad told me off for chatting to your sister. I liked your dad. How is he?'

'In a nursing home, but ok.'

'Your sister?'

'She lives on the mainland,' Chalky answers. 'She's married with kids and I'm married with twin girls.'

'It's in the genes. It'll be good to work with you Chalky. First task, we need a guest list.'

'On it,' and he jogs into the gathering darkness.

Cully smiles as he realises Lisa, Tom and Indah are staring at him. 'Let's get down to business. Tom, form two teams each with SOCO and a couple of uniforms and start processing guests. I want each person searched, contact details taken, any immediate witness stuff recorded, swabbed for gunpowder residue, phones taken and tell them they won't be getting their cars back tonight so we need keys.'

'That all, Gov?' Tom stares, surprise etched on his face. 'They won't be happy.'

'I'm not looking for happiness, I'm looking for thoroughness. We have to assume the shooter might be amongst them or one of them might be involved. Get Tizard to supply armed officers to shadow you just in case.'

'He won't like that.'

'I don't give a fuck about his feelings, tell him, it's an order. If he argues, refer him to me. Indah, you've got your task while the Inspector and I have a chat. Now go on you two, it's going to take a while so the quicker we start the better.' Cully turns to DI Lynn. 'Let's talk.'

++++

'Sorry about that.'

'What Sir?'

'Please call me Cully, Gov, if that feels better. I was off about Tizard in front of the others, not professional, but he and I have history.'

'Not to worry, he's not a favourite of mine either. Thinks he's God's gift, whizzing around on his motorbike. He does his job, but in his own way,' she shrugs.

'Ok to call you Lisa?' She nods. 'Did you go inside the hall?'

'Only to the inner doors, off the foyer.' They step into a pool of light spilling out from a hall window. Lisa takes a deep breath. She is a tall thin woman in her early thirties with short blonde hair and striking blue eyes. She wears a black overcoat and red scarf. 'The paramedics were already there. I didn't think about secondary bombing. Sorry, this is all beyond me.'

'Who was first on scene?'

'We got a treble nine call at seven ten and the patrol car was here at seven-twenty followed by the ambulances. I got here at about seven-forty. You've seen things like this before?

'I have, only eighteen months ago.'

'Shit! Of course, sorry Gov,' she's flustered, 'you and your daughter.'

'Plus two other officers, but we all lived. So, we count our blessings and the shooter died at the scene in our case, shot dead by Tizard as it happens. I can't escape the man. Let's concentrate on what's happening tonight shall we?'

'Sure, Gov. I know you've just arrived, but what's this about? Sorry, I remember your lecture at the staff college on multiple killings. It was fascinating.'

'Maybe, but it was academic,' Cully shrugs. After the last shooting, weeks after he and Linda were released from hospital Sylvia offered him a permanent post at the college, giving him more time to look after Linda through rehabilitation. Regular hours, free at weekends and much less risk of being shot again. 'Don't you dare!' Linda screamed, hobbling into the kitchen from the lounge. 'You're a cop dad, not some smart arse teacher.' He'd threatened to kick her crutch away, but she was right. 'I've no doubt,' he shakes his head, looking directly at Lisa, 'the media will label this a spree killing, postal or serial, they'll find a headline. We give killers fancy titles, but they're all murderers. Nothing changes in the way we investigate; the only difference is the size of the problems we face. We look for motive, means and opportunity. Not that we need to look far for the last two. So, that leaves motive. Any ideas, Lisa?'

'Me, I've got no idea,' she admits. 'Maybe, an angry disillusioned pupil?'

'We've never had one in this country and no school massacre since the nineties and that was a deranged adult on children and teachers, but yes the angry student is one place to start. It'll be interesting to see what Indah gets from the sixth formers. Maybe a disillusioned staff member. Perhaps an angry parent who paid a fortune, but their kid failed to make grades good enough to get to Oxbridge.'

'Oxbridge?'

'Oxford or Cambridge'

'Right,' Lisa nods, 'forgot this place is posh. I was about to say a mentally disturbed person, but anyone who does this has to be…'

'Not necessarily, not always mad or psychiatrically ill.'

'Sociopathic then?'

'Possibly,' Cully nods. 'What about a gun nut? He or she dreams, fantasises for years about what might be done and finally does it? Sorry, I'm being tedious.'

'Don't apologise, Gov, it's fascinating. Why not kill children?'

'It's the Easter break.'

'Then wait for two weeks until the children are back. There are still some borders in residence on the other campus.'

'Children with no home to go to, poor buggers. I wonder what security the rich kids have there? Maybe the risk was too great so he goes for a soft target.'

'He?'

'Normally,' Cully shrugs. 'Going back to your mentally ill offender, is he or she responsible for their actions? Ultimately, are they fit to plead? Then there's revenge. But no one has a right to take another human life,' Cully mutters, remembering his own confused conflicted feelings after Caitland and years later after Linda. 'Because there's the Rule of Law and justice system.'

'What if justice fails, Gov?'

Cully sighs deeply, recalling how anger and desire for revenge consumed him, but pragmatism saved him. Did it mean he lacked passion? Yet if he'd done something on either occasion he'd been sent to prison and Linda would have had no one to look after her. His mind flashes to his daughter, wondering how scarred she really is, scarred in places he could not see.

'Gov?'

'Sorry, I'm thinking things through. We need to get ready for a slew of cranks ringing in claiming responsibility. We're in for a tough few days, Lisa.' He smiles reassuringly at her. 'We'll be fine.'

Lisa nods her head. 'Sometimes I wish I wasn't a cop.'

'Join the club,' agrees Cully. 'Let's get back to reality.'

'Sorry to interrupt,' says Chalky. 'Here's the guest list. What next?'

'I'm liking you already Chalky. Stay with me.'

'You in charge,' demands a voice coming closer. A short man in a dark suit with thinning hair and a florid complexion appears beside Cully. 'Are you?'

'I am. I'm Superintendent Cully. Let's step over here, shall we?'

++++

'How can I help?'

'I'm Dr Inskip, the Executive Head.'

'What does that mean, the executive bit?'

'We have an early years with baby room, junior school, senior school, sixth form and border section, each with a separate head and I sit—'

'At the top.'

'Exactly.'

'How can I help you?' Cully repeats, disliking the man already, but why? Maybe he simply dislikes headteachers or teachers in general? 'What do you want?'

'This is a terrible tragedy, but I have to think of the school. Parents are ringing, demanding to know what's going on. The media is clamouring outside, we're on the news. How long will you be?'

'Dr Inskip, the shooting happened less than two hours ago. There are five dead and many wounded. This is going to take days, even weeks to sort out.'

'But…'

'Dr Inskip…' Cully changes his tone. Deep breath. Be nice, he needs this man's cooperation. Give him something to do, make him feel useful. 'You can help us. We need a list of all current senior pupils, any you've been worried about and any angry parents.'

'Worried about?'

'You've heard of Sandy Hook, Columbine…?'

'Yes, of course I have, but that's America and no child from this school would do anything like that I can assure you Superintendent Cully.' He pauses thoughtfully. 'Cully, Cully…I know that name. Are you an Islander, Cully?' The detective nods. 'Your uncle is an Alumni. He's a troublemaker.'

'That's him,' Cully agrees, aware that his uncle Adam takes his causes seriously. 'Back to business. You can't be certain Dr Inskip, that a pupil wouldn't do something like this, because none of us really know what goes on in the minds of people we are close to, let alone children we teach. You'd be surprised. Parents, staff, anyone you can think of that worried you?' Cully persists encouragingly. 'Think, please.'

'I am and will, but it's difficult to believe. I had to sack a chemistry teacher, Mr Turner before Christmas.'

'Why?'

'He had an affair with an administrator and the poor girl attempted suicide. Crystal left here and works at the court building. She was troubled. Turner is a Christian, he wouldn't do anything like this.'

'He had an affair,' Cully smirks. 'We'll need his details.'

'Of course,' he hesitates. 'What about the other events, tomorrow and Sunday?'

'You've got more things organised?' Issacs nods. 'Cancel them. We can't risk it. Do you understand?'

'Yes of course, but surely he wouldn't strike again?'

'He or she might. We don't know the motive yet. If this is someone with psychiatric issues, they are unpredictable. Sir, do you understand?'

'Yes, sorry, I'm struggling to take all this in.'

'Of course you are,' Cully nods sympathetically. 'Dr Inskip this is officer White, he's going to come with you to get what we need, including access to all CCTV. We will speak later, I promise. Now, I must get on,' and Cully walks away into the gloom. There is light spilling out from School House creating shadows across the lawn, enough to see a group of Community Officers gathered on and around a bench. 'Hello, thank you for turning out.'

'Wouldn't have missed it,' beams a young woman that Cully realises is a uniformed police officer. 'Oh God, that sounds terrible, I didn't mean anything by it,' she mumbles anxiously. 'What must you think of me?'

'I think you are keen and enthusiastic. New?'

'Newish, that obvious?'

'Yeah because you're still mixing with Community Support Officers rather than butch wooden tops.' Cully grins as shocked faces stare back at him. 'I'm joking. You're all perfect for what I need. Enjoying the job constable?'

'Yes, Sir.'

'What's your name?'

'Rebecca Shaw, but Becky is what people call me. You need me, rather us?'

'I do. Do you know who I am?'

'Oh yes, I looked you up on my phone,' says Becky. 'You're the great detective.'

'I get by. I have a task for you all.'

'Anything you want Sir.'

'Forget Sir, use Gov.'

'Yes Gov, we want to help.'

'Becky, stop it,' snaps a man at the back. 'I'm Jack, the oldest and…'

'The most experienced person here I'm guessing. Good to meet you Jack. We have a hundred or so guests that need processing. They're not happy because of what's happened, the shock and fear, but also what we're having to do to them.'

'Searching them I bet, cavity searches?'

'Searching yes Becky, not cavity, but taking gunpowder residue swabs amongst other things. I'm guessing the thing making them especially furious is that we are taking their phones and keeping their cars.'

'Ouch!'

'Exactly. We have to arrange transport. I'm thinking we or rather you could organise something around buses and taxis.'

'Like a transport hub,' says Jack. 'The road that goes by the church has a regular service and we could set up a taxi rank.'

'Perfect Jack. You're in charge. Ring the bus company and the taxi firms and get things going. We'll start escorting people across in about forty minutes, ten at a time. They will be angry, probably rarely travel on a bus and regard public taxis with suspicion. Finally, they pay, not us.'

++++

Cully takes deep breaths. He knows the target tables contained pupils from his year and in this classroom were the unwounded survivors. Sensing his reluctance, Lisa opens the door ahead of them. Entering they find four people sitting behind slopped wooden desks, well apart, not talking. The Reverend, elbows on desk, hands clasped, eyes closed, mumbling in prayer. Behind him a woman with shoulder length curly light brown hair. A well-groomed man sits a couple of desks away from her and on the far side of the room a plump woman with long black hair taps on her phone. 'I know you,' she says, lifting her head and pointing at Cully.

'We all know him, don't we Superintendent Cully?'

'From a long time ago, Judge.'

'You are something of a star and now here you are back with us in this classroom. We did French in here.'

'Not one of my strengths,' admits Cully.

'You were a history man, knew it all.'

'Drama, you were good at drama, Cully,' says the curly haired woman.

'Hi Sophie.' Even after thirty years he knows her and not just from the photograph on the back of her book. From somewhere deep inside, her smell and touch return to him and he shivers. 'You've not changed,' he mutters.

'Liar,' she smiles, flicking a strand of hair from her face. 'You ok?'

'Gov!'

'Sorry Lisa, Inspector, yes, we need to stay focussed,' Cully acknowledges.

'This is outrageous, I need to be with my husband, he's wounded,' grumbles the other woman. 'I'm Megan Simpson.'

'Settle down Megan, the police have a job to do,' Judge Patrick Le Strange says calmly, adjusting his tie. Clean shaven with short blonde hair, he is dressed in a tailored pin-striped suit. 'I would like to know about Andrew. I rang the hospital, but they said the police told them not to share information. I understand why, but, Cully, do you know, how is he?'

'I'll find out.'

'We nearly didn't come,' Patrick continues, shaking his head, 'but by chance I'm sitting here next week and we saw it as an opportunity for a break away.'

'Can we get on please?'

'Be quiet Megan.'

'Why should I Sophie? They are treating us like criminals.'

'I'm DI Lynn and everyone is a suspect Mrs Simpson until we clear you.'

'You can't think?' she grumbles. 'You can't do this?'

'Of course, they can,' Patrick glares at her. 'Always complaining, weren't you?'

'I must see Philip.'

'You will Mrs Simpson,' Lisa says calmly, 'when we've finished with you. We are moving as quickly as we can.'

'Remember spin the bottle, Cully?' Sophie grins.

'That was disgusting,' Megan groans, 'kissing people you didn't want to. I had to kiss John Carter once, ugh.'

'Don't be mean.'

'You liked kissing Cully didn't you Sophie?'

'Stop it Megan,' says Patrick.

'Loved snogging him until Jenny took him off you.'

'That was thirty years ago,' Sophie grimaces.

'Loved him.'

'In the play,' Sophie mumbles. 'You didn't do drama did you Megan?'

'No need, she's a drama queen all on her own,' offers Patrick. 'Leave Sophie alone.'

'I should be at the hospital, they might need me,' Reverend Skeets mutters.

'The Monk speaks,' snaps Megan. 'That's what we called you, remember?'

'If they need you, we will get you there Martin,' says Cully. 'How are you?'

'A little shaky.'

'I was lucky,' Sophie blurts, 'I had to go to the loo. I was in there when I heard the noise. I sat terrified, shaking until one of your officers knocked on the door and coaxed me out. Please thank her, Indah I think, she was nice. I'm pathetic.'

'Pathetic is the word,' groans Megan.

'Sophie, I'm pleased you're okay and ignore Megan, what was it we called her, Dumpy Grumps,' continues Patrick, 'she's always had a tongue like sandpaper.'

'You didn't see anything Sophie?' asks Cully.

'I didn't.'

'Always hiding away Sophie.'

'Shut up Megan,' snaps Patrick. 'You really are a ghastly woman.'

'Sean O'Leary was shot,' Sophie says softly. 'Cully, you were good mates once.'

'I was in the hall when it happened, if you're interested,' Megan pouts.

'You hid under the table,' Patrick retorts, 'emerged crying your eyes out.'

'My Philip was shot.'

'Please, we shouldn't be arguing like this, not…' Martin stutters.

'We will make this as quick as possible,' Lisa intervenes, sensing things are degenerating and they were back in the sixth form common room of thirty years ago, 'but there are procedures we need to follow. I'll take brief contact details and any immediate accounts of what happened. We need to search you.'

'I won't stand for this.'

'Then sit for it,' Patrick snaps. 'Go on Inspector.'

'Scenes of crime officers will swab for gunpowder residue and take your mobile telephones. We will keep your cars, but arrange transport. Please don't leave the Island until we say so.'

Cully moves towards the door.

'You won't forget about Andrew?' Patrick asks.

'Of course not. Do you want a lift there tonight?'

'I'm a coward, I'd rather know how he is first. I'm staying at the hotel on the high street, the school did a block booking. Here's my card with my mobile number on it.'

'We'll get back to you,' Cully tells him, 'I promise.'

++++

Feeling nauseous, Cully finds somewhere outside in the darkness where he can be sick, but resists the urge as he has done most of his life, at least since his mother died when he was eight. Since then he regarded it as a challenge, annoying grandmother when he would sit for ages on the bathroom floor leaning against the bath panel, drinking water and refusing to give in. He once overheard Uncle Adam saying it was his way of finding some control in life having been abandoned by his father and mother. Linda would tell him to talk to Sophie about it. He fumbles for his phone. 'Jade, is Sylvia there?'

'Hello Cully, she's having another ciggie to calm her nerves. How's it going?'

Cully explains, finishing with a plea: 'I need to get out of here. The gunman targeted my year-group. I knew these people,' he groans. 'Now spin the bottle has come up.'

'That takes me back,' Jade laughs, 'having to kiss boys I hated to get to the one I wanted and I married him. Here she comes. Ma'am, it's Cully.'

'What does he want this time?'

'Ma'am, sorry to be a nuisance,' he reluctantly apologises and softens his tone. 'This won't work, I know these people too well and they know me. It was long ago, but feels like yesterday,' he sighs. 'They are regressing.'

'Are you?'

'Not yet.'

'There is no one to replace you.'

'What about Amelia? She's an experienced DCI,' he emphasises. 'She comes here and I go back to where I should be, running MIU.'

'Don't shout,' she warns. 'It's an idea, but I mentioned the thing in the north, well it's a house invasion with three dead including children. Possibly a family…what do you academic types call it?'

'Family annihilation.'

'Right, horrible phrase. Amelia's up there as we speak and the gang shooting is turning out to be far more complex than expected. You've trained them superbly so I know they can cope.'

'Touché Ma'am.' He takes a breath. 'Ok, I get it, but I need extra people.'

'By morning, I promise. The Navy bomb squad are on their way. You'll make it work, I have faith in you, Cully.'

Normally, when he comes to a new investigation he goes easily through the gears, knowing what needs to be done, his thinking clear and focussed, but not this time. Tentacles of anxiety run up and down his arms and across his chest. He takes more deep breaths to control the stress. Is he having a heart attack? It would certainly be a way out. Stop, breath and do the job like any other.

Cully stands on the steps to the teaching block.

'Chalky?'

'Gov. I've got the pupil lists, staff lists and seating plan from Dr Inskip. I've got uniform collecting CCTV film. What can I do next?'

'You'll know what a helicopter needs to land safely.'

'On a frigate rolling around in rough conditions I do.'

'How about on a school field on a dark chilly evening?'

'A piece of cake.'

'You're the man I was praying for. You've got fifteen minutes.'

'Much better than manning the desk at the station,' he declares running off to find what he needs.

'Hello Becky Shaw.' She is smiling, a brunette under the uniform cap, with clear brown eyes and full lips. 'How's the transport hub going?'

'All set, thanks to Jack. He's running it so I took the liberty of chasing up computer equipment and display boards like on tele' for the incident room. I've spoken to the duty administrator at the station and she's getting things organised.'

'Great stuff. I like the fact you're using your initiative, but clear anything else with me or the DI please.'

'Will do Sir,' she mumbles, 'sorry.'

'Forget it and call me Gov please. You wanted me for something else?'

'The vicar and her team of ladies have organised coffee and cakes in the room at the side of the church hall,' Becky explains. 'People can go in and out without entering the incident room, Vicar thought it best.'

'Perfect. Please organise staggered breaks, no more than ten minutes each for our people. Tell the vicar I'll be across as soon as possible to thank her.'

'Yes,' she grins, 'I can do that.'

'Sorry, you are doing brilliantly, but one other thing, can you contact DC Harris at the hospital and ask her how Andrew Pennington is? If he's alive, get an urgent message to Judge Le Strange at the hotel, but if he's dead, tell me first. Sorry, too much?'

'No, it's just the idea of telling someone their loved one is dead,' she shivers. 'I've never done it.'

'You'll get plenty of opportunities in this job Becky, now keep hustling.'

Cully watches her hurry away. 'You've got a nice tight bum Becky Shaw,' he mutters, 'but stop leering after women younger than Linda.' A massage would help him relax. There's a Thai woman near Headquarters, but when he jokingly suggested a happy ending she slapped him telling him to get a woman of his own. She and Jamie were right, he needs to find one. Caitland even told him to find a new woman to replace her.

'What are they doing to the cricket square?'

'Dr Inskip, you creep about.'

'Cricket starts at the beginning of next term. Well?'

'Did you know a teacher called Deeds?' Inskip shakes his head. Grimacing, Cully recalls the bastard. He would have been livid to think a machine is about to land on his precious cricket square. 'We're landing a helicopter.'

'You can't.'

'Watch me.' As officers clear the fencing from around the perfectly manicured grass, police vehicles drive on to the field illuminating the scene.

Chalky makes busy with a bucket of whitewash painting a large H right in the middle of the square. Suddenly the anxiety abates and Cully, like an adolescent outwitting the adults, enjoys the moment, but doubts the feeling will last.

++++

Leaving Inskip in a state of barely contained fury, Cully walks along the path in front of the red brick of school house, arriving at tennis courts. Tennis had been his game, school champion two years running, and still is when he found time to play. It was there he'd asked Sophie out for the first time, taken her to the Saturday night disco in town.

It was January Nineteen Ninety and the DJ put on Sinead O'Connor singing "Nothing Compares 2U". Sophie is singing along close to his ear. She smells good and always does. She has grey mischievous eyes and is slender, dancing so close she must feel his excitement and his heart pounding in his chest. They drift to one of the darker corners where they kiss, deeply and longingly. He tastes her, savouring the sweetness.

Fuck! Thirty years since he'd been here, swearing never to come back and now this and her. It felt as though the years were falling away leaving him without the armour they provide against the past. Shivering in the cold salt laden breeze sweeping in off the sea he wonders how many ghosts appear in the coming days.

'Superintendent!'

'Tom?'

'Sorry, I didn't mean to interrupt. Chalky saw you walk this way and thought I'd come to update you.'

'No need for apologies, but please it's Gov.'

'We're getting on with processing the guests. Tizard is grumpy, but gave us two armed officers.'

'Good of him,' Cully all but snarls. 'I'm assuming the guests aren't happy?'

'Especially about their phones, but we're getting it done.'

'If you weren't here, where would you be Tom?'

'I...' and hesitates before answering. 'I'd be playing piano at a dance in the village hall. My wife Trudi is the organiser.'

'She'll be annoyed you're not there?'

'She's got a sound system instead. Not the same, but she's used to the demands of our job,' he shrugs. 'We've a new baby boy as well.'

'When did you meet her?'

'Gov?'

'Trudi, when did you meet her?'

'In primary school and we've been together ever since.' Managing a smile, he reaches inside his jacket and takes out his wallet. 'Here,' and passes Cully a photograph.

'Trudi is beautiful and the baby is a cheeky chap. What's his name?'

'Toby.'

'You're a lucky man Tom. I will try and let you get home as soon as I can, but back to business,' and returns the photograph.

'We've had a report of a motorbike leaving at speed along the road that runs at the bottom of the playing fields just after seven.'

'Find someone to follow that up.'

'I'll do it later, we're a bit short.'

'Delegate to a uniform,' Cully tells him, looking up.

Whatever is incoming is noisy, like an angry wasp caught in a jar.

'Wow!' Tom exclaims, as the silhouette of a Wildcat helicopter appears above the trees that edge the field, hovers before settling perfectly on the H. 'Some performance.'

'Wait until you meet the pilot. Let's go and greet superwoman.'

Pilot and Navy bomb disposal team leader Lieutenant Nadine Simpson comes up the steps two at a time from the field below. Two dogs, a spaniel called Roxy and a Labrador called Toots, trot behind, followed by two junior ratings carrying kit. 'Ah, my favourite girls.' Cully bends to pet the dogs. 'You are lovely.'

'What about me?'

'You are lovely as well Nadine,' Cully says standing. 'I'm glad it's you.'

'You promised me dinner last time.' She wears a dark blue boiler suit covered in badges and gold flashes. She takes off aviator glasses, revealing dark blue eyes. 'You owe me, Cully.'

'I've been busy.'

'Too busy for me?'

'Dinner, I swear, at any place of your choice, directly this is done.'

'I'll hold you to it,' she smiles. 'So, what have you got for us?'

'Shooter enters the hall, throws in flashbangs and starts shooting. Before I send in SOCO, I need to make certain it's safe, that he didn't leave surprises. I don't think he did. Paramedics went in to treat the wounded and nothing happened. I hate placing you all at risk.'

'Caring Cully, a new you, darling.'

'Five dead already,' he continues, 'the bodies are still in there and several wounded gone to hospital. Please take care.'

'We always do and I want that dinner. Give us thirty minutes.'

'What a woman,' says Chalky. 'Never had an officer like that when I served.'

'Chalky, the tech guys at the forensics lab will want the mobile phones directly we've collected them. Probably the quickest way is, if you could drive them there. Also speak to SOCO lead, what's her name?'

'Amber.'

'See if she needs anything taken up to the lab, the shell cases for instance.'

'There's a ferry at four this morning. I'll be on it.'

'When you get there cross the road to MIU, there should be someone there to make coffee and get you a bacon sandwich from the canteen.' He watches Chalky stride away. 'Lisa,' he calls as she appears, 'speaking of coffee, I need one and to thank the Vicar and her ladies for all they're doing.'

'No problem, take thirty, Gov.'

'I'll take fifteen, but thanks. How are the four survivors?'

'The Judge is lovely, Sophie is sweet and the Reverend is happy to co-operate, but Megan Simpson is a piece of work.'

'She always was.'

'Got her a taxi to the hospital to get rid of her.'

++++

In the church hall kitchen, ladies are serving uniformed police officers with drinks and cakes.

'Thank you very much for doing this,' Cully tells them.

'We're enjoying it, being needed, even at this hour,' says one.

'It's terrible what's happened. Will you have something?'

'Later. Do you know where the Vicar is?'

Directed to the church, Cully leaves the kitchen, skirts round the back, admires a red Vespa scooter before entering through a side door. Phone rings; his phone.

'Dad?'

'Linda?'

'Are you alright?'

'Yes.'

'For Christ's sake, why didn't you ring?' she shouts. 'It's on TV. I've been worried sick about you.'

'Sorry.'

'Your phone's been off and I've texted you millions.'

'Sorry.'

'I tried Amelia at MIU,' she tells him, 'but couldn't get through and eventually I rang Jade,' her voice rising, 'and she told me everything my bloody father couldn't be bothered to.'

'Sorry,' he mumbles.

'Basically to find out if you were alive or dead and you didn't even go to the bloody reunion. When were you going to bother to tell me that? Didn't you think?'

'Sorry.'

'Stop saying sorry. Where are you now?'

'In church.'

'Fuck!'

With clear instructions to call her the next morning ringing in his ear, Cully slips the phone away before continuing. A large, high ceilinged Anglican church his footsteps echo off the tiled floor. 'Can I join you?'

'Of course,' and she slides along the pew to allow him to sit next to her. 'That sounded fun.'

'Sorry, didn't mean to disturb you. My daughter worries about me.'

'Of course she does. You should have rung her.'

Vicar Mandy Bannon is in her early thirties, petite with shoulder length strawberry blonde hair. She is smiling. 'I often come here of an evening, it's quiet and peaceful.'

'To feel close to your God?'

'Not especially,' she sighs. 'God has got further and further away from me over the last few months to be honest.'

‘At least, I don’t have one,’ Cully admits. ‘I don’t believe you can have a god in my job,’ he pauses thoughtfully. ‘I hadn’t been here for thirty years since school and now twice in twelve months. You led the service. It was grandmother’s funeral.’

‘Ah of course, you’re a Cully.’

‘Afraid so,’ he admits. ‘When I was at school, every Monday morning we used to trail over here. It was tedious. The school services were led by Reverend Poulson. You’ll have heard of him?’

‘A terrible man. Didn’t he die in prison?’

‘It’s what you get for sucking choir boys toes.’

‘Is that all he did?’ She squeals. ‘That’s a terrible thing I said, sorry. I didn’t mean to minimise, I meant…’

‘You were thinking of what else he might have done. He did get them to suck his toes and more.’

‘Stop!’ she squeals.

‘He was a house master here for twenty years before going to a mainland church. He abused boys at the school, borders mostly and at the church before being arrested and convicted.’

‘Did he abuse you?’

‘Direct and to the point, I like that. He slippered me once for copying Jamie’s homework, but nothing else.’

‘Jamie is good at maths?’

‘That’s why he became an accountant. Oh, by the way, the Reverend Poulson didn’t die in prison, he was murdered last year, a week after he got out. Tied up, his toes cut off with secateurs and left to bleed to death. Details were kept under wraps by the investigating team, but no one was caught and to be honest I don’t think anyone tried too hard to find the killer.’

‘Old Testament justice, an eye for an eye.’

‘Is that why justice is blind?’

‘Nice,’ she laughs. ‘I doubt you came here for a confessional about school days. So, what did you come here for Superintendent Cully?’

‘To touch base, to thank you for organising the refreshments and for a few minutes reflection. Running over what I’ve done, what I haven’t, what I’ve forgotten.’

‘It must be tough to have so much responsibility. Do you ever get vertigo?’

'All the time, especially on jobs like this with new people. At MIU, I know my team and they know me, we look after each other.'

'You'll be fine,' she reassures him.

'But will they?' He shakes his head. 'I have to ask, where were you when the shooting happened?'

'Like you, at the hospice. In with Charlie and his parents.'

'That's why there's no God, letting Charlie die? How did you know I…'

'You were laughing with Jamie and I asked Sabrina who was next door.'

'Sorry, we shouldn't have been laughing when…'

'Not a problem. It's real and that place doesn't avoid things. I visit Jamie.' 'He likes this,' and she produces a thin silver flask. 'Best malt. Go on.' Cully takes it, unscrews the lid and enjoys a long swig. 'Good man.' She places a comforting hand on his. 'I remember now, we talked after your grandmother's funeral and your uncle was there, a nice man.'

'Adam, yes I need to ring him, before he also shouts at me.'

'Remember, I live in the manse if you need to talk. Ah, here comes one of your young women.'

The click of heels echoes through the church as Becky hurries up the aisle.

'Sir, you're needed. The bomb disposal people have finished.'

++++

'The only explosives used were flashbangs,' Nadine begins. 'They're not dangerous. Nowhere near as powerful as the stun-grenades the SAS use. The aim of the military grenade is to disorientate and distract hostiles in a room, giving the entry team a few precious moments in which to enter and neutralise any threats.'

'Is that what it says in the manual?'

'Piss off, Cully,' she grimaces. 'These flashbangs were just noise and are used by paintballers. You can buy them illegally or legally online or make them yourself at the kitchen table. I think these were homemade. Nothing complicated. We've recovered one that didn't go off.' She hands over a sealed plastic bag. 'Also, lots of parabellum cartridge cases we've left for SOCO, but on first sight I'd say a semi-automatic, possibly a Glock.'

'Thank you, Nadine.'

'But you need to take Toots to dinner as well as me.'

‘A double date?’

‘Skinflint. Toots likes steak, I prefer fish. I’m thinking separate dates.’

‘Why?’

‘She has a sensitive nose.’

‘Cute like yours,’ Cully grins. ‘What did she find?’

‘She’s double trained, can sniff out drugs and explosives. There is a nice leather satchel, well-worn but expensive, under the table directly inside the doors to the right. Toots got excited. I glanced inside. You want to know what I saw?’ He nods. ‘A plastic bag of white powder.’

‘Seriously?’

‘I’d say about a kilo,’ she tells him. ‘You know my number, Cully, so ring to book our dates. It has to be expensive. Don’t forget.’

Cully watches Nadine and her crew go down the steps where Chalky is waiting. He salutes and Nadine takes time to talk with him before following her team across the field to board the helicopter. He watches it take off and swing away over the town and out to sea towards the mainland.

‘Hi Cully.’ It was Sophie, coming to stand by him. ‘Always wanted to fly in one of those.’

‘I thought you’d be long gone.’

‘Wanted to see you before I went.’

‘Where are you staying tonight?’

‘With Rachel. My little sister never left the Island. Martin Skeet’s daughter is picking him up and they’re giving me a lift. Will you take my statement tomorrow?’

‘Probably best if someone else does.’

‘And will someone else take Jenny’s?’

‘I thought I’d enjoy taking down her details myself.’

‘Bastard!’ She punches him playfully. ‘You’ve not changed, Cully.’

‘I can’t take any of your statements, because I know you and there would be conflicts of interest.’

‘It’s nearly thirty years since…’

‘I know, but we have to be careful. I’m sorry about the things Megan was saying.’

‘They were true, weren’t they?’

‘Yes,’ he agrees without thinking. ‘I’m sorry for what happened to us,’ he says.

'Not your fault. Remember our special spin the bottle moment?' He nods. 'You worked hard to get the bottle to point at me and when it did…'

'Gov, we can go in,' Tom calls.

'On my way.'

'You take care,' and reaching up she kisses him on the cheek. She smells good. 'See you later please my darling Abelard.'

Cully watches her walk away. Still slim, hard bodied, she walks confidently on long legs, but there is something not right, something different. She is still adorable, beautiful and sexy, but her looks hide some deeper truth. It is in her slate grey eyes, intelligent, so quick to narrow, flicker and change, but what is it? After thirty years, what did he expect, the same girl he'd fallen in love with back then?

'Gov!'

'Coming,' he shouts back, feeling uneasy.

'One of your old flames, Gov?'

'One of many Sergeant. Right,' he turns to the assembled. 'Let's go in.'

Cully, Lisa, Tom and SOCO lead Amber stand at the entrance to the hall. They pull on overalls, shoe covers and masks.

Cully pauses on the threshold where so many years before he attended morning assembly, played games, did PE, took part in the debating society and acted in dramas. "Abelard and Heloise" had been the last play, the Christmas before A Level exams. Taking a deep breath he steps forward, the sterile suit he wears crackles. The hall is large, wall bars down one side that he remembers swing out and over which they were made to climb again and again. Floor to ceiling windows on the other side are mostly covered in black curtains, but one has been ripped in two. Ahead of them on the raised stage is a white screen ready for the film.

There are ten round tables with chairs pushed back and over. White linen tablecloths, cutlery, shattered glasses and bottles of wine are scattered all around. To the immediate right are the two tables where the victims sat. Five bodies lay there surrounded by medical equipment. Black blood spattered everywhere. Shell casings litter the floor and in several places there is charring from the flashbangs.

Beside Cully, Lisa pulls the mask over her nose. Ahead, Amber leads her team of two women and a man forward and they begin to efficiently work the scene. They are wearing white overalls with BioTech Laboratories stencilled on the back. Years before, after a series of scandals the government had closed the publicly owned forensic labs and given contracts to the private sector. Cully thought that if he were a criminal mastermind he would open such a lab and control the flow of forensic evidence at the behest of criminals willing to pay.

Cameras flash, numbered yellow plastic triangles go down to mark the shell cases, paramedic equipment is collected and bagged. 'Amber, make the leather satchel a priority.'

'Will do.' She pauses. 'Gov!'

'Amber?'

'This place card has your name on it, Cully.' She holds it up, pointing to the back of the chair where there are two bullet holes. 'Chest height I reckon.'

++++

Fifteen minutes to midnight, he muses, looking out over the fields, beyond the trees to the silhouettes of town buildings. There are few lights, most people are in bed asleep and he wishes he is, but could have been dead. He hears footsteps behind him and turning finds Indah standing there, large eyes bright with expectation. 'How are the sixth formers?'

'Hyped-up, but I've finished. I've interviewed all the ones hosting the event and two in particular. They were crossing the lawn to watch the film when they saw a figure enter the hall through the double doors.'

'Description?'

'A man wearing blackish trousers and shirt. They say he had a light on his chest.'

'He had two lights then,' reasons Cully. 'Was it bright?'

'No.'

'What else?'

'He was carrying a shoulder bag and reaching into it. Moments later they hear the noise. They didn't run. They were frozen with fear and crouched down behind a bench. They are adamant,' she continues, 'no one came out of the main entrance after the shooting started and finished.'

'Not even guests?'

'No. Another of the students was behind the screen operating the lights. She was petrified. Then someone crashes into her, knocks her down, but apologises.'

'A polite assassin. Indah you're working fast, go on,' encourages Cully.

'I've briefly spoken to the caterers. They want to know what to do with all the food? It's in the kitchen.'

'I'll think about it,' Cully says, thoughtfully. 'Anything else?'

'Have you got time to follow me?'

'I have,' he agrees, pleased for the chance to do something with this bright and extremely attractive young woman.

'Walk this way,' Indah says, enjoying the experience.

'Where are we going?'

'To the lockers. Did you have a locker?'

'No, we had to keep our stuff in satchels or cases.'

'Several of the students mention a sixth former called Lilly. They call her weird, strange, that sort of thing. That her drawings and writings are dark. I spoke to Dr Inskip. I found him in his office trimming his Bonsai which is apparently relaxing. He asked about Sophie Cairns. He didn't say why. Anyway, I got over his reluctance and he gave me Lilly's locker key. It's in the sixth form block.'

The emergency vehicles have gone.

'We can cut across the playground,' says Indah.

'Middle quad,' Cully corrects.

'Middle what?'

'Quad, short for quadrangle. Remember this place is posh. The language is there to confuse oiks from outside.'

'Does that make me an oik, Gov?'

'No Indah, I'm joking,' Cully smiles in the darkness, following her. 'Maybe these shootings were a political statement? This school represents one end of society. Oligarchs, oil sheiks, businessmen and politicians have their children here nowadays. Shooting the place up is a blow against the unfairness of society by one of the oiks.' But he is talking to himself as Indah has already gone through a corner door off middle quad. 'Indah!'

'Here are the lockers.' Glancing back, Indah realises Cully is no longer there, but glimpses a door slowly closing. She goes through it, like the wardrobe in the "Lion, Witch and the Wardrobe", her favourite book as a child. 'Gov?' It is dark, something brushes her face, she pushes through soft material. Suddenly bright lights come on. As her eyes adjust she realises she has come through curtains and is on a small stage with a dozen rows of chairs facing her, 'Gov?'

'Hello gorgeous,' comes a rough voice.

'What?' She stares out, blinking against the glare. 'Whose there?'

'Me Indah, sorry, didn't mean to scare you.'

'You didn't, Gov,' she answers feeling foolish.

'Welcome to the mummery,' he says. 'We used to rehearse in here and occasionally put on live performances for parents.'

'What did you call it?'

'Mummery.'

'Like quad, to confuse the oiks?'

'Exactly. I'm remembering we rehearsed a play in here before taking it to the big stage. Jenny Sykes was Mrs Pankhurst on her soap box and I was the cheeky chap in the crowd.'

'Jenny Sykes is on the guest list, but didn't turn up.'

'Mrs Pankhurst was—'

'I know about Mrs Pankhurst, Gov,' she snaps, but instantly regrets it.

'Sorry,' says Cully, 'not doing well, am I? You must think I'm being inappropriate, probably in lots of ways, but especially in the light of why we're here. Put in a complaint if you want Indah. Be honest,' he urges, coming onto the stage beside her. 'Well?'

'Sorry Gov, we've not had light-hearted banter these last few months. It takes some getting used to and Superintendent Harris wasn't playful, never shared much about himself and yet here you are…'

'Spilling it all out. Sorry, this is odd for me Indah, a lovely name.'

'It's Indonesian.' Now he is flirting, she thinks, but likes it. 'But, I was born on the Island.'

'How many fingers have you got?'

'Five,' she laughs, having heard the joke before, 'but I've got webbed toes.'

'I'll get myself under control,' he promises, smiling. 'Where are the lockers?'

They are fixed along the wall next to the entrance to the lower-sixth common room, at the bottom of the stairs leading to the upper-sixth. Finding a particular one Indah unlocks it and as the door swings back they see photographs of pupils with faces scratched out.

'Let's gather everyone together in the incident room,' says Cully. 'We might have found our shooter.'

Saturday

'Thank you everyone. We need to stay focussed and move quickly. We know the flashbangs were harmless distractions. The five dead and injured were all around two tables. They were probably the target. We need a chart of the hall on the wall. A large one showing positions of dead and injured and the names of who was sitting at the tables. Who can draw?'

'I can,' volunteers Tom.

'Thanks. We also know these people were from the same year, nineteen ninety, which was my final year. So yes, I know these people.'

They were gathered in the incident room where desks, computers and display boards have magically appeared curtesy of Becky and the Senior Administrator. Cully looks around at the team and it's not bad, not enough, but not bad. 'Firstly, I know we're already exhausted, but we need to keep going. Indah you start.'

'I've interviewed the sixth formers and they mentioned a girl called Lilly Crutcher. I've taken stuff from her locker. I've got it all here.' She taps a pile of material on the table beside her. 'Lots of anger about the school, other pupils and life in general. She talks about killing people.'

'The DI and you detain her at home at first light,' instructs Cully. 'What have you done with the sixth formers?'

'After speaking to the DI, I sent them home, but warned them to stay off social media until at least noon.'

'Perfect and I doubt they will for five minutes, but nice try.'

'I've applied for warrants to make an arrest and search the house,' Lisa begins. 'The magistrate was grumpy when I woke her, but agreed to sign and I've sent a motorcyclist there to bring them back.'

'You've not sent Sergeant Tizard?' Tom wonders aloud, grinning.

'That would be beneath him.'

'Where is he?' Cully asks, but thinks he might be avoiding him. 'Did he know there is a briefing?'

'He knew,' says Chalky, 'but we've started getting triple nine calls about gunmen in the shrubbery and he went to check out one of those. I think,' Chalky pauses, but senses the mood, 'he hopes to shoot someone.'

'He'd only miss,' Tom laughs.

'He doesn't always miss,' mutters Cully. 'This will get worse as the days go by. People are scared. We've set up a call centre at the station and will screen calls to get rid of cranks. You've done really well Indah, anything else?'

'I've arranged to see the caterers in the morning.'

'Good stuff. Chalky, you've booked your ferry?'

'All done and I've spoken with Amber. She's loading the van with forensic evidence to take up to the laboratory.'

'Tom?'

'We're continuing to process the guests and we're nearly finished. The transport hub has worked well'

'We'll let SOCO finish in the hall and then do a walk through,' Cully continues. 'In the meantime, I need food and we've got a feast waiting for us in the school kitchen, some of which I paid for.' Cully waits nervously for a response. 'I hate waste,' he adds.

'We can't, isn't it evidence?' Lisa complains uncertainly.

'My responsibility. Lisa, you and I will prepare and serve it in the school refectory. Another posh word,' he says, grinning towards Indah whom blushes. 'Give us thirty minutes everyone.'

'I've persuaded a uniform to cover FLO duties to let Kerry come back for a break,' says Lisa, struggling to get used to Cully's way of doing things, but liking it.

'I'm sure we can conjure up a glass of wine as well. At MIU, we always work better pissed, but seriously, there is alcohol free and fruit juice, which can't do any harm,' he smiles. 'Before we're going to cook, any luck with the CCTV Chalky?'

'Plenty of external cameras, but none inside. I've got the discs to go through.'

'Let Amber co-ordinate until you come back and we'll get uniform to watch them. Remember you're in CID so wear civvies if you want.'

'Work out of uniform, can't remember the last time I did that?'

Door opens and slams shut.

'You must be Kerry?'

'And you are?'

'Detective Superintendent Cully.'

'Where did you come from?'

'Kerry,' snaps Lisa. 'Show some respect.'

'What?' She glares at Lisa, then round at her colleagues, a look of defiance on her face. 'What?'

'Apologise now,' Lisa orders.

Kerry hesitates, but thinks better of what she might have said. 'Sorry Sir, I didn't know.'

'Now you do,' Cully states. 'A difficult night?'

'Chaotic,' Kerry sighs, deflating, slumping into a chair. In her early twenties with long black hair and wearing a suede jacket that appears too tight. Probably unfairly, she reminds Cully of a young Megan Simpson. 'As well as the people wounded by the shooter, we've several with crush injuries when they tried to flee. One is critical.' Her face is pale, ashen beneath a black fringe. 'The hospital can hardly cope and I…' she waves it away. 'I'll be fine. Is there coffee?'

'I'll get you some,' says Chalky, leaving the room.

'We're getting food,' says Lisa, glaring at Kerry.

'Good, I'm starving,' Kerry forces a thin smile.

'Where's Becky?' Cully asks.

'Found her,' announces Chalky leading Becky into the room and bringing a mug of coffee for Kerry. 'She was helping the ladies clear the kitchen. The Vicar says they'll be back early morning to serve breakfast.'

'Lisa, we need to give them money to cover things. Becky, nice, but you don't need to help the ladies, we need you at the briefings.'

'I didn't know.'

'Why is she…?' but Kerry stops herself, hiding behind the rim of the coffee mug.

'Gov,' Lisa whispers, 'Becky's only been on the force a year.'

'Every team needs a gofer and I don't see a que of uniforms asking to join us,' Cully hisses back as the door opens and closes again. 'Amber, to what do we owe the pleasure?'

'We're having food,' Chalky tells her. 'The Gov and Lisa are cooking.'

'Fantastic.'

'You and your team included,' says Cully. 'What have you got ?'

'The white powder is probably cocaine,' she smiles. 'I did the liquid test and it turned blue. Not absolute, but accurate enough.'

‘Chalky take the cocaine.’

‘Gov?’

‘With you to headquarters,’ and everyone, apart from Kerry, laughs.

++++

Lisa and Cully are both wearing aprons they find hanging in the kitchen. Cully stands at the gridle, turning duck breasts, wondering if this is the right thing to be doing? When he suggested it, told them, there is a painful silence until it sank in he is serious. They followed him obediently across to School House and into the refectory, not dining room or canteen. ‘How is the veg coming along?’

‘A few more minutes.’ Lisa hesitates. ‘This is weird, Gov.’

‘I’ve built my MIU team over several years,’ he begins, picking words carefully. ‘I know them, when to push, when to support, when to enable and so on, but as for this team I’ve got no real idea what you need. Food is excellent for bonding and we are hungry.’

‘I’ll get used to you,’ Lisa smiles, taking steaming carrots out of the oven. ‘I’ll stir some honey in,’ she says. ‘Sorry about Kerry. She’s not easy I’m afraid.’ Laughter from next door. ‘I’ll see if the team are ready.’ Lisa goes through the swing doors to the main room where Indah, Kerry, Tom, Chalky, Amber and members of the SOCO team are finishing the smoked salmon and where there is a buzz of excited chatter. ‘You all done?’

‘That is delicious,’ declares Chalky. ‘I’ll clear the plates, but then I have to go for the ferry.’

‘I’ll make you up a doggy box, you can’t miss the duck.’

Lisa and Cully serve loaded plates.

‘Fantastic,’ declares Tom. ‘This is delicious. Thank you, Gov and Ma’am.’

‘This is welcome, we needed a lift,’ says Indah, beginning to eat. ‘Tizard not joining us Kerry?’

‘He’s sergeant to you and he’s out doing his job, hunting the killer, like we should be.’

‘This beats, bagging bodies,’ says Amber and her team cheer.

‘Have they all gone?’ asks Cully, taking his place at the long table and Amber confirms the five bodies have been taken to the morgue.

Cully remembers having school lunches in this room until he persuaded his grandmother to let him bring sandwiches. The staff would sit at the window table, the borders at a table down one side and everyone else would sit on benches aside parallel long tables. The food was awful, especially the tapioca pudding with a blob of institutional jam in the middle. It was the one time he couldn't stop himself being sick.

'Eat up,' Cully encourages them, 'there's strawberry tart for pudding.'

'This is the best food I've had in ages,' Becky declares. 'Living alone, the microwave feeds me. Is this really how CID operate?'

'No Becky. This is very different to what we're used to,' laughs Tom. 'This feels cathartic.'

'Big word Tom,' Indah grins, 'but you're right.'

'Trudi, my wife's been reading a book by a local therapist. She comes out with this stuff all the time,' he explains. 'Is there another beer?'

They had found non-alcoholic beer and wine and all had a glass of something.

'What's going on?' Inskip demands, striding into the room. 'I want to know.'

'Join us headmaster,' Cully says easily, standing to greet the man at the doorway and placing an arm round him, immediately feeling the pomposity drain away. 'The team needed feeding and I imagine you've already thought of giving the food to charity.'

'I had?' He looks round thoughtfully. 'I suppose we could.'

'The publicity would do the school good, especially after yesterday, don't you agree?' Inskip is ashen faced, exhausted by events. 'I bet you haven't eaten and food will do you good.' Cully guides him to a place next to Amber still wearing her stained white overall. 'The duck is excellent, if I say so myself, and I'm guessing you like it bloody?'

'I...'

'The bloodier the better,' says Amber.

'Tom, please give the headmaster alcohol fuelled wine. He needs a large one.' Cully disappears into the kitchen as Tom pours a generous measure.

'What's he playing at?' demands Kerry in a low hiss.

'What do you mean?' Indah asks. 'Well?'

'This cooking lark. He's our boss, not a bloody chef.'

'Chef means boss in French,' Inskip muses. 'I taught French you see. No time anymore, all admin,' he laments before drinking the wine.

'It's pathetic, trying to win us over,' Kerry continues.

'He's won me over,' states Tom taking a slice of strawberry tart. 'He's a breath of fresh air after…'

'Yes?' Kerry demands.

'Our previous boss.'

'Fuck off.' Kerry stands, pushing her chair back so hard, it spins away, leaving the room as Cully returns with a plate of food for Inskip.

'There you go,' he says pleasantly, ignoring Kerry's flounce. 'I bet the Vicar can help distribute the food to charities. Great photo opportunities.'

'Yes, I'll speak to her. Thank you for this.' He cuts into the duck, blood runs, and tastes a slice. 'Perfect. Is there anymore wine?' Tom fills his glass. 'I've been thinking about Lilly, she's not so bad. Please be careful with her.'

'Of course Headmaster, kid gloves,' Cully assures him. 'You were asking Indah about Sophie Cairns?'

'I wanted to know if she was alright, she's been helpful. Not professionally you understand,' he hesitates, 'although after last night I'll need her therapeutic input. No, we asked for a volunteer from each Alumni year group to help with seating plans and such like.' He manages a chuckle. 'We didn't want the wrong people next to each other did we?'

'No, you might open old scars,' Cully sighs, thinking about his own.

'I've been looking you up on school records Superintendent Cully. You were a good pupil. Solid academically, good at sport, especially tennis, and an important member of the drama society. All the play programmes are in the archive.'

'Really, can we see?' ventures Indah enthusiastically. 'Are there photographs?'

'A long one of the whole school that year, yes.'

'Can we have it?' Tom asks. 'For the incident room.'

'No,' says Cully. 'Now we're fully fuelled, we're going back to work.'

++++

Becky volunteers to take over as FLO at the hospital while Indah stays in the incident room to co-ordinate the warrants and write up the interviews with the students. A subdued Kerry with Lisa, Tom and Cully enter the hall where bodies have been removed, shell cases and spent flashbangs mapped and collected and abandoned personal property bagged and tagged.

'The shooter comes in as the film is about to start, when he or she knows everything will be dark,' Cully begins. 'He throws flashbangs towards the front, swivels to his right and starts shooting at two tables.' The chaos and damage there reflects the panic of those being shot at. 'Nadine and Amber think it is probably a Glock or similar and it seems to have had a torch or laser attachment. Highly sophisticated kit.'

'Professional?' suggests Tom.

'Looks like it,' Cully agrees.

'According to statements, he only fires for about a minute,' says Lisa. 'Then leaves, but not the way he came in.'

'That's why he threw the other flashbangs back towards the double doors so people would look that way, but try to escape forward, adding to the confusion,' Cully continues. 'Clever.'

'He can't have left through the corner door,' says Tom. 'Because people were trying to get through there when the shooting starts. It was log jammed, that's where we got the casualties with crush injuries. The door was totally blocked.'

'Then which way?' Cully asks of them. 'The fire exit on the other side?'

'I don't think so, guests poured out of there,' Lisa points out. 'He might have gone that way, but people were panicking. He could have got knocked over, anything might have happened. A professional wouldn't have risked it.'

'And there's a camera that looks towards the art block,' Tom informs them. 'They've had break-ins and there's a gate further down. The camera covers the path all the way and there's another camera on the gate.'

'You're right,' Cully looks to Lisa and Tom, 'a professional would have planned his way out. He will have been here, reconnoitred.'

'Military,' Tom suggests.

'Or police,' Cully says, 'anyone with training.'

'But a police officer?' Kerry protests. 'Really?'

'Trying to defend him, just in case,' Tom mutters.

'Fuck off!'

'Am I missing something?' Cully stares at them. 'Well?'

'No Gov, sorry Gov,' says Tom. 'Special forces?'

'Possibly.' He turns his attention back to the stage. 'I will always love you. My heart belongs to you.'

'I didn't know you cared, Gov,' Lisa smiles.

'This way.' Cully walks to the end of the hall, climbs on the stage and vanishes behind the backdrop. 'This way,' he shouts. They follow. 'The pupil that reported getting knocked over would have been here operating lights. Come on slow coaches, there's a door at the back of the stage that leads into the main corridor. He would have been well ahead of the crush and clear to get out.'

'How did you know, Gov?' Tom asks, catching up.

'During the last Act, Abelard leaves through the middle of the audience, runs around the back and re-enters from the back of the stage for the final scene with Heloise. My line was, I will always love you. My heart belongs to you.'

'You remember?'

For a moment, Cully is absent, thinking back through the years, but catches himself, returning. 'They are in the convent where Heloise has been sent for her sins and settle either side of a grill stating their undying love for each other.'

'You were Abelard, but who was Heloise?'

'Sophie Cairns.'

'She mentioned a play,' says Lisa.

'Is she the one that kissed you, Gov?' asks Tom. 'You two have a thing?'

'Our shooter was here before last night,' Cully continues, ignoring the banter. 'Maybe a pupil, the young woman Lilly, but could she carry out a shooting like this? After emerging from behind the stage she goes along the corridor and here we are at the sixth form block. God, I remember this like it's yesterday and then where does she go?'

'Out into the lower quad, Gov, but if he's as good as we think not out the gate because there's another camera there,' offers Tom.

'Sorry, but make that disc a priority as well as the others,' says Cully. 'Then through the gardens to the front. He or she meticulously planned every move. Certainly a professional, but more critically a predator.'

'Agreed, Gov,' says Tom, 'but more importantly what about you and Sophie?'

'Some things are too private to share Sergeant Whitworth.'

++++

DI Lynn and Cully are in the church hall office with the door closed.

'You didn't mind the banter, Gov? I can have words?'

‘No need. Banter at nearly four in the morning is healthy I’d say, especially after the time they’ve had, but I’ll let you know if it goes too far. Tell me about Kerry, she’s on edge.’

‘Kerry is in an on off relationship with Tizard. He’s been warned. She’s infatuated with him.’

‘There’s something else, I can sense it,’ he says leaning in. ‘What else, Lisa?’

‘He’s married to my sister Mary. I hate him.’

‘I’m not keen on him either. Everyone on this bloody Island is connected,’ he states lightly.

‘True,’ she smiles. ‘For Kerry, there’s more. How much do you know about the sackings that cleaned out CID.’

Cully remembers it was all over the media. Headquarters installed bugs to record what was being said and six officers were sacked for racist, sexist and abusive language. Superintendent Harris was technically cleared, only sanctioned for poor supervision, Sylvia told him to retire.

‘Harris was Kerry’s dad.’ She pauses. ‘He committed suicide.’

‘Ah, so she’s had a bad eighteen months.’

‘I think the affair with Tizard has been a life raft and now he’s burst it. I thought about taking her off the case, but we can’t afford to with so few of us.’

‘Let’s not send her to the hospital too often,’ decides Cully. ‘She might feel isolated there, bring back painful memories and we must make certain she feels part of the team.’

‘I’ll keep an eye on her and…’ she hesitates, ‘would you have a word with Tom. I just feel that man to man. I was here, going through it and struggle to see things clearly. We were offered counselling, but I don’t think he went.’

There is a knock on the door. ‘Come in.’

‘The warrants have arrived,’ Tom announces.

‘Speak of the devil.’ Lisa leaves as Tom enters. ‘Close the door will you.’

‘Is this about the banter with Kerry in the hall?’

‘Partly. Have a seat. How’s Becky doing?’

‘She’s willing and enthusiastic.’

‘What about you?’ Cully smiles. ‘You’ve got Trudi and Toby to take care of and I want to make certain you’re ok.’

‘I’m fine, but neither Trudi nor I get much sleep and the job takes over.’

‘No one warns you what it’s like at two in the morning with a screaming infant, but you come through it.’

'I know.' Tom rubs a hand over his face. 'Don't get me wrong the DI is good, but we've been stretched and stressed and the previous Superintendent buried his head in the sand.'

'I don't Tom,' Cully reassures him.

'It's good having a bloke here. Lisa and Indah are great, but it's not the same. CID can be a lonely place, especially after we made the complaints and things dragged on.' Tom shifts in his chair. 'I know your daughter Linda, we did the sergeants course together. I was sorry to hear what happened. How is she?'

'Recovering. Odd being here. There is an outside chance I'm the target, but doubt it.'

'The bullet holes in the back of the chair?'

'Shook me, but Judge Le Strange could be as well. We need to find out if he's had any threats. We have to eliminate the possible to focus on the probable don't we?' Tom nods. 'Obviously we may have a drugs angle, but there's the revenge motive for past events. There was abuse here at the school. Borders in particular suffered at the hands of staff and older pupils.'

'It's useful having your insight. Gov…?'

'You're a copper Tom, ask it.'

'Did you suffer…?'

'I was a day boy, not a border. I wasn't abused, but with hindsight I witnessed it and I sometimes feel guilty I didn't do anything. Police work teaches us things, about bad stuff most people don't know and don't want to know. Emotions affect us all even thirty years later.' He pauses thoughtfully. 'Oh, and Tom, lay off Kerry.'

++++

They are sitting in Lisa's car at dawn within sight of Lilly Crutcher's house.

'This must be difficult for the Gov, coming back to his old school under these circumstances with all the memories,' says Indah.

'And the girlfriends,' grins Lisa.

'Yes and the bullying, although I doubt the Gov would have been bullied.'

'We didn't know him then and everyone has a nemesis at school,' Lisa begins, 'someone they can't forget even years later.'

'I suppose,' Indah agrees, remembering Crystal Smalls, a rank racist she hated and even now shudders when recalling her name.

'Sophie Bell was the one I had to contend with,' Lisa admits as if reading Indah's thoughts. 'The most attractive girl in the year that everybody wanted to be friends with and there I was with glasses and braces. Strange, but a few years back I saw her in the supermarket working on the tills. She was obese. I deliberately stood in her line and when she'd put my stuff through I introduced myself and smiled. I enjoyed the moment.'

'They call that schadenfreude,' says Indah, 'taking pleasure from watching someone's else's misfortune.'

'I certainly took pleasure from it,' admits Lisa, drumming impatiently on the steering wheel. 'Where the hell are they? I wonder what Lilly will have been through to make her so angry?'

'According to Dr Inskip she's always struggled to fit in,' but Indah's thoughts are elsewhere. On such a thinly populated small Island, it's surprising she's never bumped into Crystal. She wonders if the woman even remembers her? 'Not great parents either apparently.'

'At last,' Lisa groans, watching an unmarked blue van drive to a halt and disgorge four darkly clad armed officers. 'They really believe they're God's gift. Let's go Indah.'

As the two women approach the group they catch snippets of conversation.

'I've got this really good accountant,' Tizard says. 'It pays for itself, saves me a fortune in tax and I've invested a bit, the extra we make on the side from security at the festival, up at the Great Forest or the clubs at the weekend.'

'The wife takes most of that.'

'Ted, don't tell her.'

'How did you find this accountant?'

'Billy Toogood recommended him.'

'He was one of the officers shot in the custody suit. Doesn't he blame you, like Cully blames you?'

'No he doesn't and Cully is all mouth. Anyway, the accountant has sorted out Billy's lump sum, his pension and compensation and he's better off now than he was in the job.'

'Pity he can't walk,' snaps Lisa, coming up behind them. 'We had a briefing, where were you Sergeant?'

'We had calls to follow-up.'

'Try and be part of the team in future.'

The house is large, set back from the road with a short drive where two cars are parked. Lisa walks ahead and bangs on the door.

'What time do you call this?' A window is flung open above and a man's balled head sticks out. 'Who the hell are you?'

'Mr Crutcher, we're the police. We have warrants. We need to talk to Lilly.'

'I'm a solicitor, I'll bring her in.'

'Mr Crutcher, if you don't open the door we will break it down.' Swearing the man goes inside and minutes pass before the door opens revealing him in a white bath robe. 'Why the delay?'

'I needed to let my wife get up.'

'Lilly?'

'In her room.'

'We're coming in,' and armed officers lead the way.

'Why do you need bloody guns?'

'Where's Lilly's room?'

'Up the stairs, first on the right.'

'Mr Crutcher,' begins Indah, 'here are warrants to search your house and take your daughter in for questioning.'

'But why?'

'Aren't you aware of the school shooting?'

'Arnold,' shouts a woman's voice. 'Come see, it's all over the news.'

On the first floor, Lisa finds a door with a "Keep Out" sign in red pinned to it and knocks. 'Police, we're coming in,' and pushes it open. Pitch black inside and for a moment Lisa freezes, realising she ought to let armed officers go first, but the shape in the bed does not move. 'Lilly wake up.' Finding the curtains, Lisa throws them back allowing in daylight, sees two shapes and shouts. 'Wake up!'

The figures stir slowly and as the covers come off, Lisa realises they are naked. 'Get up and get dressed.'

'What the fuck! Who are you?'

'Police.'

'What the hell is he doing here?'

'Mr Crutcher, please let us deal with this.'

++++

At nine, Cully gathers the team in the incident room, welcoming new arrivals. 'Thank you for coming over from North Island.' There are some blank faces. 'It's what the locals call the mainland,' he continues, going on to outline what has happened so far. Inside him things feel less turbulent and he feels in control of himself and the investigation. He taps the chart Tom has drawn. Above has appeared the long black and white photograph Dr Inskip mentioned. Cully glances at it, in particular at the group of thirty pupils at the centre, the girls sitting the boys standing behind them. There he was between Sean and Patrick and directly behind Sophie. Someone had used red wool to link the pupils in the photograph to the people named on the representation of the two tables below. 'Who do I thank for this?'

Indah and Tom glance at each other before hesitatingly putting their hands up.

'You'll both be in detention later,' he grins. 'You've actually done well to match people apart from,' and reaching up he removes one of the pins and moves it. 'That is Carla Scutari.'

'She's was stunning,' says Tom.

'An Italian beauty,' he remembers, 'and still is apparently. She suffered flash burns to her legs, the hospital are keeping her in, but will discharge her soon.' Cully allows himself a final glance at the photograph before moving on. 'Most of you will have picked up on the fact, I used to go to this school and my last year was nineteen ninety. I knew all of them. I have to exclude myself from any direct interviews with survivors.'

'Always thought you were posh Gov.'

'Back in my day it was an awful lot cheaper, Pete. Let me introduce DC Pete Grimes, or Grumpy Gramps as he's known by us in MIU.'

'School full of posh buggers then?'

'Very posh now, ten thousand a term for borders, half that for day pupils.'

'Jesus! Perhaps the shooting was political, Gov,' Pete persists, brushing a hand over his bald head. 'The local peasants rebelling.'

'Shot guns and pitchforks maybe, but not automatic weapons. Moving on. As you can imagine we are spread thin, searching for the shooter, protecting the wounded, and dealing with the families. The Island team made progress overnight. We've had little rest. I cannot offer any opportunity for breaks this morning. This said, I want to let each of you get away at some stage today for a shower, change of clothes and a few hours kip.' Pausing he lets this sink in. 'I'd like to also welcome Sergeant Monica Aries from the Human Trafficking Unit because she speaks...how many languages Monica?'

'Six.'

'An international storm is heading our way. We await the arrival of an oligarch from London who knows half the cabinet, owns Kensington and a Premiership football club. Several other wealthy foreign parents are also expected to fly in. I understand fog has come down over the channel?'

'Pete and I just got here ahead of it,' explains Monica. She has dark features with piercing green eyes beneath a head of black hair. 'Apparently, there are no more ferries until late afternoon.'

'So, we're cut off from North Island.'

'Is this when the zombies come out, Gov?' asks Pete.

'No Pete, it's not and we have forest gremlins over here.'

'Not vampires?' Monica asks. 'Like where I come from in Transylvania?'

'No, but being on an Island slows everything down as you'll discover. Also, it means Chalky won't be back yet, but he's delivered all the forensics. Back to last night. As well as the dead we have several critical, all under armed guard. Kerry has been liaising with the hospital. What can you tell us?'

'Three are still critical with multiple gunshot wounds, another with crush injuries. The less seriously wounded are in various states, but should survive.'

'Thanks Kerry,' he smiles at her, but she looks away. 'The church ladies have got breakfast ready. There is coffee and bacon butties in the next room, but before you indulge these are the jobs. DI Lynn and Indah brought in Lilly Crutcher this morning and will be interviewing her directly after this session. It's tenuous but we need to eliminate the possibility that the shooter is a pupil. As you'll know by now the school planned a whole host of events over the weekend for the Alumni and their spouses. Those have been cancelled, but we need to manage nearly one hundred guests. Sorry Tom, but you did a great job last night and started to get to know them so I'm placing you in charge of liaison. Becky to assist you when she's available. Monica and Pete, you need to be going out to the border accommodation. Not just to deal with angry foreign parents, but talk to staff, see if anyone suspicious has been hanging around.'

'Where is Sergeant Tizard, shouldn't he be here?' demands Tom.

'He was on the raid to arrest Lilly this morning, says Indah, 'but haven't seen him since.'

‘He’s chasing up leads,’ offers Kerry, too quickly. ‘He’s working one of the alarm calls instead of coming to another briefing. He—’

‘We are short of FLOs,’ Cully interrupts the young woman before she can go further, ‘but Kerry here has done a good job at the hospital and I’d like you to continue with that…’

‘But…’

‘Let me finish. Go now, give Becky a couple of hours off and then you deserve a break before you come back here to the incident room. Only one guest didn’t turn up for the target table, Michael Carter. Contact him and then do background checks on the dead and injured apart from the Andrews, drug squad will be looking at them. Indah, once you’ve finished with Lilly, take over from Becky at the hospital, but tomorrow I want you to follow up on the people from the second group including those that didn’t turn up. Make your way through the list.’

‘That include you, Gov?’

‘Certainly does.’

‘What are you going to be doing, Gov?’ Pete asks, grinning.

‘I’ve got the autopsies followed by a press conference. Want to swop anybody?’ Silence. ‘Can I remind everyone there is a predator out there and he may not have finished killing. Be careful all of you.’

++++

‘Present are Lilly Crutcher, her father Mr Arnold Crutcher, DC Kasali and DI Lynn. Lilly you’ve had your rights explained to you and been offered the opportunity to have an independent solicitor present, but you’ve chosen to have your father, also a solicitor with you.’

‘I don’t want him here. He only deals with civil stuff anyway. Go away dad, you’re useless.’

‘Lilly!’

‘I did it, I killed them all.’ Lilly is dressed entirely in black, leather jacket, short skirt and ankle boots. Her short hair is black and she has several piercings in nose and ears. ‘Shot every one of the cunts.’

Lilly reminds Indah of herself. She was never a Goth, but her skin colour made her different and a black girl on a white Island brought challenges from the moment she sensed rather than understood the animosity even at nursery school.

It wasn't until secondary school and conflict with Crystal that she turned it around, become the predator rather than the prey.

'Language Lilly.'

'It's what you call mum isn't it? You stupid cunt, where's my dinner?'

'Lilly, you say you killed them and you certainly wanted them dead. You wrote about it,' and Indah brings a file on to the table from the pile at her feet.

'Where the fuck did you get that?'

'In your locker.'

'That's private.'

'Dr Inskip gave us the key.'

'He'd no right.'

'He had no choice,' Indah states. 'According to Dr Inskip you've struggled to fit in.'

'Did you have a warrant to take these things from my daughter's locker?'

'Shut up dad, the pigs do what they like.'

'To answer your father's question we didn't need one,' explains Lisa. 'The locker is on school property and if you look at the home school agreement, parents sign, he had every right to give us access.'

'Lilly, you didn't do it,' states her father. 'You were in your bedroom.'

'No I wasn't, you don't know anything about me,' she snarls. 'Get out.'

'Mr Crutcher, it might be best if you left us,' Lisa suggests.

'I'm not leaving my daughter.'

'You've been leaving me since I wasn't born a boy. Do what the pig says.'

'Let me take you for a coffee,' Lisa suggests standing and escorting him out of the room.

'Lilly, where were you Friday night,' Indah continues, 'if not in your room?'

'I was shooting people.'

'Lilly,' Indah persists patiently, 'you're an intelligent young woman, more intelligent than your dad I'm thinking. You've a bright future, but we need to sort this out.'

'They hate me, the kids at the school.'

'All of them?' Lilly nods. 'You've no friends?'

'One, Bethany Simpson is nice, but no one else.'

'You cut yourself,' Indah says softly and looks down to where she can see scars on Lilly's wrists below the cuff of her leather jacket.

'I used to.'

'You stopped, that's good. Something happened, something changed things?'

'I found the guys. Half a dozen of us with the same views.' Lilly is relaxing, softening. 'We talk about everything and anything and nobody judges what we say or look like. Do you know how cruel the bullying is on social media?'

'Some. Interview terminated,' and abruptly Indah switches off the tape machine. 'I was at school not so long ago, eight years, and I got bullied face to face and online. Mostly racial stuff. There was a gang of them, but a particular bitch, the leader.'

'How did you get through it?'

'I got angry and one day snapped. I found the girl in the toilets and beat the crap out of her.'

'Really?' Lilly is surprised and not a little impressed. 'Did you get in trouble?'

'No, I played the race card. She attacked me, the poor little black girl and I was simply defending myself. They expelled her and I went to university and joined the police.'

'You changed from victim to predator didn't you?' Lilly grins. 'Like in the book, that's cool,' she leans forward, conspiratorially. 'What happened to her?'

'I don't know and don't care. I overcame and escaped. I'm not saying I don't have painful memories, but I'm here doing what I'm doing partly because of her. By being successful, I was putting a finger up to her. So, we can work this through for you, right?' Lilly agrees with a nod. 'Please tell me where you were Friday evening?'

'The Goth Club, it's our joke because all our dad's belong to the Golf Club. Since we started getting together I've stopped cutting.'

'And your grades have got better, right? I looked them up. Is your boyfriend in the Goth club?'

'Yes, I love him.'

'It's nice to have a boyfriend.'

'He makes me feel good.'

'I need to speak to the other members of the club, to confirm your alibi.'

'They'll freak out.'

'I'll go myself, no sirens, nothing like that. Where will they be?'

'The café at the top of the High Street,' Lilly tells her. 'I like your nails, they're perfect.'

'Thank you Lilly. Do you want a coffee?'

'Black please.'

'I won't be long and later I could do your nails for you.'

'That would be great,' Lilly beams. 'I don't want to go home.'

'You're eighteen and don't have to. Where do you want to go?'

'My boyfriends.'

'We'll have to check it out.'

There is a sudden sharp tap on the two-way mirror that runs down one side of the interview room.

++++

'Good stuff Indah.'

'I didn't know you were there, Gov.'

'I've been watching through the glass. Is that true about the bullying?'

'I elaborated a bit, but yes. Maybe I see myself in Lilly and that's why…'

'Yes?'

'Sorry, I shouldn't have suggested I do her nails.'

'We're short staffed and before allocating duties check with the DI or me first please,' but he is smiling. 'You did it for the right reasons. Take an hour no more and then go and have frothy coffee with Goth Club.'

Phone rings.

'Cully. Slow down Monica.' He listens. 'On my way.'

Fifteen minutes later Cully drives as fast as he dare through narrow rutted east Island roads, risking life and limb by overtaking a horse drawn cart and then avoiding an old car coming at him on the wrong side of the road.

'I was about to leave for the autopsies when you called,' he explains to Monica as they walk from the car park. 'How are things?'

'Tense, but not as bad as they were. Pete and the oligarch seem to have established some sort of weird rapport.' Turning a corner the first things Cully sees are two Jet Ranger helicopters sitting on the playing field. 'Asimov and Sheik Ben Assad flew in about an hour ago,' explains Monica. 'The Sheik is inside helping his son pack. More parents on their way by plane into the Island airport and cars on the ferry now the fog is lifting. Kids are being evacuated like it's a war zone.'

‘By the look of it, it could become one.’ Two armed police officers are wide apart, kneeling holding automatic rifles at the ready while forty metres away the hands of three heavy set security guards hover over holstered pistols. ‘Pete?’

‘We were doing fine and then the mother started shouting about something and things got tense again. She’s quite a looker though, isn’t she?’ Cully glances over to where a tall blonde woman in a tight black dress with a scarlet jacket is lecturing a young woman. ‘That’s the daughter, Gov. She seems ok. Before the helicopters landed, I got chatting to one of the guards. He’s ex-job. They’ve got a cottage nearby.’

‘We’ll need to search it.’

‘The guy was fine until the chopper arrived and suddenly they turn into KGB.’

‘FSB.’

‘What?’

‘It’s renamed the FSB now.’

‘You always know stuff, Gov.’

‘What nationality are the other guards?’

‘English, but with strong Russian loyalties, based on hard cash. The ex-job guy told me they’re earning five thousand a month plus expenses.’

‘Monica said you were getting on with dad?’

‘Yeah, talking Dad stuff with Monica translating. We even had a joke, but these guards are paranoid.’

‘Ok, our guys listen to me, back off.’

‘Gov?’

‘I mean it,’ Cully shouts. ‘Stand up, walk back, relax your weapons and show them we don’t want trouble.’

‘Monica, tell the Oligarch we don’t want trouble.’

She speaks Russian quickly.

He replies, but now the daughter is talking to her father.

‘What she saying?’

‘She tells her father not to be a stupid arsehole, he should tell the guards to put down their guns and cooperate with the police. She says that things are done differently in this country and he can’t kill or bribe his way out of trouble.’

‘She’s feisty isn’t she?’

'Dad is doing as he's told.' They watch as the three guards put their pistols on the ground. Pete and the armed officers move in to take the weapons. 'He's taking his daughter and leaving,' explains Monica.

'They look like Glock's to me,' says Cully. 'Pete, get warrants and organise a search of the cottage where the guards are staying. Remove all weapons and anything else of interest.'

'Are they under arrest, Gov?'

'I'll talk to CPS to see what they want to do. Monica the Andrew's daughter Bethany is here. Make certain she's alright and…'

'She might tell us a few things about her parents,' Monica grins. 'Gov, I've been thinking. The Andrews had a lot of cocaine, if this is drugs related, I'm thinking Bethany could be at risk. We should move her?'

'Where to?'

'I know there is a safe house out west.' Cully stares at her before she speaks again. 'I could stay with her. Gov?' Still nothing. 'Gov, perhaps mum could come to, or if she objects you could authorise it under Police Powers. Gov, what do you think?'

'Yes,' he hesitates, 'sorry, can you arrange it? Thanks to both of you. I need to be going.'

As Cully walks away Monica turns to where rotor blades are turning and the family Asimov are climbing aboard. 'What was all that about with the Gov, it's like he tuned out?'

'I'll tell you later,' says Pete. 'Now, I have a house to search and you have a teenager to gain the trust of. I know which is going to be easier.'

++++

There is music and a man singing discordantly along. Cully recognises the song as "Enjoy the Silence". 'I never imagined you as a Depeche Mode fan Gerry?'

'Ah, about time, Cully. I started without you. I have eclectic tastes and I thought it appropriate as this is your class of nineteen-ninety.' He sweeps an arm theatrically over the room. 'I've never been so busy and I've only got three slabs hence a make-do trolley. I'm afraid Mr Ballard has to rest on the floor,' and points to a sheet covered shape at his feet. 'Ballard, the oil man. He was involved in the proposed exploration at the forest. Not popular with locals.'

'No loss.'

'You didn't like him?'

'No,' Cully shrugs. 'Five dead and three dying upstairs. Quite a haul so far, but I don't think he's finished.' Cully pulls back a sheet from a slab as Depeche Mode finish and Mariah Carey starts "Vision of Love". 'We snogged once,' he says staring down into the dead face of Miranda Pegg. 'She was a bitch,' he declares remembering how she taunted him about Sophie. 'Bitch,' he mutters.

'I'm guessing you were late because of the Russians. Remember I'm a member of the Alumni Association.' Gerry is in his late sixties, overweight and unshaven with dark eyes behind thick rimmed glasses. 'We talk.'

'Bloody Mafia.'

'AA allows us old farts a chance to meet up and reminisce about convent girls. You'll remember in our day, your uncle's and mine, we didn't have girls in the school. We hardly had girls at all, to be honest. We had to go to the convent dance. Those convent girls were willing once you got them away from the nuns and I married one.'

'But she was a nun!'

'She was a novice and preferred me to Christ,' he chuckles. 'Ten years, Cully, since Caitland went. Too long to be alone.'

'I've had girlfriends.'

'A string of sexual encounters apparently. Not the same.'

'Grandmother went to the convent as well,' says Cully, changing the subject. 'I miss her. I was talking to the vicar yesterday that conducted the funeral service.'

'Ah yes, she's the priest for the school as well isn't she? Not sure I approve of women priests.'

'Gerry for God's sake, things move on. What do you know about the Russians?'

'There's been rumblings about the armed guards for quite a while. Inskip knew, but wasn't going to rock the boat.'

'Well the boat has rocked and is being abandoned as we speak.'

'I'm surprised the Chief Constable put you on the case.'

'I was in the wrong place at the wrong time,' and Cully lifts the sheet on another body to find Cameron Davis staring wide eyed back at him. 'No one will miss you.'

'Agreed, a right pervert by all accounts.' Gerry lifts another sheet, 'this is Chapman, an architect, and I believe his wife has arrived to identify the body. That's why he's on a trolley so I can wheel him to the viewing room. At least, there's no facial damage for the woman to look at, unlike Bradman over there. I doubt even his mother would recognise him.' Gerry waves his hand distractedly towards the furthest slab. 'Why did you come if you didn't fancy the reunion?'

'It was Linda's idea. She found the invite in the bin. Like you, she keeps hoping I'll meet someone.'

'Have you?' Cully sighs and turns away. 'Oh, you have, an old flame rekindles, how exciting and good for you.'

'Aside from eviscerating my love life Gerry, what have you got for me?'

'Cognac?'

'We're at work.'

'You haven't been cutting up corpses my dear boy and I thought you lot at MIU were hard drinkers? The odd snifter keeps me going and it's extremely good cognac. Your uncle gave it to me'

'I'm sure it is and he did, but can we get on please?'

'Adam is very proud of you.'

'The two of you talk about me.'

'At the Lodge.'

'Shit, you still going there? No wonder you're a misogynist.'

'I'll ignore that. The Lodge isn't bad, a place to have a drink, a chat and they do a jolly good steak and kidney pudding at Sunday lunch, nothing more. We can't influence things like we used to.'

'Thank your God for that.'

'Sure you don't want a drink,' he asks lifting the bottle before pouring a generous measure for himself. He sips. 'Delicious. I understand the shooter was firing at one group. Most of the victims died from a mixture of shots. Three in one victim, four in the next and so on. Head wound in one, chest in another that sort of thing. You get the picture?' Cully nods. 'The why's are your territory not mine.' Gerry sips his drink. 'This can't be easy for you?'

'It was thirty years ago Gerry. Let me have your report when you can.'

There is a clip clop of heels getting closer.

'Oh, the bodies, I didn't…' she stutters, lifting a hand to her mouth.

For a moment, Cully does not recognise the young woman in a white dress, pale blue jacket with hair falling to her shoulders. She is stunning. 'Becky, you look great and appropriate.'

'It was good getting home however briefly,' she explains, smiling, pleased by his compliments. 'So many bodies.'

'Eventually, we all get used to it, even the smell.'

'I hope so,' she mumbles nervously. 'Oh Indah texted, she's confirmed Lilly's alibi and taken her to the boyfriends. She's back in the incident room writing stuff up.'

'You're doing a great job Becky,' he smiles reassuringly. 'The man leering at you is Gerry, he can be a pain in the brain, but he's good at his job.'

'I've got Mrs Chapman in the family room,' Becky says.

++++

The media conference is scheduled for five so journalists could catch the six o'clock news, update blogs for that evening or have copy in for next day's newspapers. Some bright spark set up a Teams link to the mainland. Not only did Cully have to deal with half a dozen local journalists in the room, but twenty faces on the screen opposite the lectern behind which he shelters.

'Sorry for the delays everyone, but as you can imagine this is a fast-moving investigation and I'm being pulled in all sorts of different directions. First question please.'

'Can you confirm there are five dead?'

'Tragically true. There were five deaths at the scene and there are others in a critical condition.'

'So, there may be more deaths?'

'I'm not prepared to speculate, but I would like to thank the efforts of NHS staff, paramedics, nurses and doctors, in dealing with this incident.'

'Nice political statement, Superintendent Cully, but…'

'Who are you?'

'Daily Mail.'

'Next.'

'I haven't asked—'

'Next.'

'Do you have any leads on the shooter?'

‘We are examining a number of possibilities, but it’ll take time.’

‘Is there a terrorist link?’

‘Nothing apparent so far.’

‘Any motive come to light?’

‘We are exploring several.’

‘Does that include a pupil at the school called Lilly?’ Cully grimaces. ‘You’ve arrested her haven’t you?’ the reporter insists.

‘No, but she’s been helping us with our enquiries.’

‘Daily Mail again. Is this another Columbine or Sandy Hook?’

‘The victims were children in those cases. Next.’

‘Superintendent Cully, is it true many rich foreign parents are withdrawing their children from the boarding unit in east Island? That they’ve been arriving by helicopter and planes to remove their children?’

‘Some have, yes, but you should speak to the headteacher Dr Inskip for more details.’

‘He won’t answer his telephone,’ complains someone.

‘Try email. Next?’

‘Is it true that there was a gun stand-off between Russian security guards and police this morning?’

‘There was a misunderstanding, no more,’ states Cully, trying a smile. ‘We worked the situation through and everything is fine.’

‘Is it true you’ve been searching a house in the village? Neighbours have seen guns being removed.’

‘There are some things I am not going to comment on at this time. Next.’

‘BBC,’ begins a face from the screen. ‘We’ve been told one of the parents is Karl Asimov the billionaire Russian oligarch. It is widely alleged he built his vast fortune from organised crime, prostitution, but especially drug dealing.’

‘I wouldn’t know about that. All I know, is that he’s a friend of the Prime Minister.’

‘Superintendent Cully, are you suggesting the Prime Minister is involved in drug smuggling?’

‘No, of course not.’

‘The nature of the attack might suggest it’s drugs related don’t you think?’

‘We are examining all possibilities.’ Cully looks around for a sympathetic face. ‘South Island radio do you have a question?’

‘Is the shooter a forest dweller?’

'Pardon?'

'The tree village is about to be bulldozed, could this be revenge for that?'

'Anyone have a sensible question?'

'Channel 4 news, coming in from London. Is it correct that you used to go to the school?'

'Yes.'

'Were you due to attend the event last night?'

'Yes.'

'Isn't there a conflict of interests?'

'Potentially, if I let it happen.'

'SKY, also stuck in London, why were you allocated?'

'Because I was on the Island.'

'But you didn't go to the reunion event?'

'No, I changed my mind.'

'Why?'

'Do you go to your school reunions?' Cully takes a deep breath. 'Next.'

'South Island Press. Are you getting help from thc mainland?'

'Some has arrived, but we've had fog to contend with. We expect more and, as you know, the Navy bomb squad came quickly last night. You also have to remember the mainland are dealing with major incidents including one in which children have been murdered.'

'So, you would admit police resources are stretched?'

'We are managing. Anything else?'

'Do you expect more shootings?'

'We hope not.'

'Will you be using a profiler?'

'No.'

'Superintendent Cully, can we talk about what happened in the mainland custody suit eighteen months ago?' asks a blonde young woman, in a square at the bottom of the screen. Behind her Cully could see a "Vogue" cover print on a white wall. 'Well?'

'Is it relevant?'

'To you, it is.'

'Who are you?'

'*Bonjour* magazine.'

'I didn't know you had a crime correspondent.'

'We don't and I'm not, but we'd love to do a feature on you and your daughter. Hero dad, hero daughter that sort of thing.'

'If there is nothing else, someone will be here to update you tomorrow.'

'Will it be you?'

'Not if I can help it,' Cully mutters.

++++

It is nearly seven Saturday evening, not quite twenty-four hours since the shooting in the school hall. In the incident room, Lisa, Tom and Kerry are combing through statements as Pete arrives. 'How did you get on with Lilly?' he asks. 'Did she do it?'

'No. We searched the house,' Lisa tells him, 'found a replica Glock 17 in her room, Satanic literature and a diary. She hates the pupils in her class, but nothing to suggest she might kill them. She's angry at not being selected to wait table at the event, especially as she missed out on all the blood and gore and the bragging on social media. Lilly didn't do it, poor kid. Where's Monica?'

'Baby-sitting Bethany Simpson. They've gone to the safe house.'

'We have a safe house?' Tom is surprised. 'Where?'

'What about her mother?' asks Lisa, ignoring him.

'Not interested. An unnatural parent if ever there was one,' mutters Pete. 'And yes Tom, we have a safe house, but it's a secret,' he chuckles.

'The world is full of troubled children,' sighs Tom. 'I'd do anything to protect my boy,' he says as much to himself as anyone else. 'We heard there was a standoff.'

'It was touch and go for a while, but things calmed down.' Pete goes on to explain the search of the guard's cottage produced semi-automatic handguns, a Glock 17, and two assault rifles. All were removed and would be tested to see if they had been recently fired. 'Otherwise we've been unable to discover anything useful talking to pupils or staff. We did watch as a procession of parents or their employees remove children. There are only four left in the unit.'

'There's nothing here,' Kerry complains, pushing papers away across the desk with such force that they cascade on to the floor. 'Shit!'

'I have good news princess,' Pete announces, picking up the papers.

'I'm not your princess,' she snaps.

'Is that because I don't have a motorbike and a big gun?'

'Piss off!'

'Enough,' Lisa shouts. 'What's your good news, Pete?'

'The Gov came back out to see us after the press conference to make certain all was well. He's gone to his uncle's for something to eat and then on to the hospital to replace Indah and will act as FLO overnight. He said to tell everyone to go home and get some rest.'

'Really?' Tom hopes it is true. 'Really?' he repeats.

'Totally Tommy boy, the Gov you will discover is a fair man and looks after his team. You can go home to Trudi.' Then he remembers Lisa. 'If that's alright with you, Ma'am?'

'I think it's a great idea.'

Tom is already standing, collecting his things. 'Pete, do you want a lift to the hotel?'

'That would be lovely. We're on expenses, so stop for a drink.'

'I mustn't.'

'Never let the wife control you.'

'Trudi doesn't and I need to take my turn looking after Toby.'

'Ah, that's where I went wrong, three wives and four kids later, never did enough at home.'

'Must cost you a fortune in maintenance?'

'I get by Tom, there are ways and means to get by,' Pete mutters. 'How was Gov's press conference?' he asks. 'He didn't say much when we saw him.'

'Ok, but suggested the Prime Minister is a drug dealer,' Lisa answers. 'I've got to do it tomorrow, he thinks it will be good for my career development.'

'He always says that. Seriously, Pete,' he mimics, 'I think it would be good for your career development. And I tell him I've got no career development, happy what I'm doing and only five years till I put in my papers.'

'I've more good news,' begins Lisa, reading a text on her phone, 'the Gov doesn't want us in for morning briefing until ten. The drug squad officer can't get here until then and we deserve a lie in. Now go everyone. I can finish off here. What's that noise?'

They all go to the main door and stare out into a blaze of orange light within which a low-loader carrying a portacabin followed by a crane are crawling into the church car park.

'Sorry,' begins Pete, 'forgot to say, the Gov ordered it, so we've got interview rooms here rather than having to traipse all the way to the station.'

'Shit, we better move the cars and then you go. One of you find Chalky, poor bugger has been watching security cd's since he got back from the mainland, and take him with you.'

Ten minutes later, a headache developing from the noise and spinning lights she returns to the incident room. 'You can go Kerry.'

'Can we talk?' she asks. 'I know people don't like me.'

'What?'

'I'm not stupid.'

Phone rings.

'Yes?' Lisa listens. 'You're kidding me. She shot a forest-gremlin? Fuck!'

++++

Uncle Adam pushes the plate across the table towards him. 'Eat.'

'It smells and looks lovely, but I'm not hungry.'

'I can imagine this case is messing with you, but you have to eat.'

'Put it in the fridge and I'll eat later.'

'You can't go on like this. You need regular food, it's fuel.'

'You sound like granny,' Cully smiles thinly.

'Coffee?'

'Please.'

'Do you have to go back tonight?' Adam Cully is nearly seventy years of age, tall with a straight back and thinning silver-grey hair. He puts two mugs on the kitchen table and pours strong black coffee. 'Well?'

'I'm FLO at the hospital.'

'You need rest. You're not superman, not indispensable.'

'Vicar Mandy asked if I ever get vertigo. Not with this case I'm not, it's more like I'm sinking through a quicksand of enveloping memories.'

'Very poetic. I'm guessing it's the people.'

'The women,' Cully corrects, smiling, 'and…'

'Yes?'

'Nothing,' but Cully wanted to talk about the safe house, yet knew it would worry Adam. He is surprised Monica even knew about it, but remembered there had been a number of high at risk asylum seekers placed there recently. 'Just the women, nothing else.'

‘Ah, they’re always a problem.’ Adam thoughtfully sips his coffee. ‘You’ve seen Jamie?’

‘I have. He’s not got long, but they’re looking after him well and he’s still controlling the world from his laptop.’

‘They looked after gran well,’ Adam says softly. ‘Cully is there something from schooldays you…’

‘No,’ Cully shakes his head. ‘I wasn’t abused, if that’s what you’re asking? Slippered once by Poulson. Compared to some I got off lightly.’ He stands and puts the mugs in the sink. ‘Just so you know, you and gran were brilliant parents and I was always able to talk to you both.’

‘You mentioned women, I’m guessing it’s a particular one, Sophie Cairns. I remember, you had gran and I worried. I can’t forgive her for that. She screwed with you.’

‘It wasn’t her fault,’ Cully sighs. ‘I must go.’

About to turn “Don’t Stop”, Fleetwood Mac, on the car’s CD player, Cully stops and flicks through the CD selector to find a Nineties compilation disc. He selects Sinead O’Connor and presses play allowing memories about Sophie and Jenny to come flooding back before Caitland’s image forces her way through. Apart from flickering street lights, a cat on the prowl, the occasional drunk forest-gremlin meandering back to the Great Forest, there is nothing to slow him. He drives fast and before the next track, Regina Velasquez Singing “You were Meant For Me”, he drives by the hospital and continues west.

++++

The White House, as it is called locally, is set back a kilometre or more away from other buildings. It is almost as Cully remembers it, although electric wrought iron-gates have been installed and are closed. Parking away from the security cameras he walks across the road, edging along the high stone wall to a convenient tree which he climbs making a mental note to get it chopped down. Settling on a branch that gives him a view over the sensory detectors that top the wall, he stares ahead. He feels a great wave of sadness roll over him as memories crowd in.

Cully remembers the paramedics coming down the stairs with a stretcher, feet crunching broken glass from where the invaders forced the front door. It was there the man in the blue coat had fallen, shot twice in the back by the protection officer whom in turn is shot dead by the woman in black. She comes next, but breaking the door open sets off the alarm and Caitland and Cully are quickly up out of bed, shooing Linda into the wardrobe with instructions to keep quiet whatever she hears. They have been issued with sidearms for personal protection, keep them handy by the bed, and both been trained to use them. Reaching the top of the stairs he sees the woman and fires, hitting her twice in the chest sending her falling into the lounge, but a large man is suddenly there and fires upwards hitting him in the thigh. The man keeps coming up the stairs followed by another with a *coffee au lait* complexion. Cully retreats towards the bedroom and men reach the landing. There is an explosion close to his head and a bullet enters the left side of the big man's neck, blood spurts like rain and he stumbles back through the bathroom door. The other is still shooting as he comes on. Cully feels his arm burn and falls back aware that Caitland is still returning fire. Then suddenly everything is quiet, the man is on his back on the landing, his arm flopping through the bannisters. Cully feels relief, but Caitland is no longer beside him. She's on her back on the bedroom floor. He tries to shrug off the memory, but it clings to him, crawling through his consciousness until he cries out with the pain of it and grabs hold of the branch to stop from falling.

Cully cannot justify his behaviour, but wants to see inside without disturbing Monica and Bethany. No, that's an excuse, he can't face going in. The small pair of binoculars he keeps in the car glovebox help. The curtains are open, something he'd speak to Monica about, and could see the two women watching television. Swinging left to the front door he is shocked to find it is half glass, something that needs changing, but it allows him to look inside, to the hallway and the bottom of the staircase where the cherubs climb the wall.

Dropping to the ground, he walks to the car and drives thoughtfully away.

++++

Thirty minutes after receiving the original call, Lisa pulls up behind a patrol car. The back doors of the ambulance are wide open and she sees, in the glow from overhead lights, two paramedics working on a body. 'How is he?' she calls.

'Once we get her stabilised we'll take her to hospital.'

'Kerry stay with the woman, see what you can find out.' Walking across the garden, Lisa enters the kitchen through the open back door. 'Police, DI Lynn, anyone here?'

'In here, Ma'am. This is Mrs Saunders, she's the one that shot the forest-gremlin,' explains a uniformed female officer.

'Have you read her, her rights?'

'Yes, but I'm not sure she understands,' she adds.

'Hello Mrs Saunders I'm DI Lynn, but you call me Lisa,' she smiles, sitting opposite the elderly grey haired woman. 'Do you live here alone?'

'My Harry is here.'

'Who's Harry?'

'My husband.'

'Where is he?'

'Upstairs in bed.'

'Ok.' Lisa looks up at the officer standing behind the woman's chair and she shakes her head. 'Do you have any children?'

'They've gone.'

'Gone to the mainland?'

'To school dear.' The officer moves across the room to the fireplace and brings over a faded black and white photograph of two children in school uniform. 'Yes, that's them,' and names them.

'Ma'am, there are post-it notes on the fridge with names and telephone numbers.'

'See if you can identify the children and ring them. Tell them what has happened, but in the meantime, we have to take her in.'

'But, Ma'am, she's…'

'I know what she is, but we have no choice. She'll be safer with us than left here. Contact the social services duty team. They may know her and we'll need a psyche assessment and an appropriate adult for the interview.'

'Yes Ma'am.'

'You've got the weapon?'

'Yes, we've bagged and tagged them both.'

'Both?'

'The forest-dweller had a wand.'

'This is crazy, but you've done well, thank you.' Lisa gets up. 'Make certain she's got a warm coat. She'll probably want her handbag. I'll follow you to the station,' says Lisa not wanting to use the portacabin.

Outside Lisa leans against her car, exhausted and the pain in her head is developing into a migraine. Getting in she finds tablets in the glove compartment and takes two, washing them down with what's left in a bottle of water. It would be easy to drive the short distance to where her parents live, let her mother fuss over her and curl up in the bed in the room that was kept "for any of you girls if you need somewhere". She doubted her parents had considered all four of them ever needing somewhere at the same time.

A few metres away the ambulance doors are closing and making an effort Lisa goes over. 'How is she Kerry?'

'Stable.'

'The shooter appears to be demented. We're trying to contact the family and we'll get social services involved. I'll follow the officers back to the station. Can you go with the ambulance?'

'Of course and, Ma'am, I do want to fit in.'

'Not now Kerry.' Lisa groans.

'I'm not stupid.'

'In that case, you shouldn't be surprised after what you did or rather didn't do? Tom and Indah put their necks on the line by doing the right thing, but you said you didn't see any harm in the banter and yet you were a victim of it as much as us. Racist, sexist you name it they said it and you told the board you heard and saw nothing. I remember one of them had his hand up your skirt, but you didn't complain.'

'My father…'

'Was pathetic, did nothing to protect us and got let off.'

'He was forced out.'

'With a lump sum and a full pension.'

'He committed suicide.'

'A coward to the end.'

'That's not fair.'

'Sorry, I'm tired,' Lisa takes a deep breath, recalling what Cully had said about being careful with Kerry. 'If you think we all hate you, then why don't you accept a transfer, go to the mainland, get away, start afresh?'

'I can't, because…'

'Because of Tizard I suppose?' Lisa snaps

'I love him.'

'What about my sister?'

'She doesn't love him and he doesn't love her. He's leaving her.'

'Is that what he tells you, you stupid slut. I'll never like you while you're hurting my family. Apply for that transfer and save us all Kerry from your childish behaviour. Now go to the hospital.'

++++

Arriving at the hospital Cully chats briefly with Indah over coffee in the canteen before telling her to go home. He then rides the lift upwards, finding Gerry waiting to go down.

'What are you doing up here with the just living?'

'Collecting Simpson's left hand.' Gerry taps the cool box he is carrying. 'A bullet smashed it and they decided to amputate. Dead stuff becomes my responsibility. I need to get this to the freezer.'

Cully watches him go before heading to the secure ward. Two armed officers open doors to let him through. Nurses move here and there glancing-up as he goes by to the curtained bed at the far end. 'Sean, I thought I'd see how you are.'

'Cully, I heard your name mentioned. I'll live apparently.' Boyish, with a round face and thinning hair Sean O'Leary is sitting up in bed, sketching on a pad. 'They operated early this morning, removed the bullet which I want as a souvenir.'

'I'm afraid it will be bagged as evidence, but I'll see what I can do. Are you up to answering some questions?'

'What do you want to know?'

'Not so much about the night, but maybe you can remind me about the Nasty Gang?' Cully pulls up a chair and sits. 'You do remember?'

'Of course I do. It's what we called them.'

'It hasn't occurred to you how the tables were divided last night?'

'Not really, but on the TV it said it's about drugs.'

'The dead and most of the wounded were on the one table where the Nasty Gang were sitting.'

'I wasn't on the table and I wasn't in the Nasty Gang.'

'I know Sean,' Cully shrugs. 'If they were the target, then you and the other wounded were collateral damage.'

'You think it was revenge, that someone from our year did this?'

'Quite a jump, but one possibility amongst several motives we're exploring.'

'Back then I wanted them dead,' Sean admits. 'We all hated them at one time or another. I was nicknamed short arse, wasn't I? Felicity used to pat me on the head and Ballard was a cruel bastard, but then you had your moments Cully. You took Rachel off me.'

'Sean, she'd finished with you.'

'Only because you kept flirting with her and you were, are taller than me.'

'Are you being serious?'

'Sort off. I'm pathetic.'

'No, you're not. You're still in shock. Schooldays really aren't the happiest days of our lives,' Cully sighs, deciding he did not want to reminisce any further and stands up. 'What have you been doing since school?'

'I went to art college, travelled a bit, trained as a librarian and I paint.'

'Which library?'

'I drive the mobile library here on the Island. I told you pathetic, I've not moved on. No wife, no kids, nothing to show for my life.'

'But you paint.'

'Not very well. Don't kid yourself Cully. I mean, look at you super cop. I looked you up on the Internet when I thought you were going to be at the event. Spectacular stuff. Why didn't you turn up?'

'I bottled it.'

'Sophie was there.'

'But no Jenny?'

'Ah, is that why you didn't come,' Sean grins, 'didn't want to cause a catfight?'

'It was thirty years ago.'

'School days are like yesterday Cully. Is Sophie alright?'

'She's shocked, but fine. Do you see any of them?'

'Occasionally.'

'Do you know a chemistry teacher called Turner?'

'Should I?'

'The Island is a very small place and we need to speak to him.'

'I know of him and the gossip. I'm guessing you know what happened. He was a fool. Crystal is vulnerable and he took advantage.'

'We can't find him, any ideas?'

'No, but my dad will know, Turner goes to his church. Dad's been supporting him through it. Turner is suing the school for wrongful dismissal. Dad's seventy, but still runs his church. He's gone fundamental. He's coming in. I'll ask him to ring you.'

'I'll leave my card.' Cully drops one on the bedside table and lifts a thin paperback. '"Abelard and Heloise" by Ronald Millar,' he reads.

'Ah, of course you and Sophie, the great romance, a bit of a coincidence,' Sean grins. 'You'll be wanting to rekindle things, will you?'

Something in Sean's voice, makes Cully hesitate, a touch of desperate hope for a negative reply and Cully gives it to him. 'No and I've not seen her.' Cully watches Sean's face relax. 'You're using the play somehow?' *What games are you playing little Sean?* 'Are you?'

'It's the theme for my art exhibition.'

Cully puts the script down, slightly shaken, notices a basket of fruit from the Island Art Society and flowers from Cordelia with three kisses on the card. 'I thought you said you were pathetic,' he says, but is thinking back thirty years. 'You paint and have an admirer with a sexy name. You didn't do art at school.'

'I didn't have your confidence.'

'When do you open?'

'In a fortnight if I'm fit. The show goes on.'

++++

Sunday

Cully leaves Sean and heads towards the canteen to get a black coffee and think, but bumps into Kerry. She explains what has happened, but the last thing he wants is to have her around and sends a grumpy Kerry back to the station to assist Lisa. 'I'll interview the forest-gremlin, no need for you to be here,' Cully tells her. He watches her flounce away before drifting down to A & E and asking after the woman.

'She'll be fine. We're going to take the shot out under local anaesthetic. It's in her arm. She's fit and healthy and will heal quickly.'

'Thank you. You remind me of…'

'I'm Mary Tizard, Lisa's sister.'

'I wasn't thinking of her, but yes of course,' Cully smiles, slightly perplexed.

'I was adopted,' Mary starts to explain, 'hence the light brown hair colour rather than blonde. I'm the youngest, there are four of us.' She is tall, thin and fox faced. 'Four girls, can you imagine it?'

'I've got one and she is,' he thinks, 'a handful.'

'We're all doing extra hours here with the school shooting. It's been chaos, we're not equipped for this sort of thing. Lisa talks about you, she's rather in awe.'

'I can't think why.'

'I can,' Mary smiles

'Can I speak to the forest-gremlin?'

'You can, if you're ok while I take out the shot.'

'For a start, it's not forest-gremlin it's forest-dweller, and I'm a healer,' calls a complaining voice from behind the screen. 'Have some respect.'

'Of course you are,' agrees Cully, liking feisty, pushing the curtain to one side and introducing himself. She is in her late thirties he guesses, tall and slender with long black hair and wearing blue jeans and a t-shirt with a pentangle on it. There is bloodied gauze covering her upper left arm. Not looking at it he writes down her details and then asks what happened, writing as she talks. She admits to being drunk, fooling about and scaring the old woman. 'I don't want to press charges. My fault. I saw it coming.'

'You did?'

'When I threw the stones yesterday morning, there was a warning I didn't heed. My fault,' she repeats.

'Ok,' Cully nods, 'but she shot you. I'll have a word, see what I can do, but CPS may insist on prosecuting.'

'She's demented, you should let her be.' She stares at Cully with dark eyes. 'Be careful Superintendent, you have an aura, there is danger ahead for you.'

'The stones?'

'You can mock, I was born with these powers and see things. Be careful.'

'We'll keep you in overnight,' smiles Mary, 'but you'll be fine. Can you get yourself into the wheelchair?'

'Sorry it's pathetic, I feel really weak.'

'No problem.' Mary lifts her and places her in the chair. An orderly arrives and pushes her away. Mary catches him staring at her. 'As a nurse you have to be strong, in every way. I need a ciggie, do you mind?' He shrugs and follows her outside to a shelter out of sight behind a tall hedge. It stinks of stale tobacco. She offers her packet, but Cully shakes his head. She lights her cigarette, drawing deeply on it. 'I know Lisa cares about me. The oldest and the youngest, we've always been close.' A mixture of smoke and chilled breath billows from her mouth. 'You must hate Steven.'

'I…' and for a moment Cully is uncertain about whom she means and then realises. 'Hate is a strong word.'

'Lisa told me and I read about what happened to your daughter and you. I'm really sorry. I should leave him.'

'You have to do what's right for you,' he says, not wishing to get into things. There is probably a chapter on marital discord in Sophie's book, if he'd read it and remembers the copy Jamie had given him is still in the car. He watches as a woman appears and lays a bunch of flowers alongside the others at the main hospital entrance, giving him an easy excuse to change the subject. 'People have started laying flowers outside the school,' he states. 'I hate to see dead flowers, teddy bears tied to railings and faded ribbons round trees.'

'It helps people.' Mary stubs out her cigarette. 'Coffee?'

‘Thanks,’ and suddenly regretting not eating the food Adam prepared adds, ‘if there’s something to eat I wouldn’t say no.’

‘No problem, come to the nurses room.’

She prepares toast for him as other nurses come in and out paying him little attention until one appears and stares at him. ‘You’re the cop off the TV. Said the PM is a drug dealer.’

‘Sabrina!’ Mary warns.’

‘Sorry Staff, but he did and you’re Jamie’s friend.’

‘And you brought me tea,’ Cully remembers.

‘You look exhausted. We can let you have some tabs, that’ll keep you buzzing all night.’

‘Sabrina!’

‘Only joking Staff. See you,’ and she leaves.

‘But she’s right about one thing, you do look exhausted. I can find you a bed,’ Mary whispers. ‘There’s always somewhere to sleep here if you know where to hide.’

‘I bet you nurses know lots of tricks.’

‘We get by,’ she smiles weakly. ‘There are things I need to tell you about my husband. Can’t now, but I’ll ring you. Promise. Don’t tell Lisa?’

Half an hour later, full of toast and coffee, Cully settles back on a hospital bed surrounded by screens. He hears noises, people moaning, staff running, alarms, trolleys squeaking, machines humming. And the smell, not calming like that in the hospice, pungent and disagreeable.

Unable to sleep he makes a call.

‘Linda, it’s dad. Sorry, it’s late.’

‘No problem. At least, I know you’re still alive,’ she groans. ‘I’m watching TV, drinking a glass of wine and I’m bored.’

‘I need a favour if you are up for it.’

‘I’m up for anything dad, stop fussing.’

‘I can’t help it, I’m your dad.’

‘I know and like it,’ she laughs. ‘What do you want?’

‘Can you get to the archives and take out the Poulson files?’

‘Of course,’ she agrees excitedly. ‘It must be hell over there.’

‘It’s a struggle and I could use you on the team. Linda…’

‘Yes dad?’

‘They are using the safe house,’ and tears erupt, ‘I couldn’t go in.’

'Dad, you need a cuddle. Talk to me please.'

++++

The psychiatrist and social services take ages to arrive and the mental capacity assessment is not complete until five that morning. Cully has rung in with an update on the Healer. In turn, Lisa tells Kerry to go home, get a couple of hours sleep, a shower, something to eat and be back for the briefing at ten.

'Don't you want me in on the interview?'

'Kerry, I'm trying to give you a break, to be nice.' In truth, she is happier doing the interview on her own and did not want the young woman anywhere near her. 'But if you don't want to…'

'None of you want me do you? I'm a ball being batted back and forth between you all.' She steps closer to Lisa. 'I get it, I'm off.'

To Lisa's surprise the mental health professionals agree Mrs Saunders is fit to interview, although the decision she thinks means they don't have to section her and find a mental health bed off Island. So, four people sit in the cramped airless interview room. Maybe the portacabin would have been better after all? A duty solicitor sits beside Mrs Saunders, an appropriate adult in a corner while Lisa faces a nervous woman. 'Betty do you understand why you are here?'

'Not really dear.'

Lisa explains slowly that police officers brought her in.

'A nice couple.'

'Do you know why they brought you here?'

'I'm in trouble.'

'Last night you fired a shotgun. Remember?'

'Not sure.'

'I must protest DI Lynn, Mrs Saunders is unable to understand what this is all about,' challenges the solicitor.

'She's had a capacity assessment and as far as the professionals are concerned she is able to answer my questions.'

'I do tend to agree with the solicitor,' mumbles the appropriate adult. 'She doesn't seem to be all there.'

'Of course I'm here, how dare you? Who are you?'

'I'm the appropriate adult.'

'I must say, you don't look very appropriate. You don't look very well.'

‘I’ve been up all night.’

‘Can we get back to the matter in hand please,’ Lisa persists. The tablets have eased the migraine, but not removed the pain in her head. She would love to let Betty Saunders go, but knows she has to follow procedures. ‘However, while your protests are being recorded we are still going ahead. Betty, you own a shotgun?’

‘It’s my husband’s.’

‘You know how to use it?’

‘Yes dear, my husband takes me out shooting pigeon in the woods.’

‘Are you a good shot?’

‘You don’t have to answer that,’ the solicitor warns.

‘Of course I do, she’s a nice young woman. Hubby says I’m a very good shot. I kill as many birds as he does.’

‘Betty, your husband is no longer with us.’

‘Was he here? Oh, where is he?’

‘Betty,’ Lisa sighs, ‘your husband is dead. He died eighteen months ago.’

‘No dear, he didn’t. He’s here, you told me.’

‘I…Do you remember seeing someone in your garden last night?’

‘I like the tree village. Terrible they are trying to get rid of it. Hubby and I signed the petition to preserve it.’

‘But someone was in your garden last night?’

‘Yes and I’m not stupid, you don’t have to speak slowly.’

‘Good, now we are getting somewhere.’

‘He had a gun.’

‘It was a woman.’

‘No dear, it was a man, I’d never shoot a woman, although Hubby once did, not deliberately and he only winged her, and it was her fault because she strayed in front of the firing line.’

Lisa takes a deep breath.

‘Did you think this person had a gun?’

‘Yes.’

‘What did you do?’

‘I called hubby, but he must have been asleep. I got the shotgun from the rack, loaded it, went out into the garden and shot the man.’

‘Why not call the police?’

'Too slow and so busy with the school shooting. My son goes to the school, he'll be going to the sixth form next year.'

'You know about the shooting?'

'Yes.'

'When did it happen?'

'Friday night, as the rugby was about to start. Hubby loves the rugby.'

'After you shot the person what did you do?'

'I rang triple nine for an ambulance.'

'Thank you.' In her head, Lisa is ticking things off. She didn't have a license for the gun so they had her on that. Good enough for a caution. More importantly Betty had taken the gun out, knew what she was doing, admitted shooting the person and knew by ringing the ambulance what she had done. That is enough to please CPS, get another caution, if not a conviction, although she doubted a jury would find the old lady guilty of anything if it went to trial. 'You've been helpful Betty.'

'Will we get our shotgun back?'

'I'm afraid not.'

'But why?'

'It's a weapon used in a crime, you haven't got a licence and you shot someone.'

'In self-defence,' the solicitor offers. 'My client was in fear for her life.'

'What about the other chap I shot?'

'What?'

'Say no more Betty,' stutters the solicitor.

'The one last week, in the back field,' Betty continues, oblivious.

'Did you hit him?'

'Winged him, I think. He certainly ran away screaming.'

'Seriously Betty?'

++++

'Thank you for seeing me so early on a Sunday morning Ms Cairns,' says Indah. It is eight o'clock and Indah is pleased to fit the visit in before the briefing as she has a busy day ahead. 'Nice place.'

'I'm always up early. Call me Sophie. I want to help. Come in please.' She leads the way down a stone flagged passage to the lounge. 'The house belongs to Rachel, my younger sister. Have a seat.' There is an Inglenook fireplace, overstuffed couches and country pictures on walls. 'Can I get you anything?'

'I'm fine, thanks.'

'I'm pleased it's you DC Kasali,' she says smiling broadly as they settle opposite each other. 'You got me out of the loo and I wanted to thank you properly.'

'I was pleased to help and the Gov already passed on your thanks.'

'Is that what you call Cully?' Indah nods. 'We were in the same year, but of course you know that. Is he a good boss?'

'I've only known him for a couple of days,' Indah smiles. It is odd following Cully's trail, exploring his background, meeting previous girlfriends. She could see why he'd been attracted to Sophie. Perhaps he still is, but why does it matter to her? She needs to focus. 'I've got a question.'

'Go ahead.'

'Why did you go to the toilet at that precise time, just before the shooting started?'

'Because I needed a wee. You think I knew it was coming?'

'Did you?'

'No.'

'Before you went to the toilet, did you see anything unusual?'

'I was chatting with Tash and then Sean O'Leary. He was trying to flirt, but is awful at it. As I went he walked over to speak to Carla. Andrew Pennington was there as well by the other table.'

'Anything you remember will be helpful?' Indah continues, understanding how others became casualties in the chaos.

'Patrick was on our table with Andrew. The seating plan was deliberately done to keep us apart.'

'Apart?'

'It was stupid teenage stuff. I was in the Nice Gang as were the others round our table.'

'The other table?'

'Seated the Nasty Gang,' Sophie grimaces. 'Stupid stuff.'

'Do you know who did the seating plan?'

'I did. Dr Inskip asked me to.'

'Really,' Indah mutters to herself, but lets it go. 'You don't live on the Island?'

'No, on North Island where my therapeutic practise is based.'

'Family?'

'Our parents are dead, they owned a hotel and I never married. Rachel is the breeder. She's with a farmer,' Sophie shrugs. 'She has four kids although you wouldn't know it to look around. She keeps it pristine. Have you got children?'

'No, work takes over.'

'Don't let it, but you're young.'

'Tell me about your work.'

'I'm a trauma therapist.'

'What sort of trauma?'

'Any, rape, death of a relative, violence, car crash and abuse. I get to see quite a few military people, paramedics, police, especially traffic officers after attending fatal accidents or ones recovering from being attacked. Anything that changes a person's life, makes them into prey.'

'Prey?'

'Victims if you prefer. I try to help people move on. Mostly group work. I simply facilitate and it's other victims that really do the work in the group.'

'Turn victims into survivors?'

'Turn victims into strong individuals that can take control of their lives and fight back, or at least defend themselves, emotionally of course. I don't like the word survivor. Here.'

'What's this?'

'My book.'

'You've written a book, how wonderful.' Indah is genuinely excited. Then remembers that both Tom and Lilly mentioned a therapy book and this must be it. Indah momentarily wishes she'd had such a book at school and perhaps she and Crystal could have read it together? Not a chance. 'You must do amazing work,' and Indah goes to give the book back.

'No, keep it.' Sophie shifts in her chair. 'You might find it useful.'

'How do you get your clients?'

'Word of mouth and I advertise, for instance, in the Alumni magazine. I'm always busy,' she smiles. 'What makes a good detective?'

'I don't know,' Indah says, taken aback by the sudden change of topic. 'On the course they say…'

'Forget the course, what do you say Indah?'

'I…'

'I'm certain you're a good detective Indah Kasali. I sense you have good intuition, empathy and understanding.'

'I suppose,' Indah hesitates. 'Probably, inherited from my mother.'

'Doubting must come high on the list.'

'Doubting, I don't follow?'

'As a police officer you have to doubt, don't you? 'Assiduous and frequent questioning is indeed the first key to wisdom,' Sophie quotes. 'For by doubting we come to inquiry; through inquiring we perceive the truth…'

'That's from a play?'

'He said it to me.'

'Who did?'

'Abelard when I was Heloise.'

'You and the Gov?'

'It was a long time ago,' Sophie looks away and back. 'You were saying about your mother?'

'She was a nurse. She retired a while ago after my father died.'

'I'm sorry for your loss and you an only child.'

'How do you know that?'

'I sense you are carrying it all, no one to share it with. Tea?'

'Please.'

'I hope you're ok with green tea,' Sophie says, standing. 'Come with me.' Indah follows obediently into the spacious, extremely tidy kitchen, watching as Sophie makes the brew. 'You need to find someone, to share with.'

'That would be nice,' Indah admits.

'But trusting someone is difficult, I guess because of your job. Everyone lies.'

'I'm sure I'll find someone eventually.'

'You will, but don't wait too long and if you get a chance grab it.' Sophie hands her a mug. 'You'll like it, I think. I always carry a packet. I find it soothing.' Sophie thoughtfully sips her tea. 'Indah, I've not been totally open with you. I disliked lots of people I went to school with, but one person in particular.'

++++

Cully stands in the church car park talking with Monica and Pete. The Sunday morning church service has finished and the few worshippers are meandering away. There have been grumblings about the car park being cordoned off, the portacabin arriving, and the church hall being unavailable, but Vicar Mandy has been firm with her flock.

'It's not that I don't trust the Island people, but I'm glad to have you here.'

'You alright, Gov?'

'Thanks Monica, I'm tired, but fine. Are you both ok with what I've asked you to do so far?' They nod in unison.

'I'm good, Gov,' says Pete.

'Monica?'

'On my way to the hospital.'

'Bethany?'

'Likes the safe house. She's going out with Chalky's wife and daughter shopping today. She's a great kid.'

'I've organised some urgent work to be done at the White House, a new solid front door and to have some trees cut down that are too close to the perimeter.'

'I didn't know you'd been there?'

'Don't forget to draw the curtains at night.'

Lisa comes over before Monica can question Cully further. Pete has given the gist of what happened ten years before, but she is keen to know more.

'Can you do without me for the briefing, I need to finish with Mrs Saunders and get her home. Social services have promised to monitor things and her children should be here soon. If ever I get like that, I hope someone shoots me,' but laughs at the irony of the comment. 'Sorry, inappropriate. Mary texted, said she met you.'

'She did and fed me toast. Good luck with Mrs Saunders.'

Cully enters the incident room and looks round. Things are up and running. Computers and telephone lines are in place, two civilian support staff have arrived, Tom's well drawn map of the scene is there under the long school photograph, joined by crime scene pictures. The church hall is small, but big enough for now and they can expand into the portacabin. Tom, Kerry, Pete, Chalky and Indah with her head in a book await him. No sign of Tizard. 'Firstly, I'd like to welcome Sergeant Claudia Davies from the drugs squad who will be following up on what was a kilo of cocaine in the satchel. Over to you Claudia.'

‘The satchel belongs to David Andrews,’ she begins. She’s tall, angular, perhaps forty with cropped brown hair. ‘We’ve applied for warrants to search his car, the house they’ve rented for the week and take fingerprints while he’s unconscious. Unfortunately, I’m told the warrants won’t be available until late this afternoon. Also, SOCO won’t be available until tomorrow because of the forest-dweller shooting. Is that real?’

‘It is Claudia,’ admits Cully. ‘This is South Island, things are different here, like in a parallel universe.’

‘We will activate the warrants tomorrow. In the meantime,’ Claudia grinning, disbelieving continues, ‘I’ll be digging into the Andrews background with help from colleagues on the mainland.’

‘Some of you,’ Cully starts, ‘will remember the Poulson case, the priest that got murdered soon after he came out of prison, well he was a teacher here.’

‘They never caught anyone did they?’

‘No Pete.’

‘Probably didn’t try hard. The bastard got what he deserved.’

‘You’re all heart, Pete. Monica is FLO today. Kerry replace her at nine tonight precisely, no later please. Then tomorrow you continue with the checks on the target group dead and alive. Any luck with Michal Carter?’

‘He’s a solicitor, but his offices are closed over the weekend and I’m chasing his home number.’

‘Good, thanks Kerry. Indah, anything? Indah!’

‘Sorry gov.’

‘You’ve not stopped reading since you got here,’ says Kerry. ‘We’re here to work.’

‘I am working. I saw Sophie Cairns first thing this morning. She wrote it. The first chapter about her life is gripping. She’s got a motive, at least for killing one of the dead, Cameron Davis.’

‘Go on,’ encourages Cully, remembering the corpse and why he hated him. He’d been expecting stuff to start coming out and really must read that first chapter if not the rest. ‘Tell us.’

‘There was an accident when she was eighteen. During the summer holidays before everyone went to university. Davis was driving. He was drunk, they crashed, the car turned over and caught fire. He got out and left her to die. I’ve checked the record, although I can’t find the crash report. She was dragged out of the car before it blew-up. Her saviour knew enough to drop her in a horse trough full of water to cool her down and then held her to keep her warm until the ambulance arrived. She is scarred down the right side of her body.'

'Who was the hero?' Pete asks with a sideways glance at Cully.

'The police record doesn't say and she wouldn't.'

'She was a highflyer,' begins Chalky. 'I remember Dad saying something about her being bright, getting straight "A's", but not going to university. She sort of dropped out of sight.'

'And the book?' Cully asks. 'What about it?'

'After the accident she did drugs and all sorts. Talks about throwing away the one chance of happiness she had, the love of her life,' and Indah looks up at Cully, before continuing. 'I'm quoting from it,' she begins. 'Poor me, they say, there is nothing that will take away the agony. Wrong, there is one thing. The only solution is to strike back with fatal violence.' Indah stands, sticks a photograph of Sophie on the glass display board and draws a line with an arrow to the picture of Davis pasted next to where his body was found. 'A suspect with a motive. Also, she did the seating plans which gives her opportunity to arrange things.'

'Excellent work Indah,' Cully praises her, feeling a knot tightening in his stomach, but gaining eye contact with her and smiling. 'Right let's get on, everyone go.'

'Teacher's pet,' Kerry hisses. 'He's too bloody good to be true.'

'Ten times better than your pathetic father.'

'Girls!' Pete steps between them. 'Times of the month?' Both young women glare at him. 'Better hate me than each other, now we've got work to do.'

'I swear, I'll kill her,' growls Indah.

'Join the que,' agrees Pete. 'Now come on.'

++++

Because Lisa has to deal with Mrs Saunders and organise the search behind the old woman's house for evidence of the second shooting Cully reluctantly offers to do the media briefing. There are many more people there in the room and on the Teams link than the day before.

Until his visit to the White House Cully had not thought about the media making a link between what happened there and the present. Now he thought it inevitable, but no one so far said a thing. At the time, there had been a media blackout and when the press office "leaked" things the story was spun as a tragic home invasion, that the wife of the family, a serving police officer, had been killed and the invaders chased off by the husband, also a serving police officer. Names were not released to protect the privacy of the family. The truth, that members of the Serbian crime gang *Groupa Europa* had come to kill Caitland in revenge for the two years she'd spent undercover infiltrating the gang in Britain and the fact she gave evidence in the trial of the gangs leader, was known to very few. The two dead protection officers were taken to the mainland and "killed" in a gang shooting there. The *Groupa Europa* bodies found their way into the Island's abattoir.

Relieved to get the press conference over with, Cully walks briskly across the car park towards his car. Phone rings. It is CPS and after a brief chat he ends the call and rings Pete. 'Hi, CPS say they want to charge the bodyguards. As we discussed, you and Chalky bring them in, charge and bail them.'

'It'll be a pleasure.'

'Try to get it done as quickly as possible. Cheers, Pete.'

Phone rings again.

'Hello.'

'Cully, Liam O'Leary here, I'm with Sean at the hospital. He says you want some information about one of my practitioners.'

'Yes, Turner, his address, if you're able to share that.'

'I can't see any harm in it, but my memory isn't what it used to be. I'll go into the church office on the way home.'

'I don't want to put you out.'

'No problem. I'm having lunch with your uncle and Gerry at the Lodge, steak and kidney pudding on Sunday is a ritual for us old guys, and can do it afterwards, if that's alright?'

'That's fine, speak to you later.'

'Superintendent Cully!'

'Yes,' he turns, his hope for a quiet lunch slipping away. The idea of steak and kidney pudding had whetted his appetite and he'd even flirted with the idea of joining the old guys at the Lodge, heaven forbid. 'Ah,' someone else to flirt with. 'Yes?'

'I'm Araminta Gold from *Bonjour*. You met me yesterday on screen.'

'And here you are in person. You didn't ask any questions today.'

'Not my thing crime, as you pointed out yesterday, I'm more society stuff.' She is petite, thin, even boyish with long blonde hair, wearing blue jeans slit at the knees and a blue leather jacket over a white roll neck. 'People call me Minty.'

'What can I do for you Minty?'

'Disappointed not to be actually here yesterday of course, because of all the action with the borders. Rich influential parents to interview, it would have been a great opportunity for stories.'

'Sorry you missed the action,' Cully mutters without conviction. 'But I can fill you in,' he brightens wondering if she might have information they can use.

'Thank you. I tried to speak to Dr Inskip, but he's a grumpy old guy isn't he?'

'He's worrying about the safety of the young people. Dead or kidnapped kids would not be good publicity.'

'Carla Scutari is out of hospital,' Minty continues, breathless. 'Her publicist has been in touch.'

'She has a publicist?'

'She's an influencer.'

'Of course she is. What does she influence?'

'Fashion, lifestyle issues that sort of thing. I mean, you must know, she's owns one of the leading lingerie fashion houses in the country. I always wear her undies,' she giggles. 'She's worth a fortune.'

'Yet comes all this way for a school reunion, intriguing,' Cully muses. 'While it's lovely to talk with you Minty, what do you want?'

'When will you allow them into the rental house?' He shrugs. 'I understand from her husband that Allison Grey arrives today. I want to ask her why she didn't come to the dinner.'

'Is she an influencer?'

'No, but she organises charity events and *Bonjour* did a piece on her a few years back with photographs. She's attractive and was draped over a Porsche 911, although I prefer your Cayman. Nice colour. We want to do a piece on the women in their luxurious rental house. I've spoken to the letting agent and she is really keen.'

'What about Megan Simpson, she'll be there?'

'I know, a great angle, a grieving widow.'

'Her husband isn't dead yet.'

'But he's close right?' she frowns. 'He's had his hand chopped off.'

'Who told you that?'

'Sources.'

'I'll kill Gerry,' Cully thinks. *'I bet you charmed him round your little figure Minty, especially if you told him about your underwear.'* He also wonders, why Alison would come to the Island after the event?

'There is something else,' she hesitates, 'Bethany Simpson has vanished.'

'I'm shocked,' Cully holds up his hands in horror. 'Probably gone clubbing or something.'

'You go clubbing?'

'My daughter does,' he tells her. 'So you've come down to the Island to do a society piece.'

'Not just one, but two, maybe more. Dom Preece owns an estate here.' Cully remembers him from school. He was only nicked by one bullet and discharged from hospital after a few hours. 'You know the sort of thing, the wounded man goes home surrounded by loving wife and children with dogs and horses. I might even get "Country Living" magazine interested.'

'Where are you staying?'

'In the same hotel as Carla of course. I like to get close to my subjects. The hotel's ok, but a bit basic compared to what I'm used to,' she laughs. 'In fact, I'm not used to well…'

'The basics.'

'And this Island is…'

'Basic.'

'And a bit strange and I keep seeing weird people and everywhere smells of pig shit don't you think?'

'I've not noticed. Is that all?'

'Not quite. I really want to do a piece on you, can I call you Cully, and your daughter Linda. I know you have a lovely place on the mainland.'

'How do you know?'

'Linda's on all the social media platforms. She's very attractive and you are photogenic. It would be great and of course we pay generously. Talk to Linda and let me know,' Minty smiles.

'Have you had lunch?'

'No.'

'Let me buy you a basic lunch in a basic local pub.'

++++

Linda is in the cellar of headquarters searching through dusty archives, firstly for the Poulson investigation and then on her own initiative for the files from the custody suit shooting. Finding both she signs them out and enters the lift that will carry her up to the third floor where MIU is based. The lift walls are mirrored and looking over the pile of manila files she holds Linda glares at herself. She has lost weight during rehabilitation leaving her too thin for her liking. Her brunette hair is cut short and there are dark rings round her green eyes where she's not been sleeping. Fox faced she cannot decide if she looks more like her mother or father?

In MIU, Linda is surprised to find DCI Amelia Fox sitting at her desk. 'It's Sunday Amelia, you should be having a break.'

'Linda, wonderful to see you. What are you doing here?'

'Dad's bidding.'

'Come and sit down, you shouldn't be carrying all that.'

'I'm fine,' but is pleased to dump the files on a desk. 'Don't fuss.'

'Sorry, I didn't mean…At least sit down and let me get you some coffee. Black?' Linda nods. 'What's he got you doing?'

'The Poulson case, remember it?'

'The pervert got his toes cut off. Served him right, the bastard,' Amelia grumbles. 'Sorry, it's the way I'm feeling, looking at dead children fucks you up.' Amelia is forty, brunette with intelligent green eyes, wearing white t-shirt and jeans. 'Linda, there are more files here than for one case.'

'It's our shooting.'

'You shouldn't be reading those.'

'I'm not doing anything wrong.'

'Of course not and I didn't mean ethically, but are you ready sweetheart?'

'It hurts physically, there's not much wrong with my head.'

'Sorry, I didn't mean anything, I'm only looking out for you.'

'I know Amelia. You always did. Where's that coffee and do you have anything to snack on?'

'I'm not a good host am I?' Amelia prepares the coffee and biscuits. 'There you go. Did you have breakfast?'

'No.'

'Then I'm taking you to the canteen for lunch. You need looking after.'

'I won't argue,' Linda smiles her thanks. 'Why didn't you and Dad make a go of it, you seemed good together?'

'Did you have counselling?' Amelia asks, changing the subject.

'Dad saw an advert, an old school friend and she is good, listened, didn't preach and helped me through.'

'What about Cully, did he get help?'

'What do you think?'

'I know he thinks he's superman, but he needs to talk to someone.'

'He used to talk to you.'

'Stop it Linda, we're not getting back together.'

'You can't blame me for trying,' she laughs, but then seriously. 'Poor dad, he's experienced so much loss, his mum, my mum, granny and when I got shot I think he thought it was happening again, another woman leaving him.'

'But you didn't,' Amelia speaks softly, crouching down beside her. 'I do feel guilty about ending it, but two cops together rarely works.'

'Amelia, I'm not suggesting…Now get up or you'll get stuck down there. How are your knees?'

'They get stiff, but it's nothing, not like—'

'Me,' and reaching down, Linda helps Amelia up. 'You don't need to dance around it. I was shot twice, could have died if it wasn't for Pete Grimes, feared I wasn't going to walk again, but I can and I fucking well wish people would stop fussing.'

'Sorry, sorry Linda,' and Amelia pulls a chair over and sits. 'I do sometimes wonder if your dad and I could have made it work. Don't let the job take over Linda,' she sighs. 'Maybe he'll get back with an old flame from school, there must be someone.'

'Plenty, but that brings personal crap from schooldays as well and the case is complex enough. I shouldn't have persuaded him to go to the reunion.'

'But he sometimes visits the Island, he took me once.'

'He doesn't go much, but it's not so much the Island, it's…' she pauses, 'it's what happened to mum and earlier when he was at school. That Island fucks up the Cully family one way and another.' She sips her coffee, thoughtful with both women accepting the silence. 'You met Adam?'

'Yes, and we walked up to the cemetery, to the Cully graves. I saw a different side to him that day.'

'I love that walk,' smiles Linda. 'Dad's a softy under the tough exterior. He's got a friend in the hospice at the moment and visits as often as he can. I should really go, he's my Godfather.'

'You've experienced a lot of loss as well Linda,' Amelia says kindly.

'I know, but I talk about it. Chiefly to you and Sophie Cairns, the counsellor. But Dad is fine at this moment,' Linda laughs. 'He texted me to say he is having lunch with Araminta Gold, a journalist from *Bonjour* magazine.'

'What sort of name is that?'

'Made-up, I guess. She's been after me about doing an article on us at the family home.'

'Well the house is lovely and I can see the angle, daughter and Dad hero's.'

'Amelia you should have been a journalist, that's exactly what she said.'

'Will he agree?'

'She's young, attractive and I'm guessing will charm him.'

'I love the house,' Amelia sighs.

'It could have been yours.'

'Stop it Linda,' she laughs. 'Otherwise, how is he?'

'Stressed. The situation sounds horrendous, but so does your home invasion, two children dead?'

'Three, the baby died this morning.'

'Shit! Sorry, that's horrible for you and the team. Any suspects?'

'A relative we think, an honour killing. The mother married the wrong guy. Tell me about the Poulson link'

'He was a teacher at the school, slippered Dad once, and maybe there's a connection, or at least we need to make certain there isn't. Dad thinks the shooting might be revenge for historical abuse, but there's also a drugs link.'

'Two strong motives. And the other case?' Amelia asks pointing at the files.

'Dad will be furious, he's so protective, but it's time I put any demons to bed. I'm reading the files tonight and going down there tomorrow, to walk things through.'

'Not on your own you're not. I'm coming with you.'

'But you're snowed under.'

'It's time I let the snow melt and I want to look after you.'

++++

Paperwork, paperwork and more bloody paperwork.

'Pete!'

'Gov?'

'I said go easy on the expenses. Two cognacs after dinner last night, really?'

'I was thirsty.'

Grey veils of showers sweep across the channel from the mainland, whipped up by cold northerly winds. Cully sits in his overcoat, turning pages with one hand while holding a cup of coffee for warmth in the other. He'd exchanged texts with Linda, pleased she's found the Poulson files and telling her he was having lunch with Minty. The lunch, as he'd hoped, turned out to be useful because the young woman knew more about some of the victims than the team, or at least Kerry, had gathered. For instance about Allison Grey and another victim, Miranda Pegg being an expensive escort enjoyed by men and women of power.

'Kerry, apart from the Andrews, anything interesting in the background of our dead and wounded yet?'

'One second, Gov, while I finish this,' she calls across the room. 'Thanks, you've been really helpful. Yes sure if I'm ever in your region you can buy me dinner.' Kerry puts the receiver down, grinning broadly. 'I've got something.'

'You look happy,' says Cully.

'I am and sorry if I've been a wet blanket, Gov, but I'm feeling good today, got a date later if you'll let me get away please, Gov?'

'Fine. What have you got?'

'I've had an amazing phone call. You'll not believe this,' she bubbles, coming into the church office where Cully sits. 'That was a colleague from over the water; I persuaded him to go and interview Allison Grey.'

'But she wasn't there,' says Cully.

'How did you know?' Kerry pouts. 'I thought this was my…'

'Sorry Kerry, I guessed,' he lies, recalling what Minty had said. 'Go on.'

'Her husband is and…'

'Come on Kerry spit it out, I'm all ears.'

'Mr Grey has the regional Porsche franchise. You and he have something in common, Gov,' she smiles and for the first time Cully sees why men are attracted to her. 'He has half-a-dozen garages. He's worth a fortune. He's much older than her. They've been married twenty years, but no children. Apparently, according to him, directly she saw the news about the shooting she jumped in her 911 drove this way, to be with her lover and quote "nest of perverts".'

'Lover?'

'Carla Scutari. Husband doesn't want, to quote, "the slag whore back". According to him his wife and Carla have been at it since school days. These group get togethers are a regular thing, once, twice a year. The husband is a pragmatist, his was a marriage of convenience, she got to share his money, he's got to fuck a beautiful younger woman and have her on his arm as eye candy, but enough is enough.'

'I guess she'll be here today or maybe tomorrow. I know there is fog in the channel again. Good stuff Kerry. Anything else?'

'Not a lot of interest in most of them, Gov. Ballard is in the oil business and spends most of his time in the USA. A bit dodgy perhaps, but nothing significant. Bradman was an archaeologist, but totally uninteresting. Pegg never married having lost her fiancée in a flying accident.'

'Nothing more recent about her?' Cully wonders aloud, thinking about what Minty told him.

'No and Chapman, the architect, run of the mill family man.' Cully nods and smiles, but knows Kerry has skimmed the surface 'Felicity Taylor?'

'Still critical and the hospital are not hopeful. Her husband and children are with her. It's her third marriage. The one of interest is Davis.'

'Indah has told us about the car crash with Sophie.'

'But that's not all. Indah didn't get everything, did she?'

'We know he's got convictions, dangerous driving and drink driving offences from the crash, got eighteen months suspended sentence and was banned for three years. Ten years later he was done for ABH,' Cully reads from a report he found on his desk, 'on a young woman and recently a sexual assault. I get the impression there is other stuff, but was never caught. The ABH took place at the Island rugby club where he played and the sexual assault was there as well only three years ago, a seventeen year old waitress at an event there.'

'You already knew this?' Kerry pouts, trying to keep her anger under control. 'Indah did this, didn't she? It is my task to do this, not Indah's.'

'We're a team Kerry,' Cully snaps. 'She's simply following up the link between Sophie and Davis. The other stuff you've got is really good,' he lies, 'and I appreciate it, but don't push it. Play with the team or leave it.'

'You and DI Lynn share a script?'

'Steady,' but Cully quickly softens his tone, tries a smile and leans forward in his chair. 'Might be good for you to move on. Think about it and I can help you get a good post on the mainland. Now, back to business. Go and see the seventeen year old waitress, but briefly, unless her father, brother or boyfriend turn out to be homicidal nutters.'

'Shouldn't Indah do that?'

'Kerry,' he warns.

'I'll go on the way home.'

'Thanks and please feel free to take the rest of the afternoon off, you've had a hard time. Think seriously about my offer, but remember, I need you to take over from Monica at the hospital at nine, no later, tonight, can you do that?'

'Of course,' she grimaces.

A few minutes later he watches her leave.

'Did I hear her?' asks Lisa appearing from the kitchen. 'I bet she's seeing Tizard.'

'Probably,' agrees Cully.

'I thought he'd dumped her.'

'Of course he did. It'll be part of his game plan,' says Cully. 'Rejection, attraction, rejection and so on. Have you ever been fly fishing?'

'No.'

'My uncle used to take me. You reel in, you let out until the fish is exhausted and then you net it.'

'Shit! Something you've done?'

'With fish, not women. Kerry is vulnerable and he only has to click his fingers for her to come running.'

'I hate him and I don't trust her,' Lisa groans before taking a deep breath. 'I overheard him talking about the extra money he earns from small jobs on the side, but I'm sure he's into something else. He's always had money to spend on his women, motorbikes and guns. When he and Mary first got together, there was always cash to spare.'

'Any idea what?'

'No,' she shrugs. 'How's the forest-gremlin?'

'Healer,' corrects Cully, smiling. 'She's recovering.' Which pleases him, because he likes her. 'The Vicar wants a memorial service Friday, to help the healing process, she left me a note,' and he passes it to Lisa.

'Signed with a kiss, Gov,' Lisa grins. 'I'm off to see Mrs Saunders. I've spoken to CPS and they say prosecute.'

'Afterwards, go home, Lisa and get some rest. Chalky, anything on the CD's?'

'Not a thing so far, Gov. The shooter has been bloody careful.'

'Anybody got anything I can do that doesn't involve paperwork?' Cully shouts.

++++

'Don't ask and you won't get, Gov.' Later, as she leaves, Lisa hands him a sheet of paper. 'What you wanted, a trip to the ordinary. Not a pupil from your year so no conflict. I've been going through the preliminary statements we took from the guests two nights ago. Diana Kent says a man helped her up when she fell at the door that got log jammed and he was carrying a bag over his shoulder. Just seems odd.'

Cully takes the coastal road east. Sinead O'Connor on the CD player, the heater turned up against the cold and wipers working hard to clear the rain. Passing the school boarding complex that is quiet after the excitement of the day before, he soon arrives at the address for Ms Kent. Parking opposite the common with its cricket pitch and clubhouse, a hundred metres from the beach, where his mother had taken him the summer before she died. Driven there in her old green Ford Anglia with a picnic, they'd built sandcastles and he'd hunted for crabs in the rock pools while she rested. In hindsight, the disease that killed her was already there, sapping her energy, and useless doctors saw it too late. Forty years before! Where the hell had all those years gone? Don't dwell, he tells himself getting out, relieved the rain has eased and crosses to a row of narrow cottages.

'Ms Kent? Sorry to turn up like this. I'm Superintendent Cully.' He shows his ID. 'Have you got a few minutes?'

'Of course, come in and please call me Diana.'

'You've a lovely place here.' He follows her through to the cosy front facing lounge. 'I grew up in a house like this,' he says.

'You're an Islander?'

'I am. Is it obvious?'

'No, but you are a Cully and there are quite a lot of you about. Tea or coffee?'

'Tea please.'

'Won't be a tic.' He watches her slip into the kitchen at the back of the cottage. She is five years younger than him, brunette and petite. 'I hope you like cake, I've made lemon drizzle. You went to the school. I remember you now, you were a prefect. You were nice, not like some of them. Alumni Association?'

'Not my scene.'

'Nor mine. It's odd seeing the names on the news. I remember Cameron Davis because he kept coming on to me.'

'But you'd only have been thirteen.'

'There speaks a policeman and a father.'

'I've a daughter.'

'We never had children.'

'I'm sorry.' What a trite thing to say he briefly thinks. 'Tell me about it?'

'He kept coming over to me and my friends, a real creep, him and Chapman.'

'Sorry about that. Chapman?'

'They were a pair, but you can't arrest them now, they're dead and good riddance. It's funny isn't it, how much we understandably miss as children and then see things when we get older,' she muses thoughtfully. 'As young people, I think, we only see what's directly in front of us.'

'Maybe that's for the best. This is lovely cake.'

'Thank you, I love baking, but when you're on your own. Sorry, I'm divorced and I don't see people. Stupid I know, but I'd hoped to re-connect with an old flame and we were sitting next to each other and getting on well when the shooting started. He's staying at the hotel in town. He's there for the week.'

'You should contact him.'

'Maybe,' she brightens. 'I could, couldn't I?'

'I know this is difficult, but can we go back to last Friday.' She nods. 'You were on the table with pupils from ninety-five?'

'It's a good crowd. Some of us keep in touch and we'd been out for a drink before walking up to the school. I was a bit drunk. We were waiting for the film to start and suddenly the noise.' Diana shivers. 'The bangs and then the shots.'

'What did you think?'

'I didn't, I froze. People were screaming, running and I tripped and fell. I was terrified and then there was a hand, a strong hand pulling me up.'

'Did you look at his face?'

'Not really. I was crying.'

'But it was a man?' She nods. 'In your statement, you said he had a bag?'

'I noticed it as he pulled me up, over his shoulder. It seemed odd.'

'What did he look like?'

'Not young, maybe your age,' and she laughs, 'I didn't mean, well you know.'

'I do. His face?'

'It was all so quick. I didn't see his face. I'm sorry.'

'Not a problem,' but it is, because there would be no photofit and another investigative avenue is closed. 'What about his hand when he helped you up?'

'Rough, callused,' she nods. 'Why is this important?' She stares thoughtfully at Cully. 'Oh my God, you think it was him, don't you?'

'Not really,' he minimises, in an effort to reassure her, 'but like you, the bag seemed odd when you told the officer about it. If he was the shooter, I doubt he would have helped you up. He would have been in too much of a hurry to get away. It was probably one of the other guests saved you from getting hurt, maybe this old flame of yours.'

'It could be, couldn't it?'

'You might bump into him at another event.'

'I doubt I'll go. I'd be too nervous.'

'Talk to people and you will get over the shock. Don't bottle it up,' he advices.

++++

Indah prides herself on efficiently organising her work, managing her time and travel as best she can. After her visit to Sophie and then the briefing, she'd researched Davis and put her report on Cully's desk before setting out to interview Judge Le Strange at the hotel and Preece at his estate.

She now drives west along the coast road that runs atop the cliffs that drop to the rock-strewn shoreline. The inhospitable sea is dark, grey rain clouds sweep in. She rarely comes this far, the place is bleak, wind-swept and with little evidence of civilisation, but at least there are no tourist coaches. They will arrive after Easter, blocking the roads, slowing traffic and disgorging elderly travellers at various mediocre attractions.

Indah is strangely relieved to reach the village. There is plenty of parking in the square and leaving her car walks to the pub where Cully says he was Friday evening. Personally, she thinks it crazy having to check his alibi because there is no way the Gov is involved, but she understood it's necessary to avoid questions later and to shut Kerry up.

‘I’m DC Kasali,’ she announces, showing her ID across the bar. ‘Could I speak to the person on duty Friday evening?’

‘That was me,’ he smiles. The bar is empty apart from one customer and his dog nursing a bowl of water in a far corner. ‘I’m always here.’

‘You’re the landlord?’

‘With my wife Betsy,’ he says. A large man, balding with a beard. ‘She’s outback cooking. I’m Barry.’

‘I need to ask if you remember one of your customers from that evening.’

‘We were busy, rugby fans and forest-gremlins. Made a lot of money that night. Without nights like that we’d go out of business. As you can see we’re not rushed off our feet.’

‘Do you have CCTV?’

‘No love, not something we’ve ever thought about and too expensive. Can I get you something?’ Indah hesitates, but is hungry and orders a tuna sandwich and coffee. ‘Is this about the school shootings?’

‘Just checking where people were.’

‘Confirming alibis, like on TV?’

‘That sort of thing,’ she agrees.

‘Suspect?’

‘No.’

‘Man or woman?’

‘Man,’ she says, then hears a voice she recognises, turning towards the television, fixed to the far wall. ‘Him.’

‘The cop doing the press conference?’ He questions, surprised. ‘Why does he need an alibi?’

‘It’s procedure, we need to clear everyone.’

‘Right, I’m with you, there was something online about the lead guy actually attending the school.’

‘He wants us to be thorough.’

‘Betsy!’ Barry shouts.

‘Coming, what is it love, I’m busy?’

‘This young lady wants to know about Friday night, about the cop on TV, was he here?’

‘What are you talking about?’ Indah explains. ‘Oh him, the good looking one? Cully, did you say Cully?’ Betsy asks. ‘They’re everywhere on the Island, own a lot of it, posh bastards.' She chuckles, showing a row of yellowing teeth. 'What is it you want?'

'Was he here?' Indah repeats.

'I think so, but we were busy.'

'Superintendent Cully used a card to pay,' says Indah.

'The cookbook, he was the one reading that bloody big book. Where is it?'

'Under here,' Barry says and hefts it up on to the bar with a thump.

'Take a seat, have your sandwich and coffee and I'll check our card receipts.'

Half an hour later Betsy comes over as Indah finishes her lunch and pulling out a chair sits down.

'He was here. Here's the receipt. He ordered fish pie and a gin and tonic. I make the fish pie myself. I remember him. When his pie was ready, I took it over. He was nice. Complimented me on it. He forgot his book, but he's a generous tipper. He paid and then put a tenner in the tip tray.'

'What time was this?'

'Here's the credit card slip.'

'Thanks.' Indah stares at the slip before leaving.

'Shit,' the time is wrong. Where was Cully between eating his meal and getting to the school? 'Fuck!' Why leave the book? Kerry will love it. Stupid bitch, sometimes she really could kill her.

Indah puts the cookbook in her car before walking the short distance to where the Reverend Skeets is staying with his daughter, but he's out, visiting a friend at the hospice. His daughter would give him a message and she was sure her father would contact Indah as soon as he got back.

Taking a moment to herself Indah sits on a bench at the harbour side, watching a yacht easing through the narrow entrance and out to sea. Gulls swoop and call overhead. She is tired, but enjoying every moment. She's not felt so alive in ages if ever. It's for this she joined. Then there is Cully. She isn't the only woman interested in him, Sophie of course and she's seen the way Becky looks at him, but Becky gives off mixed messages, and she's heard the gossip about Amelia Fox. He could have any of them. She thinks a lot about Cully and wonders what she is doing? She isn't like Kerry, or at least hopes she isn't. Her mother tells her there is no shame in a woman attaching herself to an older man to get what she wants, to fulfil ambitions. If the woman happens to find the man attractive, then why not have some fun along the way? 'Is that how it was with you and dad?'

'I was an impressionable young nurse and he was this sophisticated successful doctor, but then I fell in love with him. So, be careful what you plan for Indah.'

Phone rings.

++++

Leaving Diana Kent, Cully walks down to the beach and skims a few stones out over grey waters, thinking about what else she'd told him. She'd mentioned the memorial service, which Vicar Mandy had already floated as an idea on her blog, hoping the police would allow it to go ahead. She likes the vicar, 'She's feisty, not too Godly and punches above her weight, literally, if you know what I mean?' He admitted he didn't and it was what she went on to say that surprised him.

Then there was the stuff about Sean O'Leary.

Cully thinks about these things as he drives and an hour later he has completed another rather subdued media conference.

His phone rings. 'This is Cully.'

'It's Liam O'Leary.'

'Talk of the devil. Sorry, I was thinking about Sean. He and I should meet for a pint, talk over old times.'

'He'd enjoy that. I've got Turner's address,' and shares it.

Ending one call starts another. 'Where are you Indah?'

'I've just visited Skeets. He wasn't in, but spoke to his daughter. Also the pub where you were Friday night. They've given me your book. It's bloody heavy.

'*La Rousse* is my cooking bible and I'd hate to lose it. You are being thorough,' he compliments her, but aware of what she'll have discovered. 'I'll explain later.'

'Explain what?'

'You know what Indah, but for now…'

'I need to talk times with you.'

'Sure, but later,' he persists. 'Thanks for the report on Davis.'

'I like to keep on top of things.'

'You certainly do. You're out in the wild west. Good,' and he shares an address. 'I've found Turner, the chemistry teacher, the one sacked for having the affair. Meet you there.'

'On my way.' She is thrilled. Twenty minutes later the passenger door of Indah's car opens and Cully climbs in beside her. 'What time is it?'

'Five pm,' he tells her. 'Still Sunday and less than forty-eight hours since the shooting. It feels longer,' he admits.

'It certainly does.'

'I'm sure you are exhausted Indah, I know I am.' It starts to rain again. Drops pummel the car. 'What a bleak place.' They sit in thoughtful silence for a few moments. 'How did your earlier visits go?'

'Interesting, Gov,' she smiles with amusement that extends to her large brown eyes. 'You know about Sophie. I saw Judge Le Strange first, he's lovely. Preece next. He's been discharged to his estate. They had nothing particular to say. I did bump into a girl called Minty, apparently she knows you.'

'Came across her at the media conference yesterday. I love this. Listening to the rain drumming on the roof, sitting here isolated from everything.'

'Gov?'

'Sorry, miles away.' Wishing he's, what? With Sophie, but here he is with Indah. Forget Turner, take Indah for a drink and see what happens. 'Indah, about Sophie…'

'Gov, we ought to get moving.'

'Too right,' Cully slaps his thigh hard to focus. 'That's Turner's cottage over there.' The place is small, two storeys with a slate roof and whitewashed walls. 'With love and attention, it could be really nice like…'

'Yes Gov?'

'Nowhere important.' The rain is easing, but the clouds are thickening and blackening which suggests there is more to come. 'I've checked the registration of the van in front there and it's Turner's.'

'We must call for armed backup.'

'We can't wait Indah.' Heavier droplets are already falling. 'Let's go.' Leaving the car Cully sees a woman filling a large canvas back with hedgerow plants. 'What are you doing here?'

'Foraging for healing herbs. Be safe policeman,' she shouts.

'You'll get drenched,' he calls back.

'It's only water.'

'What did she mean by you keeping safe, Gov?'

'Nothing. Come on.'

They walk towards the front door when an explosion rattles windows and a plume of smoke rises from behind the cottage.

'Get down Indah, behind the back of my car. Healer, take cover,' but she has already vanished into the hedgerow.

'The back?' Indah calls, running.

'Because that's where the block is and more likely to protect you,' he shouts. 'Just do it. Nothing must happen to you. Go.'

'Shit, Gov!'

'I'm getting closer.'

'Gov, you can't. Regulations say we should wait for backup.'

'You stay there.'

Bending low Cully runs towards the side of the cottage. There he hesitates before edging forward and glancing round the corner. The garden is large and unkempt. A blinding light flashes ahead of a loud bang, but Nadine is right, these things were soft compared to the ones used by special forces. He needs a moment to clear his head before moving forward, taking cover behind a bush. A man he assumes to be Turner has his wide back to him. 'Turner, armed police. Turn round.' The man does nothing and Cully repeats the warning, but louder. Slowly he turns, facing Cully open mouthed. He is holding a long poker, glowing red hot at the tip. 'Put it down,' Cully orders, getting closer.

Turner swings the poker, catching Cully on the right hand as he moves in, but Cully keeps going, bringing his knee up into the man's groin. Turner yells, his overweight body folding to the ground, releasing the poker against Cully's jacket. 'Hands above your head.' Turner obeys, not speaking. Cully moves in behind him, pulls his arms down behind his back and handcuffs him.

'Indah,' he calls, 'all clear.' She appears from round the side of the cottage, runs to him, and hugs him. The hug lasts a long time. There is a smell of burning flesh. 'You're hurt.'

'It's nothing.'

'I have a quick question,' she mumbles. 'Is it ok to be terrified?'

++++

'Excuse me?'

'Yes, sorry.' Monica is exhausted, furious Kerry has not appeared to take over from her at the hospital and wanting large glasses of wine, but mostly worried about Bethany alone at the White House. 'How can I help?' she asks the woman.

'You're a police officer?'

'Yes.' Monica stands in reception. The woman in front of her is tall, late forties, attractive with long blonde hair. 'How can I help?'

'I need information.'

'About?'

'A victim of the shootings.'

'Anyone in particular?'

'Carla Scutari, I'm her friend Alison Grey.'

'She's been discharged.'

'So soon?' Surprised. 'That's good,' but not convincing. She smiles, revealing gleaming white teeth. 'My husband left me a voice mail, that the police are after me.'

'Not after you,' Monica corrects, 'but we do need to speak to you.'

'I wasn't there, I've only just arrived on the Island.'

'Even so, but tomorrow will do. You must be a good friend to have come especially.'

'Thank you for your help, I must go, I'm staying with a friend and she's expecting me.'

As Alison leaves Kerry appears.

'Where the hell have you been?' Monica snaps. 'We agreed nine and it's nearly ten.'

'I couldn't get away.'

'Why? Because he had his teeth into you? The young woman puts a hand up to her neck. 'Get something to cover it up and start behaving like a police officer instead of a whore.'

'You don't know me and you're not my boss.'

'I'm your superior officer,' Monica reminds her.

'You overners think you're better than us Islanders.'

'Of you maybe and what's a fucking overner?'

'You're from even further away aren't you?'

'You don't like foreigners, is that it? Are you a racist, like your father?'

'Fuck off and he wasn't a racist just... You mainland cops think you know it all.'

'Maybe we do Kerry. Now listen and let's get the handover done. Felicity Taylor died this evening and I've been dealing with her husband and sons. Luckily, Pete came over, because he's a team player, and took some of the heat. They've gone and things are quiet. Alison Grey turned up. Carla Scutari has gone to a hotel with Simpson's wife.' Monica continues apace, anxious to get away. 'Araminta Gold has been sniffing around trying to get a story for her magazine.'

'Which one?'

'Does it matter?' she sighs. 'Simpson is still in a coma, as is Pennington who they'll be moving to the mainland. Sean O'Leary is still here, but recovering. He's got some visitors. Now, do your job Kerry.'

'I'm going to get a coffee, I hope that's ok with you?'

Kerry walks away as Pete appears round a corner.

'And dress like a bloody police officer,' Monica shouts after her. 'That skirt is too short and button your blouse.'

'Tizard loves it, I bet,' says Pete. 'A bit harsh weren't you?'

'I've had a shit day, Pete.'

'I know Monica, but she's young.'

'She's a police officer and she needs to grow up. I want a drink, but I need to check on Bethany. Let's get out of here.'

'I'll drop you at the safe house,' he says, 'and on the way I'll tell you more about the Gov.'

Finding the toilets Kerry stares at herself in the mirror and in particular at the livid scarlet bite on the side of her neck. She couldn't even remember him doing it, the orgasm so intense. She fell asleep, waking alone with him already gone. Maybe Monica is right, she is a whore. The door opens and closes behind her. In the mirror, Kerry watches a nurse enter a cubicle. Minutes later she emerges and starts washing her hands in the sink beside Kerry. 'Nasty one. Guys are bastards, if it was a guy?'

'It was.'

'It's just that I saw you arguing with that woman outside the secure ward.'

'She's a colleague, she thinks I'm a waste of space.'

'Are you?'

'I suppose I can be.'

'I can cover that up for you if you'd like? Give you something to reduce the swelling. Follow me.' She leads the way to a dressing station where she dabs on cream before applying a plaster. 'There, much better. Take these tablets as well, they'll help.'

'Thanks, let me buy you a coffee,' Kerry smiles.

'That would be good. I'm on a break if you want to talk?'

They sit in the canteen. Beyond are a group talking loudly about art. Amongst them sits Sean O'Leary, still in his white hospital gown. Next to him a tall woman he calls Cordelia.

'Been with the guy long?' the nurse asks.

'Too long,' Kerry yawns, feeling her eyes grow heavy. 'I can't let go.'

'He's married. He'll never be yours Kerry.'

'How'd you know my name?'

'My names Mary by the way, Mary Tizard and I'm going to kill you if you don't leave my husband alone, understand?'

++++

'Interview with Graham Turner,' begins Cully for the benefit of the tape. 'Present are Reverend Liam O'Leary, DC Indah Kasali and Detective Superintendent Cully. Do you understand why you are here Mr Turner and understand your rights?'

'Yes.'

'You don't want a solicitor?'

'No.'

'You're facing a range of charges from assaulting a police officer to—'

'That was an accident,' he interrupts.

'This look like an accident?' Cully holds up his hand which Indah has bandaged over the green poultice of herbs the Healer masticated before smearing it on the burn. It stings, but no more. 'And you've ruined my jacket.'

'You got me in the balls.'

'I slipped,' Cully grimaces. 'Moving on, you also face offences under the Fireworks Act, Pyrotechnic Regulations, various Standards and under the Anti-Terrorism Act.'

'I'm not a terrorist. This is bullshit.'

'Don't forget your attempt to kill DC Kasali and myself.'

'I didn't try to kill you. I didn't know you were there.'

'I shouted warnings.'

'I didn't hear you. I'm partially deaf from the bangs.'

'You do that to yourself?'

'What?'

'The side of your head, looks nasty.'

'I got shot.'

'By whom?'

'Whom, very posh.'

'Who shot you?' Cully asks again.

'The stupid old woman that lives out back of me.'

'So, you were out testing your flashbangs. Go to A & E or see your GP?'

Turner shakes his head. 'No, they'd have to report it to the secret police. You lot,' he scoffs.

'Who treated your wounds?'

'I'm not saying.'

'In my other job with the Murder Investigation Unit on the mainland, we know about the horsebox hospital, is that where you went?'

'Not saying,' he repeats, folding his arms. 'How did you know where I lived?'

'Intelligence,' Cully says, catching the look of horror that passes across O'Leary's face. 'You weren't difficult to find.'

'Spy satellites I guess?'

'Something like that,' Cully smiles. 'DC Kasali here has been exploring the dark web.'

'You advertise there Mr Turner,' begins Indah. 'You offer your flashbangs at five pounds each and get lots of orders. Feedback is good. You were a chemistry teacher so you know what you are doing, but it's illegal.'

'The state attempts to stop everything a free citizen should be able to do.'

'You don't like government, do you? I've been reading your blog,' Indah continues. 'I'm building a nice terrorist case here. You're anti-government, anti-everything and you make explosives. I think the anti-terror squad will love you and the way things are at the moment should get you sentenced to life.'

'Bullshit.'

'Tell me about your customers,' says Cully, 'especially recent ones?'

'I don't grass to the authorities.'

‘Ever sell to an American?’

‘No. Why?’

‘I’m told people can disappear into Guantanamo.’

‘I have to object,’ states O’Leary. ‘This is becoming absurd.’

‘Mr Turner,’ continues Cully, ignoring O’Leary, ‘we are dealing with multiple murder and on top of everything else I doubt you want a conspiracy to murder charge.’

‘I had nothing to do with that.’

‘You hate the school. You’ve said all sorts of nasty things on your blog.’

‘I’m not against the kids or ex pupils, but if I’d had a chance to do that bastard Inskip then that would be different.’

‘Turner,’ O’Leary warns.

‘Threat to kill on tape, this gets better,’ Cully grins. ‘You’re suing the school?’

‘They sacked me for no reason.’

‘You had an affair with a vulnerable woman.’

‘Crystal wasn’t vulnerable,’ he laughs and Indah feels her stomach turn over. *‘It couldn’t be?’* ‘Brittle maybe,’ continues Turner, ‘and liked to say she was hard-done-by, but I never promised her anything. We had fun and then suddenly she wants me to leave my wife.’

‘You refused.’ *‘Balding, poor skin and plump,’* Indah wonders *‘what any woman, even Crystal Smalls, if it’s really her, might see in him?’* ‘Is that why she attempted suicide?’ she demands.

‘The suicide thing was attention seeking, but it all came out. My wife left me and I’ve not seen the kids in months.’

‘Poor you,’ she snaps, but catching a sideways glance from Cully changes tone. ‘We believe your flashbangs were used in the attack on the school. Have you anything to say about that?’

‘Nothing to do with me.’

‘Help us and if CPS agree we might reduce some of the charges,’ Cully states.

O’Leary leans across and whispers to Turner.

‘Some of your guys for a start,’ Turner grins.

‘Police?’

‘Yeah, surprised? Your armed response people like to use them for training.’

‘You know a Sergeant Tizard?’

‘Him and an officer called Joe.’

‘How many did you sell them?’

‘Hundreds over the years.’

‘Who else?’

‘The paintballing people. They are good customers. Maybe fifty each order.’

‘Business is good and no VAT or tax to pay,’ Cully smiles. ‘Whoops, that’s more law you’ve broken.’

‘You said…’

‘What about an individual, maybe one you’ve not seen before?’

‘There was a guy, bought twenty last week.’

‘Description.’

‘Late forties, thin, five ten, but it was dark.’

‘Hair colour?’

‘He wore a hat and I didn’t see a car before you ask.’

‘Voice?’

‘Well spoken, a bit posh like you and the kids at the school. A woman from the mainland. I posted a dozen to her.’

‘Mr Turner you keep on giving and while I’ll check I’m sure it’s an offence under the Post Office Act, sending incendiary devises by mail. Anyone else recently?’

‘A woman, long curly brown hair, about your age,’ he tells Cully. ‘Another woman took ten away on her red scooter.’ Turner yawns. ‘Are we finished?’

‘Description of the last woman?’

‘We need to stop now,’ states O’Leary. ‘He’s co-operated.’

‘The description of the woman first and then we can take a break.’

‘That’s easy, I know her.’

Monday

Outside the interview room, Liam O'Leary catches up with Cully as Turner is taken from the portacabin to the police station and a cell. 'I've told Turner he needs an experienced criminal lawyer. 'You will meet with Sean for that drink won't you? He's not got many friends.'

'Things are hectic, but after we've closed the case.'

'Thank you for not dropping me in it with Turner.'

'Not a problem. Cordelia seems interested in Sean?'

'She's nice,' O'Leary nods. 'He needs to grab the chance with her.'

'How's Sean's sister?'

'Patsy is well,' Liam beams. 'She got her law degree, is married with two children and is a successful corporate lawyer in the city. She quickly outgrew the Island.'

'You must have been disappointed Sean didn't complete his degree?'

'A long time ago,' he frowns. 'The woman Turner identified came as a surprise to you, didn't it? I saw your face Cully.'

'You don't miss much. I can't imagine why she should want flashbangs, but we'll find out.' Phone rings. 'Sorry, I've got to take this.' He watches O'Leary walk away and thinks: '*Oh yes, I'll definitely be seeing Sean again'*. 'Hi Amber, what have you got?'

'Ballistics have confirmed it was a Glock 17. Twenty-eight parabellum bullets recovered.'

'Two clips worth. Firing twenty-eight shots with reasonable accuracy and changing clips in just a minute makes him a professional predator,' Cully reasons. 'Anything else?'

'Ballistics have searched police records and…'

'Yes Amber?'

'They've discovered something,' she hesitates before telling him.

Two minutes later Cully rings the Chief Constable. 'Sorry to ring so late.'

'Not a problem, I've been expecting your call. You've just been told that the striations on the shell casings from the school hall are a perfect match for those on the shells from the custody suit shooting. It's the same gun that wounded Linda and you. The ballistics report is computer generated and I get it first.'

'You don't trust BioTech?' he asks still trying to take in what she is saying. 'I sense there is more.'

'Forensics should never have been privatised and BioTech have made previous mistakes, but not this time. Cully I'm sorry.'

'What for?'

'I've not told you before because I care about you.'

Cully leans back against the wall and as he listens sinks slowly to the floor.

Sylvia takes them back ten years to the shooting at the White House. The gun that fired the bullet that hit Caitland went missing. It turned up, or at least bullets fired by it, a year later in a gang shooting on the mainland, then again two years later when a financier staying on the Island was murdered. Two years after that a drug dealer was killed with it and then another. None of the victims were connected. Then eighteen months ago Cully's team from MIU, the drug squad and armed officers from the mainland and the Island came together as a task force to intercept and arrest a gang smuggling in drugs, weapons and young women. The operation was successful until officers got to the custody suit. The Glock 17 was used in that shooting when one of the prisoners tried to escape.

'Sylvia…' but does not know what to say.

'The man that shot you and Linda there did not belong to *Groupa Europa,* but an Albanian syndicate. What we've got is an armourer who leases out the Glock,' Sylvia states emphatically, 'something we've come across before.'

'Tizard?'

'Probably,' Sylvia agrees quietly. 'Tizard was certainly there ten years ago and might have picked up the Glock. He could have been renting it out over the years. He was there eighteen months ago and could have given the gun to the Albanian to help him escape. He knows guns.'

'What aren't you telling me?'

'He isn't the only connecting person. I'm ashamed to say I did wonder back then if you took the gun Cully. I would have understood if you'd kept it for personal protection. Sorry. There are two others that link things, none of whom I especially fancy for it, firstly an officer Joe Dabell from the Island and SOCO Amber Green.'

'Amber...'

'She was a junior technician on the White House clean up. She worked with the task force and was there in the street after the Albanian was shot. Green is Amber's married name. Her parents are Serbian. I'm probably being racist, but the Andrews were doing business and owe a lot of money to Eva Djokovic, of *Groupa Europa UK.'*

'There's one other,' begins Cully, 'Pete Grimes.'

++++

Lisa Lynn knew she needed to get herself a life. Here she is at two o'clock in the morning walking the deserted corridors of the hospital like a mad woman in a horror film. She is searching for Kerry. '*Where the hell are you?*' she wonders.

Lisa did not leave the incident room until gone midnight when Claudia and Chalky were still working. In the office, she is staring at the computer screen and a list of seven names she'd gleaned from police and prison records and intelligence sources. She could not believe how many Island people advertised to kill people. Claudia appeared at the open doorway. 'You should get off.'

'I should, but let me ask you something first?'

'Anything.'

'Would you hire an assassin off the Internet?'

'Not me,' Claudia admits, 'but if you're desperate you'd do anything to get rid of your wife, husband, partners lover, the guy you owe money to and so on.

'Would drug dealers hire a local killer?'

'No way. They've got their own people to deal with problems such as the Andrews.'

'So, what I'm doing is a waste of time?'

'In finding the shooter, but in demonstrating that we've done everything we could to find him to the Chef Constable, it's background.'

'You are cynical Claudia and I like it.' Lisa smiles at her. 'Chalky,' she calls.

'Yes Ma'am.'

'Any luck?'

'There are hours of this stuff, Ma'am.' They have sequestered CCTV covering Friday morning to the end of the day after the killings from the ferries that travel back and forth between the Island and mainland. 'We've got the list of cars coming and going and so far no registration is coming back dodgy. The same for passengers that paid with cards, but some paid with cash. We need more eyes, Ma'am.'

'I've tried.'

'I know, people don't want to help,' he sighs. 'I need a break.'

'Go home and continue with it tomorrow.'

'If this guy is the pro we think he is, he's not going to make a mistake leaving a trail is he?'

'You're right Chalky, but we need to sift through it all.'

'The Gov asked me to check to see if Turner went to the mainland the day he was shot by Mrs Saunders,' Chalky explains. 'He did, returning the next. The idiot paid with a credit card. I'll send Gov an email.'

'Good. Now go Chalky and get some rest, you to Claudia.' She watches them leave before turning to a pile of papers. A flood of complaints about people not getting their phones back, but she'd spoken to HQ and it would be several days yet. 'Fuck!'

Lisa knew that if she went home she'd end up opening a bottle of wine, watching television or playing poker on one of the Internet sites she frequents. It is the reason the bank froze her overdraft and her credit cards are nearly maxed out. She needs help and wonders if Sophie would take her as a client?

The hospital offers a refuge where she could find her sister for a chat although they'd inevitably argue about Tizard. Apart from her niece and nephew the only brightness in her life is Claudia and then only if she is correctly reading the signals.

At this time of night, there were no other cars on the road and apart from scavenging foxes she sees no one until she reaches the hospital.

Phone pings. It is a text from Monica.

I hope you don't see this until morning. That you're asleep. I didn't want to forget to say, but Alison Grey turned up at the hospital. She asked about Carla Scutari and appeared annoyed she'd been discharged, or (and this is my gut) annoyed that she is still alive!

Also, Pete thinks I was hard on Kerry, I called her names, but she turned up an hour late for handover. Sorry.

I would have called her worse, Lisa answers. *Now go to sleep Monica.*

Phone pings. A text from a gambling site offering her a twenty pound credit to play.

She forces herself to ignore it.

Still to find Kerry, Lisa heads back up to the secure ward where she asks an armed officer if he has seen her? 'Not for ages, Ma'am. She went off to have coffee with a nurse at about ten and hasn't come back.'

Lisa knows where the nurses rest room is and heads there. Opening the door the room is in darkness and she's about to close it when she hears snoring. Flicking on the light she sees Kerry asleep on the couch.

++++

'I'm taking you to hospital,' Indah declares, 'to prevent it becoming sceptic.'

'You pouring cold water over it helped.'

'Like you did with Sophie, dropping her in the horse trough.' *'Of course it was you,'* she thinks, but he doesn't answer. 'Is something wrong, Gov?'

'The Healer's poultice helped of course,' he smiles, avoiding her stare.

Devastated by what Sylvia has told him, Indah found him sitting on the floor and immediately decided he is suffering from delayed shock from the burn.

'That was weird, the Healer being there. She predicted…'

'Rather sexy I thought,' Cully grins, trying to lighten things, but actually wanting to scream. 'The chewing that is. You dressed it perfectly.'

'I know the basics from my parents, but I'm still taking you to hospital. Let's go. I've been reading "Murder on the Orient Express",' she tells him as they head out to her car.

He wanted to tell Indah everything, but knew he couldn't. He could only talk to two people Sylvia and Linda and Sylvia had told him to ring her back later.

'I got a uniform to bring your car to the church car park from Turner's,' Indah tells him. 'She was so excited I think she took it a few extra miles.'

'You really are efficient. Remind me about Agatha Christies book.'

'Not so much the book, but the premise. You must have wondered when Turner was listing his customers.'

'You've lost me,' he admits.

She wanted to say bastard, but stopped herself. Of course he had and now he is teasing, testing her or both. 'Gov!'

'Speak to Vicar Mandy as a priority. I don't like where this is going Indah,' in so many ways he thinks.

'It's going to the hospital,' she says, helping him on with his seat belt.

++++

At A & E, Sabrina treats him, but there is little to do. The green poultice has reduced the swelling and sooths the pain to such an extent that Cully refuses pain killers. Sabrina admits she and her mother often visit the Healer in the forest. Gently and reluctantly refusing Indah's offer of her spare bed he takes a taxi back to the church car park, picks up his car and drives to his uncle's. Cully climbs into bed with a white terrier curled into the crook of his knees and telephones Sylvia.

'I've had Internal Affairs on it for ten years and they've not come up with any hard evidence against any of them, but Tizard remains the prime suspect. I have to pull you out. If you weren't already compromised, you are now.'

'Let me finish here Sylvia.'

'You were desperate to get away not long ago.'

'It's different now.'

'What if you were the target? I do read the crime scene reports Cully. There were bullet holes in the back of the chair where you could have been sitting.'

'Not according to the original seating plan. Someone switched the name cards, but that's another issue. I should have been sitting next to Sophie.'

'Sophie?'

'An old school friend.'

'Oh God Cully! You haven't have you?'

'No.'

'I know you want to.'

'What?'

'I know things about you Cully.'

'So you should after nearly thirty years Sylvia,' he smiles remembering when they first met. An undergraduate on a police scholarship, serving in uniform during the university summer holidays, he was allocated to a patrol car. Sergeant Sylvia Greening told him she would be driving and while they cruised the streets he got to know her. She was the only officer that did not make fun of him, tease him about his posh boy accent or the fact he would be the beneficiary of accelerated promotion when graduating. They recognised ambition in each other and he followed her upwards. 'Sylvia, you're quiet.'

'I'm thinking, remembering about us,' she explains. 'Apart from Caitland, you've never settled on anyone, even Amelia. You've become a tom cat Cully, any woman will do.'

'Love you to Sylvia.'

'I know you do. Let Internal Affairs handle the armourer investigation Cully, you concentrate on the school shootings. Stay away from Tizard. Understand?'

'Ma'am.'

'But I'm giving permission for you to carry a side arm for personal protection.'

'Thank you, I was going to suggest it. I'd like Pete, Lisa, Monica and Chalky to carry as well, we are short of armed officers.'

'Sure about Pete?'

'Yes.'

'Ok, agreed. One other thing,' she pauses for effect, 'never again suggest the Prime Minister is a drug dealer. The police commissioner is furious. On the positive side, a Judge Le Strange rang to sing your praises.'

'Nice of him. He's sitting here from Tuesday. We need to give him protection in case he's a target. I'll allocate Pete to it. It'll keep him out of trouble.'

'I'll get the paperwork done for the guns'

'Another positive, Ma'am, we've made an arrest. The guy that made the flashbangs was a disgruntled teacher.'

++++

Getting Pete up early at the hotel is surprisingly easy as the man rarely slept beyond five and when he knew what it's about became fully alert and excited.

Despite his hand, Cully is able to drive them to meet the six am ferry, receive and sign for the steel box from the escort that brought it over the water.

Cully wonders if he has over-reacted in his call to the Chief, but Mrs Saunders shooting the Healer added a veneer of justification to the argument.

At six-thirty, they sit at Uncle Adam's kitchen table.

'You didn't need to get up so early Adam. I could have cooked the breakfast.'

'Not with that hand you couldn't and you're not eating properly as it is. My nephew is stupid and stubborn, Pete.'

‘I know.’

‘Mother would expect me to look after you. Anyway, once we’ve had breakfast I can go up to the allotment. How do you like your eggs, Pete?’

‘Fried and sunny side up please Mr Cully.’

‘Adam please.’

‘This is good of you.’

‘I like the company and you can fill me in on the juicy bits my nephew refuses to share.’

‘No, he can’t,’ Cully objects. ‘You’ll only share it at the Lodge,’ he sighs.

‘You went to posh school Adam?’

‘I did, Pete.’

‘A family tradition?’

‘Yes, although Cully’s mum didn’t, because in those days there were no girls, just chaps.’

The smell of frying bacon fills the kitchen and soon the three of them sit at the large kitchen table eating the substantial fry. ‘Great black pudding,’ says Pete.

‘I make it myself, but getting the blood can be difficult, bloody health and safety.’

‘Know what you mean Adam, paperwork and rules get in the way of proper coppering.’

‘You two will start sharing war stories in a minute.’

‘Did you serve, Pete?’ Adam asks.

‘In Belfast and a bit in the desert.’

‘Ah, I was in Belfast and the Falklands. I’ll never forget…’

‘Jesus! I’m joking.’

‘You never fancied the military, Gov?’

‘No Pete. I’ve been shot often enough being a police officer.’

‘Something I would hate is having to deal with the media,’ Adam changes the subject. ‘Mind you I am famous because of you Cully. At the allotment yesterday evening and when I took Angus out for his walk, people came up to me, people that know me asked “is that your nephew on TV?” and strangers ask me if I’m related to you. Apparently we look alike.’

‘They saw the media conferences?’

‘They did and it’s in the papers, on the news and over the Internet, especially as you accused the Prime Minister of being a drug dealer. It’s the biggest story the Island has had since, well I don't know when do I Angus?' There is a yap in reply. 'Good boy. More tea, Pete?'

'I'd love to, but we need to get going, Gov.'

Standing, Adam lifts the plates and slides them into the sink. 'Don't forget the box, Pete and I may be getting old, but I know what's in it. You boys going to start a war?'

'I hope not,' Cully sighs.

'I'll take the box to the car,' says Pete. 'Thanks again Adam.'

'No problem, come again and we can open a bottle and talk about army times without being interrupted.'

Adam watches Pete leave before turning to his nephew.

'Glock 17's in the box?' Cully nods. 'You've used a Glock, haven't you?'

'When I was with armed response and on cases since.'

'Including at the safe house.'

'Adam…'

'You've never talked about it and I won't push you. You were always a good shot.'

'Grandmother hated us going out shooting.'

'She still cooked the game we shot. God, could she cook,' Adam grins. 'Remember the jugged hare?'

'Superb and the roast pheasant,' Cully recalls, grinning.

'How could I forget?' Angus is round his ankles, wanting to be taken for a walk. 'I can get pheasant and vegetables from the allotment if you'd like?'

'I'd love it, but I can't guarantee getting here anytime.'

'I'll slow cook it and we can heat it up when you get here. We'll uncork a bottle or two of Chateau Laffite Rothchild 2009 to wash it down.'

'That's twelve hundred pounds worth.'

'What's the point of having it if you don't drink it and anyway you're inheriting the cellar when my time comes.'

++++

'Thanks for picking me up.'

'Dad rang to ask about the Poulson file, if I'd got it.'

'But you didn't mention the other files?'

‘Of course not, but ballistics have confirmed the Glock 17 used in the school shooting is the same weapon used to shoot Dad and me.’

‘Did Cully tell you that?’

‘No, but I have my contacts,’ Linda smiles, recalling her early morning conversation with Sylvia. Ever since the White House shooting Sylvia had been there for her, a sort of surrogate mother alongside her great grandmother. Linda tells her what she’s planning, gets her approval, but is told to take care. ‘It’s an outrageous coincidence if it is,’ Linda continues. ‘The gun was lost according to the files, lost between the shooting in the custody suit and where the gunman was shot dead. The gun vanished. A member of the public might have picked it up and recycled it.’

‘Unlikely.’

‘Agreed, but two cops I know of link that shooting and the one on the Island, Sergeant Tizard and Officer Dabell. So, off we go. It’s great to be able to drive again,’ Linda announces with enthusiasm. ‘The automatic gearbox helps, but the rehab has been good and I’m taking a reduced dose of the pain killers. Dad is worried I’ll get addicted.’

‘He doesn’t know we’re doing this?’

‘God no, I thought I’d tell him when I have to.’ They chat for the thirty minute journey. ‘Here we are,’ but instead of driving into the police compound she parks on double yellow lines on the street. ‘We won’t be here long,’ she smiles thinly, recognising some reluctance in herself. ‘Let’s go through what happened. The gunman shoots the officers, me and dad.’

‘You were unlucky.’

‘Wrong place, wrong time, I’d only come down from CID to say hi to dad,’ Linda sighs. ‘The gunman turns and runs out of the custody suit through the open door.’

‘God, this was appalling.’

‘Worse, the gate to the car park was also left open.’

‘Deliberate?’

‘Not sure, probably incompetence and macho shit blinding them to basic security measures.’

‘Let’s walk,’ Amelia suggests. They go down the quiet narrow street that leads to the main road. ‘There’s a clear line of sight from the gate of the car park to the end of the street. Nowhere to hide.’

Reading from the notes she has taken from the file Linda describes what happened. 'The shooter runs carrying the Glock, until Joe Dabell, chasing, shoots him once. Tizard passes Dabell and shoots him again because in his statement Tizard says the Albanian was about to shoot him. The man falls, according to the diagram, here by the lamp post. There's no drain, no where he might have dropped or hidden the gun. Again, according to the record other officers get to the scene within seconds, but did not see the gun. Someone took it.'

'But why Linda?'

'Confusion, panic, I don't know. Maybe he already had the idea to pass it on, sell it, or keep it for himself as a trophy. The report suggests the Albanian hadn't been searched properly and what if one of the officers gave it to him to help him escape?'

'Maybe the custody suit door and the car park gate were left open deliberately,' Amelia suggests.

'SOCO were there quickly and several ambulances arrive. Paramedics treat us inside and check the shooter for life signs, but do not see a gun. Internal Affairs organised a finger-tip search, but no one can find the Glock at the scene,' Linda adds.

'It has to be a police officer doesn't it?'

'What if the gun was underneath him? He fell on it. If that was the case, then it could have been taken by SOCO staff or paramedics, but most likely a police officer.'

'Agreed,' says Amelia, 'and from what you've said, my money is on Tizard. How's Cully dealing with him?'

'Avoidance I think, on both their parts. Tizard is a cowboy, going out on wild goose chases at every opportunity. South Island has been seized by panic and so far they've received a lot of calls, all a waste of time, but all needing to be followed up. It keeps Dad and him apart. You should read Sophie Cairns book. I can see Dad in the opening pages.'

'Maybe he is.'

'Perhaps,' Linda smiles.

'I'd be worried.'

'About what Amelia?'

'They might start shooting each other.'

++++

'Pete, bring it into the office. I need to talk to DI Lynn before the briefing.'

'Gov.' Pete places the metal box on the desk and leaves.

'What's that?' asks Lisa, looking up from where she is reading through notes from the Saunders interview. 'What's in the box?' She taps it. 'Gov?'

'Guns. Last night Amber rang me. She'd received the ballistics report. It is a Glock 17 and they've matched the weapon to the one that was used to shoot Linda, me and the other officers eighteen months ago.'

'Jesus!'

'I've spoken to the Chief and agreed we've got an armourer operating locally leasing out weapons. Our school hall shooter is still out there somewhere. We've had the Healer shooting and Turner might have had a gun instead of a hot poker.'

'How is the hand?'

'Fine.' he dismisses it. 'Armed officers took an hour to appear because we're stretched,' Cully explains. 'We can't take risks.'

'I hate guns.'

'But you've done the course and scored in the top one per cent, I checked.'

'I wish I'd missed the bloody target.'

'You didn't. You, Pete, Chalky, Monica and I will carry. Also we don't tell people about the link to my shooting, only that the Chief Constable has given us permission to carry for personal protection and because we are short of armed officers.'

'Tizard won't like it.'

'Why because we'll offend the exclusive machismo around armed units or because he'll be scared I'll shoot him.'

'We could both shoot him,' she smiles. 'There's something else. I sent Kerry home last night after I found her asleep at the hospital.'

'Oh.' Cully remembers Mary finding him a bed where he slept for several hours. 'Did she say anything?'

'Something about a nurse, but I didn't listen too hard. Stupid bitch!'

'Lisa!'

'Sorry Gov. I've not slept. What are we doing about Tizard and the flashbangs?'

'I've informed the Chief Constable. She's telling Internal Affairs. Let them deal with it,' he says reluctantly. 'I suggest we don't say anything about Kerry to the team. If they ask, she's off sick.'

'Listen up,' says Cully entering the Incident room. He briefs them on what happened the evening before, about Turner, flashbangs and the injury to his hand. 'Tom is over there now, going through the cottage. We've got a list of his customers to follow up.' Cully pauses, surveying the expectant faces. 'The Chief Constable has sanctioned my request that those of us that can, carry a firearm for personal protection.' He repeats the reasons he gave Lisa and names the officers that will carry. 'Moving swiftly on. Indah can you handle the bail hearing for Turner. I can't see any objection to bail, but the magistrate might agree to a tag.'

'Gov, I'm already in court with Mrs Saunders,' says Lisa, 'and I know Indah has got an interview arranged.'

'Cheers, Lisa. Where's Becky?' People don't know. 'When she appears, I'm sending her to the mainland to take Judge Le Strange to the hospital where his partner is and then to take evidence up to BioTech forensics.'

'Always good to have a gofer,' says Pete.

'Yes, but I'd like to give her something meatier.'

'I bet you would, Gov.'

'Thanks for that Pete and you can FLO at the hospital.'

'Gov, you know I hate all that touchy feely stuff and my last wife said I lacked empathy.'

'You do, but the hospital is yours.'

'Monica could do it.'

'No, Sergeant Aries is taking Bethany to see her dad.'

'A taxi could do that,' Pete grumbles.

'Get over yourself, grumps. Monica, how's Bethany?'

'Fine and she knows more about her parents than they'd want her to. She is disgusted by them and is clearly the adult. The good thing is she is resilient and once her A levels are done she's off to live with an aunt in New York before going to university. We've settled into the safe house just fine and remember to draw the curtains.'

'Claudia, warrant for the Andrews car and rental house?' She nods. 'Remind us why we are searching the rental house, they didn't move in?'

'But the Andrews went there Friday morning to leave their bags.'

'You think they might have left something?'

'Exactly. SOCO can't be there until early afternoon, they are backed up with everything else. I'll go there then.'

'Mind if I come along?'

'Not at all, Gov. We're beginning to get some intel' on the Andrews, especially the husband. He's been buying large amounts of cocaine once or twice a year according to our sources. We've got their financials. I'm waiting for more details and phone records. He seems to use one City drug dealer, Eva Djokovic, a really nasty piece of work.

'You've now got plenty to use in the interrogations. I can't get involved, bloody conflict of interest. Chalky, sorry, but you are our go to tech guy so keep on with the CCTV this morning.'

'The school discs have all been done, but we've now got even more stuff from the ferries, but I'm not seeing anything helpful.'

'Thanks for the info' on Turner about crossing to the mainland. It suggests he did go to the horsebox hospital after being shot by Mrs Saunders. Lisa once court is over I need you to co-ordinate the interviews for late this afternoon in our new portacabin interview rooms,' Cully announces cheerfully. Groans all round. 'I suggest you and Claudia take Megan Simpson, Monica, after you've dropped Bethany back to the safe house, you and Tom take Carla Scutari. You'll need to let him know. Indah, can you keep me up to date with the door to door please?'

'Only one thing so far, Gov, an elderly chap living opposite the back of the church saw a fire after seven Friday evening. He's annoyed, the smelly smoke blew over his place, but he didn't see anybody there. He says he knew you and something about a gnome.'

'You need to see the Vicar, Indah. Speak to her about it.'

++++

'Becky!'

'Gov, sorry I missed the briefing, but I went to see Lilly.'

'Indah says you're doing a good job with her, but we need to consider a referral to social services. Baby-sitting is not really our business.'

'Sorry Gov.'

'I've been looking for you. I've not had a chance to thank you, for what you've done as FLO and working with Tom and getting guests away as quickly as possible over the weekend. You must be exhausted.'

'No, too excited. Sorry, that sounds terrible, I keep putting my foot in it. It's no problem, Sir.'

'Gov will do fine and I like your enthusiasm and envy your energy. Do you have any commitments?' She looks back blankly. 'Can you work through, or do you have children, a family that need you? You'll get paid overtime.'

'I can work every hour you want,' she says excitedly.

'Do you have your own car?' She nods. 'Good, because we don't have a spare police vehicle. You'll get mileage of course. We need you to take items of evidence for further forensic examination, including the shotgun used to shoot the Healer and the explosives taken from Turner. Can you drive me to the hotel and I'll explain what else I need you to do.'

Arriving they find Judge Le Strange enjoying coffee in the bar.

'Patrick, there you are. Are you still intending to sit in court tomorrow?'

'I can't let people down,' he responds. 'I'll be there.'

'We will add protection at the courthouse. Only a precaution. But today you should be there when Andrew wakes up after his operation. This is Becky, you've spoken on the phone when she told you Andrew was alive. She is going to drive you to the hospital, leave you there before picking you up and bringing you back this evening. Ok Becky?'

'Yes Gov, but Judge, I'm afraid I've only got an old Punto.'

'But this must be taking you away from your duties here on the Island?'

'No Judge, the Gov wants me to take evidence to forensics at the BioTech lab.'

'He obviously keeps you busy,' Patrick smiles. 'Now Becky call me Patrick. You are doing me a wonderful service and as long as you don't tell the Superintendent here I intend buying us each a proper drink on the ferry, a gin and tonic perhaps? And I'm starving. I hope the food has improved.'

'They do a tasty bacon sandwich Judge.'

'I've told you, Patrick please,' he insists, 'and perfect, let's get going.'

'I just need the loo. Won't be minute.'

'I can't believe I'm going on an adventure with a beautiful young woman. Never expected to say that,' and winks at Cully. 'Thank you, you didn't have to do this. I met with DC Kasali yesterday to give my statement. You do surround yourself with handsome young women, but then you always did.'

'Also I owe you for speaking favourably about me to the Chief Constable, it balanced up that I misspoke in relation to the Prime Minister.'

'But it's true,' Patrick laughs. 'Thinking about your girls, there was Sara, Virginia, Rachel and Sophie and Jenny squabbled passionately over you.'

'I'm back,' Becky announces.

Cully watches them leave.

'That was good of you,' Sophie appears beside him, smiling.

'Partly self-interest, he's a useful ally,' Cully admits. 'I'm keeping him sweet.'

'You always were Machiavellian. Did I ever meet Virginia or Sara?'

'I don't think so,' he grins. 'Where did you come from?'

'I'm here to work. I got a call from Diana Kent,' she explains, pushing back a strand of curly light brown hair. 'Apparently you said she needed to talk and encouraged her to make contact with an ex-boyfriend. I never saw you as a matchmaker, more a matchbreaker.'

'You're the second person to hint at that. Sean O'Leary said it when I visited him in hospital yesterday.'

'He can be a little bitter and you did take Rachel off him.'

'I did not, she'd dumped him.'

'Is that what she told you?' Sophie grins. 'My sister has always been a liar.'

'Exactly why are you here?'

'People from the shooting have got together with others and want me to facilitate a group discussion. Pathetic really, none of them are physically hurt, but emotionally. They've booked a room. I'm not charging for this introductory session.' She pauses in thought. 'You look weary. I've moved into the cottage on Rachel's farm until this is over. Let me cook you dinner tonight?'

'When this is over you can.'

'And breakfast?'

'Sophie,' he changes the subject. 'Why didn't you let me see you after the accident?'

'Don't Cully, far too long ago.'

'You gave Indah your book.'

'It was self-indulgent, but she would have got to it eventually. You'll send her back to me.'

'Leave her alone,' Cully warns her.

'She's your type Cully, but rather young.'

'If I'd been quicker to get to you, it wouldn't have happened.'

'Not your fault and you saved my life that night.'

'Then why didn't you let me see you?'

'Leave it. I was damaged goods. We're not talking about it. You know she fancies you?'

'Who?'

'Indah, hero worship, I'd call it. Mind you so does the one that's just left.'

'What Becky? She's a kid.'

'You've always underestimated your effect on women.' A faint smile plays on her lips. 'Your self-effacing modesty adds to your attraction. Buy me a drink?'

'I'm on duty and I thought you had a group session?'

'Not for another hour and I fear I might need a drink to get through. "But do you, Abelard, never see Heloise in your sleep? How does she appear to you?" she recites and flutters her eyelashes comically. 'Now buy me that drink.'

++++

Indah walks by the pink and white Vespa gleaming in the sunshine and in behind the church to the community garden. 'Hello Vicar.'

'You must be Indah, we've not met and please call me Mandy.' Mandy stops digging. 'Spring is a wonderful time and I'm making the best of a lovely morning. The ladies have done a great job here. It was a mess when I came to the Parish.'

'What would you do without your ladies?'

'Struggle to survive. They are lovely, but elderly and I am conducting many more funerals. Fewer and fewer coming to services. Nobody under thirty. Can't remember when I conducted a wedding. The church is dying.'

'Isn't that true of Christian religion generally?'

'Probably,' she smiles. 'Gosh, a philosophical discussion this early?'

'My father used to say I was godless,' Indah mutters. 'Doing this job you stop believing.'

'I understand that,' Mandy nods. 'How did Indah end up on this racist intolerant Island? Sorry, that's terrible of me, I'm rather knotted at the moment.'

'My dad was a GP here. How did they react to a female Vicar?'

'Nothing to my face, but I heard the mutterings. Where was your dad from?'

'Indonesia, Java to be precise.'

'Beautiful I imagine.'

'Very, we used to go back every couple of years, but Dad died and mum is not so well nowadays.'

'I'm sorry for your loss.'

'Losses, I think I've lost them both.' Indah moves away to the oil drum and looks inside. 'You burn everything?'

'Everything we can't compost. I've been digging the ashes in, dust to dust, ashes to ashes.'

'There's nothing left in the drum,' Indah muses. 'We still need to take it. Your neighbour said he saw a fire Friday evening here in the garden at about seven fifteen. The killer might have escaped this way.'

'He's our neighbourhood snoop. Have you seen his regiment of gnomes? He's a pain. Sorry, not very Christian of me. Did we break a by-law?'

'Not as far as I'm aware, but were you or your ladies out here then?'

'I wasn't and by six they've normally snuggled down in front of the TV with a glass of sherry.'

'I don't see other fire damage, so the drum seems a likely suspect.'

'Be my guest and arrest it.'

'I'll get a couple of uniforms up here to take the drum. We also need SOCO to search where you've dug in the contents.'

'Sorry.'

'Nothing to be sorry about, you didn't know.'

Indah uses her phone to arrange things as they walk to the kitchen door and go inside where two of the ladies have the urn bubbling. Beyond can be heard the noise from the incident room. 'The drum is being collected and SOCO will look at the garden when they've got time. I'm afraid the garden will be taped off.' Indah is reading a notice pinned to the cork board on the wall. 'You've had to cancel things to let us use the hall.'

'Needs must and a school slaughter takes precedence over bridge, indoor bowels, quilt making and Pilates.'

'Slaughter?'

'Haven't you seen the press?'

'No time.' Indah looks back at the notice board. 'I do Pilates when I can, it keeps me supple.'

'I bet,' Mandy smiles. 'How's the portacabin working out?'

'Not one of the Gov's best ideas, it's cold, cramped and smells of wet rot.'

'You like him don't you?'

'He's a good boss.'

'That's not what I mean,' she smiles.

'Tea for you Dear,' one of the Ladies hands a mug and biscuit to Indah.

'Thank you. There is something else. You bought flashbangs from Turner.'

'Ah, have I broken the law?'

'Technically, you bought explosives from an unlicensed retailer. Not serious, but why?'

'I felt sorry for him. The young woman he had the affair with is not the innocent people make out. She knew what she was doing, entered the relationship with her eyes open and she'd no reason to tell his wife, the affair was over.'

'You know this how?' Indah asks, but is thinking about Crystal. It sounds as if she's the same nasty, manipulative person she always was. 'Sorry, what did you say?'

'Confession,' repeats Mandy. 'She used to come to the church and talk to me. I can't say I liked her, but my job is to listen to whoever comes in.'

'Turner's not much of a catch is he?'

'No detective,' she laughs. 'I never understand why people are attracted to other people. That's not totally true, sometimes it's obvious isn't it?'

'What do you mean?'

'You know what I mean Indah,' she smiles. 'You could do worse than attach your wagon to that particular star.'

'You sound like my mother.' Indah sips her tea, watching Mandy over the lip of the mug. 'You said you felt sorry for Turner?'

'Of course he was wrong to do what he did, but he lost everything including income. I bought ten of the things to put fifty quid in his pocket. I've still got them. Do you want them?'

++++

The house is on the northwest coast overlooking the sea where the channel between the Island and the mainland is at its narrowest. There is a creeping sea mist and gulls circle above. Claudia picks Cully up from outside the hotel with news about the search of the Andrew's car. 'Baby formula?'

'To mix with the cocaine, doubling the amount,' Claudia explains. 'It's not even their Jaguar, it's hired, all for keeping up appearances.'

She follows Cully's directions only to find the chain ferry across the river is out of service and they have to go the long way round to the house, with her cursing the state of the roads and slowness of other drivers. 'How do you put up with this place?'

'I'm only visiting,' Cully mutters.

The grounds are large, edged on the landward side with a high wall and gates, while a wide drive cuts through manicured lawns to the house. Estate agents blurb would call it substantial and well-maintained. There is plenty of parking and Claudia pulls her car in beside the SOCO van already there.

The interior is bright and modern, light streaming in through glass skylights.

'Nice place,' Cully remarks. 'This is where Minty wants to set her article.'

'Pardon, Gov?'

'Sorry Claudia, talking to myself.'

'Forgot you're an only child, Gov.'

'You know another?'

'Knew another, my ex-partner. She used to drive me mad,' Claudia sighs, 'talking more to herself than to me.'

'Is that why you ended it?'

'No, found her in bed with the bitch next door. I've moved on,' Claudia tells herself. 'This place is special isn't it?'

'At five hundred a day, it should be,' answers Cully. 'Anything Amber?'

'Nothing,' she sighs, blonde hair pulled back in a tight bun, 'but we've only just started and we're short staffed. Did you send the shotgun and explosives to the lab?' He nods. 'That's one thing I don't have to think about. I'm exhausted. I need more help and the lab facilities here are crap. Isn't there anyone else mainland can spare?'

'I've tried.'

'Try harder,' Amber grimaces. 'We'll need eight hours to do a thorough job here.'

'We can't give you that long,' Claudia complains.

'We won't let them back until tomorrow,' Cully suggests. 'How's that?'

'Better, but if you want my opinion, there's nothing here of interest. There's nothing in the Simpson's baggage and the place has been cleaned by the professionals the rental agency hire. We could be doing other things.'

'We still need it done,' Cully smiles. 'You have family on the Island?'

'What?' Amber is startled by the question. 'Yes, why?'

'Just chatting Amber,' his smile broadening. 'Someone mentioned your parents are Serbian, not somewhere I've ever been. Thanks for all your hard work.'

'Everything here is posh and expensive,' Claudia remarks.

'There's even a hidden toilet in the hallway,' Amber replies. 'You should try it Cully, for dumping your bullshit. There's a bidet with warm air to dry your bum.'

'You've tried it?'

'Let me get on.'

'I've only known you three days and I love you already,' says Cully sarcastically. 'You were there after my daughter and I got shot weren't you?'

A phone rings. Claudia takes the call, listening for several minutes. 'Gov, we've got more on the Simpson's finances and they're in big trouble. Their business folded six months ago, they declared themselves bankrupt, the bank are about to take the house, cards are maxed and they owe school fees. Most significantly the word on the street,' she pauses loving the phrase, 'is that they owe dealer Eva Djokovic at least thirty thousand pounds for Posh. Ninety-seven per cent pure Columbian.'

'Is this Eva Djokovic a member of a gang?'

'Yes Gov, *Groupa Europa.*'

'Never heard of them,' he lies, but making certain Amber is within ear-shot. 'What nationality are they?'

'Serbian.'

'You could translate for us Amber.'

'Piss off Cully,' she growls.

'What business were the Andrew's in?' Cully asks Claudia.

'Wine trade. They had a shop in Kensington and a warehouse in the suburbs.'

'Any idea how and why it went under?'

'None, but we're still digging. There is an accountant to track down.'

'Thirty thousand is a lot of cash when you've got nothing.'

'Exactly,' Claudia agrees. 'In the interview with Megan Simpson, shall I ask about life insurance?'

'Why?'

'He dies, wife survives and she pays off the debts including Djokovic.'

'Perhaps Dumpy Dumps organised this whole thing. That's what we called Megan Simpson in school.'

'Cruel.'

'But true.'

'The best place to hide one murder is amongst several,' Claudia argues.

'It's a stretch, but it needs to go on the list of motives, maybe at the bottom.'

'What if Dumpy Dumps and Eva got together?'

'You're stretching things Claudia, that goes right at the bottom, let's get back to the facts,' Cully reasons. 'I suggest we let the women have the house back tomorrow afternoon unless the interviews throw-up anything significant. They'll need protection. A couple of armed officers should do it.'

Cully's phone pings, he looks down and sighs. He yawns. 'Can you drive me please?'

'Sure thing. And Gov, you need sleep.'

'Before we go,' begins Cully, 'someone show me this hidden loo.'

After using it, Cully climbs into the car beside Claudia and they set off.

'Convenient local shops,' he comments as they drive by a row of stores. 'Watch out!'

'Stupid idiot!' Claudia sounds her horn, but the scooter rider doesn't even look round. 'Bloody delivery drivers. They're an absolute menace.'

'I haven't had a pizza in ages,' Cully sighs. 'A meat feast with chilli, celeriac coleslaw with a good Chianti. Something the Andrews could have supplied by the caseload. I wonder what happened to their bankrupt stock?'

++++

'Jenny Sykes, I'm DC Indah Kasali. I rang.'

'Yes of course,' and she stands back. Tall, thin with long blonde hair caught by salt laden wind gusting in off the sea that she brushes from her fox face. 'I think you need to see Tash Brown as well. She's here, I'm looking after her. We've been friends since primary school. Can I get you a tea or coffee?'

'Coffee would be good, thank you. You have a lovely place here and great views.'

'I find the sea restful.'

'Even in winter?'

'Not so much I suppose. Do you mind dogs?' A white Jack Russell lays in a basket in the kitchen corner, opens an eye to study Indah, but does not move. 'He's tired, we did a long walk along the cliff this morning.'

'Isn't that dangerous?'

'Not if you're careful.' Jenny sets a tray. 'You've seen other people?'

'Yes, several,' and Jenny asks after everyone, people Indah has met.

'Sean O'Leary, he was wounded. Would it be ok if I visited him?'

'Of course,' Indah says. 'You don't want to know about Sophie?'

'Why would I?' Indah is intrigued by the sudden change of tone. 'Please, come through and meet Tash.' The woman sits in an armchair with her plastered ankle supported by a stool.

'How is it?'

'Mending.' She has a head of curly blonde hair. 'Have you caught him?'

'Not yet, but we're following several lines of investigation.'

'Are we one of them?'

'No, just talking to people that were there or didn't go,' Indah reassures her. 'Jenny, can I start by asking why you didn't go to the event?'

'I changed my mind.'

'Tell her the truth Jenny that you didn't want to see him.'

'Him?'

'It's nothing and it's not true. I've no idea why I accepted the invitation in the first place.'

'One hundred pounds is a lot of money to waste,' Indah comments.

'To see him,' says Tash. 'Tell her.'

'But you went Mrs Brown?'

'Ms and yes I did. We were both going until Jenny changed her mind, but I wasn't about to waste the money. Do you know what's happening to all that food?'

'Tash,' warns Jenny, 'people are dead.'

'I believe the headteacher and Vicar are distributing it to various Island charities.' Indah takes a deep breath, thanks Jenny for the coffee and moves on. 'Where would you have been sitting?' Indah asks, seeking a different line of questioning. 'Jenny?'

'On the nice table, I believe between Patrick and Andrew.'

'Nice table?'

'You know about our group names?'

'Remind me,' Indah smiles.

'Nice and Nasty, a joke most of the time.'

'Joke?'

‘Not always,’ adds Tash.

‘Ms Brown can you tell us what you remember?’

‘Call me Tash. I don’t remember much. The lights went down, the film about to start and then there were loud bangs, shouts and screams. I thought it was a practical joke and then someone pushed me to the ground. He fell on top of me. I remember the terrible pain in my ankle and blacked out. I woke covered in blood, so much blood. I’m lucky, I’m alive.’

Indah sips her coffee. ‘I suppose, you didn’t see Phillip Simpson with a leather satchel?’

‘That old thing, I’m sure you remember Jenny. He always brought it to parties filled with booze nicked from his father’s shop.’

‘The same satchel?’

‘Yes. He and Davis were all conspiratorial about it on Friday night. Watching them brought back memories of that horrible beach party,’ Tash grimaces. ‘It’s absurd that thirty years later I still feel a stab of pain about how cruel they were.’

‘I’m sure the detective does not want to hear about school days,’ says Jenny.

‘The Nasty Gang?’ Indah persists. ‘Tell me about it, please.’

‘We were always excluded from their special group. For a start, they had lots of money, most of us didn’t.’

‘Sophie,’ Indah persists, aware that this whole investigation is turning into a soap opera, yet she is fascinated and not a little bit about Cully, *‘but he’s twice your age’*, comes a voice. *‘It’s only fantasy.’* ‘Things between her and you Jenny?’

‘Is old history and has nothing to do with now,’ Jenny gets up, crosses to the window and stares out at the ocean. ‘If you must know, we’ve not spoken since the summer we all left, not that we’ve seen each other.’

‘What happened?’

‘It doesn’t matter.’

‘It was stupid teenage jealousy all round,’ begins Tash. ‘Cully and Sophie had started going out together while they were in that play.’

‘Abelard and Heloise,’ offers Indah.

‘But Jenny won him over.’

‘Tash stop it,’ Jenny snaps. ‘Do you remember that terrible brown uniform we used to wear at the convent and the nuns?’

‘We heard about a beach party,’ Tash continues, ignoring her friend, warming to her subject, ‘but when we got there it was the Nasty Gang, they all laughed at us turning up. It was humiliating. It was obvious Cully and Sophie had been arguing. Rachel was already there with the Nasty Gang and Sophie demands her sister tell her the truth.'

'About what?' asks Indah leaning forward.

'That Cully had been fucking Rachel. She was a fifteen year old tart, easy meat and the Nasty Gang liked young girls.'

'Anyone in particular?'

'Chapman, the creep. Can't believe they let him become an architect. He was always touchy feely,' Tash sighs. 'Anyway, Rachel was drunk and she tells her sister Cully fucked her, every which way. Sophie slaps Cully. It wasn't true, just gossip. Jenny, do you remember who started it?' Silence. 'Jenny?' She shakes her head in reply, turning away from the window. 'Cully was furious, demanded Rachel tell the truth, but the Nasty Gang started jeering at Sophie who ran away. Cully steps forward and punches Simpson hard to the ground, fends off Davis and lands one on someone else before we pull him off. Sophie had vanished by then while we all walked up to the pub.'

'You and Cully, Jenny?'

'Got together that night,' answers Tash.

'You originally met Cully at the school?' Indah persists, hardly able to hide her interest.

'No, before then,' says Tash. 'You met him at one of our convent dances for the first time,' Tash reminds her. 'You let him snog you. You didn't stop talking about him. Then we moved to the posh school six form and met him again and he invited you to a disco, but you didn't go.'

'Please shut up Tash. I'm sure the detective has had enough of hearing about our teenage stuff. She wants to know if there was anything else you saw Friday night, don't you?'

'I know Sophie slipped out just before the shooting started,' says Tash. 'Don't you want to know about what happened the summer after the beach party Detective?'

'No Tash, she doesn't.'

'Tell me,' says Indah.

++++

Lisa is feeling relaxed and confident. She isn't gambling and hardly drinking. She'd not admit it to Cully, but arriving at the school Friday evening overwhelmed her with stress when she thought she might have to run things and triggered one of her headaches. Then came the call from the Chief and relief flooded through her relieving the pain. She likes Cully, and while he can get on with tedious management stuff she can concentrate on what she enjoys, being a detective and there is no better place than being in the interview room facing a person of interest. Especially an arrogant self-important person like Megan Simpson.

Reaching out she switches on the tape recorder, waits for the bleep and begins. 'Present in the room is Mrs Megan Simpson, the duty solicitor, Sergeant Claudia Davies and Inspector Lisa Lynn.'

'I should be at my husband's bedside, not sitting here.'

'Inspector, I'd like to clarify something?' asks the solicitor. 'My client understood this is to be a statementing process, but recording the interview suggests you have something more in mind?'

'It's a complex case and we need to keep things on record.'

'In that case, I reserve the right to advice my client to withdraw her cooperation if necessary.'

'Of course.' Lisa liked Claudia and they had spent a productive time in the incident room planning the interview. 'Sergeant Davies, over to you.'

'I'm interested Mrs Andrews as to why your friend Carla has arrived here with expensive City lawyers and you have the duty solicitor. I'm sure he's good, but it seems odd.'

'Convenience. My lawyer is not available.'

'Not paid his bill? You have a lot of unpaid bills. We've been looking at your finances. You and your husband are broke?'

'I really don't…' the solicitor starts. 'Did you have a warrant?'

'Here,' says Claudia passing the paperwork over. 'You should also know that we've searched your car. Here's the warrant for that as well.'

'This is an ambush,' complains the solicitor.

'How dare you,' Megan bristles.

'We dare Mrs Simpson. We will talk about what we found in your car in a minute, but let's get back to your finances. Your debts are massive, you have no income and you owe your drug dealer Eva Djokovic thirty thousand pounds.'

'Stop there, I need time with my client.'

'Of course.'

Thirty minutes later they return.

'Did you get a tea or coffee?' Claudia asks.

'Yes, but it's revolting and this room is freezing.'

'I have to agree with Mrs Simpson,' begins the solicitor, 'surely this could have been done at the station, not in a damp portacabin?'

'Sorry about that,' begins Lisa. The two women detectives have discussed strategy during the break. 'Let's get back to the drugs we found in your husbands satchel.'

'It was planted there.'

'His fingerprints were on the plastic bag containing the drugs.'

'How did you get his fingerprints?'

'We took them.'

'While he's unconscious and he's only got one hand poor baby.' She is outraged. 'How dare you? He could be dying and you interfere with him.'

'Did you have a warrant?'

'We did of course,' and Claudia pushes more paperwork across the table.

'Do you have a baby?'

'No.'

'Then why, when we searched your car, did we find two tins of baby milk powder.'

'I've no idea.'

Claudia makes an exaggerated note of the denial. 'Remember we are interviewing Carla in the next room and Allison Grey's husband has told us about the parties.'

'What parties.'

'The drug and sex parties you all enjoy once or twice a year.'

'Rubbish!'

'What about Alison Grey?'

'I haven't seen her in years. She didn't attend the parties.'

'So there were parties?'

'Reunions,' Megan corrects.

'Friendships that go back thirty years. Just the group of you?' Megan is blushing. 'Exclusive?'

'I suppose so.'

'Why would someone want to kill you all?'

'What?'

'Surely, you must have thought about it. The six dead were all at your table. It does seem the gunman targeted your table.'

'Six?'

'Sorry, didn't you know, Felicity Taylor died on the operating table. That leaves your husband, Carla, with minor burns and you totally unscathed.'

'I was lucky.'

'Or knew what was going to happen?'

'Don't be absurd.'

'Tell us about the Nasty Gang?'

'That's a long time ago. Stupid name. They were stupid. They were stupid children.'

'We need to talk about your drug connections,' Claudia changes direction, 'what do you know about Eva Djokovic and *Groupa Europa?*'

'That's enough officer, we are ending things here.'

Back in the incident room, Lisa is lost in thought. According to Monica and Tom Carla Scutari, closely protected by her expensive London lawyer, had given nothing away in her interview.

From where she is sitting, Lisa can see Cully in the church hall office, partially hidden behind the computer screen. Perhaps he's playing a computer game, gambling or looking at porn, but doubts it. No, this case is personal and he wants it done and dusted. Like others in the police, at least the ones she had spoken to, she is surprised he had survived in the force let alone in life after what happened, but then he had Linda to care for and he is an undoubted favourite of the Chief Constable.

++++

Cully is reading Indah's report on the interviews with Jenny and Tash. She'd not gone into detail, but reading between the lines it is obvious they, probably Tash, talked about the beach party and events from that summer. While Cully doesn't care about Jenny, he does about Sophie. Picturing her, he sees the teenager in school uniform, bright slate grey eyes, shoulder length naturally curly light brown hair, asking to borrow his rugby shirt. 'Why?'

'Netball, we're in a tournament and we need a change of kit. I'll wash it before I give it back.'

'Maybe I'd prefer you didn't.'

'Perv.'

'Can I come and watch?'

Going online, Cully searches for Sophie and there is plenty there about her book including high praise from critics. He must read it. Carla is everywhere. He remembers her, dark hair, attractive, aloof, highly intelligent, goes to LSE, builds a fashion empire, but never marries or has children. Cully surfs the net for some of the other women, but there's not much. As for Allison Grey, there are several photographs of her, one half-naked draped over a Porsche 911 from several years back.

Then he goes to the note about Michael Carter left by Kerry and there's a contact number for his work. Cully rings, explains who he is and is quickly put through. 'Michael, you probably don't remember…'

'Of course I do and you're all over the news.'

'I'll get straight to it Michael. Why didn't you come on Friday?'

'If I had, I might be dead.'

'Good point, but why didn't you?'

'I couldn't face it.'

'Understood. I didn't go either.' They chat for a while, before Cully brings them back to the main issue. 'You were part of the Nasty Gang.'

'Jesus Cully that was then, things change, I've changed.'

'Did you go to these parties?'

'At the beginning, I went to a few, but I met my wife up here, got a job I love, had children and caught settled bliss. I know in school I was a bully, especially to John my brother, but that was then for Christ's sake.'

'Do you see John?'

'No, he's never forgiven me. I tried to apologise to make amends, but he wouldn't have it and we went our separate ways. He joined the army.'

'What wouldn't he forgive you for?' Silence. 'Michael?'

'I verbally tormented him, but Poulson got to him and John blames me for not protecting him. I really didn't know what was going on.'

Twenty minutes later Cully puts the phone down.

A new message appears on the computer screen from Indah.

Draft Notes on Detective Superintendent Cully

The CCTV confirms he came across on the ten am ferry from the mainland, then met his uncle for lunch at the restaurant in the village. He had veal and a glass of Brunello. The waitress says he tipped her a tenner. He told his uncle he'd decided not to go to the reunion, but would go to his wife's, mother's and grandmother's graves. He drove to catch the ferry, leaving time for a drink and something to eat. The landlady remembers him. I recovered the debit card receipt and once again he left a generous tip. The Chief Constable confirms what time she rang him as does his mobile phone.

++++

Indah appears in the doorway smiling.

'You've seen Vicar Mandy?'

'She wanted to help Turner. I believe her.' She settles into the chair opposite him. 'You've read my report on my visit to Jenny and Tash?'

'I have. They were always close.'

'Both convent girls apparently.' A wistful smile plays on Indah's lips. 'They told me about the beach party and the one you all attended in the summer. It was after that party Sophie was burned in the car accident with Davis.'

'We were kids as far as the first was concerned and the second, well that gets more complicated. More importantly for now, has my alibi checked out?'

'You read my notes?' He nods, pointing at the computer screen. 'If I didn't know better,' she chuckles, 'it looks like you were constructing an alibi.'

'I was,' he grins, 'for Linda. I knew when I saw her she'd give me grief for not going, accuse me of bottling it which of course is true, but at least I could tell her what I'd done instead.'

'I spoke to your uncle on the phone, he sounds nice.'

'He is. Am I in the clear now?'

'More or less.'

'More or less,' he repeats.

'You told me to be thorough and we need to shut Kerry up.'

'Indah, that's beneath you. What's left to do?'

'You know exactly, we need to talk about your timings and Kerry mumbles about making certain. She's jealous. You've replaced her father.'

'I suppose, but I'm not like him.'

'God no, you're so…But,' she pauses, 'you gave the Chief Constable the impression you came from the pub to the school, but you didn't did you?'

'No and I'm sorry.'

'Where were you?'

'You've gone all serious, I'm seeing a different side to you Indah. I'd hate to be interrogated by you, I'd be putty in your hands. I'm happy to tell you, but I'd rather take you tomorrow?'

'Fine.' She's strangely relieved and happy to go along with his suggestion. 'Oh, and I forgot to give you your book back. You could kill someone with a blow from it.' Indah smiles, hesitates, wondering if this is a right moment and then speaks. 'Ever had a beef Rendang?'

'Don't think so, but it sounds delicious.'

'Dinner tomorrow night at my place,' she blurts, suddenly worrying she's gone too far. 'I make a really good curry.'

'I'm sure you do Indah and that would be wonderful.'

'Great,' she smiles, relieved.

'Anything more?'

'I could get your cookbook dusted for fingerprints, put you in a line-up, but won't waste resources, whatever Kerry thinks. She's been checking up on me, on you.'

'How?'

'You don't ask why?'

'You've told me why,' says Cully, 'she's jealous, wants to undermine me, the team, the investigation.'

'She would love us to fail, to get revenge on all of us,' she says quietly.

'Because she blames you, Lisa and Tom and the system for her father's death,' he concludes. 'Indah, there's a temporary posting coming up at MIU, would you be interested?'

Thirty minutes later.

'Listen up,' calls Cully loudly, stepping out of the office. 'Pub.'

'Pub,' comes the chorus.

Tuesday

Cully is keen, for it to be a day of visits and interviews, of straightforward normal police work, of course carrying guns makes a difference, as do forest-dwellers and healers, but he is determined to keep it low key.

'Breakfast, fry up'

'Please uncle.'

'Good lad, you slept in.'

'I did, felt I deserved it as I've been giving everyone else time off and we had a bit of a session last night. I got a taxi back.' Cully pets Angus as the dog rolls over to expose an expanse of pink belly. 'There you go boy, walkies later.'

'Don't use that word, you know how excited he gets.'

Earlier, sitting up in bed Cully rings Lisa at eight, asks after her.

'Slight hangover, nothing more,' she says. 'I really enjoyed last night. It's a good team.'

'Any news from Kerry?'

'She rang in sick. She's obsessed. Tizard's bored with her. He'll move on.'

'To whom?'

'He's a predator and hasn't found anyone vulnerable enough to seduce yet. There have been at least three others I know about, an administrator at the station, a social worker and many years ago Amber.'

'Seriously?'

'It didn't last long and it was before she got married.'

'Indah and Tizard?'

'No, she's far too wily. She presents as this rather innocent girl, but is hard inside, intelligent, able and ambitious. You like her don't you Cully?'

'I'm not crossing that line however much I might want to,' he smiles, but knows he's fooling himself.

They go on to discuss what needs to be done. He reminds her that Pete is on close protection duty with the judge. Lisa reluctantly agrees to visit the women in their hotel.

Cully agrees to contact Becky which he does, enjoying her enthusiasm. 'Really me? Of course, I'll get ready right away.'

'I'll make tea,' says Cully, reaching for the kettle.

'We always used to be a good team.' Adam thought for a few seconds. 'I miss it. Having people in the house and doing things together.'

'Once this is over, I'll get Linda over. She can continue her rehab here.'

'Maybe she's ready to get back to work. Don't smother her Cully.'

'I try not to,' he sighs. The kettle boils furiously and Cully takes down the tea pot and box of leaf tea. 'No tea bags?'

'You must be kidding, you know they only put dust in bags. Now be a good lad and remember to warm the pot.'

'Tea cosy?'

'In the draw, grandma's.'

'Got it. You impressed Indah when she rang.'

'She seems lovely and I hope I said the right things?'

'You told her the truth uncle.'

'She was charming and clever the way she got the information out of me.'

'She simply asked you a few questions and you answered them, but yes she is clever.'

'Why do you need an alibi?'

'I don't, but I was one of the four guests on one table that didn't turn up and there was one who didn't appear on the target table. We have to check everyone.'

'Ah, of course, the Nasty Gang.'

'You shouldn't know any of this and I can't discuss it.'

'It's all over the Internet. Do you think you'll catch this shooter?'

'No.'

'No if's and but's?'

'A professional attack. He was off the Island before anyone knew what was happening, but we keep going. After breakfast, can I use the study?'

'Of course.'

Breakfast cleared away Cully goes into the study while Adam takes Angus walkies. A Teams media conference has been arranged by HQ and turns out to be remarkably straight forward. There are fewer interested journalists than before and no sign of Minty. The story is fading from the front page and no longer figures in the first half of television news. Afterwards there is a telephone call with Dr Inskip, reassuring him that things are going to plan and he should be able to release the school buildings and grounds shortly.

Cully receives a call from Patrick Le Strange before emerging as Adam and Angus return.

'Good walk?'

'I've just been invited to dinner by the woman at the bakery and to lunch by another walking her Cockapoo, bloody mongrel. Angus seems quite keen on the bitch, but I'm not certain about the woman. It's all because of you.'

'No, it's not. It's Angus,' says Cully, dropping to his knees and petting him. 'The girls love you, don't they?' He barks. 'I'm having lunch with a Judge Le Strange.'

'You are taking it easier today. That name rings a bell.'

'I was at school with him. His father owned the quarry out west and a few acres of the Great Forest.'

'Ah that Le Strange.'

'I saw the placards in your study. When's the protest?'

'This afternoon, you could come if you want.'

'I'd like to, but I'm busy. Uncle, try not to get in too much trouble and don't get arrested again. I may not be able to pull strings next time.'

++++

'Shit!' Lisa ends the call. 'That was Tizard.'

'What's wrong?'

'He rarely calls me, Ma'am. He's up to something.'

'You just don't like him. What did he want?'

'Permission to take the early evening off. He'll come back on at ten.'

'Did you give it to him?'

'I did, although he's probably…'

'Seeing Kerry.'

'Now you make me feel like a pimp Claudia, against the interests of my own sister,' she groans. 'What am I?'

'A pimp,' Claudia giggles.

'Thanks.'

'Do you want me to come in with you?'

'No, I'll do this, but don't go away,' says Lisa.

Climbing from the car, Lisa walks into the hotel. She is nervous about what is likely to come, but in the distance sees a friendly face and starts to relax.

An armed officer stands at the reception desk, chatting to the receptionist. Lisa coughs and the man swings round. 'Sorry Ma'am.'

'All quiet Joe?'

'Yes. The women are through there having coffee.'

They were in the lounge overlooking the gardens at the rear where Lisa could see the second armed officer patrolling. She touches the Glock at her hip, hating the feel yet accepting the need. They did not see her standing there. She watches, studying them closely. At first sight, Megan Simpson did not fit, short, dumpy with black hair she would not appear on any page of *Bonjour*, but the other one is built for it. Carla Scutari is tall, slender, short black hair, perfect skin all enhanced with plastic and Botox.

'Good morning, I'm DI Lynn. I already know Mrs Simpson of course.'

'Oh it's you,' Megan grumbles. 'She's the one that interrogated me.'

'Ladies, I'm sorry to disturb you, but if I could have a few minutes of your time.'

'I've had enough of being questioned.'

'Let it go,' smiles Carla thinly. 'Come and sit down. Coffee?'

'Thank you.'

'The madeleine's are surprisingly delicious,' she says without any hint of an Italian accent. 'They were a favourite of Proust, the French novelist.'

'I was expecting to find Alison Grey here as well.'

'We've not seen her.'

'She arrived Sunday. She was at the hospital, she was asking after you Ms Scutari. She said she is staying with a friend?'

'That'll be Sophie. We've not spoken in years.'

'You had a falling out?'

'You could say that,' Carla admits. 'How can we help you DI Lynn?'

'We said yesterday that you could move into the rental house this morning, but we would ask that you delay your move until this afternoon?'

'You've already asked us to wait a day more than we wanted,' Megan complains.

‘I appreciate that, but our forensics team are finishing. We needed to make certain there are no surprises waiting for you.’

‘Or drugs?’ snarled Megan. ‘Are you sure we hadn’t built a crack kitchen in the cellar?’

‘We’ve searched and you didn’t,’ says Lisa.

‘Don’t be silly Megan,’ says Carla. ‘I’m sure the detective knows we don’t touch that stuff. It rots the brain and ruins the complexion.’

‘You can’t keep us here,’ Megan complains.

‘We could, but we would like your co-operation. You could go to the safe house, it’s very secure.’

‘Is that where you’ve kidnapped Bethany to?’

‘We didn’t kidnap her, we placed her there for her protection.’

‘Megan,’ Carla interrupts, ‘you’ve booked the house for a week and it’s a lovely place with a pool and sauna. We can have some fun, not a good word I know in the circumstances, but at least relax after what’s happened.’

‘We will continue to keep you under protection,’ says Lisa. ‘This afternoon you will be driven there by police officers and armed guards will be outside the house from the moment you arrive.’

‘Is that necessary?’

‘The killer is still at large.’

‘What if we want to go shopping?’ Megan asks.

‘There isn’t a shop on this Island I’d want to visit,’ says Carla.

‘To eat then,’ Lisa suggests, ‘there’s an excellent French restaurant close by.’

‘The French one does home delivery,’ says Megan.

‘Megan darling, you’ll be suggesting we order a take away pizza next.’

‘I wouldn’t. The kitchen is well stocked.’

‘Descent champagne?’

‘Of course.’

‘When can we go?’

‘I suggest you have lunch here, the food isn’t too bad,’ Lisa suggests.

‘I need to go to the hospital to see my husband.’

‘Of course and Bethany, you’ll want to see her?’

‘Not today, maybe tomorrow.’

‘She could join you at the house, rather than staying at the safe house if you prefer, there’s plenty of room and she’d enjoy the pool.’

‘No.’

'Another alternative is that one of my officers and his wife, they are foster carers, could take her. They've got daughter's Bethany's age. You could visit.'

'Do you have children, DI Lynn?'

'No.'

'Then leave the parenting to me.'

'Bethany is seventeen and I'm sure…'

'I said no and she's my daughter.'

'Of course, but we have Powers of Protection for now and Superintendent Cully is determined to protect all of you and will do what it takes.'

'Good for him, but he couldn't protect his daughter could he?'

Lisa is thankful to get away.

'Shit!' Lisa gets in her car. 'What a bitch.'

'Went well then?' Claudia asks.

'Megan Simpson couldn't give a shit about Bethany.'

'Monica says she's a bright kid. She'll be fine. Lunch?'

++++

Becky could not believe what is happening, one moment she is walking the beat through the town, bored and wondering if she should have joined the Navy or become a hairdresser when suddenly she's investigating mass murder, drug running and actually attending a proper briefing like on TV. Cully is totally wonderful and appreciative of her. She'd researched everything about him on the Internet and he is the real deal, good looking, charming and intelligent. She knew he'd been married, but widowed. He had a daughter Linda. It's on the Internet about the shooting in the custody suit. What a hero! Of course she'd seen the way Indah looks at him and he her, but there is nothing wrong with competition.

Pulling up opposite the yacht club with the marshes on her right and the harbour on her left Becky climbs out and crosses the road. She'd been home, managed to get sleep after the pub which had been great because she felt a real member of the team. She'd dressed differently than before. At the hospital, she'd wanted to be approachable, able to comfort relatives as FLO, but today she needed to be a tough copper, wearing a black dress with black jacket and flat black pumps if she needed to chase someone. A brunette, her shoulder length hair is tied back in a severe bun and she wore her police ID on the blue safety lanyard that came apart should a villain grab it from round her neck. Over her shoulder is her black bag containing her mobile, notebook and pepper spray.

At the gate, there is a keypad and she presses the call button. A few moments pass before a man speaks. 'Yes?'

'Detective Constable Rebecca Shaw,' she announces clearly and proudly. 'I rang earlier.'

'Oh yes, come in.' There is a buzz. Becky pushes the gate and walks along the path towards the main door. Gulls screech overhead as they follow a trawler out of the harbour.

Cully rang her that morning before she left home, asks her to do the visit and repeats what Diana Kent had told him. 'See if he knows anything about these alleged sex and drugs parties Alison Grey's husband talks about. Ask the steward what you think you need to. Don't second guess yourself. You'll be fine.'

'Mr Wicks, thank you for seeing me.'

'I can't think what it's about.'

'Mrs Kent, your neighbour, told us you saw an incident here at the club.'

'She's a busy body.'

'You saw a woman push someone into the water. What exactly did you see?'

'I don't remember, it was years ago.'

'Come on Mr Wicks, please tell me?'

'I thought it odd, this young woman in a collar turns up. I thought she was a stripper or something, she argues with Mr Chapman and pushes him off the pontoon.'

'You now know who she was, or rather is?'

'Yes, I've seen her picture in the local paper, the Vicar woman Mandy Bannon.'

'You didn't think to contact us at the time?'

'I suppose I should have done, but didn't get round to it.'

'What do you do here?'

'I look after the place, clean up, run the bar.'

'Did you see or hear anything else?'

'I shouldn't say.'

'Why?'

'It's their business.'

'Any idea why she pushed him?'

'No, I said, they were having an argument.'

'What about?'

'I don't know.'

'You don't remember much do you?'

'I'm getting old, I forget things.'

'Who else was here?'

'It was a private hire?'

'Hired by members?'

'Yes and guests.'

'Which members?'

'I...'

'Why was the Vicar so angry with Chapman that she pushed him in the water?'

'I don't know.'

'You must have some idea Mr Wicks. Did something happen?' Becky had read Cully's notes from interviewing Diana Kent and Indah's from talking with Jenny Sykes and Tash Brown. 'Tell me about Chapman?' Silence. 'Was he with a young girl that night?'

'Maybe.'

'Was this a drugs and sex party with under-age girls?'

'I didn't see anything.'

'Mr Wicks, what was the argument about?'

'Years ago a girl called Debra fell in the harbour and drowned, but I don't really remember much about it.'

'Accident?'

'The police and the coroner thought so. I don't remember details.'

'You don't remember the incident or you don't remember if she was pushed?'

'I don't remember.'

'You are loyal to the club and its members aren't you?'

'I've been here a long time. I'm due to retire.'

'Are they going to pay you a large lump sum when you go buying your silence?'

'Silence?'

'About what happened. But you are starting to remember aren't you? You will remember everything and you will make a full statement. I'm taking you in now.'

'No, I'm on duty.'

'Do you want me to arrest you for obstruction,' Becky asks, producing handcuffs in a way she had been practising in front of the mirror. 'Your choice mate?'

++++

The morning is bright if cold, the sky a pale blue with thin strings of cloud crawling across it. Slowing he swings the Porsche into the car park, finds a space and reverses in.

'This is where you were Friday evening?'

'It is,' he confirms. 'Coming?' Cully asks, climbing out and buttoning his coat against the chill. He waits for Indah to join him before slipping his arm round her narrow waist. 'You ok with this?'

'Yes, very.'

'Good.' Pushing through the door, Cully introduces Indah to the receptionist and explains they have come to see Jamie. 'How is he?'

'Since the weekend he's been happy, chatting and joking when he's not sleeping. Never seen him like this before.'

'Visitors?'

'Several. You want the list?'

'No,' says Cully.

'But I will,' says Indah. 'Could you make a copy?' The receptionist agrees. 'Thank you.'

'We'll go through.' Cully leads the way down the corridor where they meet a nurse. 'Hello Sabrina, how are you?'

'Good. How's your hand Cully?'

'Much better thank you. We're here to see Jamie.'

'He'll be pleased to see you both.'

'You brought Cully into A and E the other night didn't you?' Sabrina looks at Indah. 'You were in the waiting room. You make a nice couple,' Sabrina smiles before walking on.

'Nice couple,' Indah bristles. 'Did you hear that?'

'I did,' Cully grins. 'Let's meet Jamie.' Cully pushes open a door. 'Indah, meet my best mate Jamie, the best accountant money can buy.' The man sits up in bed, features gaunt, ashen, his back against several pillows. Wires connect him to machines that hum and tubes to bags that hang from steel posts around him. 'Looking at porn Jamie?'

'Later Cully,' Jamie says closing the laptop. 'This thin machine,' he begins patting it, 'connects me to the world. You've brought a guest.'

'This is Indah Kasali, a member of the team. She's investigating my alibi.'

'Always in trouble aren't you Cully?' He coughs. 'You want to interrogate me?'

'Not interrogate Jamie, can I call you that?'

'Of course Indah, come and sit next to the bed so I can see you properly.' She does so. 'You are beautiful,' he sighs wistfully. 'Now, please ask your questions.'

'Cully was here with you Friday evening?'

'Yes for over an hour after six, reception will have recorded the exact times.'

'I've asked for the list,' says Indah, glancing at Cully.

'Sabrina came in when he was here.'

'Yes, she did,' Cully remembers. 'She brought me tea.'

'Nice of her,' remarks Indah.

'I know that tone,' Jamie splutters. 'Water please Cully.'

'I can do it.' Rising, Indah brings a glass of water to Jamie's pale thin lips. 'I know you were at school together,' she states. 'So, you knew the people in the school hall. Any thoughts about what happened?'

'They deserved it, every one of them. They bullied and abused, left victims in pain for decades.'

'Even so.'

'Fatal violence is all that works,' he mutters.

'Sophie wrote that,' Indah says, glancing at Cully. 'You've got lots of cards and flowers. These are beautiful,' and she reads the card, 'Ali Grey with plenty of kisses. Cards from Sophie, the Judge, John Carter with a big thank you written in red and one from Vicar Mandy.'

'Indah, you shouldn't,' Cully says.

'Of course she should,' states Jamie, 'she's a detective, inquisitive, thoughtful and a beautiful woman.'

'One last thing, what did you mean by you know that tone?'

'The sound when women buzz around Cully.'

'Buzz, really?'

'Buzz, buzz,' he repeats, 'but I'm sorry, I'm tired, can we stop please?'

'Of course,' Indah says, leaning forward and kissing him on the forward. 'I'll be back,' she whispers.

'Good, now buzz off,' he chortles.

Outside the room Indah grins broadly all the way down the corridor.

'He's lovely. Why did you keep it a secret?'

'I didn't want him bothered by…'

'DC Kerry Harris?'

'What?'

'She was in here yesterday,' explains the receptionist, 'not a nice girl. She was asking about you and Jamie and the people that visit him.'

'You didn't?'

'Of course not, no one gets by me and she didn't get near him, but I had to take a call and she had a good snoop at the visitors book. Talking of that, here's the list,' and she hands it to Indah.

'Sorry, I'll have words,' says Cully, 'she had no right to be here.'

Back in the car Indah reminds him that she'd said Kerry is snooping about.

'I'll speak to her. Am I in the clear now?'

'You always were, Gov.' Phone rings and Indah answers, listens before slipping her mobile away. 'That was the DI, she thinks Alison Grey is staying with Sophie. Carla says she hasn't seen Alison in years. Maybe the husband got it all wrong?'

'Maybe some of it. Looking back, I'm sure there was something between Carla and Ali.' Cully pauses thoughtfully. 'Are you coming to join us for lunch?' She shakes her head and he breathes in her scent. He wants to touch her, run his fingers through her black hair and kiss her. 'No?'

'You boys have a good lunch. I've got shopping to do, drop me in town please.'

'When are you going to see Sophie again?'

++++

'You've not brought any women with you Cully, I'm disappointed.'

'Next time, I promise.'

'I've met, let me see, Lisa that first night, Indah when she took my statement and Becky of course, all lovely.'

'And today I give you Pete.'

‘More my type, a tough man with a big gun,’ he laughs. ‘You are attractive, Pete.’

‘I am?’ Unexpectedly delighted, Pete grins. ‘Thanks Judge.’

‘How was your morning Patrick?’

‘Straightforward, but this afternoon has a rather bitter custody battle for me to rule on. Some parents are truly awful. I’ve booked us a table across the road. Pete, where are you going?’

‘To get a sandwich.’

‘Don’t be silly, we’re having lunch together. Now come on, lunch on me.’

They leave the courthouse and walk across the square to the pub where they are directed to a corner table. Given menus they quickly order. ‘Are we going to be naughty and have drinks?’

Pete glances at Cully.

‘A lemonade for Pete, white wine spritzer for me, thank you Patrick,’ says Cully.

‘I’ll join you with the spritzer. Not to worry, Pete, after I’ve finished and Cully is nowhere to be seen we can have a proper drink.’

‘Once you’ve got the judge back to the hotel and after you’ve secured your sidearm you can have the rest of the evening off, Pete. You two can go out on the razzle.’

‘I’m too old for that Cully,’ Patrick laughs. ‘Do you remember the disco we went to?’

‘And the convent school dances?’

‘Yes and painfully I remember trying to like girls, fighting my natural instincts.’

‘That’s tough judge,’ Pete says.

‘I was lucky to be living in the Nineties when things were better than before, but my father, a stern backward looking man, would never approve.’

‘He never knew?’

‘He was told. Mummy knew, but it was our secret until the letter arrived, but the bitch is dead isn’t she?’

‘Which one?’

‘Felicity Taylor.’ Cully nods. ‘Good.’ Patrick is quiet for a while. ‘Have you heard, Andrew is on the mend?’

‘Good news,’ says Cully, but will not be distracted. ‘Patrick, tell us please.’

'After the beach party, Felicity wrote a letter to my father, telling him I'm,' he pauses and emphasises, 'homosexual. Directly after A Levels he told me to get out of the house and never darken his door. We never spoke again.'

'I'm so sorry Patrick, really I am.'

'The bitch,' states Pete. 'Judge, why would she do that?'

'Spite, I suppose. The Nasty Gang were all vile and Felicity was horrible. She's been married three times to older men and the first two died.' Patrick suddenly laughs. 'I saw that look, the one the two of you exchanged. I'm not stupid. I know I've just confessed to being a suspect.'

'Join the list,' says Cully. 'Here come our drinks. Patrick, your father owned part of the Great Forrest didn't he?'

'Yes, sold it to the oil company, made a killing apparently. Why?'

'There's a protest today at the Tree Village and my uncle is involved.'

'Mmmm. There are court proceedings later in the week,' but leaves it there. 'It's terrible to admit, I don't regret any of the Nasty Gang dying.' Patrick sips his drink. 'I'm an awful gossip. They've not got any better since leaving school. I could list their crimes and misdemeanours. You know about Davis?'

'Yes, the Simpson's financial problems and Miranda Pegg.'

'She is, was a whore. Miranda made money on her back, has serviced some of my colleagues, literally on the bench and even made a couple of porn films.'

'I've got a feeling you know more.'

The Judge talks. Bradman, an archaeologist, claimed to have dug up Anglo-Saxon jewellery, went on TV, wrote a book only for it to be proved he planted the stuff. Ballard did dodgy oil deals and was involved with the plan to explore for oil in the forest. 'With him dead, the oil exploration plan is more or less dead as well. Chapman was a nasty little perv. You've heard the stories?' Cully nods. 'Carla is a publicity whore.'

'Michael Carter didn't turn up. Do you remember him?'

'He was a bully. His brother John got the worst of it. They were salt and pepper, but to be fair I understand Michael has changed, settled down. They never got on. I think John joined the army. I'm sorry Alison didn't come, I always liked her. You used to walk home with her Cully.'

'She let me. I felt lucky to do so. We should have come to you in the first place, you know more than we do.'

'Pete, Cully was our hero. Remember the beach party Cully?'

'I can't believe people haven't forgotten.'

'No one forgets the fight. The slap that went round the Island.'

'Don't stop now Judge please,' Pete encourages him, grinning.

Patrick repeats the story Tash had told Indah. 'I fell a little bit in love with you that night Cully. I mean face slaps and punches, wonderful. It was like having our own Steve McQueen.'

Phone rings.

'She did what?' Cully listens. 'Lisa, be gentle with her. I probably shouldn't have sent her on her own. Get her to take his statement and send him on his way. Using her to chauffer the women later, will remind her what she is.'

'What's happened Cully?'

'Your friend Becky went out to do an interview and ended up arresting him, cuffing him and bringing him in.'

'Is he complaining?' asks Pete.

'He is.'

'What fun you have,' Patrick laughs. 'Don't be harsh with her, she was a perfect companion with me.'

'So Pete, how have you found court?'

'Impressed with how you deal with a mixed list Judge.'

'This afternoon, I'll keep the focus on the children and listen to them. Children are far more aware of things than a lot of people give them credit and childhood pain never leaves you, does it?'

++++

'DC Kasali, nice to see you again. Come in. Green tea?'

'Thank you.'

'I'll let you have a packet.' Sophie fixes her with her slate grey eyes before turning away. 'It is soothing. Ok to talk in the kitchen, I'm preparing lunch? Do you cook?'

'Mum insisted I learn. I used to spend hours at the kitchen table watching her. The way to a man's heart, she says, but that's my mum, planning my future, encouraging me to find the right man.'

'Joining the police part of her plan?'

'No,' Indah laughs. 'Far from it. I was expected to marry a doctor, dentist or lawyer. She now just about remembers me when I visit. Dad dying pushed her to the edge.'

'I'm sorry Indah,' but the sympathy is not sincere. 'You've not identified the shooter yet?'

'I can't say.'

'Of course not, silly me. Cully drives you hard?'

'He's professional.'

'You defend him, that's nice.'

'The Gov…'

'Cully,' Sophie corrects. 'That's what we used to call him. He loved it, gave him a sense of mystery, like Morse on TV. Maybe, it's what made him become a detective. It was sort of sexy.' She is quickly cutting tomatoes in thin slices. 'I always use a very sharp knife,' and adds them to lettuce in a glass bowl.

'Sophie,' Indah realising this discussion is straying away from what she's there for, although she wants to know everything about him, changes the subject. 'When I was here before, you told me that you'd been in an accident with Davis? I've looked up the records and it's all there. He was charged and got a suspended sentence.'

'He should have gone to prison.'

'Agreed. Did anything else happen that night?'

'What makes you ask that?'

'In your book, you talk openly about being raped by someone from school, I'm assuming it was Davis and maybe that night.'

'You're a good detective.'

'Just doing my job.'

'You're dedicated, I can tell.' Sophie takes a deep breath, the knife hovering above spring onions. 'This isn't easy, but I have to live by my own mantra,' and she starts chopping, 'be honest and let it out. Davis raped me before the crash.'

'I'm sorry. Did you report it? The book doesn't say, just hints at things. Sorry, I'm such a plod. No empathy there.'

'Don't worry. It was nearly thirty years ago? I did speak to a sergeant the next day in hospital, but he wasn't interested, dismissive even.'

'Do you remember his name?'

'It was so long ago, but I think his name was Harris. He pointed out that Davis and I had been to school together, I'd gone to the party, we'd both been drinking and apparently taken drugs which I have no memory of and maybe I'd encouraged him. I'd been wearing a short skirt.'

'That's awful, I'm sorry.'

'In truth, on the night of the shooting, I went to the toilet, not because I needed a wee, but because Davis kept staring at me. I'd not seen him in decades, but suddenly it was like that horrible night all over again. Ah! Stupid.' The knife has caught her finger and blood trickles across the cutting board. 'Fuck.'

'Let me,' and reaching for a tissue Indah wraps it. 'It's not deep, put it under the tap.'

Sophie does so, the bloody tissue disintegrating and swirling down the drain. 'Perhaps, you should have been a nurse.'

'That's what Cully says,' and Indah tells Sophie about the incident at Turner's cottage.

'Well aren't you the little Florence Nightingale,' Sophie mutters, but taking a deep breath forces a smile. 'Lucky Cully. As for Davis, I'm pleased he's dead. Does that make me bad?'

'No. You approve of fatal violence?'

'Ah, that's what I wrote, but you take it out of context. I went on to say that we may wish it, but it would be wrong.'

'Even if you can't get justice?'

'Define justice?' Sophie turns her eyes on the other woman. Any softness has gone, replaced by something swift, cunning and predatory. 'More tea?'

'No, this is fine,' but Indah is unnerved. 'You must have hated Davis?'

'I did, but also myself. I felt it was my fault, I'd probably led him on. I know now of course about how a victim feels. I didn't think any man would want me because I was dirty. The man I loved I locked out.'

'Cully?'

'No comment.'

'Remind me,' Indah persists, 'what age were you when you were assaulted?'

'Raped. I was raped. I won't let the women and men I work with hide behind anything. I was eighteen when I was raped.'

'You never told anyone apart from the police sergeant?' Sophie shakes her head. 'There's nothing on record.'

'I'm not surprised, he wasn't interested. You do believe me?'

'Totally, and we know Davis had convictions later, including one for sexual assault.'

'I know. It was in the local paper. It gives me even more of a motive. Do you think I knew what was going to happen in the school hall?'

'You said you didn't,' Indah states, turning things over in her mind. 'Do you know Vicar Mandy Bannon?'

'Did she say I do?'

'She may have hinted at something,' Indah lies, aware she is fishing. 'She's the priest at the church and school.'

'I know who she is.'

'You won't say if you know her?'

'You forget what I do.'

'You've worked with her?'

'No comment. Please Indah, you have to understand, confidentiality is key to everything I do. You'll need to get a warrant.'

'We will,' Indah sighs. 'You know Jamie?'

'I do, he's my accountant. He's everyone's accountant,' she laughs, but the sound is hollow. 'He's the best. Was there anything else?'

'Keen to get rid of me?' Indah grimaces. 'I think,' she hesitates, 'you need to come in for a formal interview.'

'Of course. If that's our formal business over, you can ask about Cully.'

'I don't know what you mean?'

'You do know what I mean young lady.'

'What about your sister?' Indah changes the subject. 'What about Rachel?'

'What about her?'

'Didn't Cully go out with her first?'

'She was a fifteen-year-old whore. You could say I picked up her leavings.'

'You slapped him.'

'Jenny spread poison about him and I stupidly believed her.'

'Are you're sure it was her?'

'What?'

'Nothing. Cully saved your life didn't he?' No reply. 'Did you see him after the accident?'

'No. He wouldn't have wanted me, I was damaged goods. He tried, rang, sent flowers and letters, I've still got them, but I didn't respond. Then he married remember? What was her name, his wife?'

'Caitland.'

'And you fancy him, don't you?' Sophie is grinning. 'You smile with your eyes when mentioning his name.'

'I think we're finished.' Indah gets up, moves to the door before turning back. 'One last thing, is Alison Grey staying here?'

'Yes, I am, but I've got a lunch date, can we make it quick?'

++++

'Sorry about Sophie, she likes to analyse people.' Alison appears happy, moving her hands in the air. 'Does it to everyone,' she smiles.

'Even you?'

'Me more than anyone, I'm a mess you see.' Alison is tall, slim with long blonde hair pulled back behind her head in a pigtail. She is wearing sexy designer gear, leather jacket and short skirt, that Indah thinks suits a night out on the pull rather than a lunch date. She looks and even smells sexy. 'But I'm close to being sorted. Now, what did you want to ask?'

'My colleague Sergeant Aries met you at the hospital. She says you were asking after Carla Scutari, that you appeared disappointed that Carla had been discharged?'

'I was tired, I'd had a long journey.'

'You're not friends anymore?'

'We're not close.'

'You used to be, close that is, at school and maybe afterwards?'

'Cully tell you that?' she smiles. 'We were close once. He's quite something isn't he?'

'I'm not here to talk about Superintendent Cully.' Sophie had left them in the lounge to talk. She could be heard in the kitchen finishing lunch. 'Your husband tells us that you've been seeing her regularly ever since. That you are lovers and attend regular sex and drugs parties together with other Alumni, the Nasty Gang?'

'He's a fantasist,' she laughs. 'You are direct. I like that.' She crosses her long legs, allowing Indah a glimpse of stocking top. 'I'm bisexual and Carla and I were lovers, but she moved on.'

'Left you behind. That must have hurt?'

'I got over it.'

'With Sophie's help?' Indah assumes.

'But of course,' Alison nods, smiles, 'she's amazing and helps all of us find resolution. You've read her book?'

‘How’d you know?’

‘She told me she gave it to you. Did you read the chapter about sexual attraction?’ Alison pauses. ‘Of course you did.’ She leans forward, her cleavage inviting. ‘Sophie wants Cully back.’

‘I’m not stopping her.’ Alison throws her head back, pigtail swinging, laughing before settling back. ‘Can we get on please?’

‘Who are you trying to seduce dressed like that?’

‘Not you, although you’re cute and I understand why Cully wants to fuck you, and it’s none of your business.’

‘Back to what your husband says.’

‘It’s an excuse I’ve used to get away. He thinks I go to the parties, but I escape from him for a few days twice a year. He’s a pig.’

‘You married him.’

‘Ouch! Sophie says you have a long sharp tongue Indah, I bet Cully loves that,’ she laughs. ‘Ask my sister about my breaks away.’

‘We will.’ Indah pauses, trying to think, confused by the attraction she feels for this woman. Deep breath. ‘I’m getting to realise Sophie helps a lot of people like Jamie?’

‘You’ve met him?’

‘Today. I saw the flowers you sent him, nice.’

‘He’s my accountant and is, soon to be my ex-husbands. He’s the best, but we will all miss him as a friend much more than as an accountant.’

‘He and Sophie seem to be at the centre of things?’ No reply. ‘Aren’t they?’

‘We support each other,’ Alison smiles. ‘Is that all, I have someone to seduce,’ she giggles.

‘That’s all for now,’ Indah says standing. ‘I could give you a lift,’ she suggests, keen to know where Alison is going.

‘No, but thank you, I’ve already ordered a taxi. In fact, I think that’s it now.’

‘Of course,’ Indah accepts, but cannot help asking: ‘Where are you going?’

‘To see an old friend. Goodbye.’ She steps close to Indah, her pigtail brushing against Indah’s lips and she’s gone.

In the hallway, Indah hears Sophie say something and Alison reply with: ‘I’ve got to do this.’

Indah hurries by Sophie, out the front door and into her own car as the taxi starts to edge away. Starting the engine she is about to follow when Sophie comes to her window and taps on the glass. ‘Yes, what is it?’ Indah sighs, lowering it.

‘I’m in a rush. I have to go,’ but it was too late the taxi has gone. ‘Shit!’ She takes a breath. ‘What is it Sophie?’

‘Give Cully my love.’

++++

After lunch, Chalky arrives at the hotel in an unmarked police car to take Megan Simpson to the hospital while Becky, feeling chastened after being warned by Lisa, takes Carla directly to the house.

Megan sits silently in the back of the car, saying nothing despite Chalky’s best efforts to start a conversation.

At the hospital, Megan sits next to her husband’s bed listening to the machines that keep him alive. Staring blankly at his right arm where bandages disguise the fact his hand has been amputated she wonders what is to become of her?

‘Your bloody sister rang last night. Calling from New York demanding to know why no one had told her about the shooting. She’d found out on the Internet and how were you? What about Bethany, is she alright?’ ‘*What about me, Megan had wanted to shout, how am I? Broke, scared and thoroughly pissed off.*’ ‘I’m coming over,’ she mimics her sister-in-law’s American accent, ‘can’t get away for a couple of days, but I’ve booked my flight.’

‘Would she lend us the money to pay the debts?’ she asks her comatose husband? ‘Of course she wouldn’t,’ she answers herself, ‘she’d be horrified and give her another reason to take Bethany away.’

There had been a text that morning which Megan ignored.

‘You won’t believe what’s happened. Cully took Bethany into a safe house under something called Police Powers and that bloody DI Lynn even suggested they foster Bethany, bloody cheek. I said no. I should get over to see her I suppose.’ She looks across to the bedside table where there is a large handmade card. ‘Get Well, Daddy,’ it reads with colourful flowers all around. ‘I know, some woman called Monica brings her here. She rang me, wanted to know if I wanted to join them, make it a family thing. I wish people would mind their own business.’

‘What’s happened to us?’ she sobs suddenly. ‘Where did the money go? It drained away so quickly. I thought Jamie was a good accountant. Everything was perfect and now I’m terrified. Philip, you’ve left me with this mess and I don’t know what to do. They know about the parties, about the drugs and about Eva Djokovic and that woman scares me shitless.'

Megan leaves him, joining Chalky outside, again sitting in the back seat, staying silent until they come to a halt behind a line of traffic.

'What's going on?' she demands.

'It's a protest march against the oil company's plan to clear the Forest Village,' Chalky explains.

'The what?'

'It's a squatters village in the forest, it's been there for years. It's rather good actually. Yes there are homeless and travellers there, but artisan craftsmen have moved in and there's a café and it's become a tourist attraction.'

People crowd against the car, carrying placards, pushing, shouting and glancing in.

'Can't we get away,' she screeches.

'They mean no harm.'

'Just get me out of here please,' she screams.

'Sorry, we had to come this way. The ferry across the river is out yet again,' he sighs. 'Getting clear,' says Chalky, blowing air into his cheeks.

They arrive at the house and Chalky comes to a halt beside the police patrol car. Not speaking Megan gets out and goes into the house without a backward glance.

Getting out Chalky leans down.

'How are you lads?'

'Good,' says Joe. 'This morning we were guarding these woman over at the hotel and now at the house, it's easy. Don't you agree Ted?'

'Agreed.'

'You searched the house before the women went in?'

'Of course. Now you're in CID Chalky, you think you can check up on us?'

'Just chatting,' Chalky shrugs and walks away. He notices Megan watching from a ground floor window. 'Strange woman,' he mutters, climbs into the car and drives away.

Megan watches.

Coming into the house she'd been surprised to find Alison Grey there, dressed for seduction, talking with and touching Carla. They paid her scant attention before taking a bottle of champagne from the fridge and going upstairs.

Megan feels she did well during the police interview the day before. Calm most of the time, but outraged to discover the police had searched the rental house without informing her, but laughed off any questions about the parties. The solicitor had been useless, but she could not afford better unlike her so called friend Carla. She pours herself a long vodka.

Philip had been stupid bringing the cocaine to the dinner. He wanted to show off to Davis. He'd said Djokovic was fine waiting for her money, but she clearly wasn't. They owed her for three deliveries. Over thirty thousand plus interest. Pure uncut. Philip argued it was good business to get the best, cut it themselves with baby milk powder. It would triple their money. Now there would be no money and no Philip and she is going to have to find the money before they came to finish the job. 'Bloody Eva Djokovic, a fucking Serb.' The party guests were mostly dead and no chance of them paying their share now. 'Shit! Shit!' She would speak to Carla and maybe she would give her some cash. Megan giggles. What little money they have left is nearly gone, just enough to keep up appearances this one last time.

Above she can hear Carla and Alison humping. Was that still a word? Do lesbians hump or did they call it something else? Scissoring isn't that a word? God, she hoped Bethany wasn't going to be a lesbian.

The front doorbell rings.

++++

The taxi drops Minty at the end of the drive as another car leaves and because the taxi driver sees the police car and does not fancy explaining his lack of documents. She pays, tips well, thanks him warmly and walks up the drive pulling her pink wheeled suitcase. She feels good. She has sold the interview with Preece to "Country Living" and she believes she can convince Cully to agree to a piece with Linda. To top it all, here she is on the verge of a career changing scoop, several scoops if she plays her cards right.

'Hello boys,' smiles and bends down to look in the open driver's window of the police car. The men jump, having not noticed her progress up the drive. 'Sorry, did I startle you?'

'No, just doing paperwork,' one says, dropping a tabloid newspaper into the footwell, sweeping away cardboard chip containers and ketchup sachets from the dashboard. 'What can we do for you love?'

'I'm guessing I've to check in with you guys,' she smiles ignoring the "love". Minty dresses deliberately upmarket compared to Sunday, wearing a tight black Armani dress, a matching jacket and designer stilettos. She has a shoulder bag containing tablet computer and phone. 'How you doing?' she asks lightly.

'Who are you?'

'Araminta Gold, I'm a journalist.' She shows her Press Card. 'I've an appointment with the women inside.'

'Spell your name, we have to write it down on our board.' She does so. 'Come on, I need to check you over.'

'Really?'

'Afraid so.' Joe gets out. He is short, maybe five-eight, shorter than a police officer on the mainland, skinny, but with a developing paunch. He search's her thoroughly up and down and she shivers at every touch. 'You're clean.'

'I know. Are we good?'

'Just look in your bag and the suitcase.'

Sighing Minty opens her bag and then settling the case on its side opens it. He kneels. Disgusted she sees dandruff on his shoulders and watches as thin fingers go through her things, deciding she'll not be wearing the "Scutari" underwear until washed, might even throw it away. 'Finished?'

'We have to be careful,' he mumbles standing. 'Just protecting the women,' he adds as she walks towards the front door. 'That's our job.'

'A very important job it is to,' she calls back, unable to suppress the sarcasm.

'A bit of alright,' Joe says climbing back into the car.

'Too skinny.' Ted is older than Joe, taller and wider with thinning grey hair and sits behind the wheel. 'I like a bit of meat on my women.'

'Like your Margaret?'

'There's enough and too much. She's on another diet. Chocolate?'

'Please.'

'The previous one was alright.'

'The blonde?'

'Yeah,' and glances at his clip board. 'Alison Grey, she's hot, dressed like that, asking to be fucked.'

'She was nervous?'

'What's happening would make anyone nervous.'

'At least, we've got these.' He pats the automatic rifle resting across his lap. 'We didn't see Gold coming did we? It could have been the shooter, he could have shot us both like in the movies.'

'He's long gone. Tizard says it was a drugs hit from the City. But yeah you're right, we should turn the car round to face the driveway.'

'Then we won't see the house.'

'Then half round so we can see both, but later I need a piss,' says Joe, climbing out of the car, leaving the rifle on the seat, and walking towards distant bushes, shadowy in the dusk.

Joe returning, buttoning up his flies, walks towards the car. 'Nothing is happening tonight,' he says. 'Saw a fox. Bloody thing was watching me piss.' Silence. 'Mate.' Ted is slumped forward over the dashboard, red stain across the side of his head and face. 'Jesus Christ!' Joe goes for his rifle, but it's gone from the front seat. Stepping away from the car he stumbles back on to the ground. Fear rising he goes for his side arm, fumbling in panic. 'Fuck! Fuck!'

It is then the laughter starts, guttural, booming from the car.

Confused, Joe is transfixed before realisation dawns.

'You bastard!' he growls. 'I thought you were dead.'

'That was the idea,' Ted sobs. 'You should have seen your face.' He wipes away tears and tomato ketchup from his face. 'Come and sit in Joe. More chocolate.'

'Bastard. Where's my gun?'

'On the back seat.'

'I should bloody shoot you,' he grumbles. 'You've got ketchup in your ear.'

'Wait until I tell the lads.'

'Don't you bloody dare.'

++++

Doorbell rings again.

'I'm coming.' Megan is unsteady on her feet, takes a while to get there. 'Oh it's you.'

'Is this still ok?' Minty hopes.

'Yes, come in. Leave your suitcase in the hall and I'll show you to your room later. I thought you'd have a photographer with you?'

'This is a preliminary chat.'

'Do you want a drink?'

'What's that noise?' Her face contorts. 'Oh God!'

'It's real, not porn, if that's what you're thinking. Come through.'

'I thought it was just you and Carla.'

'She's not wanking either,' Megan slurs, enjoying the chance to say the word. 'Not wanking,' she repeats. 'Alison turned up.'

'I didn't know they were a couple,' Minty is already thinking of another by-line. Diversity is all the rage and she wondered if she could get Carla and Alison to agree to a photo shoot in skimpy gear, cuddling on the sofa, by the pool in swimsuits. Megan is clearly drunk, she can get her talking. Reaching into her bag she takes out the tablet and phone, switches them both on and starts recording.

'You say Alison just turned up?'

'Not that I mind women doing it. I'm broad minded, I don't want you to think I'm a prude,' she laughs, 'but they haven't seen each other in years, decades.'

'Why is she here?'

'You'll have to ask her.'

'I will,' Minty nods. 'This is a lovely place,' she says walking to the French windows, looking out into the illuminated garden that runs back beside the covered pool. 'We can get some great photo's. Maybe in the pool. Is it heated?'

'Yes and there's a sauna and jacuzzi.'

'Fantastic.' Minty settles on the over-stuffed couch. 'The police officer outside searched me, it was horrible.'

'We're having nothing to do with them. Alison suggested we take them coffee, but once you start with something like that, it won't stop, they'd be wanting to use our loos next.'

'Why is she here?' Minty tries again.

'God knows. Maybe just for a fuck, but it messes up our plans, Carla and I planned dinner at the French place down the road. We'd booked, but will be late now. I thought you might claim it on expenses?'

'Yes, of course, but Alison?'

'You didn't answer before, drink?'

'Please.'

'Vodka alright?'

'On the rocks.'

'No problem. They'll be finished soon. To be honest I'm jealous.' She drinks. 'I'm worried about Philip.' Very worried, in fact, there is no life insurance because they could not afford it. 'He's going to die,' Megan laughs and hiccups. 'How much are you going to pay us for the feature?'

'Depends how interesting it is. You went to school with Cully didn't you?'

'Yes. You've met him?'

'He took me for lunch the other day. He's rather nice.'

'I don't really remember him,' she lies easily, 'he wasn't part of my friendship group.'

'Really?' She smiles. 'I'd love to know more.'

'Is that what you mean by interesting?' Megan hands Minty her drink. 'Tell me what you want?'

'Secrets are interesting.' Minty puts the glass to one side with no intention of drinking it. She needs to be sober. 'Gossip and scandal. For instance, I've been trawling the names of the dead and found some interesting stuff about Ballard.'

'He's a crook, was a crook. Dodgy business stuff with the Arabs. He is, was connected with the forest clearance.'

'That's what the protests are about?'

'I suppose, but who cares really?' Megan asks, standing and pours herself another drink. 'It's only a few trees for Christ's sake.'

'Some people feel very strongly about it.'

'Not really *Bonjour* magazine territory is it?'

'I work for *Bonjour*, but I freelance and it seems to me there are plenty of stories bubbling around at the moment on this Island. Ironic isn't, the most boring backward place in the world and suddenly there's lots going on.'

'If you say so.'

'You must be worried sick though. How's your daughter?'

'Bethany is fine. Everyone seems to care more about her than me. I was the one that was shot at,' she complains. 'You're not drinking.'

Show willing, she tells herself, takes the glass, sips, mouth puckering at the undiluted spirit. 'Do you have any tonic?'

'In the fridge. The kitchen is through there.'

Minty leaves the lounge, relieved that the noise from above has stopped. Like Megan she'd not had sex for weeks. There had been a moment at lunch with Cully when she thought about it with him, but he's twice her age and she is not that desperate. The fridge is huge and swinging open the door finds a can of tonic. There is a noise behind her, excruciating pain down her back before blackness.

++++

The door opens, but the chain remains on. She looks out.

'What the hell do you want?'

'Is that anyway to speak to your senior officer Kerry?' He is smiling. 'I'm here to see if you're ok.'

'I'm off sick,' she glares through the gap between door and frame. 'The DI sent me home Monday.'

'Because you were asleep on duty.'

'That bitch of a sister drugged me.'

'Do you have proof of that?'

'Fuck off! You'll cover it up whatever I say. First Tom comes to visit and now you. Is the DI coming later?'

'She might.'

'Suddenly you all care?'

'Do you want to come back to work?' he asks. 'Can I come in?'

'Might as well.' The chain falls and the door swings open. She wears a towelling robe and apart from a tooth-floss thin string thong is clearly naked underneath. 'Getting an eyeful Sir?' She giggles. 'Drink?'

'No thanks.'

'You can take your gloves off. Fancy gloves for a fancy car. I bet Indah loves it.'

'Leave her out of this.'

'Touchy. You planning to charm me?' She is filling her glass with red wine. 'You've got little Indah eating out of your hand. You'll have her eating your cock next.'

'I hear your love life isn't so good,' says Cully. 'Tizard's dumped you.'

'Bastard!' Not certain if she is talking about Tizard or Cully, Kerry slumps down on the sofa, spills red wine, swears and reaches for the bottle.

Cully gets to it first and fills her glass. 'This one is empty, do you have another?'

'Want to get me pissed?'

'You already are. Another bottle?'

'Kitchen.'

Cully leaves her, walks towards the back of the cottage to find the kitchen where there is a wine-rack with several bottles. He picks one. Returning, he notices a length of rope and a pair of handcuffs hanging from a peg.

'Like a bit of bondage, Sir?' Kerry is leaning against the wall watching him. 'Want to tie me up?' The robe parts to reveal her breasts. 'Want me?' She moves closer. 'You can do anything you want.' She stumbles and leans against the wall giggling. 'Well?'

'I like my women sober.' He pulls her robe closed and ties the belt tightly before using it to lead her back to the couch. 'Sit.'

'Am I your bitch?' she giggles. 'Why do you need an alibi?'

'I don't.'

'I've read Indah's sweet report.'

'It is only a draft.'

'There are certainly gaps,' she declares. 'What did you really come over for?'

'To visit people and attend a school reunion.'

'You've fooled everyone, haven't you? They think you're something special.'

'Finished, Kerry?' He smiles thinly. 'I'm told you are trying to undermine the investigation, to get revenge for what happened to your father. True?'

'Get out.'

'Not yet.' He opens the bottle and places it next to her on the low table by the couch. 'You've not answered my question.'

'Sure you don't want a drink?' She asks filling her glass and drinking. Wine trickles down her chin, dripping scarlet blots on to her white robe. 'I don't know what you're up to, but there is something odd with you.'

'I'll take odd, it's better than some of the things I've been called.'

'Everyone hates me.'

'You shouldn't take things so personally.'

'It's hard not to.'

'Kerry, you really are very drunk,' he states the obvious. 'I'm sorry the way things have turned out for you. You need help?'

'I'm not weak, I don't need your sympathy or support.'

'Of course you don't.'

'You think sorry helps? Everyone said sorry after Dad died, but no one means it do they?'

'What about Tizard, does he mean it?'

'Fuck off!'

'Don't ever go to the hospice again Kerry, there's nothing there for you,' he warns. 'Understand?'

'Is that where your secret is?' she snarls.

Kerry's mobile is on the low table. She sees his look, but Cully bends and snatches it up before she can, glancing at the screen as he does. 'You've been texting?'

'Leave it.' She stands unsteadily, swings for him, but he steps away and she falls on the floor, her glass spinning away, smashing against the hearth, 'Bastard!'

'You've been texting Tizard all evening, but he's not replied. You shouldn't beg, it's beneath you,' he says reading. 'You know he's moved on, fucking a slag in town. He's had plenty of women, including Amber apparently.'

'Piss off!' She struggles to get up from the floor. 'Give it to me.'

'I thought he'd finished with you. You know he's with her tonight.'

'Bollocks! He'll come back to me,' she sighs, managing to crawl on to the couch.

'You thought he'd leave Mary for you. He was never going to do that was he?'

'Why do you hate him?'

'I don't, but I want him punished for what he did to my daughter.'

'The inquiry cleared him. It wasn't his fault your precious daughter got shot.'

'Perhaps.' Cully glances at the screen before texting.

'What are you doing?'

'Trying to help.'

'None of your fucking business, now get out.' Kerry grabs for the phone, but he steps away and she falls to the floor again screaming. 'Get off my phone, you bastard!'

'One last text,' he says, tapping.

'Get out!'

'I've not finished yet.' He reaches for her, grabbing her wrists, pulling her up, against his body. 'Let's get you sorted.'

++++

'You know Superintendent Cully arrested Turner don't you?'

'Yeah.'

'I bet Turner's dropped us in it about the flashbangs,' says Ted.

'That's down to Tizard, we just take orders don't we?'

'Even so, there'll be a stink, especially with Cully, a high flying honest cunt if ever there was one.'

'An Islander, you'd think he'd cut us some slack,' says Joe.

'Got shot didn't he?'

'Several times apparently.'

'Bloody careless of him,' Ted laughs, but thinks. 'Poor bugger had his wife killed.'

'I remember, Tizard and I were on the team,' says Joe thoughtfully.

Suddenly there's the whine of an engine and a scooter comes to a halt a few metres from the police car. The rider gets off, takes a large box from the carrier at the back and slips a strap over his shoulder.

'Help you?' Ted emerges from the car. 'What do you want?'

'Pizzas for the house and you.'

'For us?'

'The women inside ordered them.'

'Take off your helmet please.' He obeys, is young, pale skinned with acne and short cut hair. 'The women rang you?'

'Not me, but the shop. I simply do the deliveries. Is that a real gun? Wow, this is connected to what happened at the school isn't it?' He's excited. 'Wait until I tell my mates.'

'What's your name?'

'Brian.'

'We need to search you and your bag Brian.'

'Go ahead, the meat feast and the hot Mexican, my favourite, are for you with slaw and cheese filled dough balls. The balls are amazing, my girlfriend works in the kitchen and they use a local goats cheese and Gruyere. I didn't take the call, but apparently they wanted you to know they appreciate what you're doing. Can I hold the gun?'

'No.'

'It's a Heckler-Koch right?'

'The women said they appreciated us?'

'Yeah. Here's your stuff and there's a complimentary litre of cola.'

'Thanks.'

'Come on guys can I take them the food? The house ordered a boring vegetarian, an Italian and a seafood, but no sides. I don't want it to get cold. I won't get a tip for cold food. Look I only get paid on deliveries, so can we move this on please guys?'

'Go ahead.'

Brian walks away towards the house, rings the bell and a moment later the door swings open. The guy steps inside and out of sight. The police officers tense. 'I should go and check.'

'Don't be so impatient Ted, give him a few moments. This stuff smells amazing and I'm starving.'

'Margaret has band any and all take-out.'

'She got you on the diet to then?'

'In truth, I need to shed a few pounds, but not tonight. Let's enjoy the food. Relax. How often do we get an easy gig like this?'

'Yeah and I bet Tizard is riding Kerry Harris right now.'

'Don't blame him, she's a bit of alright. I bet she's a screamer. I would, wouldn't you?'

'Certainly would. Pass the dough balls mate. Tell you what, that' Becky Shaw's not bad either. She got a really tight arse,' says Joe. See, he's coming out.'

Helmet on, with the bag over his shoulder and the door closes behind him. Walking by the car he waves, climbs on the scooter, and goes to start it. There is a moment when nothing happens. Then the engine turns over, hesitates and starts. The pizza guy drives away leaving the officers to enjoy the food.

'Don't understand how Mary puts up with the Sergeant do you?'

'My Margaret works at the hospital, in the canteen, and says Staff Nurse Mary Tizard is not an innocent victim,' begins Ted. 'She's a bright bunny, intelligent and attractive and will be dumping the Sergeant when she's ready.'

'I wonder if she knows about all the extra money he earns?'

'If she does, she'll gut him financially. Margaret also reckons Mary has another man, probably a doctor. She saw him go outside with some bloke the other day for a cigarette if you know what I mean,' and laughs.

'That'll leave him free to be with Kerry.'

'You're joking, he's bored with her. He's trying to pull that SOCO woman.'

'Amber, she'll break his balls if he tries anything,' Ted laughs. 'He used to fuck her years ago, but she'll not let him anywhere near her now.'

'He's got a new woman in town, a right slapper, but married to a fucking psycho. We've arrested him.'

'Not?'

'Exactly, the Sergeant is playing with fire.'

++++

Lisa sits with Claudia in the bar of the hotel where the mainland team are staying. 'I felt awful when I got to the school and thought bloody hell if this is down to me, I can't do it.'

'I would have wet myself.'

'I did,' admits Lisa, 'just a dribble.' They laugh. 'Cully makes it ok. He's an enabler. Doesn't think he's God's gift which makes a change from Harris.'

'Cheers to Cully.' They lift and chink glasses. 'I'll get another bottle.' Claudia goes to the bar, comes back, fills their glasses and sits down. 'It must be difficult for him, all these people he knows and the memories. I don't get the impression he enjoyed school.'

'Did any of us?' Lisa sips her drink. 'Why don't you come and stay with me; this place isn't exactly the Ritz. I've a nice spare room and you're welcome.'

'I'd love to, Lisa, but my boss rang, they want me back on the mainland tomorrow. Sorry. I've really enjoyed working with you and we've still got tonight.' They hold hands under the table. 'The mainland is another world, but it's not far away.'

Phone rings.

'Hi, sorry to disturb you, but just wanted to say I popped in on Kerry. I'm worried about her. She was drunk and all over the place.' There is some noise in the background. 'I'll feed Toby. Trudi, let me run you a bath and pour some wine. You can relax this evening. I'll take care of everything. I'm here now until tomorrow morning. Are you hungry?'

'What's got into you Tommy?' a young woman's voice asks.

'Sweety, I'm sorry if I've been a pain the last few days.'

'Tommy it's fine, I knew what I was getting into marrying a cop.'

'Tommy,' giggles Lisa, feeling the effects of the wine. 'Not to worry I'll ring her. See you Tommy,' and she hangs up. 'I'm hungry.'

'What do you fancy?'

'Well,' smiles Claudia, 'I could kill a steak.'

'Bloody I bet.'

'Naturally, and you, Lisa?'

'As bloody as it comes.'

++++

Leaving Kerry's west Island cottage Cully drives thoughtfully towards Indah's town house. He is aroused by Kerry, undoubtedly an attractive young woman and temptress. When he pulled her up, she forced her body against his, lifting her leg so her thigh rubbed against his side before kissing him with an open mouth.

Parking the car, he knocks on the red door.

'Sorry I'm late, everything is such a rush at the moment,' he begins as the front door opens, but all he can do is stare open mouthed and hand over two bottles of Burgundy Pinot Noir taken from Uncle Adam's cellar. 'You look amazing,' he stutters and all thoughts of Kerry vanish. As Indah later explains, she is wearing the kebaya, the national costume of women from Java. Calf length it is made from a pale blue sheer silk, with strategically placed white lace brocade of embroidered flowers. She turns and he follows unable to take his eyes off the contours of her hard body.

'Please open the wine the meal is ready.'

Sitting opposite each other she asks about his upbringing and relaxed, he's happy to share. 'After mother died, gran wrapped me in love and took me to live with her. It was the first time she saved me. The second was when Caitland went and she turned up at our house and took over. I'd been about to resign to look after Linda, but there was gran bless her. She moved in, let me do the job and became a mother to Linda.'

'Your mother was Adam's sister?'

'Yes. His wallet saved me as well, kept me in school.'

'You've been through a lot Cully.'

'So have you what with the bullying you suffered, your dad and now your mum. More wine?' She nods, holds up her glass and he pours. 'Nice to have an evening off and I couldn't be spending it in better company. Thank you for all the trouble you've gone to.'

‘No trouble,’ she grins. ‘I need to talk to you about Sophie and Alison, about my visit there today, but tomorrow, tonight is for relaxing. The new suit looks great on you,’ she compliments him.

‘Good old M & S.’ He’d hung the blue jacket over his chair. ‘I threw away the one Turner burned.’

‘You and Monica seem close.’

‘Monica is a colleague and mate like Pete.’

‘That Minty woman was after you today, she rang before I left the incident room. Wanted you to know, she is staying at the rental house tonight.’

‘She’s doing a story on them and wants to do a story on Linda and me for *Bonjour*. We may do it and if in your roundabout way you were trying to find out if I’m attached the answer is no, although Linda is on at me to find someone.’

‘I’m surprised.’

‘And you?’

‘Only to the job,’ she blushes. ‘I don’t want to talk about work, but Kerry is still getting on my nerves. She’s been to the pub. Spoke to the landlady, after me. Kerry says the landlady didn’t recognise the photograph of you she showed her.’

‘Do a line up.’

‘Don’t be silly. She’s crazy. Sorry, she also sent me a text, says the cemetery closes after you say you left.’

‘She’s been busy, but she’s right. I don’t drive into the cemetery,’ he explains, sitting back, smiling, ‘but park down the hill before walking there, following the same route along which gran took me. I always do, it brings back happy memories. But do whatever digging you want Indah.’

‘No more, I’m done and fuck Kerry.’

‘Kerry isn’t a problem anymore,’ he says taking her hand in a way he hopes is reassuring. ‘You’ll do well at MIU,’ Cully tells her.

‘I’m looking forward to serving under you,’ the innuendo explicit. ‘It’s real then, the job?’

‘Totally. The six-month period to cover maternity leave is yours and once you’re in we don’t let go. We recruit the best.’ He’s aroused by her, but doesn’t want to spoil it with a wrong move. ‘That is wonderful. I’m full up.’

‘You’ll stay tonight?’ She leans towards him. ‘No one will know.’

‘It’s not that I don’t want to.’ He totally wants to, but there is a very small voice in his head warning him, ‘I want to protect you.’

‘You’re sweet, but I’m an adult and can make my own decisions.’

'I know, but I'm compromised enough on this investigation and I don't want to drag you down. Look what's happening to Kerry.'

'I'm not her.'

'I know and I didn't mean…'

'I know what you meant. Stay, please.'

'Indah, you are far too precious,' he says, feeling her long fingers entwining with his. 'You are lovely, but let's take things a step at a time.'

'Stay.'

'You don't give up do you?'

'Not if there is something I want,' she grins. 'My bed is—'

Phone rings and Cully reluctantly reaches for it.

'I'll get dessert,' she says, standing, swirling away in a cloud of blue silk.

'I'll deal with this quickly,' he says watching her leave the room, 'promise.'

Wednesday

The waters of the channel are dark while in the distance North Island is silhouetted against the sky. There is a sprinkling of lights over there. Cully parks his car, takes a moment absorbing the view before getting out and walking towards the police tape. He can smell Indah's perfume and hopes no one else will, but then sees the ambulances and all thoughts of her drift away on the breeze. Not for long, he hopes. For months, there had been no sniff of sex with anyone, lusted after Becky, surprised by the rekindling of feelings for Sophie and then in one short evening he'd been sandwiched between two offers. A fantasy if ever there was one! Admittedly one had been drunk and not a little desperate, but his desire for Indah is becoming an infatuation that he is desperate to satisfy.

A uniformed officer lifts the tape for Cully to duck under. He hears raised angry voices ahead. 'What's going on, Lisa?'

'I've only just got here myself.' She walks away from the group huddled at the end of the drive. 'Sorry, lost it with the idiots.'

'What's going on?' Cully repeats.

'At the change of shift, the new officers knocked on the door to introduce themselves and make certain the women were ok. The lights were on, but no one answered. They rang the number they had for Megan Simpson and got no reply. They went around the building and through a side window they saw a woman lying on the floor of the living room. There is blood. They called me as duty officer. I'd forgotten, I'd had a drink, but got a taxi. Sorry, gov.'

'Shut up!' Cully snaps, knowing he is on the edge if not over the alcohol limit himself and very frustrated. 'Sorry, but stop saying sorry.' Annoyed that his evening had been interrupted. 'I texted Indah and told her to go to the incident room.'

'Poor thing, she really needs a night off.'

'We all do,' agrees Cully. 'Kerry wasn't answering.'

‘I know. Gov. I was...She’s still off sick. I’ve rung Tom. Officer Miller called Sergeant Tizard before he called me.’

‘But you’ve not gone in?’

‘The team are reluctant to go in without Tizard.’

‘You’re the senior officer on scene, Lisa.’

‘I know, but without him or you, I’m sorry. I bottled it, maybe the drink.’

‘Stop saying sorry, these things happen and it’s bloody difficult in these situations. Don’t worry about it.’

‘Sorry Gov,’ Tom joins them, out of breath. ‘I was at home and had to get Trudi up. She wasn’t happy. She was in bed asleep.’

‘Tommy, you smell of baby sick,’ says Lisa.

‘Sorry.’

‘Will people stop saying sorry, but yes you do Tom. Right, let’s take a moment to come down a few notches. We go in now,’ states Cully.

Cully leads Lisa and Tom back to the group where Pete has appeared.

‘Where is your Sergeant?’ Cully demands.

‘On his way.’

‘Constable Miller, we can’t wait any longer.’

‘Sir, a few more minutes.’

‘No, now, for Christs sake. Go now.’

Four armed police officers jog up the drive followed, at distance, by Lisa, Tom, Pete and Cully. The lead officer carries a ram that he swings back and hits the reinforced door. He has to hit it three more times before wood splinters and it swings open. ‘We’re in,’ and the armed officers enter.

Pete and Cully both draw pistols as they move across the foyer. Lisa follows, but keeps her gun holstered. ‘Careful everyone,’ she calls, not a little nervously.

‘Mind the suitcase,’ warns Pete, pointing to a pink case leaning against the wall. ‘Smell it, Gov?’

‘Yeah. Spread out,’ Cully shouts. ‘Pete upstairs please.’

‘In here,’ shouts Miller.

Megan Simpson lay on the ground looking up at the ceiling, a hole in her forehead and another over her heart. ‘She’s been executed,’ Cully mutters. ‘Let’s get SOCO in here.’

‘Amber is coming,’ responds Lisa.

‘Gov,’ Pete shouts, ‘up here.’ Cully leaves Lisa with Megan’s body and takes the stairs two at a time. ‘In here, Gov.’

'Jesus!' A black haired woman, Cully assumes to be Carla, lay under a blood soaked sheet. 'She's dead.'

'But she's not,' Pete says.

'Alison,' Cully moans. 'What the hell are you doing here? Paramedics, up here now!'

Pete and Cully leave as they arrive. 'What the fuck's going on, Pete?'

'Beats me, Gov.'

'This guy is good. Two shots each, but why not Alison Grey?'

'He wasn't interested in her. Maybe he thought she was dead. She was hidden under Carla.'

'Gov,' Lisa calls up from below. 'Tizard's just arrived.'

Cully takes a deep breath before walking slowly down the stairs as Tizard appears at the front door. 'Where have you been?'

'What's going on? You've forced entry without me.'

'Where the fuck have you been?' Cully demands.

'You shouldn't have gone in without me, I'm team commander.'

'Not much of a commander,' Cully tells him as he reaches the foyer. 'Well?'

'The bike cut out.'

'Then use a car.'

'Still quicker on the bike.'

'Not tonight obviously. Where are the two officers that were on the first shift?'

'I'm guessing they went home when the others arrived.'

'You don't know?'

'I'll find out.'

'Get them to report immediately to the incident room.'

'They need a break.'

'Don't we all Sergeant, but I need to talk to them. This happened on their watch and they have to report not hide away.'

'They need a break,' he repeats.

'I don't give a damn Sergeant, there are two dead women here and I need to find out what went wrong.'

'I'm sure they did their duty.'

'Get them into the incident room. I'm contacting Internal Affairs.'

'No need for that.'

'Tizard, are you disobeying my orders?'

'No, I'll get them in.'

'Good and we don't need you here anymore.'

++++

Cully moves into the kitchen, pulling out a chair from under the breakfast bar. The place is all white tiles and polished steel. He would love to cook there, create something wonderful magical for…ah, but for whom? Indah of course. Thoughts about other women have faded.

Beyond his fantasies about Indah, there is something niggling at the back of his mind, but tiredness and the magnitude of events keeps getting in the way.

What was Alison doing here? He hoped he would get a chance to ask her.

Is this about drugs, abuse and the Nasty Gang or something unrelated?

Shit! Minty of course. 'Listen everyone,' he shouts, leaving the kitchen. 'We're looking for another woman.'

'Who?'

'Araminta Gold.'

'The journalist?' asks Lisa. 'She's here?'

'The pink suitcase will be hers, too tacky for the women,' explains Cully, 'and where is the officer's log, her name will be on it? Tom, where have you been?'

'Out the back. There's an indoor swimming pool, a jacuzzi and a cabin of some sort.'

'Did you look inside?'

'No, I'll go now,' Tom vanishes.

'Nothing in the cellar,' Lisa calls from below.

'Gov!' shouts Tom. 'In the sauna.'

'Get paramedics, quickly.' Cully hurries through the kitchen to the pool where he sees Tom at the far end, crouching in the doorway of the sauna cabin. He is kneeling on the floor beside a body. 'Well?'

'She's alive. I think she's been tasered. Her wrists and ankles are tied.'

'Let the medics take over.' Cully leaves them to it, returning to the lounge where Amber is kneeling beside Megan's body.

'Cully, when is this going to stop? I can't keep up. My whole team are exhausted.'

'I know, but this might be the end of it.'

'I fucking hope so. Gerry is on his way.'

'I didn't think he made house calls. I bet he wasn't happy being called out.'

'Actually, he was, mentioned something about a chapter for his book.'

Moving from the lounge Cully watches the paramedics wheeling Minty away.

'How is she?'

'She'll be ok,' says Tom. 'I've bagged the tape used to tie her wrists, ankles and gag her.'

'Perfect.' Cully stands in the foyer watching the ambulance pull away. 'Why are these here?' There were unopened pizza boxes on the hall table. 'Pizza?'

'I'm hungry, what flavour?' Pete asks coming down the stairs. 'We could reheat it.'

'Why did the women order pizzas when they've got a fully stocked kitchen?'

'I'm surprised,' begins Lisa, 'after what they said when I saw them. Carla said something like, "I don't do fast food".'

'Maybe they decided to slum it,' says Pete, opening the top box. 'An untouched seafood pizza with garlic. I hate cold prawns.'

'I hate garlic,' says Lisa, 'you get bad breath.'

'They wouldn't order them, especially before a *Bonjour* interview. They'd want to be sophisticated, drinking Dom Perignon and eating caviar.'

'There's an excellent French restaurant down the road and an Italian in town, they could have gone to either,' says Tom.

'These women wouldn't have ordered pizza,' says Cully. 'I asked before, where's the visitor log the officer's used?'

'Here, Gov,' says Lisa, producing a clipboard.

'At least, they kept a record,' and he reads. 'The pizza guy brings the cops pizza and then takes it up to the women who let him in. Not neat eaters,' he flicks away dried tomato. 'The women wouldn't have ordered pizza for the cops, not their style. Tom.'

'Gov?'

'Did I see a landline phone in the kitchen? See what the last number dialled is?'

Minutes later Tom returns. 'It was the pizza place, last called at five thirty. I let it ring. They confirmed the order, paid for by a Mr Simpson on a credit card, but more importantly they want to know if we've seen their skiving pizza delivery guy.'

'According to the visitor list he arrived at eight and left at eight minutes passed. Lisa, we've searched everywhere haven't we?' She nods. 'Amber!'

'What now Cully? Not another bloody body? You know I could have been a librarian?'

'You would have been wasted.'

'Wish I was.'

'The secret toilet in the foyer, of course,' he shouts.

'Cully there are four other toilets in this house if you need to go,' she grumbles coming to join them. They pull back the front door which had crashed against the wall and Cully pushes a faded square of panelling before stepping away, allowing Pete space to kneel down beside the lifeless body.

++++

Lisa and Pete follow the ambulances to the hospital, arriving as Alison Grey is taken into surgery. They are told her chances of survival are slim. Pizza guy Brian is placed in a cubicle in A & E while Minty Gold is taken to the secure ward for further observation. As they wait to question them a nurse waves, smiles brightly and comes over. Lisa introduces Pete to her sister. 'Can you hold off on talking to Ms Gold? She's physically fine, but emotionally traumatised. We've given her a sedative.'

'Of course. Mary, I need to see the possession box for Philip Simpson.'

'In the office on the ward.'

'You look done in, have you had a break?'

'Listen to who's talking,' Mary smiles thinly at her sister.

'I know, but have you?'

'I took some hours off this evening, I mean yesterday evening. Got away from the hospital.'

'I'll talk to Minty later shall I, Ma'am?'

'No Pete, I'll take her when she's ready, you take Brian.'

Pete steps into the cubicle.

'I'm DC Grimes. How are you feeling?'

'Like shit. Did he really taser me?'

'We think so.'

'I should get one for protection when I'm out delivering.'

'They are illegal,' Pete warns.

'Then how did he get one, was he a cop?'

'Why do you say that?'

'Cops have them. You hear stuff on the Island about the cops over here. Those CID guys got sacked, the cops outside were more interested in stuffing their faces than watching over me and there are always corrupt cops on TV, aren't there?'

'What can you tell us about him or her?'

'Think it was a him. Didn't smell like a skirt. Not much to tell. It was all very quick.'

'You stepped inside?'

'I know we're not meant to, but there were cops outside. He had the cash ready.'

'Did you see his face?'

'No, he had his back to me, getting the cash.'

'Do you normally carry your helmet to the customers door?'

'Recently, since I had one nicked from the bike.'

'But the police were there.'

'Habit and I said, they were more interested in the food.'

'What else can you tell us?'

'Not a lot.'

'What was he wearing?'

'Jeans and a blue shirt, I think, but it happened so quick.'

'Which is basically your uniform?' states Pete, confirming for him, how clever the assassin is. 'Isn't it?'

'I suppose and he must have taken my jacket.'

'Anything else?'

'He wore gloves, I remember. Yeah, those thin latex ones they use in the kitchen at work.'

'Did he say anything?'

'I think he said sorry when he tasered me.'

'Accent?'

'I was being electrocuted,' Brian protests, 'but posh I suppose.'

'Anything else?'

He was a generous tipper. 'Top pocket ten pound note.'

'We need the tenner,' says Pete opening a plastic bag. 'Pop it in.'

'I'll get it back?'

'Probably, but I can't say when.'

'Shit! The only way to make money on this job is with tips and that's the best in ages.'

'Here.' Pete hands over a fiver. 'Best I can do.'

'Cheers.'

'You must have heard us enter the property, you didn't make a noise. You could have kicked the door.'

'I thought it might be him coming back.'

'But we shouted police.'

'Yeah right, I told you he might have been a cop. What about my scooter?'

'We're looking for it.'

'How can I do my job?'

'Sorry, but can't be helped. Borrow one.'

'I don't know anyone.'

'Stop complaining Brian and be pleased you're alive. I'll get someone to take you home.'

Outside the cubicle, Pete sees Lisa and Mary emerging from the lift. Lisa is carrying a shoebox.

'Anything, Pete?'

'The shooter is a clever bastard, sorry ladies, but he really is.'

'Pete, interview the staff at the Pizza place.'

'They'll be closed and Tom spoke to them on the phone.'

'Pete, do what you think best,' she concedes tiredly.

'Ma'am.'

Lisa opens the lid of the box and looks inside. 'It's empty. No wallet, keys or anything else. This killer is far ahead of us. Pete forget the pizza place, Becky can go tomorrow. Instead wake the agent and find out how many keys Megan Simpson had.'

'It'll be a pleasure, Ma'am,' Pete leaves.

'Mary can you do me a favour?'

'What else are sisters for?'

'Give me a ring when Minty Gold is fit to be spoken to.' Lisa hesitates. 'Did you give Kerry something to make her sleep?'

'No.'

'I know when you're fibbing Sis.'

'I shouldn't have, but I was angry, but she's not a problem anymore.'

'Steve's in deep trouble. Bring the kids and stay with me, please. It's a big house. What time does your shift finish?' Mary tells her. 'I'll come when the children are home from school and pick you all up. No argument.'

'I'm not arguing, Lisa. I'm done with them both.'

++++

Three o'clock in the morning and Cully is still at the rental house, sitting on a bench at the deep end of the indoor swimming pool. Yawning he stares into the clear depths of the water thinking. He has been talking to the Chief Constable, outlining the mess they are in. First, they let Alison in and then Minty. Then Pizza delivery guy Brian turns up. The officers confirm who he is, but don't speak to the women to check they ordered the food. He gives them a tempting feast to scoff on. Unsuspecting, Brian walks to the front door, rings the bell and it opens. He's invited in, against pizza house regulations, but there are cops a few metres behind so no worries and the front door is left ajar. The shooter uses a taser and pushes him into the loo off the hallway, ties and gags him, takes off Brian's jacket, puts it on and then the helmet and takes the scooter keys. Picks up the food bag and leaves. Waves to the cops and heads off. 'My responsibility Sylvia.'

'Bollocks, it's bloody Tizard, I'm going to see he's hung out to dry, don't you worry about him,' and she hangs up.

'We found CCTV from the house opposite of him driving away, but then we lose him,' reports Tom appearing from the house. His voice echoing from the high ceiling. 'But we've found the scooter down by the ferry.'

'He's well away, probably on the mainland by now. The idiots let him ride away.'

'They didn't know there were corpses in here.'

'My career amongst them.'

'Surely not, Gov. We couldn't have expected this.'

'Even so Tom, it makes us look bloody stupid.'

'What if Brian had left his helmet on the scooter and not taken it in?'

'It was a risk, but we believe the shooter wore a balaclava at the school hall. He simply pulls it over his face. Lots of bikers wear them and I doubt Laurel and Hardy would have noticed. I'm wondering how the shooter got in, in the first place, but I'm guessing somewhen during late afternoon, hides and waits.'

'The officers should have searched the place before the women entered?'

'It's one of the many questions I and Internal Affairs will be asking. The shooter could have killed Minty, delivery guy, the officers and finished off Alison if necessary, but didn't want to. This was a professional hit which brings us back to drugs, Eva Djokovic and *Groupa Europa*. We have a chemical chain reaction.'

'A what?'

'Once the chain is in motion it is unstoppable. Simpson buys the drugs, he doesn't pay, the dealers get angry and take action at the school and then here. Not only do they kill the Simpsons, but send a warning to anyone else tempted to not pay in the future.'

'Is the killing finished then?'

'I hope so, but Phillip Simpson is still alive. We need to tighten security around him. Tom, go home and come in late this afternoon, you must be exhausted.'

'Thanks, Gov.'

'When you see your wife, blame me for everything. If that doesn't work, my uncle Adam has a spare room.'

'Cheers, Gov.'

Tom leaves as Pete arrives.

'How are things at the hospital?'

'Chaotic, the place isn't up to rotating murder victims. Have you spoken to the DI?'

'Not yet.'

'Simpson's possession box at the hospital is totally empty, wallet everything gone.'

'Shit!'

'I rang the rental agent.'

'I bet she wasn't happy.'

'Not happy about anything, Gov. Fucked off being woken, but more upset about the loss of advertising. Carla's publicist did a deal. Forget the rent and Carla would push the agency on her blog. On top of that, the *Bonjour* article would have been superb publicity. She is pissed about any damage. Apparently getting blood stains out of expensive carpets is a nightmare.'

'Not worried about the victims?'

'Not as you'd notice. I didn't mention we battered in the front door. I asked about keys, but there aren't any. There is a code to get in. It changes every twenty four hours and the computer sends the new code as text to the occupiers. In this case, the Simpson's.'

'No one else?'

'No, but the Simpson's could also have got in using fingerprints, there's thumb print entry as well.'

++++

Leaving Amber and Pete to work the scene Cully drives along deserted roads to the hospital thinking about Indah in that outfit and without it. He rings her mobile to thank her for the meal, apologises that things had been cut short and up-date's her on events. Her tone tells him there are others in the incident room and it's difficult to talk. 'Chalky and Becky are here.'

It is probably for the best that things with Indah had not gone further. There were so many reasons why it shouldn't, not least he's her superior officer and he didn't want to be another Tizard. Who is he kidding? Adrenaline fuelled investigations like this one leave emotions raw and throw people together. It had been one such that started things with Amelia.

Finding Monica, acting as FLO, he makes certain she feels able to tell Bethany about her mother and liaise with the aunt coming from New York. They agree that under the circumstances Bethany would be better off with Chalky and his family.

Then finds Mary, asking if there is any way she could keep him up-dated about Alison? Of course she would. Taking the lift to the basement, he rings Sophie. 'Sorry about the hour.'

'Shit Cully, I need my beauty sleep.'

'You're beautiful enough as it is,' but does he mean it? Compared to Indah she… 'We need your help.'

'What do you want?'

'You need to get over to the hospital,' and he explains. 'But one question first. I thought they were over years ago, why were they together last night?'

'She's confused.'

'She's confused?' The lift doors slide open. 'I'm confused.'

'I'll be right over,' and she hangs up.

'What now? Christ! Why can't people leave me alone?'

'Hi Gerry.'

'Sorry, I didn't know it was you, people are in and out of here all the bloody time. Never any peace to do some cutting. I didn't mean to snap, but it's not only Amber that's exhausted. What time is it?'

'Five and I appreciate you.'

'I'm sure you do Cully.' Gerry is slumped in a chair in his small office to the side of the mortuary. He is sipping from a glass of cognac. 'I've not started on the autopsies yet, if that's what you're after? I've just got back from the scene. I was about to start cutting, but needed a pick-me-up.'

'There's no rush.'

'Want one?'

'Yes please.'

'Help yourself.' Cully finds a dusty glass, wipes it with a rag and pours himself three fingers. 'Top me up will you?' Cully does so and moving a pile of books on to the floor sits down. 'The one that survived is in surgery. Did you know her?'

'I used to walk home with her and fantasise about what would never be.'

'Ah, young boys and their sticky dreams.'

'What's puzzling is that she was there at all and why only shoot her once?'

'You'll figure it out. You'll solve the Alison conundrum and you never know if she's survives you might get lucky.'

'I doubt it, she's gay, or at least bi.'

'So there's hope.'

'Has Carla arrived here?'

'The attractive dark one?'

'Yes. Alison and she were a couple a long time ago, but I thought they were over.'

'Shit a double bloody waste. I was developing quite a daydream about her.'

'Gerry, you don't…?'

'No, I don't, but the dead can still be attractive.'

'Can I have a look at her?'

'You can and you'll see what I mean. Don't mind if I stay here, do you? Need to take the weight off.'

Cully goes to the steel table with channels running down either side for blood to drain away and pulls back the sheet. 'Jesus Gerry, what happened to her?'

'Forgot to warn you,' he shouts, 'the bullet pierced her breast implant on the way through.'

'Back to front, yeah?'

'Yes, both bullets. One through the back and the other through the back of the head.'

'So, he was probably standing behind her in the doorway?'

'Looks that way.'

'Carla was astride Alison, riding the strap on.'

'Cully, for Christs sake I'm an old man,' he laughs. 'There's a clear exit wound where the breast was so the bullet kept travelling and into your Alison, but talking to upstairs it didn't hit any vital organs and was a through and through. She's lost lots of blood, but if she fights she'll live.'

'She probably saw him,' Cully says. Phillip Simpson's hand, 'Have you still got it?'

'Of course, we have to keep everything for the coroner, not that the poor bugger is dead yet of course, but according to my colleagues it won't be long.'

'Where is it?'

'In the freezer.'

Before leaving the hospital, Cully makes certain they knew to place Alison in the secure ward and checks security surrounding Philip Simpson.

Once in the car and driving towards the incident room he rings Pete. 'How are things?'

'Fine apart from Amber grumbling about the workload.'

'Where are you?'

'Outside, having a coffee.'

'I need you to go into the kitchen and search the fridge and the freezer.'

'What am I looking for?'

'Simpson's left hand.'

++++

Arriving at the incident room Cully exchanges smiles with Indah and asks Chalky if he and his wife still feel able to take Bethany.

'Of course, poor kid.'

'It'll be better than the safe house. Will you liaise with Monica. I'll renew Police Powers to cover our backs. Becky?' No response 'Becky!'

'Sorry Gov.'

'Will you go to the hospital and replace Monica as FLO?'

'Yes Gov.'

Cully finds Lisa sitting quietly in the office.

'You alright?'

'I need some time off, just a few hours later today please?'

'Of course, take whatever you need. Can I do anything?'

'I'm bringing my sister and the children back to my place. I thinks she's seen the light at last.'

'She's lucky to have you. Why don't you get off now?'

'Too much to do and I'm not picking them up until the kids are out of school. How is Alison?'

'Should be ok. Remind me about the arrangements for the women.'

'Megan Andrews went via the hospital. I arranged for Becky and Chalky to do the chauffeuring. Becky confirms she dropped Carla off at the rental house at three. Chalky arrives with Megan at four-thirty. The police car with two armed officers were already outside when Becky got there. You need to talk to Becky, she's really upset.'

'Haven't you?'

'I have, but they listen to you.'

'They listen to you.'

'Not in the same way. They believe everything you say.'

'Scary.' Cully takes a seat as his phone rings. 'You've only found the thumb. He will have cut it off and dumped the rest of the hand somewhere. Get uniform to take it back to the mortuary. Yeah, it's how he gained entry, bloody clever. Thanks Pete.' Cully explains to Lisa. 'Gerry admits security in the mortuary is poor and what with all the comings and goings anyone could have slipped in and taken it.'

'Like a police officer?'

'Is that what's bothering you?'

'Tizard's involved, I know it. There is something else,' Lisa continues, 'but you'll think I'm being vindictive, even paranoid.'

'Vindictive and paranoid, it must be bad. What is it?'

'Look.' She shows him the empty hospital box. 'Everything has gone from Simpson's box, in particular his wallet.'

'Pete told me. We've confirmed the pizzas were ordered by a man or woman using Simpson's credit card. The wallet could have been taken by paramedics, hospital staff or his wife, anyone gaining access to the office.'

'Again like the mortuary, but including police officers.'

'It is chaotic, but ok,' Cully responds thoughtfully. 'Keep going.'

'Kerry is in the hospital a lot, right from the beginning.'

'Slow down, Lisa. Where is she by the way?'

'Please think about what I'm saying.'

'Megan could have removed anything and everything from that box if she'd wanted.'

'We haven't found any of her husband's stuff on her.'

'I can see where you are going with this, Lisa.'

'It's just between us so far, right?' He nods. 'The caller and possibly the killer if they are one and the same, or not, knew the times the women would be returning to the house with the officers. He or she…'

'Or they…'

'Knew the officers would be outside and knew when the change would take place. They entered the house before the women and escort arrived and knew to leave before the shift change.'

'I have to agree, he, she, is well informed,' he agrees, recalling that he and Claudia talked about the arrangements in front of Amber. 'It could be anyone.'

'But how did they know?'

'We don't know yet, Lisa.'

'What if it was a cop, Tizard for instance?'

'Lisa, slow down.'

'He had access to the flashbangs, to the Glock 17 used to shoot you and Linda.'

'But why?'

'He was paid.'

'You are making huge leaps. I know we both dislike him, that he's a rule bender, but corrupt?' Cully opens the door to the office, but turns to face her. 'Accepting the killer got the thumb and the credit card, we need to find out how the killer found out about the timings. In the meantime, we need to talk to Laurel and Hardy.'

++++

'This isn't fair,' complains Joe as Cully enters. 'I've been waiting for ages.'

'It's been hectic. To reassure you this is between us, nothing is being recorded, but I wanted a word before the people from the IA get here. You'll need a union rep of course and maybe a lawyer.'

'I will?'

'Come on, you know the drill, you've had dealings with them before after the shooting in the custody suit.'

'I'm sorry about that.'

'I'm sure you are. What do you think IA are going to want to talk about?'

'Me and Ted messing up.'

'Certainly that and they are going to want to talk about flashbangs aren't they?'

'I don't know what you mean.'

'You know Turner has given us a full statement.'

'It was the Sergeant's idea, to use them in training. There are some derelict buildings where the army used to be in the forest.'

'Tell them that, that it was Tizard's idea.'

'I will.'

'Now about last evening, let's run through it, so you've got your story straight. How many people did you let into the house?'

'Three Alison Grey, Araminta Gold and the pizza guy.'

'Did you check with the women that they were expecting them?'

'No, but I saw Carla Scutari greet Alison and Megan Simpson greeted Gold at the door.'

'The pizza guy?'

'They opened the door to him and let him in.'

'What if I told you we think the women were dead before the pizza guy arrived?' Joe slumps into a chair. 'You are in deep shit,' Cully emphasises. 'Why didn't you walk them up to the door or check with the women first?'

'We assumed...'

'You should never assume anything, should you Joe?'

'Was one of them the killer?'

'No.' Cully pauses. 'Did you see the pizza delivery guy when he left?' Joe nods, clearly unsure. 'You gave a description of the young man that went in, but it wasn't the same person that came out.'

'It wasn't?' Cully doesn't reply, letting Joe think things through. 'He had his helmet on and we were…'

'Eating pizza.'

'The women bought it for us.'

'No they didn't.'

'What?'

'Let me explain something to you Joe.'

'The pizza delivery guy that brought the pizzas was genuine, but the one that left was the shooter. We're assuming the killer was already there in the house when you arrived. Not your fault, but—'

'How did he get in?'

'More importantly,' Cully begins softly before raising his voice, 'why wasn't he found when you searched the house before the women entered?' Cully swings round. 'You did search the house?'

'Yeah, of course we did, standard procedure.'

'You don't sound convinced.'

'I'm sure we did.'

'Upstairs, downstairs and the cellar?'

'Yes, every room and the pool area.'

'You were in a hurry?'

'The Carla women was impatient to get in.'

'An attractive, sexy women so you wanted to please her.'

'I suppose.'

'And hall toilet, did you search it?'

'I didn't know there was one.'

'Did you read yesterday's briefing paper?'

'The toilet was mentioned in there?'

'It was. A complete description of the rental property and plans. There's a sauna and jacuzzi in the pool area. The journalist was found bound and gagged in the sauna. At least, she wasn't killed and the pizza guy was simply tasered. So they were lucky, but not the three women and I suppose you and Ted were lucky as well.'

'Why?'

'We're dealing with a professional predator. If you'd told him to take his helmet off, he'd probably have shot you both, after all you were sitting in the car stuffing your faces, easy meat.'

‘If you put it like that, Gov.’

‘I do. I’m thinking the shooter was hiding in the toilet or maybe in the sauna.’

‘Shit! I’m not saying anything more. I want my union rep.’

‘Did Sergeant Tizard brief you?’ No answer. ‘DI Lynn is currently interviewing your colleague and you know how this works Joe. One of you talks, that person gets the deal, maybe a simple suspension, while the other gets hung out to dry, loses his job, pension and everything else. Your choice.’

‘I’m not a criminal, you’re talking to me like I’m a scumbag.’

‘You let two women die and another is critical.’

‘I’ve got a wife and three kids.’

‘Ever heard of Eva Djokovic or *Groupa Europa*?’

‘No.’ Cully believes him and anyway can’t see him as the armourer. ‘I’ll trade you.’

‘What have you got to trade?’

‘Tizard,’ Joe states with a grin.

++++

Lisa sits while Cully stands in the doorway of the church office discussing how the informal interviews with Joe and Ted had gone when Indah appears.

‘Gov, I know how the shooter knew where they’d be,’ she declares excitedly, slipping into the office, brushing her hard body against his, smelling of meadow flowers. ‘Social media. Araminta Gold is all over it with every detail of her life, especially the last few days and Carla and her publicist never stop posting stuff, including times of arrival. The shooter only had to look to know everything that is going on, the when, where, how and why’s.’

‘That easy?’

‘Very easy,’ Indah smiles.

‘Sorry, I know I’ve given you enough to do already, but can you write it up? Please do a timeline. It’ll take the pressure off us, we can’t be blamed for leaking the info. When are you seeing Sophie again?’

‘Tomorrow.’

‘Have you seen or heard from Kerry?’

‘Not a word.’

‘Anyone heard from Kerry,’ Cully asks stepping into the main room, but no one has.

'I could pop in on her later, Gov, offers Tom.'

'That would be great,' Cully thanks him. 'Trudi alright after last night?' Tom nods in response. 'Tell Kerry she's either in here or off sick. I'll get coffee for everyone.'

Cully slips through to the kitchen where Mandy is frying bacon. 'That smells great.'

'I thought you all deserved brunch, but it's not healthy.' She flips the bacon. 'You could butter some rolls. Is it true?'

'About?'

'You know what Cully?'

'Yes, two dead so far with another one serious.' He starts to butter. 'Shall I put tomato sauce on each?'

'That smells amazing,' Pete declares coming into the kitchen. 'Brown sauce on mine,' he adds cheerfully. 'I'm starving. We really appreciate this, Vicar.'

'Mandy please, Pete. What have you been up to?'

'Can I say Gov?'

'Might as well, she's become onc of thc tcam.'

'SOCO have finished at the house and Amber and I agree your theory about the bullet Alison caught fits with the blood splatter. The thumb has gone to the hospital and I've got uniform combing gardens, bins and drains for the hand. Shall I pour coffee?'

'Please, Pete,' says Mandy, looking pale. 'Hand?'

Pete explains. 'They used the thumb to get in.'

'Have you seen Kerry?' Cully asks Pete.

'No Gov.'

'Briefing in twenty minutes.'

'But first...' and Pete carries bacon rolls through to the incident room followed by Mandy with a tray of coffee mugs. 'Cully.'

'Yes Mandy?'

'I know things are horrible and difficult, but the memorial service. I need to know.'

'Anybody have any objections?' Cully looks round the room as people take a bacon roll and coffee. 'No objection, so go ahead. We will allocate security. Nothing too visible, but officers will be armed.'

'Of course, I understand. One other thing, will you do a reading please?'

'Why me?'

‘Please.’

‘I will,’ he reluctantly agrees. ‘Monica, I’ve found something simple for you to do?’

‘I don’t like the sound of that. What?’

‘Dr Inskip needs reassuring.’

‘Gov, no.’

‘Just go and charm him please. You’ve been FLO all night, so after that go and get some rest. You can keep using the safe house if you like or go back to the hotel, up to you.’

‘Stick and carrot,’ she smiles.

Slipping out the back Cully finds Lisa and Mandy, like guilty schoolgirls, smoking and giggling behind a stone buttress. ‘Caught you, detention later.’

‘You’d be so lucky,’ Mandy quips.

‘Lucky, lucky, lucky,’ sings Lisa and both women laugh.

‘I led her ashtray,’ says Mandy. ‘Get it?’

‘I’d given up, but I needed one,’ explains Lisa, ‘and I hate to see a woman smoking alone.’

‘Your sister smokes,’ Cully smiles.

‘We all did at one time or another.’

‘All?’

‘There were four of us girls. I was the oldest and Mary the youngest. Mary was adopted. I was so pleased because the middle two were close and suddenly I had a mate.’

‘Mandy, any siblings?’ asks Cully, having read Becky’s report on her visit to the yacht club.

‘I had a sister, but she died.’

‘Sorry Mandy.’

‘It’s ok,’ she sighs. ‘Do you want one?’ Mandy offers the packet. He shakes his head. ‘At the seminary, we all did a little cannabis. It was so boring and the odd puff helped with things and takes you closer to God.’

‘You met him?’

‘Her. God is definitely a woman.’

‘Agreed,’ says Lisa. ‘My sister has just rung, Araminta Gold is ready to be interviewed. I could see her and then do the autopsies, Gov?’

‘Perfect, Lisa and then get ready for your guests.’

‘Thanks Cully.’

++++

Thinking they should set-up the incident room at the hospital, Lisa slips into the canteen, collects three cups of coffee and heads towards the secure ward. She talks with the armed officers on the door while they drink the coffee. Inside she asks after Alison Grey before pulling back a curtain on another woman.

'Don't I get to see Cully?'

'You'll have to put up with me Ms Gold. I'm DI Lynn.'

'Call me Minty, everyone does, but can I just finish this?' She continues typing on her computer tablet. 'Such an incredible scoop.'

'What are you doing?'

'I'm writing my story for tomorrows paper. Not sure which one yet, but I've got The Times, Sun, Telegraph and the Financial Times on the hook and they are prepared to pay thousands for it. I was actually in there when it was all happening.'

'You could have been killed.'

'Exactly, like a war correspondent.'

Lisa stares at the young woman and she could sort of see why Cully, describing her in the pub, called her fit if you like your women thin without obvious tits. 'Too thin for me,' Pete had said, 'and I like my women mucky.'

'Posh can be mucky,' said Cully, obviously not a little drunk.

The cut glass accent made her posh, but the only thing mucky about this young woman are her ethics or was it morals, maybe both?

'Two people were killed,' Lisa reminds her.

'Tragic I know, but I'm a journalist and have to keep focussed on what an amazing story this will make. I might even win an award, like a Pulitzer.'

'That's American.'

'Well whatever our alternative is.'

'You write for *Bonjour* magazine.'

'Not after this gets published. Television of course and maybe a book. I'll need protection, armed protection.'

'Why?'

'Because I'm a witness and the killer may come after me.'

'If he'd wanted you dead, he'd have shot you or turned the thermostat up on the sauna and let you cook to death.'

'That's a horrible thing to say.'

‘Did you have this computer in the house?’

‘Yes. I took notes on it and even recoded some stuff on it and my phone.’

‘Perfect,’ and Lisa takes the machine from her.

‘What are you doing.’

‘It’s evidence. Where is your phone?’

‘In my bag.’

‘I’m taking that as well.’

‘You can’t.’

‘Yes I can. You’ve told me you recoded stuff on them and our tech people can go through it and find all sorts of evidence. Secondly, you’ve helpfully written your statement for me and thirdly the machines were in the house and are therefore evidential items of interest.’

‘This is absurd. I’ll get *Bonjour’s* lawyers on to it.’

‘If you do that, they’ll demand the story won’t they?’

‘I’ll get another computer and write it. I’ve got until six tonight to get it in.’

‘Good luck, I’ll leave you a receipt.’

Lisa walks to the nurses station.

‘Mary can you do me a favour?’ She nods and Lisa whispers about what she wants her to do. ‘Can you do that?’

‘Of course. Until well after six?’

‘Perfect, I know you know how to sedate someone,’ but Lisa is smiling and both sisters laugh. ‘Remember I’m picking you all up later.’

‘We’ll be ready.’

Lisa heads to the lift and takes it to the basement and the mortuary.

Gerry is whistling as she enters.

‘Ah, the lovely DI Lisa Lynn.’

‘You sound happy Gerry.’

‘Enjoying my work. What have you got there?’

‘Tech.’ She puts the items on a bench and explains.

‘Young women nowadays,’ he laughs. ‘Do you want a cognac?’

‘I’d love one, but better not.’

‘Any news about the hand?’

‘Afraid not.’

‘At least, we got the thumb back. Embarrassing, but I’ve been on at them to make this place more secure.’

‘The two dead women?’

'Not much to tell you. Both were shot with, if not the same, then a similar weapon to the one used in the school shooting. I've spoken with Amber and we agree the two women in bed were shot first. Carla Scutari has had a lot of work done that must have cost her a fortune. As for the lone woman in the lounge, she was shot after them, or should I say executed, head and heart. Eight murder victims in days, remarkable, I'm thinking of writing a book.'

'Not you as well,' Lisa sighs.

++++

Looking up Cully finds Indah standing in the doorway, grinning.

'Coffee?' she asks.

'Please. Is it just you and me now?'

'It is,' she smiles, leaving, returning with coffee minutes later and closes the door. She sits, crossing her legs, allowing for a flash of stocking top. 'What can I do for you, Gov?'

Cully sighs.

'You know very well, I hope we can continue from where we finished last night?'

'So do I.' She stands, coming round the desk, leaning back against it close to him. 'Now?'

Cully reaches out a hand, but there is a crash in the incident room as a door swings back and Chalky calls out that he's back. Giggling Indah retreats to the chair.

'Back to work,' Cully grins, adjusting his clothing. 'Have you finished with my alibi?'

'Oh,' she is blushing, 'there is one thing. You'll be getting a speeding ticket. The camera caught you travelling at forty coming here Friday evening. I'll fix it.'

'No you won't Indah.'

'But you were speeding to get here on police business.'

'Even so. I will appeal, but I don't want any favours, but thank you for the thought. Anything else?'

'One day I'd like to do that walk to the cemetery, I've never been up there.'

'I'll take you. You mentioned "Murder on the Orient Express?"'

'I did.'

'Have you finished reading it?'

'Yes.'

'Have you read Becky's report about the yacht club?'

'I have.'

'Any thoughts?'

'Are you testing me?' she grins.

'Well?'

'The girl that drowned, Debra is related to Vicar Mandy.'

'I'm guessing it's her sister. She therefore has a motive to kill Chapman. According to you, and I agree, Sophie had reason to kill Davis. What if there are others, like Patrick Le Strange, and they got together?'

'A conspiracy?'

'Exactly. I telephoned Michael Carter and asked him why he didn't come to the do. Same as me, he says and he didn't want to be associated with the Nasty Gang. He admits to being one of them at school, that he was mean, but says he has changed and wants nothing to do with them. I asked and he said he'd been to a few parties years go, but nothing for ages.'

'You believe him?'

'That's where you come in. Check him out please. He has a brother John, who was also in my year. Not so bright. He'd been held back. He was a bully, but bullies can be victims as well, and according to Michael he was in the army. They don't have any contact, haven't for years. What if our conspirators hired someone like John Carter to do their bidding?' He pauses. 'Is it something you'd be interested in following up as a priority?'

'Certainly is.'

'Tonight...'

'Yes?'

Phone rings before he can tell her that he wants to see her.

'Cully here' He listens. 'Tom, did you get some rest? Tom, slow down.' Listening. 'Get out of the cottage and stay out. Do nothing.'

++++

'You cut her down?'

‘I had to.’ Tom sits in his car, ashen faced. The light is beginning to fade from the day and Cully is aware they need to manage things. ‘I couldn’t leave her hanging.’

‘It’s ok, you’re human and any of us would have done the same,’ but doubts it. ‘Not your fault Tom. We go in carefully, don’t touch anything, you understand?’

‘I can’t see her again.’

‘Yes you can Tom, you’re a cop and that’s what we do. Now move.’

Cully leads Tom through the open door of the cottage that lets directly into the sitting room where Kerry’s lifeless body lies under a rug.

‘You covered her up?’

‘She was naked.’

‘Even so, you’ve messed with the crime scene.’

‘Crime scene?’

‘You know what I mean Tom,’ Cully sighs. ‘Did you touch or disturb anything else?’

‘I don’t think so.’

‘You need to be sure.’

‘I am.’

‘That’s good Tom. We’ve got to leave now. We have to secure the cottage, get SOCO here and I need to ring the Chief Constable to get Internal Affairs to take over as Kerry was one of us. You know we can’t investigate the death of one of our own. Now come on, let’s get you outside. Move.’ Cully pushes Tom and propels him out of the cottage. ‘Tom, when you got here today was the door open?’

‘Unlocked, but not open. I knocked but there was no answer. I tried the handle and it opened. I went inside and saw her hanging there.’

‘I want you to sit in my car and record your report on your phone about what you found, every detail please. Go.’

Cully glances down the side of the cottage where in front of the garden shed, next to the black wheelie bin he sees a plastic box spilling over with wine bottles. The shed door has a large padlock that seems out of place.

‘Everything alright?’

‘Sir?’ Cully walks over to the garden fence where an elderly man is standing smoking a cigarette. ‘I know its’s a dirty habit. Peggy, my wife won’t let me smoke indoors.’

'I'm Superintendent Cully.'

'You're Kerry's boss and that young man?'

'Is Sergeant Whitworth.'

'He's upset isn't he? What's happened to Kerry? Look I know what you are thinking, that I'm some interfering old man with nothing better to do than snoop.'

'That's what I'm thinking Mr…?'

'Blake.'

'Mr Blake I appreciate your interest and colleagues will want you to make a statement.'

'She's dead isn't she?'

'What makes you say that?'

'Peggy and I knew Kerry's parents. It was tragic when her mother died from cancer and then a year later her dad hung himself. After your high-ups scapegoated him.'

'Is that what she told you?'

'Kerry struggled with it all, drinking, different men, she was vulnerable. Did she commit suicide?'

'Mr Blake…'

'I know you can't tell me. I'm guessing others will come in to investigate.'

'My colleagues will want to speak to you. I have to go now.' Cully turns away and takes out his phone. 'Hi Amber, it's Cully, I have some bad news that I need you to act upon.'

'Sure you can trust this Serb?' she snarls.

'Sorry, I know how busy you are with the events last night.' He goes on to explain. 'So, we need two SOCO that preferably don't know her to work the scene. I'm going to call Lisa, tell her what's happened and get a uniform to stand guard. I'll wait until they arrive.' He ends the call only to make one to the Chief Constable.

Minutes later Cully gets back in his car. 'We need to wait until uniform and SOCO arrive and then I'll take you home.'

'No, I want to work.'

'We don't expect you in this evening.'

'I want to work.'

'Did you dictate your report?'

'Done it.'

'Good.'

'That bastard.'

'What bastard?'

'Tizard drove her to this.'

'We don't know that.'

'Did you speak to the Chief Constable?'

'I did. She wasn't happy.'

There is a sudden tap on the driver's window and there is Mr Blake carrying two mugs of steaming black coffee. Cully let the window down. 'Peggy thought you might like refreshments, coffee and choc' biscuits.'

'Thanks.' Cully takes the mugs, handing one to Tom.

'Biscuits,' and he produces two wrapped biscuits from his pocket. 'The chap on the motorbike used to call regularly you know, but not so much recently. Used to be a bit, well noisy when they were inside together, the dividing wall isn't that thick.'

'Was he here last night?'

'Maybe, but there were several visitors yesterday evening and you,' he points at Tom, 'were here weren't you?'

++++

The coming hours were some of the most challenging Cully has faced in a long while. Firstly, it takes ages for uniform and SOCO to arrive to take over the scene. Then he takes Tom, despite his objections, home, meets Trudi and Toby and shares a cup of coffee. By way of his mobile, Cully has another conversation with the Chief Constable and an initial telephone discussion with the lead officer appointed to investigate Kerry's death.

In the incident room Indah, Monica and Chalky are talking in low tones as Cully enters. 'Gov, is it true?'

'I'm afraid so.'

'Suicide?'

'That's how it looks, but we'll know more after the postmortem. Internal Affairs have already been allocated to investigate. I've taken Tom home and I want Lisa to have a break with her family. Monica, I hate to ask…'

'I'll make certain the scene is preserved, Gov, no problem,' she says, getting-up. 'I saw Inskip for you, he's being understanding,' she smiles.

'Chalky, can you manage here?'

‘Gov. Bethany is settled in at my place. The wife and the girls will look after her.’

‘Pete has gone back to the rental house. Sorry, we are so short staffed.’

‘Gov, I’m here.’

‘I’ve not forgotten you Indah, not for a minute. This is going to sound awful, but we can’t let this tragedy distract us from the shootings. Indah, you need to keep going and see if you can locate John Carter, Michael Carter’s brother.’

‘Gov, but I could replace Becky at the hospital, she’s struggling and with Kerry’s death…?’

‘Indah’s right, Gov,’ says Monica, pulling her coat on. ‘You can’t leave her there.’

‘Come on then Indah,’ says Cully, ‘let’s go.’

They drive fast. It’s an automatic and Cully drives with one hand on the steering wheel. He’s a teenager with Sinead O’Connor on the stereo and holding the hand of beautiful young woman, feeling more alive than he’s done in ages.

At the hospital, Indah suggests Cully goes in and sees Becky on his own. ‘But don’t let her distract you.’

Promising to be quick Cully enters, takes the lift up to the secure ward where he finds Becky sitting outside. ‘How are you?’

‘I’m ok,’ she says.

‘I’ve been meaning to speak to you.’

‘About the man I arrested?’

‘Actually, I’d forgotten about that, but now you mention it.’

‘I shouldn’t have. I got angry and over reacted.’

‘You did, but enthusiasm is no bad thing. Take a deep breath in future.’

‘Yes Gov. There is something else?’

‘DI Lynn said you were upset. You took the women to the house Becky, that’s all you did. You had nothing to do with what happened.’

‘I know really, but so many dead.’

‘I’ve got more bad news,’ and he gently tells her about Kerry.

‘It gets worse, doesn’t it?’

‘Indah is ready to take over here. You can go home Becky and I’ll see you tomorrow morning.’

‘Home to an empty flat,’ she sighs. ‘I suppose you don’t fancy a drink?’

‘Not tonight Becky, maybe another time. Now please go and get some sleep.’

‘No, I need to work, to be here. To be doing things’

'I'll look after her,' says a calming voice.

'Mary, I'd say good to see you, but things are pretty awful.'

'I know about Kerry. They've brought her body in and news spreads. It's the Island Cully, what do you expect?' She hesitates. 'I'm not pleased, if that's what you're thinking?'

'I wasn't,' he smiles. 'What's the news on Alison Grey?'

'She's comfortable. Sean O'Leary is being discharged in the morning.'

'Araminta Gold?'

'She's just woken up,' says Mary. 'She's furious. Something about missing a deadline. She says she's going to sue the hospital and the police.'

'I'll deal with her. Becky, let Mary make you coffee and toast.'

Entering the secure ward Cully finds Minty.

'What do you want?' she demands.

'I've been told you're upset.'

'I bloody am. Your DI Lynn stole my tablet.'

'She took it as evidence.'

'And some nurse doped me and I've missed my chance of a Pulitzer.'

'You're not American and you can submit your article tomorrow.'

'It won't be fresh and other papers will have it by then,' she sighs. 'When will I get my stuff back?'

'When we've finished with it. I'm sure DI Lynn gave you a receipt.'

Exasperated, Cully walks away, takes the lift down to the foyer where Indah is waiting. 'Becky wants to stay which means Indah, we are free. Fancy a quick drive and a walk.'

'It's dark.'

'No it's not, there's a full moon and I've got a torch.'

++++

'Do you have any friends at school you've kept in touch with?' He asks as they drive. 'Anyone?'

'No.'

'Very definite?'

'Just the way it went.'

'Sean O'Leary was a good mate and we got on really well, or at least I thought so.'

'But?'

'I'm beginning to realise he resented me and still does.'

'About what?'

'School stuff,' Cully says not wishing to talk about other women, with a woman he wants. 'I'm sure he moved the seating cards Friday night to put himself next to Sophie on whom he's got a crush and me near the Nasty Gang table.'

'To get you killed?'

'I doubt that, but he's still consumed by school stuff. Here we are,' and he pulls into the side of the road next to where the old football ground used to be. 'I went a lot, especially after mum died, one of her work colleagues used to take me. This was back in the day when football was a proper contact sport. I think I can still remember the team,' and he names eleven players. 'The kit man used to live next to gran and his wife washed the shirts. They hung on her line Monday morning. I used to dream of wearing one.'

'Did you?'

'Only when I bought one from the club shop. I've still got it. Now, I'm being really tedious.'

'No you're not. I like to know about you. Where are we going?'

'This way.' Climbing out of the car he takes her hand and leads the way up the lane, along a short length of tarmacked road and up a narrow dirt path edged by tall trees. Dry leaves crunching beneath their feet they head along a tunnel of overarching boughs. It grows steadily darker, the torch a poor spike of light and Indah clinging tightly to him.

There is a screech.

'What's that?'

'Only an owl.'

'Only?' She grips his hand harder. 'And that, something ahead.'

'A badger. Come on.' They are climbing, the narrow torch beam criss-crossing the path. 'See the moon,' and there it is ahead of them. Suddenly they are free of the trees and on a level path through farmland. Arriving at a stone arch, but find the gate locked. 'We can go over where the wall is crumbling,' and Cully helps her. 'We're here.'

'Where is here?' Cully swings the torch beam in an arc. 'It's a graveyard.'

'Not any graveyard Indah, it's where my family live.'

'Live?' she asks nervously. 'Really?'

'It's what I used to say about mum when I was a child. It helped. We can sit here.' They sit on a wooden bench. 'Look over there.'

'It's the river, like a ribbon of silver. It's beautiful. You can see the sea and beyond the mainland twinkling with diamonds,' she smiles. 'You used to come here with your grandmother to care for your mother's grave?'

'Let me introduce you to the three Cully women.' Using the beam of the torch he illuminates each gravestone in turn, beginning with Adam's mother and his grandmother, then his own mother and finally Caitland.

She touches his arm, breaking him free of the narrow alley of memories that would lead to darker places. 'You don't talk about your wife,' Indah begins tentatively. 'Or what happened.'

'What do you know?'

'Rumours and gossip, but nothing really. Lisa warned us all not to mention it soon after you arrived. She likes you, didn't want us to intrude into something that is not our business and a long time ago.'

'The only person I've properly talked to about this is Linda,' he admits, neglecting to mention Sylvia.

'Sorry.'

'No, I'm told it's good to talk,' and they cuddle closer. 'Caitland was a career police officer, enjoyed the action, the risk while I was always more cerebral.'

'The great detective,' says Indah.

'She couldn't resist the opportunity to go undercover. She loved Linda, but being a mum was never her thing,' he sighs. 'Going undercover, deeply undercover, means you surrender everything about yourself. You become the new person. If you don't, you'll fail and probably get killed. If you do you say goodbye to everything you've left behind. You have to do what you have to do to survive undercover and for a woman,' he hesitates, 'well you can imagine what. Caitland was undercover for two years. The three of us met occasionally, but things changed and Linda and I got used to being a one parent family. Then came the court case, Caitland gave evidence and the three of us were whisked away to the White House. We were awkward together and Linda resented being taken away from our home, her school and friends, but we worked at it and after several weeks we began to feel like a family again, until they found us.' Taking a deep breath he tells her about *Groupa Europa*, the gun battle and aftermath. As he talks Indah wraps her arms tighter around him, bringing her legs up over his lap, 'I suppose ever since Caitland went undercover I've built my life around Linda and the job.'

'And, you're an only child. I know exactly what that's like,' she reasons quietly. 'We fool ourselves into thinking we don't need anyone else.'

'Coming here has always given me peace. I learned to tether my sanity to a happy family life. My grandmother was my attachment figure. Then after Caitland went, my Linda became everything. Then Linda got shot and suddenly I was cut adrift. I constantly worry about her. I blame myself.'

'But it wasn't...'

'I know,' he snaps. 'Sorry, I can be difficult Indah.'

'I know, it's one of the things I like about you. Mad, bad and dangerous to know, isn't that what they say? What about what happened to you?'

'I've been shot before and apart from the odd ache I'm fine, but when it's your own child you fail to protect.'

'Hardly your fault.'

'Emotional logic goes out the window when you have them. I'd do anything for her. I don't know what I'd have done if she'd died.'

'Being a parent sounds scary.' She puts her arms around his neck, kisses his throat softly and whispers. 'I can make anything better, if you let me?' She cups his face, brings it close to hers and kisses him. 'Did you bring me up here to have sex?'

'Yes,' he admits, 'but it's cold, or I'm too old.'

In reply, Indah takes his hand and draws it up under her skirt.

Thursday

'That meal was superb, even at gone midnight.'

'And your companion is stunning.'

'Sorry that's the second time I've brought an unexpected guest.'

'I'm enjoying it and you can bring Indah whenever you want.' There is a log burner in the long shed and opening the glass door he holds bread against the flames with a toasting fork. 'She is stunning, charming and clever. Her eyes are hypnotic,' he says reversing the slice of bread on the fork.

Cully bends and rubs Angus on his offered belly before stepping outside. 'It's lovely here in the morning.' He looks out over the well-ordered allotment to the valley below where an early morning mist flirts with the ground. A figure moves, dances towards him. 'It's well cared for.'

'The allotment committee keeps a tight rein on things.'

Indah escapes the mist, arrives beside Cully and they kiss.

'I should be feeling guilty,' she says.

'What for?'

'After more deaths yesterday and Kerry, I shouldn't be enjoying myself, feeling this way. Do we have to go back?'

'You want to run away?'

'Yes please,' and laying her head on his shoulder yawns. 'I hardly slept. Is your uncle ok with us sleeping together, it's his house?'

'He is fine and I think he's in love with you already.'

'I love toast,' she declares entering the shed.

'With homemade marmalade?'

'Wonderful,' says Indah. 'This place is perfectly idyllic. Do you normally come here at eight in the morning?' she asks.

'Sometimes earlier when I can't sleep. I like the quiet. I've also got everything I need here.' Adam pours milky tea into a saucer before placing it on the ground for Angus. 'Too early for you my dear?'

'Not at all, everything is perfect,' She grins at Cully. 'I'm experiencing so many new things.' She sips her tea. 'Pheasant, expensive wine, perfect toast and the view from the cemetery on the hill is wonderful,' she teases, thinking she'd never made love in a graveyard before, but wanted to again. 'Can I have more please?'

'Of course,' and Adam lances a slice of bread with the fork. 'Cully took you up there did he, things must be getting serious,' he chuckles.

'I meant to ask,' begins Cully, wanting to divert the conversation, 'how did the demonstration at the forest go?'

'Very well, there were several hundred of us there. The oil company thugs threatened, but backed off. Lots of positive media coverage. I'm ashamed to say Ballard being killed may help us, he was the driving force behind the rape of the Great forest. Cully, you need to relax, you keep checking your phone.'

'There's so much going on, I can't afford to miss anything,' but puts the phone away. Angus yaps, demanding more tea which Adam gives him. 'Tell me about the allotment, how's it coming along?'

'I've taken over the next one along when he died. I should have a farm when I've finished my land grab.'

'You should keep chicken.'

'I'm thinking about it. Here's your toast Indah?'

'Wonderful.' She takes the slice, smears it with butter and marmalade, takes a bite, licking dribble from her chin. She catches Cully staring at her and licks her chin again. 'Thank you for last night, I've never had pheasant before or drunk wine from a six hundred pound bottle.'

'It's very good to have you here. I hope the bed was comfortable?'

'Adam!' Cully sighs. 'I thought you'd pulled the woman with the Cockapoo?'

'Seriously, not sure about her.'

'That's where he gets it from, from you,' laughs Indah.

'What?'

'Saying seriously all the time.'

'I do that?' Cully asks, not realising.

'Yes, you do,' she grins.

'Can I ask you some questions about the school?'

'Of course my dear.'

'Cully says you left the Alumni Association?'

'I did, because we were a friendly relaxed association and then the new headteacher Inskip arrives. The horrible little man, decided he'd hijack it and use it to raise money for the school. I've no objection to raising money, but it's become corporate and…'

'Not fun anymore?'

'Exactly. I still get the Alumni magazine,' and he picks one up from a pile near the wood burner and hands it to her. 'You might find it interesting. Anyway, us older ones still meet and we're thinking of declaring UDI, an independent group.'

'Good for you.'

'I'll join you,' says Cully, feeling side-lined, but pleased the two of them are getting on so well. 'In my day, the fees were ok, well I assume they were, you paid.' Adam brushes the comment away. 'But now only sheiks and oligarchs can afford them. Inskip is focussed on business.'

'But, I think he'd rather be teaching French,' Indah says, remembering the conversation the night of the meal in the refectory. 'I think he's a sad man.'

'He needs someone like you to cheer him up, we all do,' Adam nods to himself. 'More tea?'

'Sorry, I need to take Indah home and then collect Tom,' says Cully.

'I'll take Indah,' says Adam. 'If she'd like to stay a while longer?'

'Of course I would. You could take me to court. I've got warrants to apply for.'

'I'd find that interesting.'

'Good.' She goes over to Cully and kisses him with marmalade lips. 'See you later, Gov.'

++++

Cully drives Tom into the church car park.

'You need to talk to someone.'

'I want to work.'

'You sound like Becky,' he mutters. 'Maybe later.' Getting out, he sees the Vicar. 'Mandy, just the person we need.'

'Cully, how're you?'

'Not so good,' and he explains about Kerry.

‘So sorry. This week gets worse and worse. I didn’t know her, but I can imagine how you all feel.’

‘Tom found her, can you find time for him?’

‘Of course.’

‘I have to warn you that you’ll need to make a statement.’

‘No problem. Come on Tom lets go and hide in the manse and I’ll make us some proper black coffee. Have you had breakfast?’

‘No.’

‘Then I’m cooking up a fry. Come on.’

Cully watches them walk away. He takes a deep breath, knowing what is to come.

The incident room is quiet. They have moved everything off the display board and on to the wall where there is more space. Tom’s drawing of the school hall crime scene has been joined by one of the rental house. Above is the long black and white school photograph and three red strands of wool now link it with the diagram of the house. Each picture has numbers and letters next to it. 1 and 2 signify which table they sat at. Then D for Dead, W for wounded, F for failed to attend and M for motive.

He turns to the team.

‘You all know about Kerry. She was one of us, a member of the team and will be missed. If any of you want time out, then let me or Lisa know and you will get it. Counselling will be available, but if you want someone to talk to right now the Vicar has offered. Those of you who have met her know she’s not going to get all religious on you, but is a good listener. You can sit in the church for somewhere quiet if you want.’ Cully lets this sink in. ‘Kerry’s cottage was secured last night, SOCO are in and her body has been removed to the mortuary. The Chief Constable has requested IA investigate and they will be here later today.’ He pauses, aware of a chill in the room. ‘She has also contacted them about the failings in respect to guarding the rental house. IA will be based at the station, not here and they will be given every curtesy by us, understand?’

‘Gov,’ comes the chorus.

‘Chalky, can you arrange pick-ups and book overnight accommodation for them.’

‘Gov.’

‘Our priority remains what happened Tuesday night at the house. I know it’s difficult, but we must be focussed. SOCO have finished at the crime scene and

Lisa is running things there. We're gathering CCTV from surrounding streets and carrying out door to door. Pete, over to you.'

'I got to thinking.'

'Steady, Pete,' warns Monica.

'The Gov called Michael Carter and Indah has been working on it as well, He was due to come to the event, yet didn't, but he's got a brother. The Gov has asked me to follow up because of my army links. John Carter was in the army for a lot of years, but left under a cloud. If we are talking professional, then he has the training and the skills. The army are always reluctant to share and I suggested to the Gov I go north to where he was based and speak to them in person. I've booked a ferry to go this morning.'

'Thanks. Tom is taking things badly and is talking to the Vicar at the moment, but wants to work. Pete, take Tom with you.'

'Go off Island, he'll have palpitations. I'm more than happy to go on my own. I don't need babysitting,' he grimaces, annoyed.

'Pete, what's wrong with you? Do I need to give you a direct order?'

'No Gov, sorry.'

'Better for Tom than sulking around here. While you're at it, you can drop off Araminta's computer and telephone at BioTech.'

'Claudia, over to you.'

'Thanks, Gov. We know that the Simpson's were buying cocaine from Eva Djokovic to supply the parties Megan was organising for the Nasty Gang. City police initially thought they owed her about thirty thousand, but now think it may have been more as they were supplying various social groups and members of a tennis club they belong to. Yesterday evening the City actioned warrants against the home of Eva, her business and a warehouse she owns and had results in all three places, seizing drugs, guns, cash and fake documents. Nothing as yet to tie Eva to the Simpson's, but it's a great result.'

'Claudia is having to go back to the mainland, but will be continue to follow up on the drugs links. Thanks Claudia. Simpson and Alison Grey are still at the hospital under guard. Becky has agreed to go home to rest. I've found a uniform to cover, but Chalky can you replace her this afternoon please.'

'Sure.'

'Monica can you type up Tom's report in draft on finding Kerry, it's recorded here on his phone. He's left it unlocked.' Cully bends closer. 'I'd appreciate any editing you might feel necessary.' Turning back to the room. 'Indah is in court and I need to go and see Vicar Mandy when she's finished with Tom.'

++++

Later, Cully finds Mandy in the church kneeling before the alter, bathed in dappled red light spilling through the stain glassed window above the alter. He assumes she is preying and slips quietly into a pew several rows back. Mandy stands, crosses herself and turning sees him sitting there.

'To what do I owe the pleasure of your company, Superintendent Cully?'

'How's Tom?'

'Shocked, but I think your idea of sending him off to the mainland is a good one. It gives him something else to worry about.'

'You back in touch with God?'

'Any port in a storm,' she shrugs coming to sit next to him. 'You look serious Cully.'

'Mandy, we have to talk.'

'That sounds official. If you want to talk about Kerry, we can—'

'Becky Shaw went out to the yacht club and spoke to the steward.'

'Becky seems like a bright young woman.'

'She is, if a little too enthusiastic.'

'What did the steward say Cully?'

'You know Mandy, don't you?' She nods. 'Why did you take up this post?'

'I needed to start somewhere and having the stipend at the school was an advantage financially. Cully, it's obvious you know, so ask the bloody questions.'

'You mentioned the other day, that your sister died. Debra went to the school, was a border for two years through the sixth form, wasn't she?'

'She was.'

'You didn't tell us.'

'You didn't ask.'

'Mandy please help me.'

'It's about what happened last year and what I did?' Cully nods. 'The job here coupled with the chance to get into the school was an opportunity for me to find out how Debra died. It was six years ago, she was only twenty. Mum died a while back, but before she did she begged me to find out what really happened. You know Debra drowned in the harbour after a party at the Yacht club?'

'I'm really sorry.'

'She was my younger sister, three years younger. She was wild. My parents hoped by sending her to board here it would settle her down, make her take her studies and life seriously. She did well enough with A Levels to be offered a University place.'

'You say wild?'

'Since she was thirteen, running away, shop lifting, drugs, drinking and sex with older men. You would have liked her Cully.'

'Ouch!'

'Sorry, bad attempt at humour,' she pauses. 'My parents tried everything. I wasn't always around. I took life too seriously, did well at school, went to university and trained for this. Perhaps, I was trying to be her opposite, the good daughter, but ever since her death I've felt guilty, could I have done more?'

'Probably not.'

'That's true, but it still eats away at me.'

Cully recognised that in himself, the gnawing guilt. Could he have done more for all of those he didn't protect? Then realises he's not been listening.

'I grabbed the opportunity to come here and began to find out things,' Mandy is explaining. 'At the time of her death, the police wrote it off as an accident and the coroner agreed. To be fair she was full of drugs and alcohol and they said she'd gone outside and fallen off the pontoon.'

'Who said?'

'Other party goers.'

'Let me guess, it was a Nasty Gang party.'

'Going to University had not been such a good idea, she'd started taking drugs again. Then I discovered friends she'd made here at school had invited her over for get-togethers and parties. She was dealing by then, small amounts, but she was popular for what she could supply.'

'You talked to her friends?'

'Yes, and that's when I found out about the Nasty Gang parties and the fact she'd been going. One of her mates, Karly and her had been paid by the Simpson's to go and...he joked he wanted to see them in school uniform'

'Have sex?'

'Yes. Cully, my little sister was prostituting herself.' Tears were running down her cheeks and Cully reaches out to take her hand. 'I'm not saying they killed her, but they let her die.'

'I'm so sorry Mandy, but we will need to take a formal statement.'

'I know and I should have told you.'

'What happened between you and Chapman?'

'Karly told me they were having another party at the yacht club. These get-togethers have been regular for years. I've remained in contact with Karly, helped her through things. Got her into rehab, that sort of thing. Selfish really, I think she became a Debra substitute for me. Karly had been contacted to see if she could recommend any girls, supply more like her and Debra, but she refused.'

'They didn't want Karly?'

'Too old apparently, bastards.'

'We need to talk to Karly.'

'Can I ring her first?'

'Of course. Back to Chapman?'

'I went there, to the yacht club. Security wouldn't let me in because it was a private party. I slipped round the back and waited for what seemed ages, people came out and in, to smoke or kiss and grope and then a smallish guy came out and recognised him from the Alumni Facebook page. He was with a very young girl, groping her with her telling him to get off. I intervened. She went back inside and I followed him on to the jetty. I told him who I was. I accused him of abusing my Debra. He pushed me away and I pushed back. He fell in with an almighty splash. It was great and then a man's voice shouted and I, like a bloody coward, ran away.'

'The steward saw you.'

'I was surprised Chapman didn't make a complaint to the police.'

'He couldn't afford to, not with interests in young women. I'm so sorry about all this, but we do need that formal statement.'

'Relax Cully. I have to do this. Let's go to the vestry now, the ladies can bring us some tea and cake, and I'll write it all out.'

'One final question have you had counselling and with whom?'

++++

'Everyone drives fast over here, don't they?' Tom announces, not a little nervously, 'And everything is big.'

'I suppose so,' Pete grins. 'Island life is certainly different.' Pete is trying not to drive too fast, especially as Tom squeals when he overtakes. 'When did you last come over?'

'Two years back, for the sergeants course. That's when I met Linda Cully.'

'Nice girl, she'll go far like her dad.'

They had driven north via the modern glass and steel building that are the BioTech laboratories to drop off Minty's computer and phone and are now entering the army town. 'Tom, I can drop you in town. The shops are good and you could buy something nice for Trudi and Toby. I can visit the army base.'

'You want to get rid of me?'

'No, I'm just…It doesn't matter. Here we are.'

The barbed wire topped fence runs along the side of the road and within there are rows of two storey brick accommodation blocks. Reaching the gate there is a tank on a plinth surrounded by flags. An armed soldier approaches, Pete explains who they are, they show ID and they are told to wait.

'How long were you in the army?'

'Ten years,' says Pete.

'Is that where you learned to shoot and work with guns?'

'I suppose.'

'What were you?'

'Infantry Sergeant Major, this regiment as it happens, 2nd Battalion.'

'But you never met Carter?'

'Not that I remember, but I'm older and he was in 1st Battalion.'

'Sorry Pete, I don't mean to…'

'No problem Tommy.'

The barrier lifts ahead of them and the guard waves them through, pointing to a parking space. A few minutes later an adjutant appears, leads them to an office and asks them to wait before a senior officer arrives. 'Would you gentlemen like coffee?'

'Thank you, but no thanks Colonel and thank you for meeting with us,' says Pete, recognising the rank.

'You've come a long way. I've been following the shooting story.' He settles behind the desk. Tall, blonde and somehow a bit like Chalky. 'I'm guessing you think John Carter is involved?'

'We do.'

'Carter was a troubled soul. He survived for a good number of years, but his anger always bubbled beneath the surface and occasionally exploded.'

'Isn't that what you want in a soldier Colonel?' asks Tom.

'No it isn't. Maybe once, when you wanted men to charge with bayonet fixed and overrun a trench, but it's the last thing you want nowadays. War has become technical, computers and such like. We need brains rather than brawn.'

'Carter?'

'He made slow progress, spent a few nights in the guard house before, after nearly ten years, becoming a corporal and a few years later he made sergeant. I thought he was settling down, making a go of it. He was tough on the squaddies, but fair.'

'Something happened to change things?'

'His wife left him.'

'There is a wife.'

'A town whore. Sorry, uncalled for.'

'I had one of those,' mumbles Pete. 'A great shag, but useless as a wife.'

'You've served?'

'Yes Sir. Here, in the 2nd Battalion.'

'Ah, I thought I recognised the name, Sergeant Major wasn't It?'

'It was Sir.'

'And a hero.'

'Not really, just doing my duty.'

'A bit more than duty Sergeant Major Grimes.'

'Just Detective Constable now Sir.'

'Once a soldier always a soldier. Good man. Bloody sand got everywhere.'

'It did Sir.'

Suddenly the atmosphere changes. The Colonel relaxing, smiling and is happy to share.

'While Carter didn't fit in, he still survived for twenty-five years?'

'He was useful. You know what I mean Sergeant Major?' Pete nods. 'Never up to joining SAS, but even here in the regular army we need things done he was willing and able to do. But three years ago, he became difficult to manage and then we got lucky.'

'Lucky?'

‘Carter got injured on patrol in Afghanistan when an ID exploded. It allowed him and the army to part company without further trouble.’

‘Trouble?’

‘There was an allegation that he’d assaulted a local woman. No action was taken and he left with a lump of compensation.’

‘Cover up?’

‘It was convenient for all concerned.’

‘Apart for the woman in Kabul?’ Tom pushes, despite a warning glance from Pete.

‘She was compensated.’

‘But no justice?’ questions Tom.

‘War is shit Sergeant Whitworth.’

‘Any idea where Carter is?’

‘No, but his wife will know.’

‘I thought you said…’

‘They are not together, but they keep in touch.’

‘Never divorced?’ Tom wants to know.

‘Of course not,’ says Pete. ‘Stay married and the money tap stays on, right Sir?’

‘Right. The compensation, pension the one time army quarter she lives in from when the Ministry of Defence sold off the estate.’

‘Do you have an address?’

‘I’ll get it for you,’ and making a call the adjutant quickly appears at the door. ‘We need some information. But it will wait until after lunch. You’ll both join me won’t you, for lunch in the Officers Mess?’

++++

As Indah listens to Judge Le Strange giving his ruling she fumes, especially as Sophie keeps glancing across at her smiling triumphantly. ‘The police have applied for warrants to examine the patient files of therapist Sophie Cairns and her telephone and e mail communications. Those acting for Ms Cairns argue that these are confidential medical records and should not be disclosed under any circumstances. Indeed, they add that the police are on a fishing expedition. I’m sorry, but I cannot rule on these applications because of my intimate knowledge of those involved on both sides. However, this is simply a delay and I have already requested an independent judge attends from the mainland, or the police might themselves seek a transfer to the mainland.'

'The court will rise.'

Indah retreats from the court room and goes down the steps towards the toilets, but she hears footsteps behind her. She turns. 'Are you following me Sophie?'

'Don't be absurd. I need the toilet.'

'Bladder problems?'

'What do you mean by that?'

'Like the night of the shooting,' Indah reminds her.

'Bad luck not getting the warrants.'

'Only a delay and Judge Le Strange is right to say he can't rule, it would be unethical and open to appeals.'

'You are sweet Indah, but it's only a sugar coating isn't it?'

'What do you want?'

'To go to see Alison at the hospital, nothing else.'

'Why didn't you stop her?' Indah asks.

'Stop her?'

'You knew where Alison was going didn't you?'

'She didn't tell me.'

'Liar.' At a glance, Sophie might pass for late thirties, but they are close and in the glare from the overhead florescent lights Indah can see the fine lines on her face and neck. Indah reminds herself Sophie is late forties and smiles. These feelings are a surprise and for a moment wants to apologise, but doesn't. 'Did you know what would happen in the house?'

'How would I?'

'You know more than you're letting on.'

'Do you have to see Jenny again?' Sophie asks, changing the subject. 'Do you?'

'The two of you should make-up, not continue this crazy feud. I like her.'

'Top of your game, landing punches, but sticks and stones. Perhaps, you should give her my love, be the one to bring us together, when you see her again?'

'I won't be.' Indah is suddenly enjoying the banter, wanting to dominate the older woman. 'The Gov might,' Indah begins, 'she left a message for him, that she wants to see him.' '*Where did that come from?* Indah wonders. A lie, a stab and yes Sophie flinches. 'Now, I must go Sophie.'

'Did I catch you at the wrong time?'

'We've booked an interview, I'll see you then.'

'I've been obsessing about him. Do you think about him, imagine being under him or on top, or bent double over his desk, which is it?'

'In a graveyard actually, did he ever fuck you there under the stars?'

'I…'

'Maybe you need counselling,' Indah suggests and makes to move away, but Sophie steps in front of her. 'Let me pass.'

'In a rush?'

'I've work to do,' and glancing up and down the corridor Indah realises they are alone. Looking back at Sophie, she shudders, feels that it is some kind of warning, but cannot put a name to it. Her slate grey eyes are cunning, even malevolent. 'Get help Sophie,' and attempts to sidestep her, but the woman is quick and blocks the younger woman's way.

'Not so fast.' Sophie smiles. 'You want him?'

'I'm not talking about this now.'

'Abelard is still very sexy.'

'He's not Abelard, he's Cully, or the Gov, but he's not some character in a play.'

'I have plans.'

'Of course you do and you're worried I'm going to upset them?'

'I might be, but you'll not keep him long Indah. Are we competing?' Sophie laughs. 'You'll win the sprint, but not the marathon.'

'Whatever you say Sophie,' and Indah passes her this time without obstruction. 'At least, I'm not damaged goods,' she hisses walking on.

Indah is going to have to think, objectively and in cold blood about what she does next, but for the moment she needs to pee. Toilets are in the basement and after emptying her bladder Indah stands washing her hands. A door opens, there is movement behind her, something whips against the back of her legs and she screams, crumpling to the ground.

++++

After an excellent lunch and armed with John Carter's wife's address, they drive through town into an estate of small identical squashed-in semi-detached houses. There Tom and Pete find the address they want, introduce themselves and follow the woman through to a small neat living room. 'Why do you want John?'

'To eliminate him from our enquiries.'

'Really,' she laughs. 'What's he done?' A blonde woman in her forties, she is attractive, trim and well dressed. 'I'm not surprised. He can be a handful, but means well. He suffers from PTSD, that's what the shrink says after the roadside bomb. He's always been brittle, but the counselling helped.'

'Counselling?'

'Yes, he's positive about it. I haven't seen him so together for ages. He suddenly has purpose.'

'What sort of purpose?'

'Green issues for one.'

'Really?'

'He's been on protests, campaigned for natural sources of energy such as wind power, solar and so on to replace gas, oil and nuclear. That's why he went to the Island.'

'Island?'

'To live in the tree village, to help protect the forest and the village against the oil company. He's totally focussed, almost obsessed by it. I admire his zeal, I've started to care about him, love him again.'

'Is he still there?'

'I'm surprised you don't know,' she smiles. 'As far as I know he is.'

'Does he have any friends?'

'He's always been a loner, a bit secretive, but I always assumed it was because of the army. Soldiers keep it all inside, locked up, that's why we get lots of domestic problems. But the counselling helped a lot.'

'Do you remember who with?'

'No, sorry, a woman I think. He used to carry her book with him in an old rucksack.'

John Carter's wife gives them the most up to date photograph she has from three years before. 'Thank you,' says Pete. 'I, I mean we, really need to find him. Here's my card, get him to contact me please.'

'You are quiet, Pete,' says Tom once back in the car, driving out of town.

'Too many memories, most of them bad.'

'Sorry.'

'I've moved on. She wasn't what I expected.'

'Not the army base whore?'

'Exactly. We can still make the next ferry.'

'Not too fast, Pete,' begs Tom as they overtake a lorry. 'I'll ring the Gov, let him know we're on our way back.' Tom taps in a number. 'Gov, we've found Carter. He lives in the forest village. Would you believe he's been on the Island all the time? We're on our way back now.'

'So, how's the mainland been?'

'It's another planet,' Tom complains.

'Put me on speaker. Can you both hear me?'

'Yes Gov.'

'How reliable is the wife?'

'I believe her,' says Pete. 'She's got no reason to lie.'

'Right, we'll meet with you on the edge of the forest.'

'And Gov, John Carter had counselling with a woman, but the wife couldn't remember the name.'

'Sorry, I've got another call coming in. Sorry, you two, got to go, meet you by the forest,' and the phone goes dead.

Forty minutes later they drive into the ferry terminal.

'Home soon,' Tom declares.

Pete follows a line of cars on to the ferry.

'We're on board,' Tom says, opening his door to get out. 'Pete, come on.'

'One call.' Pete taps. 'Hi Indah, it's Pete,' he says on her voice mail. 'All good, but can you do me a favour?' He quickly explains what they have discovered. 'John Carter's wife is convinced he had psychological help after he left the army, can you look into it please?'

'We have to get out of the car, Pete,' Tom insists. 'They want us out.'

'We're the police,' Pete objects. 'Just a quick text.'

'Pete, please,' Tom pleads.

'Yes, of course, sorry.' Waves his apology to the ship's crew waiting to cast off and follows Tom up the stairway. 'Slow down.'

'Coffee?'

'Please and a rum.'

'We're on duty.'

'Tom, be a good lad.'

In the lounge overlooking the car deck, Pete watches as the ferry eases away from land and into the channel. There is a blue sky, the sea is calm and gulls cry as they follow the boat, or is it a ship? It is odd, because when he came over with Monica a few days before he felt a pang of regret leaving the mainland and yet now he is pleased to be going back. He remembers the text he was about to send when Tom hurried him.

Sorry Indah. About John's brother Michael. I'm wondering if he knew he's on the Island? I, we need to find him asap. Owe you. Pete.

++++

Sophie could understand why Cully is taken with Indah, stunningly beautiful, intelligent and feisty, yes he would enjoy her. He would fuck her, but it wouldn't last. Where did that leave her? She wanted him, but couldn't risk the pain of losing him again. Indah wasn't a problem, a passing phase, but Jenny, she is the problem. Why did she want to see Cully?

Parking high on the cliffs over-looking the sea Sophie sits and waits. She watches the car ferry getting closer before climbing out. The breeze brings salt off the sea and she licks her lips. Leaning back against the car, she looks around, but there is no one else about. She can wait as long as it takes, after all she's already waited thirty years.

'Jenny!'

The Jack Russell barks, pulls on his lead and Jenny tells him to be quiet.

'Sophie, what do you want?' she demands, swinging round, long blonde hair catching round her face in the breeze. 'Are you following me?'

'Of course not. We need to talk.'

'How did you know I'd be here?'

'Tash has always had a big mouth, like you.'

'What do you mean by that?'

'Did you really want him that badly?'

'What are you talking about?'

'Cully.'

'There's nothing to say.'

'You've asked to see him.'

'No I haven't.'

'I know you have.'

'The only person I've seen is DC Kasali.'

'But...' Sophie hesitates. 'The clever little bitch.'

'What?'

'Nothing. Something I'll deal with later.'

'Back then I obsessed on him, but I regret it now. I'm over him and have been for a long time and you should move on. Go home Sophie,' and Jenny turns away.

'Don't turn your back on me. You had plenty to say back then. What you said was poison and destroyed us.'

'For Christ's sake Sophie, forget it, it was thirty years ago, we were kids. We talked trash all the time, saying things that weren't true.'

'About Cully and Rachel.'

'I didn't start the story.'

'But you took it, embroidered it and threw it in, stood back and waited to see what happened. You got what you wanted didn't you? Broke Cully and me up and fucked him at the first chance you got.'

'What if I did?'

'I can see through your strategy now.' Gulls circle squealing overhead. 'Bitch!'

'Sophie, there was no strategy, I was a teenager playing stupid games.'

'You were so desperate to give him your cunt.'

'Yes we fucked. He took my virginity in a bloody bus shelter for Christ's sake. It was cold and uncomfortable for what it's worth. Not my finest moment.' Jenny pauses thoughtfully, angry, spiteful even, wanting to win. 'But after that we never stopped.'

'I don't believe you Jenny.'

'You poor cow Sophie.' Jenny grins. 'Cully and I had so much sex.'

'Liar.'

'He'd come in my cunt and my mouth.'

'Liar.'

'And once, blissfully painfully, up my arse.'

'Bitch. Liar.'

'Maybe I am. Did we or didn't we, you'll never know, because you can't trust a word that comes out of his mouth. Thirty years Sophie, let it go.' The wind caught her words, throwing them back in her face. 'I don't want anything to do with him, you can have him.'

'Why didn't you go to the event at the school?'

'Stop this, I'm not answering anymore stupid questions.'

'I need to know things.'

'Ah, but you've hardly fucked him have you?'

'I have, it was blissful, the weeks before that bloody "off to university party".'

'And that's it, the reason you hold on to this dream of being together with him?'

'There's something else that connects us.'

'What?'

'Something far more precious.' Sophie looks away over the sea. 'You wouldn't understand.'

'Why did you go to school event that night Sophie?' Demands Jenny, stepping closer to her. She is a little taller, threatening. 'Let me answer for you shall I?' She grins. 'You must have been devastated he didn't turn up to the event. You mentioned the word strategy. I bet you had a strategy that night. Play with your hair, giggle, touch him and let him touch you. He might have left with you, Heloise and Abelard walking into the sunset, how perfect. You'd take him home to fuck. You're so needy, you'd let him do anything he wanted to you.'

'Even when I wank I think of him,' Sophie mumbles.

'You poor cow Sophie. Now I'm going home, come on Paddy,' and the dog starts to pull on the lead, 'there's a good boy.'

'Wait Jenny.'

'What now?'

'At the party, you were all over him.'

'You were flirting with every guy there, including Cameron Davis.'

'He dumped you for me,' Sophie grins. 'Someone drugged me that night.'

'You're a crazy bitch.'

'Stop it!'

'Why, what are you going to do?' Jenny leans closer. 'Pathetic bitch.'

Sophie slaps her. Jenny screams and there is a sudden laceration, blood coursing through her eyebrow, dripping down her face and to the ground in large drops.

++++

'Indah, what's happened to you?' She steps back, allowing Cully to enter. 'Indah?'

'I was assaulted.' He helps her to the couch and sits next to her. 'Thank you,' and kisses him, whispering, 'Adam's here.'

'What happened?' Cully asks, his face creased with concern and gently pushes hair back from her face. She smiles briefly, but cannot hold the look. 'You're in pain.'

'Only my legs and knees.'

'What can I get you?'

'Cognac and cuddles please, lots of both,' and lays her head against his shoulder. 'I'm so pleased you're here.'

'Here we go,' announces Adam appearing from the direction of the kitchen carrying three well filled glasses. 'I'm just sorry I didn't catch the woman.'

'Woman?'

'I think it was Sophie,' sighs Indah taking a glass and drinking. 'I didn't actually see her, she attacked me from behind. The warrants were turned down and then she and I had an argument in the corridor.'

'What about?'

'About you,' she manages a warm smile that reaches her dark brown eyes. 'We both said things we shouldn't have. My fault, I behaved unprofessionally. She must have followed me into the loo.'

'A woman ran by me,' says Adam, 'but I didn't think anything of it. Then I heard poor Indah shouting and went in to find her curled up on the floor.'

Indah sips her cognac. 'That's what they teach us on basic training to curl up to protect vital organs,' she explains, reaching out and taking Cully's hand. 'She was whipping me with a soaking rolled up towel, very school bully and it stung like hell.'

'My poor girl,' Cully grimaces at the thought of it. 'I'll get Sophie arrested immediately,' he says indignantly, standing. 'Bloody woman!'

'No please Cully, I don't want people to know.' She's alarmed. 'I feel such a fool and it's really nothing, mostly shock and my fault, I provoked her.'

'We can't let her get away with this,' Cully says softly. 'Adam, will you do a statement?'

'Of course.'

'Cully, it won't look good for you, she'll stir things even more.'

'Let her, I don't care about me,' and he sits back down.

'You should,' she says.

'And he's used to it,' Adam cuts in, chuckling, 'women fighting over him and I've never liked Sophie. She caused you so much heart ache.'

'It was thirty years ago,' Cully protests.

'Even so, refusing to see you after you saved her life, for Christ's sake, it wasn't on, bloody woman.'

'Adam.'

'Sorry, but it's true.' He finishes his cognac, reaches down to the bottle, refills them all. 'I'm so pleased he's found you Indah, he needs to settle down.'

'Adam, we only just...'

'I know, I know, but an old man can hope.'

Indah laughs, a light musical sound.

'You two are so alike,' she tells them, 'and Adam, sometimes you just know don't you?'

'Yes,' he nods, settling back in the chair.

'Tell me about Cully when he was a boy, please,' urges Indah.

'It'll be a pleasure and then I'll cook lunch, soup?'

'Perfect. Adam brought a box full of vegetables,' she explains. 'It was such a wonderful day and then bloody Sophie,' she sobs. 'I haven't replied to Pete's voice mail or text,' says Indah,' or continued to chase up on Michael Carter.'

'Not surprising,' says Cully, taking a drink from his cognac. 'What did Pete want?'

'He's desperate to find John Carter?'

'Desperate,' wonders Cully aloud. 'Indah, take the day off. I'll deal with Pete.'

'What will you tell him?'

'That you've been assaulted.'

'But Cully...'

'He's right, my dear, it's the game you're in.'

'Game?'

'You are police officers and cannot allow anyone to assault you, let alone that woman.' Adam loosens his tie. 'You can't let this go and you need feeding, I'll make soup,' and he's gone into the kitchen. 'Apron?'

'Behind the door,' Indah calls back, grinning. She slides along the couch, cuddling into Cully. 'Stay and look after me.'

'You know I can't, but about us, I'm worried what people might say about you.'

'I don't care.'

'You should, you've got your whole career in front of you.'

'But have I got you in front of me?'

'Of course'

Cully's phone rings.

'Yes, what is it?'

++++

'We should wait for backup.'

'All we're doing is seeing if he's still there,' says Pete.

'Even so, if he's our shooter, he's bloody dangerous. Anyway the light is fading. We should wait.'

'Ok,' and Pete reluctantly pulls into a layby before the entrance to the forest.

Twenty minutes later Lisa stops her car behind them followed by two vans with armed police and dog team. Tom and Pete get out and walk back to meet her. She tells them, she will go in alone to explain to the forest-dwellers why they are there. 'Cully says the Healer is the leader.'

'Where is he?' Tom asks.

'Alison Grey walked out of hospital. He's on his way.'

'Typical Gov,' Pete grins, 'sorting out the women. We wait for him?'

Lisa hesitates. At the rental house, Tuesday evening she'd failed to act, to be decisive and the Gov had reminded her that she was the senior officer on scene as she is now. 'We go in.'

'The Gov'll miss the excitement,' Pete comments.

'We don't want excitement,' states Lisa. 'I'm going in first.'

'Ma'am you shouldn't go in alone,' says Pete, 'Carter might be there.'

'I don't want a riot.'

'I get that, but I'm coming with you.'

'I love this place. Mary and I come to the café for coffee and chocolate brownies.' They walk along the track leading to the village. The word WELCOME is carved into an imposing sign above the entrance. There is music, the sound of children's laughter, the smell of wood smoke and a heady whiff of cannabis. 'We took the children on the tree top walk. It's enchanting. That's why I don't want to upset the residents.'

'At least, there won't be any oil drilling now,' says Pete.

'There won't?'

'Not after this morning. With Ballard dead, there was no one to represent the oil company in court and my mate Judge Le Strange granted an injunction in favour of village residents and supporters. It's all over the local news.'

'That gives us another motive,' Lisa says thoughtfully.

'Can I help?' a woman emerges from the first in a horseshoe of huts. There is one selling clothes, one where a potter can be seen at work, another with metal sculptures outside, a plant stall and a place selling handmade jewellery. 'Police?'

'You must be the Healer?'

'Cully sent you.'

'How did you know?'

'It's in the stones. This is not a good place for you.'

'What do you mean?'

'It's dangerous.'

'Are you threatening us?'

'Of course not,' she smiles. 'We don't want trouble.'

'Nor do we. This isn't a raid. We want to speak to one person and only one.'

'You've got guns.'

'So, has he. He's a person of interest in the school shootings. John Carter, is he here?'

'I've not seen him today, but his place is up there,' and she points into the tree canopy. 'I hope you don't mind heights.'

Lisa calls in armed officers.

'Sergeant Tizard, up there.' She points to where a lattice of rope ladders and walkways lead to several tree houses. 'His is the highest one. Apparently, he built it to be out of the way.'

'You can't expect us...'

'I thought you were action man.'

During the coming half-hour, Lisa watches with amusement as Tizard and his men struggle to climb up to the platforms. She stands in a pool of dappled light. Birds sing and she wishes she were there for some other reason. The Healer stands with her, explains that that evening there is to a party to celebrate the court decision. 'You should come.'

'I might do that.'

The light is fading and Tizard moves cautiously ahead of his team along walkways connecting platforms that wobble with each footfall, towards the house. Heads appear from windows and doorways before being told to get back. Reaching the tree house identified by the Healer they shout a warning before going in. 'Empty,' Tizard shouts minutes later.

'The dog won't go up there,' calls the handler. 'Sorry Ma'am. He's old and not good with heights.'

'Search down here then.'

A while later Tizard appears on the ground, walking over to where Lisa is standing. 'The place is clear.'

'Sure?'

'Doubt me?'

'Absolutely.'

'I want to sec Mary and thc kids.'

'I'd speak to your solicitor if I were you.'

'Bitch!'

'Whatever,' Lisa shrugs. 'IA want to see you. If you were a goose, I'd say you were cooked, now get out of my way. Tom, we've done what we can, we wait until morning to continue the search, it's too dangerous in the dark.'

++++

'Alison, it's good to see you.' He sits on the bench beside her. The oil drum has been removed from the community garden behind the church, but there is still police tape surrounding the patch where Vicar Mandy was digging. Street lights illuminate the place and opposite there is a row of terraced houses with small front gardens. It is on the way to where Alison used to live. 'Can't believe this place is still here,' says Cully.

'I liked you walking me home especially as it was out of your way.'

'The four of us, you, Jenny, Sean and me.'

'Why did you never try anything?'

'Didn't want to make a fool of myself and you were way out of my league.'

'Stupid boy,' she laughs. 'How did you know I'd be here?'

'The hospital rang, said you'd walked out against advice. You got a taxi and I rang the company. I rang my spy over there in the house with the gnomes.'

'Ah, I saw the curtains move. I remember,' she smiles. 'Is it the same man?'

'It is. We interviewed him during the house to house. He's still got the gnome I broke, glued together.'

'Oh my God, he remembers you?'

'He's fine.'

'You threatened him, told him not to peep at me again or you'd smash another gnome. Always the hero Cully.'

'You're bleeding. I've called the ambulance.'

'I won't go back.' She touches the place, stares at the spreading stain. 'I want to die.'

'I'll get you sectioned if necessary.'

'God, power mad Cully. You know don't you?'

'I made some phone calls.'

'Of course you did.'

'You were pregnant,' he says softly.

'We, Carla and I, found a clinic in Copenhagen and chose a sperm donor from a catalogue. The doctor used what looked like a turkey baster to impregnate me. I got pregnant. I lost him. It was our fault.'

'Why?'

'Carla and I were living together, I thought happily. We had a plan to have a baby, or at least I thought we had a plan. It was the same day I discovered I was pregnant that she told me she didn't want a family with me. She walked out that night.'

'Ali,' Cully begins softly, reaching to take her hand. 'I'm so sorry.'

'Carla,' she squeezes his fingers, 'invited me to the launch of her first lingerie range.'

'You went?'

'I thought…I don't know what I thought. I was twenty weeks pregnant.'

'Carla came over to me, smiling. I told her it was our baby and she told me she didn't want it. She told me I could keep it or get rid of it. We argued and I ran out. I'd drunk too much, crashed the car and lost the baby. I couldn't have more children.'

'You must have hated her?'

'I've wanted her dead for a long time. She killed our baby.'

'You shouldn't have come, should have remained away. I've read Indah's report of your interview with her. Your husband, told us you are still in a gay relationship with Carla, but that's not true?'

'I've let him think that, but I've not seen her in twenty years.'

'You married him, a man?'

'I did, I really don't know why. Self-loathing, punishing myself. Every time he stuck his cock in me, I told myself I deserved it. I don't go to Nasty Gang parties. I wouldn't, I was in your gang Cully, the Nice Gang. Stupid childish names,' and she squeezes his hand hard. 'Sorry. Anyway, I go to my sister's. She said she rang the police?'

'She spoke with DI Lynn and told her that you went to stay with her when Frank thought you were at one of the Nasty Gang parties. You and she are close?'

'Yes.'

'She's never married?'

'No and she's not gay and we're not in an incestuous relationship.'

'Wow! That is some jump Ali.'

'This is the Island, people jump to conclusions and I try to pre-empt them. I hadn't had sex with a woman in nearly ten years until the other night.'

'If you hated her, why go there, why dress the way you did, have sex with her, unless…' A siren is fast approaching. 'Jesus Ali, you wanted to die with her, didn't you? You knew what was going to happen at the house.'

'Even after thirty years Sophie only thinks of you Cully and I dreamed of having sex with Carla one more time. Love and hate, either side of the same coin don't you think?'

'Did Sophie know what you were doing? She stopped Indah following you? Is she part of this conspiracy?'

'There is no conspiracy, just coincidence.'

'There's no such thing as coincidence. Was it John Carter that shot Carla?'

'I didn't see.'

'I bet he didn't expect you to be there. You getting hit was a mistake.'

'No comment. Here's my ride,' she tries to stand, but collapses into his arms as the paramedics reach her.

++++

Tom stands in front of Lisa, impatiently moving from one foot to the other, beaming. 'A quick look, Ma'am, please, I've got a torch?'

'She's right,' the Healer says stepping forward. 'You're expecting a baby.'

'How do you know that? We've only just…'

'But it's you that's at risk. Don't go up there,' but Tom ignores her, walking towards the ladder. 'Don't go.'

'Tom, wait,' Lisa shouts. 'Slow down.'

'It's fine, Ma'am, please I can do this.'

'Take care and take an armed officer.' Lisa relents nervously. 'Pete, ask around to see if anyone down here knows anything.'

Lisa looks up, watching distant lights in the shadowy forest canopy.

'This is amazing,' Tom declares, moving quickly along a walkway. 'What do think Ted?'

'Crazy people,' he wheezes, out of breath. 'Why would you want to live up here?'

'Didn't you have a tree house as a kid?'

'No, I hate heights.'

'I'm going to build one for my Toby.'

In the hut, there are shelves covered with cooking pans and utensils, tins of food, a few books and lots of paper. Ted stands in the doorway, holding his rifle nervously across his body while Tom begins to sift through a box of documents with light from his torch. There are diagrams of the school, typed sheets detailing the attack and a programme for that night's event. He finds a bodycam and a laptop computer and holding them tightly suggests they go back down.

'Thank Christ for that,' moans Ted.

There is a sudden creaking above, branches fall followed by a body that roles in the darkness. Upright the figure charges towards Ted, throwing him backwards out of the door and over the edge of the platform.

Tom moves forward, raising his torch beam to look at the face. A man with a tightly cropped blond head and a shot gun swinging wildly stares back. He fires once, twice and goes out the door, along the walkway before vanishing downwards.

Children scream as the man swings to the ground.

'Carter, armed police,' Pete shouts, 'put the gun down.'

'Go to hell.' Raising the shotgun he fires, but it's high and wide. Pete returns fire, but Carter is away, running into the trees with Pete chasing and repeatedly firing.

'Tom?' shouts Lisa. People are shouting. 'Tom?'

++++

'Suicide?' Becky wonders.

'We've found the dog over here,' calls a uniformed officer from amongst the rocks at the base of the cliff. 'Not pretty, I'm afraid.'

'Any identification?' Monica asks.

'Nothing in her pockets and no bag,' says Becky. She is trying to disassociate—isn't that what they call it?—but she is struggling as her hands travel over the mangled corpse.

'There's a disc on the collar,' and the officer brings it over to them. 'We've had people fall of the cliff before, one or two a year. The edge crumbles easily.'

'So maybe she was chasing her dog and they both go over,' Becky suggests.

'Where is SOCO?' Monica sighs. 'How long before the tide comes in?'

'Two hours before it reaches the body I'd say.'

'What does the disc say?'

'Paddy lives at this post code,' and he writes it down. 'What do you want to do?'

'DC Shaw and I will visit Paddy's address. I'd like you to stay with the body until SOCO arrives and make certain her body is removed to the mortuary before the tide comes in.'

'What about the dog?'

'Bag it.'

The two women take the steep path up to the top of the cliff. 'I wonder what she was thinking when falling?' asks Becky.

'Really?'

'Just wondering. You know how when you stand at the edge of a high building, you get tempted to jump.'

'No I don't, I never stand at the edge of anything tall. I hate heights.'

'You suffer from vertigo Monica?'

'I suppose,' she sighs. 'The address is only a few minutes away. I suggest we leave the car here and walk. It'll clear our heads.'

'Do we need to?'

'You realise there might be a husband or a family member at Paddy's address Becky. Have you ever done a death notification visit?'

'No in truth, I've not seen a dead body before, close-up that is. I saw the ones at the school hall and under sheets at the mortuary, but they were well away and it was like a film or on TV, unreal.'

'You should spend some time with traffic, that'll get you used to it. I'll lead if there is someone at the house.'

'You've done this before?'

'Too many times.'

The house sits snugly in a cluster of buildings overlooking the sea about a mile away from where the body lay on the rocks waiting to be photographed and removed. The front garden is neat and colourful. There are lights on. At the front door, Monica knocks and they wait.

'No one in. Maybe she lived alone,' Becky suggests, feeling relieved, trying not to run.

'I can hear someone coming,' says Monica. 'You'll be fine Becky. I'll get you into an autopsy next.'

'Shut up!'

The door opens slowly.

'Yes,' the woman yawns. She appears to have been asleep. 'What do you want?'

'I'm DS Aries and this is DC Shaw.'

'Police again?'

'Again?'

'A DC Kasali was here at the weekend to talk to Jenny and me about what happened at the school.'

'You are?'

'Tash Brown.'

'You've broken your foot?'

'Ankle, during the shooting. Surely you know all this.'

'It's not about that.'

'Not forest-dwellers, bloody people, the sooner they're cleared out the forest the better. That woman deserved to get shot.'

'Which woman?'

'The healer woman. A load of nonsense.'

'Ms Brown, does Paddy live here?'

'Yes he's Jenny's dog. She's out walking him now, but she's been much longer than usual.' She's suddenly alarmed. 'Has something happened?'

'Could we come in please?'

'What's happened?'

'We need to come in, please.'

An hour later Becky sits in the passenger seat of the police car staring out to sea admiring the way Monica had dealt with Tash, empathy and firmness combined. She'd sat with Chapman's wife at the hospital after the woman had identified the body of her husband, but hardly saying a word. She'd so much to learn. Tash Brown listened calmly, before bursting into tears. Monica moves to sit next to her, places an arm round her shoulders, consoles her, and explains there would be a need for a formal identification, but that could wait until tomorrow. In the meantime could Tash contact Jenny's daughters or did she want her to do it? No, she would do it right away.

SOCO arrives in the car park and goes down to do what they do. Then with the help of a team from Cliff Rescue haul the body up from the beach using an a-frame winch and ropes, just ahead of the fast encroaching tide. Becky admires the skill of it all. She needs a drink, a large glass of wine. Shit! She's forgotten about Tom. It had been over the police radio. He could be dead. No, he mustn't be. She wanted this, real police work. A couple of days back she'd been happy arriving at the yacht club, being allowed to do something beyond goffering for the team, but maybe she wasn't cut out for it? More than one glass of wine and sex, she needed sex. Not love making, but hard fucking. There had been no one for eighteen months. She had offers, but not from anyone she wants.

'What's up?'

'Sorry, miles away.' She'd not noticed Monica climb into the car beside her. 'I was useless there. You were brilliant.'

'No you weren't. Stop doubting yourself. You've had more experience in a few days than most get in years. You'll be good.'

'I hope so.' Becky dreads the fact the investigation is coming to an end, that the team would be breaking-up. There is a rumour Cully might be coming across as Superintendent in charge and that might give her a chance of moving up into CID. She is new and normally would not stand a chance, but no one wanted to work in the Island CID after the scandal and sackings and if she kept in Cully's good book then why not? She wonders what she might have to do to keep in that book? A blacked out mortuary van appears and takes the body away. Becky watches in the rear view mirror as the constable puts a bag with the dog in the boot.

'Shall I ring the DI?' Becky asks.

'She'll call when there's something to say.'

'We need to tell Cully about this, don't we?'

'Later. He's got enough on his plate as it is.'

'I feel so helpless,' Becky sighs and wipes away a tear. 'What do we do with the dog?'

'Burn it.'

++++

Cully reaches the village clearing as paramedics work on Ted. Briefly he asks two of the large male forest dwellers to encourage people back, to give them space, but Cully does not need telling the police officer is dead. 'Lisa!'

'Gov,' she stumbles over to him. 'I'm not up to this.'

'That makes two of us, but we are here and have to get things done.'

'This is my fault. I let Tom go up there.'

'No it's not, I should have been here.'

'As well as all this, we've lost Indah.'

'She's been assaulted. Not badly, shocked mostly. I've asked for CCTV. I think it was Sophie.'

'Jesus, Gov, what's happening?'

'Where's Tom?'

'Up there,' and she points towards the tree canopy.

Climbing slowly upwards, crossing a walkway, Cully sees men holding lanterns, people bent over a body and his heart sinks. The Healer stands back to allow paramedics to take over. The first thing Cully notices is the amount of blood smeared across her front. She is ashen and exhausted. Seeing him, she shrugs, tears running over smeared cheeks and retreats into the darkness. He edges forward, enters the house, notices the moon through the hole in the roof, lifts Tom's abandoned torch and briefly searches the place. Slipping the things he wants into a canvas bag he carefully returns to the ground where he finds Pete sitting forlornly on a log. 'My fault, Gov, I should have remained with him.'

'No one's fault, Pete. You thought it was clear. Ted was with him.'

'How is he?'

'Dead I think. Tom is being worked on.'

'The Healer took control. She's something else. What if Tom dies?'

'He won't. Where do you think Carter was hiding?'

'On the roof.'

'The dogs?'

'Useless.'

'Gov,' begins Chalky, appearing through the trees. 'It looks like he made his escape on a motorbike.'

'Damn. We had that report on the night of the school shooting, of a motorbike speeding away on the lower road. Maybe it was Carter. Pete, you shot him?'

'Twice I think, as he was running away. There is a blood trail. I should have killed him, wanted to. I emptied the clip.'

'You'll get your chance,' Cully says placing his arm round his shoulders. 'Pete, are you up to working?' He nods. 'Then the crime scene belongs to you and Chalky.' He tells them. 'But I need your gun Pete, IA will want it.'

There is sudden silence and looking up they see a stretcher being lowered on ropes towards the ground. A gentle breeze rustles the trees and a low humming begins as the forest-dwellers gather, many carrying burning torches, forming a semi-circle. Cully feels something touch him deep down inside and Chalky mutters something about magic. The police officers join the semi-circle, allowing the stretcher to land before several step forward to carry it to the ambulance.

'Jesus, Gov what was that about?' asks Pete.

'Forget Jesus, Pete, feel the power of the forest.'

'Seriously, Gov?'

'Don't you start,' Cully tells him.

'Amen,' says Chalky.

Cully hitches a lift in the ambulance transporting Tom to the hospital where he is rushed into resus. Cully is told to wait outside. Seconds later the wheeled stretcher carrying Ted goes the same way.

++++

Standing in A & E Cully rings the Incident Room.

'Monica?'

'Gov, we know, it was on the police radio and Chalky rang. Becky and I have just got back and I need to brief you.'

'Later please.'

'Sure. How is he?'

'Not good.'

'Lisa?'

'Gone over to see Tom's wife Trudi and get her into the hospital.' He goes on to explain about Indah. 'Ted's wife is here, I've spoken to her. Sorry, I've got to go.' Another call. 'Linda, that you?'

'Hi, Dad, I've been following things on police radio. It sounds horrendous.'

'I need your help.' Cully tells her what has happened. 'Can you get here? I'm worried about Pete. The IA people will swarm all over him and I know no better Union Rep' than you.' He listens. 'Great, fend them off at least until tomorrow. See you soon, love you.'

Why did he send Tom to the mainland? Pete could have gone on his own. Don't be absurd, it was routine. It was Tizard, he'd failed to clear things properly. Fuck! Tom had little Toby and apparently Trudi is pregnant and is about to become a widowed single mum. No, stop projecting. It's going to be ok. 'Isn't it?'

'What?'

'Where did you come from?'

'My shift just finished. You look lost,' says Mary.

'I'm totally lost,' Cully admits.

'Can I give you a lift somewhere?'

'Anywhere.'

'Sorry, the car's a mess.' She takes toys, empty coffee cups and chocolate wrappers off the front passenger seat and throws it all into the back. She takes a perfume bottle and sprays the inside of the car and herself. 'My house isn't much tidier, but Lisa keeps a tidy place. You must think I'm a slut. Perhaps I should be. You want to go somewhere particular?'

'Somewhere quiet.'

'I know exactly the place,' and she drives. 'Worried about your friend?'

'Much more worried about Tom, but also concerned about Ali. Crazy, I hadn't seen her in nearly thirty years, but she wants to die and I don't know how to help.'

'Maybe you can't.'

‘She’s also a suspect,’ and Cully explains the emerging conspiracy theory.

‘You’ve spoken to Ted’s wife?’ Mary asks.

‘You know her?’

‘It’s the Island, everyone knows everyone else and most of us are related anyway,’ she laughs. ‘You and I probably are, way back.’

‘You said you wanted to speak to me about your husband?’

‘I’ll come in and make a statement. I can bury him.’

‘I’ll attend the funeral,’ he smiles in the darkness. ‘Internal Affairs will want to speak to you,’ he adds. Then realises where they have got to, high up overlooking the channel, mainland lights twinkling in the distance. ‘I know this place, we used to come here and…do stuff.’

‘So did I,’ Mary admits. ‘Everyone does. Tell me Cully, do you want to do stuff with me?’

‘I…’ and for a moment Cully is tempted, it’s a long while since he’s had sex in a car, but smiles in the darkness when he thinks of Indah. ‘Not tonight, but talking would be good.’

An hour later his phone rings and taking it from his jacket pocket Mary gives it to him. He listens. ‘Sorry Mary, I have to go.’

Friday

Cully is dropped at the hospital by Mary, arriving he finds Chalky and Pete smoking under the canopy at the entrance and Indah sitting silently in the waiting area.

'I let you sleep,' Cully explains as Indah lifts her head off his shoulder an hour later, a line of dribble leaving a trail over his jacket lapel. 'You've been dreaming. You make little whimpers. It's cute,' he smiles and wants to kiss her, but resists.

'What time is it?'

'Nearly three.'

'Sorry I rang you.'

'I'm glad you did, you dragged me back. I was lost.'

'Where were you?' she asks removing a sweet rapper from his hair, but before he could answer she remembers. 'Oh God, I know why we're here.' She sits upright. 'Any news?'

'He's back in theatre. They didn't get all the shot, first time round.'

'But they have scanners,' Indah shouts. 'They shouldn't make mistakes. It's bad isn't it?'

'The surgical team are good here.'

'It's been two hours. A long time for them to be operating isn't it?'

'Try not to worry.'

'Easy to say.'

'Importantly, how are you?'

'Legs are stiff, ache a bit, but otherwise I'm fine. Adam makes delicious comforting soup and I got some sleep. Where is everybody?'

'I sent Chalky back to the incident room. Monica and Becky were called out on a job late yesterday afternoon. Lisa and Pete are in the canteen.'

'What job?'

'An accident'

'Didn't you want to join the others in the canteen?'

'I had what I wanted asleep on my shoulder.'

'You're lovely darling and now you're making noises. Your tummy,' she lays her hand there, 'is rumbling. Let's find them and get some food.'

They board the lift to the third floor and embrace, breaking apart when the doors slide open. They find Lisa and Pete pushing food around their plates.

'Not really hungry,' Pete admits. 'Thanks again, Gov, for Linda. She got here in time to keep the dogs away. Interview tomorrow at Headquarters.'

'They didn't stay?'

'Didn't fancy it. Desperate to get back to the mainland. Linda is a fearsome union rep. She'll be there tomorrow. She'd make a great lawyer.'

'Lawyer?'

'She's doing her degree, I thought…'

'Certainly, be safer than this bloody job,' Lisa exclaims. 'Anyone seen my sister?'

'She went off duty,' says Cully. 'I gave your gun to IA.' Pete nods. 'It's just procedure,' he reassures him. 'As is the interview with Internal Affairs. Where is Linda?'

'Curled up on the couch over there,' answers Lisa. 'Let her sleep Cully.'

'Tea or coffee anyone?'

'Black coffee all round please, Gov,' says Pete. 'We've got CCTV footage of Carter getting on a ferry and getting off the other side. He's a tough bastard, he's wounded, but keeps going, a real soldier.'

'You admire him, Pete?' asks Indah.

'No, but respect his tenacity.'

'He's heading for the horsebox hospital,' Indah suggests, 'like Turner.'

Time goes by, hardly speaking, sipping at cooling coffee. Pete gets up, announces he's going for a walk, refusing Cully's offer of company. Lisa says she's going to ring Mary.

'Is Pete alright?' Indah asks, the two of them alone.

'He will be.'

Cully's phone rings.

'Hi Monica?' He listens. 'Are you sure? No sorry, there is no news on Tom. We're still waiting, but I'll let you know directly there is something.'

'What's happened?' Indah demands.

'We'll discuss it later.'

'No.' Indah sits upright, glaring at him. 'What's happened?' He hesitates. 'Cully?'

'Jenny Sykes is dead. She was walking her dog and fell over the cliff, possibly chasing the animal. I need to get to the incident room.'

'I'll drive you.'

'Do you mind if I ask Linda?'

'No,' Indah pouts, but only for a moment. 'Understood,' she smiles and he feels her hand squeeze his thigh.

'You go home,' he tells her.

'Come to me later. Whatever time you want. Here's a spare key,' and she slips it into his jacket top-pocket. 'I had it cut just in case.'

Cully gets up, walking over to where his daughter is lying full length on a couch. He stares at her, marvelling at how peaceful she appears. She stirs, blinks and smiles. 'Dad?'

'Thank you for supporting Pete.'

'I've always liked him and he did save my life remember?'

'How could I forget?' Because he never does. It wasn't something MIU would normally be involved with, but Sylvia asked Cully to supply some bodies so he, Pete and a couple of others joined the other elements that made up the task force. The operation had gone well with eight arrests and a dozen trafficked women removed to a safe place for processing by Monica. There had been guns and drugs seized and he remembers Claudia being there. Pete and Tizard brought the Albanian gang leader back to the station.

'Dad!'

'Sorry.'

'What's happening?'

'I've got to go back, there's been a death, probably accidental, but I need to be there. Would you drive me?'

'Of course. Tell me about the stunning black girl? You obviously fancy her.' Linda swings her legs off the couch, stands and stretches. 'There you go, hardly a twinge,' but sits back down.

'Linda!'

'It's cramp, nothing more.' Linda nods towards Indah. 'She's lovely.' She stares at him. 'Oh my God, you've fucked her already.'

'Shhh.'

'She's a junior officer, but then so was Amelia,' Linda whispers, smiling.

‘You’ll be my union rep please?’

‘Of course, Daddy,’ she smirks. ‘It’ll be fun having a young stepmother.’

‘Stepmother? No. I thought you were trying to get me back with Amelia?’

‘I’m trying to get you with somebody, anybody. Introduce me.’

‘Walk with me,’ he helps her up. ‘You ok?’

‘The pain comes and goes, but I’m fine. Good to be on your arm though. Perfume, I can smell it on you. It’s “Forest Glade”, I like it. Have you two done it here in the hospital tonight?’

‘No! I’m so proud of you,’ he smiles.

‘And I need to confess something anyway. I’ll tell you when we’re driving.’

‘Indah, this is Linda.’

‘Hi, great to meet, well not under these circumstances. Ah, here’s the doctor.’

‘Tom is out of surgery,’ she announces. ‘We didn’t want to leave any iron in there did we? But,’ she pauses, ‘he is in a coma and remains critical.’

++++

The fire burns bright, flames reaching high into the night sky.

‘You alright constable?’ Pete asks.

‘It’s all a bit weird, if you ask me.’ Reflections from the fire play across his face. He sits on the veranda of John Carter’s tree house, automatic rifle across his knees. Yellow police tape flutters in the gentle breeze and somewhere close by a police radio chatters. ‘But Carter’s gone right?’

‘Yes.’ Pete tells him about what the CCTV on the ferry has recorded. ‘He’s wounded, probably dead in a ditch. Sorry about Ted.’

‘He was a good bloke.’

‘Where’s your partner?’

‘In the car. Thought it better we split, just in case.’

‘Wise.’

Pete looks out at the scene thirty metres below. Around the blaze sit at least fifty forest dwellers, men, women and children. The healer walks amongst them, exchanging a few words with each adult, stroking the hair of the occasional child, halting before a woman and two children. In the firelight, Pete recognises them, they witnessed the shooting and he remembers the heart wrenching screams of the youngest child. ‘They’ve not disturbed you or the scene?’

‘No. Been nice, brought tea and chocolate cake.’

'You're not feeling strange, light-headed?'

'No, why?'

'Thought they might have put some extra ingredient in the cake.'

'Shit! You don't think…?'

'No, relax. I'll take a walk around.'

An urban dweller all his life, Pete could not remember even being in a forest at night. It unnerved him, but strangely pleased him. He climbs down to the ground. The dark sky is full of stars and mixed in with the smell of wood smoke and cannabis is a scent he assumes comes from the trees, bushes and plants that surrounded him. He'd wandered well away from the clearing and turning met a wall of shadowy undergrowth. For a moment, he feels panic, even reaches to where his Glock should have been, but AI have taken it as they always did when an officer fires his or her weapon. 'Don't be stupid,' he mutters aloud.

'No, don't be, walk towards my voice.' The voice is calm, authoritative and he knew it instantly and there she is, smiling, large eyes bright in the gloom. 'Pete what are you doing here?' In truth he isn't quite certain. 'Wanted to check on the officers,' he lies.

'We're not going to hurt them, this isn't "Wicker Man".'

'I didn't think you were, but that is a good film and it was a policeman they sacrificed.'

'Edward Woodward,' she says. 'I enjoyed it.'

'You did, I thought…'

'What, that it would offend me? I saw it years before I was fully aware of my powers and many years after it was made. I'm not that old.'

'I didn't think you were,' he smiles. 'Do you mind me being here?'

'No, why should I, the forest belongs to everyone, that's the point.'

'But you're burning trees?'

'You should arrest us for murder shouldn't you?' she laughs. 'We coppice the forest and burn the stuff we remove. It helps the forest, we care for it.'

'Right, of course, sorry.' He hesitates. Loud joyous singing has begun in the distance. 'I thought you might blame us, the police for what's happened.'

'I don't blame.'

'What's happening?'

'A simple ceremony to appease the trees,' she states, but sees the look on his face. 'To help us all relax and move on. Come and join us,' and she leads the way back.

'Will they be ok?' He nods towards where the mother has her arms around her two children as they sit either side of her. 'I can't get the scream out my head.'

'By the way, the kids scoffed the barbecue we had earlier I'd say they were getting over it already.'

'Barbecue?'

'There's plenty left if you're hungry, Pete,' she laughs. 'Ah, you thought we eat bowels of stewed plants we collect from the forest floor and lichen we scrape from the trunks of trees. Some here are vegetarians, but a lot of us enjoy steak and sausages. How about you?'

'Yes, I do.'

'Why are you really here, Pete?'

It's the way she said his name, softly that touched him somewhere, he did not know even existed.

'I wanted to thank you,' Pete says.

'What for?'

'Treating Tom, keeping him alive.'

'I'm not sure I did that, but thank you.' She takes his hand in hers. 'You are very troubled, Pete, I can feel it. What have you done?'

'Nothing I can talk about,' he shakes his head. 'I can't go on calling you Healer, what's your real name?'

'Real name?'

'Sorry, I'm stupid.'

'No, you're not.' She reaches out her other hand and brushes his cheek. 'Samantha was my birth name.'

'Oh.'

'You expected something more whimsical, like Primrose or Willow?'

'I'm not sure what I expected, but I like Samantha. I like you a lot, I mean…'

++++

Cully lets himself in using the key Indah has given him. It is five o'clock in the morning and he is carrying the bag containing the bodycam and laptop he took from the tree house not wanting to risk leaving it in the car, but places it by the front door to take away later.

Indah has left lights on and a trail of clothes for him to follow up the stairs where her lace pants hang on a door handle. He undresses on the landing and quietly slips in. The room is in darkness and he hears the sound of rhymical breathing.

Trying not to wake her he climbs carefully into bed, but she is suddenly there, reaching for him with clever fingers, her head disappearing beneath the covers and he is in her mouth. The feelings are exquisite and for a moment he thinks he's going to orgasm, but laughs aloud as he remembers the World Cup winners mantra he'd used as a teenager to keep from coming, Argentina, Uruguay, Uruguay, Argentina, West Germany, but then her mouth is climbing and he is no longer in a bus shelter with Jenny or against a wall with Sophie. He's with Indah and this is grown up love making, kissing her, rolling over so he's on top and inside her and she is shouting something wonderfully obscene.

As Indah sleeps against him he recalls the conversation with Linda in the car as she drove him from the hospital to the incident room. 'You did what?'

'Amelia was with me.'

'She should have known better.'

'Dad, I'm not a child.'

'But…'

'Dad, you can't teach me anything about being careful.'

'Especially since you stopped listening,' immediately regretting it. 'Sorry, stupid thing to say. Sorry.'

'Apology accepted. You're stressed.'

Cully looks out of the window at the passing darkness listening to his daughter explaining she had taken the custody suit shooting files from the archives as well as the ones on Poulson. She explains about the trip back to the scene of his and her shooting and the report she and Amelia had written for IA and which Sylvia had signed off on.

'Anyone else get involved?' he asks.

'Stop being stupid,' she snaps pulling into the church car park beside the portacabin. 'Jesus, Dad, was that your idea?'

'They hate it, I know it was a bad one,' he sighs. 'Sorry, I'm too protective and thank you for everything you're doing to help. Anything about Poulson?'

'Nothing significant, but there's a short witness statement in the file from a woman, saying she saw a car parked outside the church with two men in it, one of them had blond hair. She couldn't give a registration or make of car. Want my advice, Dad?'

'I do.'

'Go and see Indah and let her fuck your brains out.'

'What time is it?' Indah asks sleepily.

'Nearly six,' he tells her, kissing the top of her head and breathing in her perfume. 'I should be going.'

'I want to make love again,' she breaths, climbing over to straddle him. 'God, that's so good,' Indah shouts rocking backwards and forwards on him.

An hour later Cully reluctantly tries again to get away.

'I've got evidence to look at.'

'Look at me,' and she throws back the covers, rolling on to her stomach.

Kissing the nape of her neck, he moves down her spine, a vertebrae at a time, licking her bottom with his tongue, the back of her thighs and then behind her knees.

'That tickles,' she giggles.

'You poor love, your bruises where she hit you are dark.'

'Sophie is a dangerous bitch, but I don't want to talk about her.'

'Perhaps, but she didn't do this, did she?' Indah turns over, pushing herself up, staring at him. 'We need to talk about Crystal Smalls, don't we my darling?'

++++

'The one thing it doesn't do is let you forget the pain,' begins the commentary in a weak, rather hollow voice. 'The dream was to shoot them in the school hall where the brutality took place. Boys in blue blazars over white shirts and school ties. Girls in white blouses with short blue skirts cut above pink knees. Savouring the looks of terror, the begging and then fire, watch blood blooming scarlet, all part of the fantasy. Destroying the images that haunted day and night for thirty years. They were no longer children, but still recognisable and still dirty people deserving death. The following short film, all our own work, is dedicated to every victim there has ever been. Enjoy.'

There is no further commentary, but an electronic, computer game sound track in the background behind the real noises of the slaughter.

The bodycam switches on as he crosses the lawn in front of school house. Waiting until the film is about to start the shooter enters through back doors, the hall is in darkness and shadowy people stare forward at the screen, unsuspecting, waiting for the performance to start. Deep breath, press the button on the watch and throw the cluster of flashbangs far into the room. There is momentary silence and then thunder claps and the first scream. Swivelling to his right he sees them and fires. No need to hurry, savour every shot. The semi-automatic Glock 17 efficiently fires a clip that contains seventeen rounds. He fires, replaces it with practised ease, and then empties the second towards targets picked out by the laser light fixed to the bottom of the Glock, amazed that it is possible to buy such a thing on Amazon. All is engulfed in shouts of shock and terror as people realise what is happening. People falling backwards, dying at ones command. Screams as people run, falling over each other to get away.

The night goggles are perfect, essential to make certain one hits the guilty, but knows there is collateral damage, hits people that never caused harm, but did stand by and let it happen, did not intervene, even laughed. No regrets, no guilt, it was always going to be this way.

Text bubbles have been added above the victims as they fall. Cameron Davis, rapist. Ballard, corrupt. Felicity Taylor, homophobic poisoner. Pegg, whore. Chapman, paedophile. Simpson, drug dealer and so on.

Watch alarm goes off. He's been there sixty seconds. Needs to leave. Time to go. Turning a man with short blond hair, fixed grimace and darting eyes that convey his panic bumps into him, falls to his knees and looks up. 'No, please.'

Fuck! He is sure the second clip is empty, but fate brings them together. 'This is for the trees.' Head shot and the man falls backwards and the last to the heart, although certain there is no heart there to hit.

Must go, forward not back, trotting, not running with the stream of panic. Throw the second lot of flashbangs back towards the double doors, the way in. Still dark in here, but night goggles off and drop in shoulder bag with gun. Balaclava and gloves off, heading towards the stage. The corner door is log jammed as expected. All that planning working perfectly, thinking through the moves over and over like chess.

Breathing steady, feels good, even able to help a woman to her feet. Up on the stage through the curtains, bumps into someone. They scream and fall. No matter, but apologises. Keep going.

Into the lit corridor, running past classrooms screaming anguished memories. Well ahead of the crowd, but can hear them coming, yelling, desperate people. Left through the sixth-form block out into the lower quad, but remember stick to the wall. The CCTV covers the gate so not that way, through the gardens behind the junior school and over the wall and across the road.

Slow down, walk up the hill, across the road and in behind the church. The shed is set back and the door unlocked as expected. Inside strip off shoes, trousers, and shirt. Underneath are running singlet and shorts. Running shoes are on the floor ready, as are peaked cap and headphones. Outside, tipping the clothes into an oil drum, empty petrol over them and light it. Flames reach upwards and for a moment transfixed by the violence of the fire.

Quick stretch, arms and legs. Shoulder the canvas bag. Jogging away from the church, along back roads, calming, allowing the adrenaline to settle and enjoying the high of it all. Running is always an escape from the pain, pounding hours along deserted roads.

++++

Showered and changed into fresh clothes, Cully sits in the garden sipping slowly from a mug of black coffee. There is mist on the hills in the distance, leaching colour from the landscape and threatening to cut east from west Island.

After he leaves Indah, he drives away before finding a quite pull-in and opens the laptop. He recognises it of course, knew the password is stencilled on the back because the owner is becoming forgetful. The icons on the front screen are explicit and he watches the first film of the school shooting before opening the second that records the shooting in the rental house. He has no doubt the films were about to be published online.

'Didn't hear you come in.'

'Ah, and I didn't hear you coming. You shouldn't creep up on people like that uncle Adam,' Cully tells him. 'You've not gone to the allotment already?'

'Later, but how is Tom?'

'Critical.'

'I heard about Jenny Sykes on the radio. I remembered you used to go out with her. Grandmother and I came to see you in that play at school.'

'Oh what a Lovel War?'

'No, you were lovers in it.'

'"Abelard and Heloise", that wasn't Jenny, that was Sophie.'

'Ah, her again, sorry, but I suppose,' he begins reluctantly, 'you and Sophie looked good together.'

'We were, but fucked it up. It was a long time ago Adam.'

'Love, sex and betrayal are never a long time ago Cully.'

'Deep stuff.'

'I can do deep stuff,' he chuckles. 'Have you arrested Sophie yet for the assault on Indah?' Cully shakes his head. 'Don't let her get away with it. Indah is delightful and I want to see her again soon,' Adam grins. 'It's good to have Linda here.'

'She was my chauffer last night. I hope she's slept well. Has she talked to you about leaving the police?'

'No. Why?'

'Something Pete said, that she'd make a tremendous lawyer.'

'She would. Would you mind?'

'No. Should I talk to her?'

'She'll talk to you when she's ready.'

Phone rings.

'Sorry Adam, have to take this.'

'No problem, I'll be in the kitchen if you want me.'

'Chalky?'

'Just so you know Internal Affairs are planning to interview Tizard this afternoon at Headquarters. Monica and Becky are on their way to observe the autopsy of Jenny Sykes. Sorry about her, Gov.'

'I hadn't seen her in thirty years,' but Cully is relieved not to see her one more time dead on a slab. He is happy remembering her as she'd been, squealing in a bus shelter. Memorable, but it was the only time they had sex. 'Most importantly, any news on John Carter?'

'County say they visited a vet in a horsebox, if that makes sense to you, and after a little friendly persuasion the woman admitted she treated him late last night. Removed two bullets and patched him up before sending him on his way, but she doesn't know where. She's admitted treating Turner as well. They are charging her. Do you think he's coming our way?'

'He'd be foolish, we've got the ferries covered, but we have to be careful.'

'Vicar Mandy has asked for you to contact her.'

'Thanks, I'll be there shortly.'

Cully finds a number from the list and calls.

'Mandy?'

'Cully, this whole thing gets worse doesn't it?'

‘Things certainly aren’t getting any better.’

‘How’s Tom?’

‘Critical.’

‘Do you want to cancel the memorial service?’

‘I’ve thought about it and I will speak to the Chief Constable, but I’m guessing she’ll be in favour of going ahead. I’m asking for extra security from the mainland.’

‘Hardly what I had in mind, the church surrounded by a load of macho men carrying big guns.’

‘Macho women as well Mandy,’ he corrects her softly. ‘We might find him by then and it’ll be fine.’

‘Fine is the best we can hope for.’

Coffee mug empty he places it on the table in front of him beside Sophie’s book and feels familiar hands on his shoulders. ‘You’ve been reading it?’ she asks.

‘I’ve started it,’ he admits. ‘The first chapter.’ He is there, her lost love, as is the rape and the car crash, the fire and then the drug abuse and her fucking men to get a fix. Picking up the book he turns to the place Indah has drawn attention to. ‘You’ve read this bit?’

> “There are two types of people, predators and prey. Too often prey remains prey. Too often the abused and vulnerable do nothing, cannot overcome their fears and learn to fight back, to become the predator. Individually that is how we feel, isolated, in pain, ashamed, it’s our fault we let this happen, unable to sleep and above all dirty. The abuse need not have been major, a physical violation or emotional trauma, but could have been something that many would regard as small, such as an insult or slap. Context is all. How do we deal with it? Forget the justice system, the so called Rule of Law, because it rarely works and when it does it fails to reward with finality. Talking therapies provide momentary relief, like a palliative that thins the pain. Nothing really works, victims repeat over and over. Poor me, they say, there is nothing that will take away the agony. Wrong, there is one thing. The only solution is to strike back with fatal violence. Of course as a therapist I would not recommend this to anyone and we are bound by our ethical codes

to report anyone we fear might be about to do so, but through psychological training we can…"

'I have and it gives an understandable if distorted reason to act doesn't it?'

'Oh yes it does. Glad you're here sweetheart.'

'Pleased to be here and to help out yesterday, it made me feel needed.'

'You are needed.'

'You know what I mean. Uncle Adam is making me tea and toast, like you and I used to share in bed after mum. You saw me through it then.'

'We saw each other through.'

'Have you seen Pete?'

'No Linda, why?'

'He went for a walk late, didn't he? Just want to make certain he's not going to miss the interview with IA. I'm meant to be picking him up,' she explains. 'We're on the eleven o'clock ferry.'

'You enjoy this legal stuff don't you?'

'I do,' she agrees.

'I need to tell you something about what happened at the White House.'

'Here we go,' Adam announces, interrupting, placing a tray with tea and toast on the table, pulls up a chair and tells Linda to sit. 'Another coffee Cully?'

'No thanks. Can I walk Angus?'

'Of course.'

'It'll help me relax and think.'

'You'll need these?' says Adam.

'What?'

'Shit bags.'

++++

The hospice is quiet, nurses move about as if floating on air. It is a place of peaceful tranquillity. They nod in recognition, smiling at Cully as he walks along to the room. Entering, he sits next to the bed. 'Hello Jamie.'

'I guessed you'd come, just in time to arrest me before I die.'

'I'm not here to arrest you.'

'I'm really dying now Cully, no more remissions. My symptoms are getting worse, headaches, nausea and drowsiness amongst others.'

'I want you to tell me something Jamie?' Avoiding the tubes, Cully holds the man's thin hand, not wanting to hurt him. 'Where is John Carter?'

'I don't know.'

'I got his, or rather your laptop. You gave it to him, I recognised it, that's why you bought a new one. I've seen the films. Your handy work?'

'The bodycam John wore transmitted everything to me. You turning up to visit meant I couldn't watch it live, but I enjoyed every second of it once you'd gone.'

'Shit Jamie, did you have to do things this way?'

'How else were we to get justice?'

'We?'

'John and I.'

'What about Poulson?'

'I killed him.'

'How?'

'I found him in the vestry. The bloody church were taking him back, forgiving him, fucking hypocrites. He didn't recognise me.'

'Just you?'

'That's what I'm saying. I wanted him to apologise, but he wouldn't, he laughed. I hit him over the head with a large bible I found there. Tied him in a chair and gagged him. Waited for him to come to and cut off his toes with a pair of secateurs I found in amongst things women use for flower arranging. I watched him bleed.'

'It must have been incredibly painful for him. Why did you want to inflict so much pain?'

'Have you been raped? Of course not. The pain, the humiliation, the shame never leaves you.'

'I can't believe you did this alone. What about Carter? We have a witness that says there were two men in a car outside the church.'

'You and I both know witness statements are rarely credible.'

'What about reporting the original abuse?'

'To whom?'

'Other staff? The headteacher?'

'Jim Curtis was nice enough, but he was naïve.' James coughs, guttural and wet. 'I remember Sophie and Jenny fighting over you,' he smiles thinly.

'The police, someone might have listened to you?'

'Seriously?'

'What about the church?'

'The church covers things up and as far as the school was concerned he was the church.'

'Your parents?' Cully asks gently.

'Never,' Jamie splutters. 'I was a border. That tells you all you need to know about them, they didn't care about me.'

'Everything about the murder you've told me was in the media Jamie.'

'You're right, but the police keep stuff back. There was a glass I used to drink from. My prints will be on that if you haven't lost it. I also turned back a page of the bible. I remember it was the Old Testament, Numbers 32:23, "Be sure your sins will find you out". Do you blame me Cully?'

'Poulson deserved it.'

'My fault he slippered you.'

'I shouldn't have copied your work.'

'I offered it to you.'

'I should have stood up for you Jamie.'

'Rubbish Cully, you didn't understand what was going on and no one saw abuse back then. You were a kid.'

'Where is Carter?'

'I've no idea, he's gone rogue. Why aren't you arresting me?'

'Because I don't want you to die in prison, better here. Anything more you want to say Jamie?'

'There's lots, but not yet. Martin Skeets comes to see me. I've asked a favour of him. He's agreed and I'd like Indah to be there please. Sorry, I'm getting tired. You'll come again?' Jamie squeezes his hand. 'I love you Cully. Look after Linda.'

'Of course I will. I'll be back.'

'Like the Terminator. Would you do it for me, if I asked?'

'See you soon Jamie'

'Don't leave it too long, I might not be here.'

Cully drives north away from the hospice before taking a sharp left close to the rental house where the women died and there ahead of him is the ancient cable ferry that crosses the river that flows down the centre of the Island. Reluctant to take the Porsche on, but it is the quickest way back to Adam's and Angus is getting hungry and bored. As they wait for rusty chains to slowly drag the clunking flat bottomed ferry across the river Angus places his front paws on the dash and barks excitedly. Edging aboard dirty water comes up through the steel planking and as they cross smoke rises from the engine house. Cully climbs out paddles to the rusty railing and at the centre of the river drops the canvass bag containing the laptop and bodycam into the river.

++++

Eventually arriving at the incident room mid-morning, Cully is not surprised to find more bunches of flowers set against the wall of the church hall, several with messages of support for Tom. Stepping around them he enters to find Lisa and Chalky sitting at desks in silence. 'Morning,' he says.

'Gov.'

'Anything I should know about?'

'Headquarters believe Carter is heading north away from us,' says Chalky.

'But a boat was stolen early this morning close to where he visited the vet,' says Lisa. 'He could be trying to get across to us. The Coast Guard are searching for it.'

'We need to monitor things. I'm going to use the office, ok, Lisa?'

'Sure, Gov.'

Cully settles behind the desk, finds the number he wants on the Internet and calls.

'I appreciate it was a long time ago and there are issues of confidentiality, but this is important. I've explained who I am.' Cully listens. 'I could put my request in writing, but that would take time and I'm sure the university does not want to obstruct a police investigation into a mass shooting at a school.' Listens. 'Someone will ring me back, thank you.' Cully replaces the receiver with a sigh and little hope. So is surprised when he receives a call ten minutes later. 'Superintendent Cully.'

'Hi, This is Professor Margaux Bright and I shouldn't really be talking to you.'

'But you are.'

'I'm intrigued and the name you mentioned rang a bell. Is this off the record?

'Totally Margaux.'

'Smooth Superintendent Cully.'

'Just Cully.'

‘The thing on the Island looks gruesome.’ He agrees. ‘Sean O’Leary is involved?’

‘He’s a person of interest. Why did his name ring a bell?’

‘Will you do some teaching for me?’

‘Now who’s being smooth and yes I will,’ he agrees readily as he enjoys teaching and has been told he’s good at it. ‘Let me know when.’

‘I can only pay expenses.’

‘A good dinner will suffice.’

‘Smoother still. I was only a junior lecturer. Sean was my tutee. I remember him because he was a little shit and I had to fight the male Mafia to get him sent down. Luckily he failed a couple of end of year exams. I got the impression he’d been pushed into doing law by family.’

‘He had. What did he do?’

‘Two of my female tutees complained he was getting familiar and then a regular drug search found cannabis and RHB in his room.’

‘The police were informed.’

‘Of course not, the university liked, still likes to keep these things in house. I could see where it was going, what he was up to. He claimed the RHB was for body building.’

‘A bit late in his case.’

‘Mean Cully, but true. He argued everyone had pot which was true. He was given a verbal warning, but I kicked up.’

‘That made you popular.’

‘You can imagine. But he failed the papers, ironically including ethics. He went, but only after a colleague agreed to do a reference for art college.’

‘I’m guessing, no concerns were passed on.’

‘Not officially,’ she laughs.

‘About the teaching, send me some dates and I’ll get back to you.’

Cully makes a call to the art college, but instead of going through the academic route, doubting he’ll find another Margaux, goes direct to security. There, odds are there might be an ex copper and indeed there is. Accepting the need to chat about the job Cully eventually establishes the guy had only been there a few years, but going back through the computerised records there is nothing about Sean, yet there had been rumours about date rape drugs circulating in the union and local clubs.

Returning to the main room Cully is pleased to find Indah there.

‘I know,’ Indah sighs. ‘I’ll be there next week.’ She listens with growing annoyance. ‘I can’t see how she misses me, when she hardly recognises me. Goodbye,’ and drops the receiver on to the cradle.

‘Are you alright?’

‘No, yes, just exhausted, but in a very nice way,’ she adds in a whisper.

‘It’s certainly been a grim few days,’ begins Chalky. ‘I couldn’t help but over hearing, about your mum?’

‘Yes?’

‘My dad hardly recognises me.’

‘He was a great teacher and used to organise indoor games if it was raining during break time,’ says Cully, smiling at the sudden memory. ‘We used to race cars down a spare blackboard leaned up on some books. Not that he’ll remember me, but give him my regards please.’

‘Will do, Gov.’

‘Indah, go home and get some rest and be back at four.’

‘No Gov, I had all that time yesterday.’

‘You were assaulted.’

‘Sophie is coming in. I have to see her.’

‘Ok, if you’re sure.’

An hour later Cully has called the Chief Constable and they’ve agreed the memorial service should go ahead. Later he sits back from the screen with the Teams media conference over and done with. It had not been too bad. Most of the questions concerned Tom, the search for Carter and the memorial service.

As Cully is beginning to relax Monica and Becky come in. Ashen faced Becky is silent and sits at a desk in the corner. ‘Becky go and get some rest and see you here at four for the pre memorial service briefing.’

‘I don’t want to be alone.’

‘Monica?’

‘Becky come back with me. Go and wait in the car.’

They watch her go.

‘Stupid to ask, how was it?’

‘Jenny Sykes is a mess,’ Monica states bluntly. ‘Gerry was in a foul mood, but eventually stated the obvious, that she died from multiple fractures after falling from a great height. He said to tell you, no more bloody bodies, especially people he knows.’

‘He knew her?’

'So he says.'

'What about Becky?'

'She struggles, but she'll be alright. I'll look after her.'

'See you at four Monica, not before, and thanks.'

++++

Sophie leaves the cottage Rachel has lent her, driving trying to resolve the issues that left her with little sleep the night before. Her first visit is to see Alison, a true friend over all these years, at the hospital. Cully always fancied Alison from a distance, "out of my league", he once said, "by several rungs". His interest in her did not worry Sophie. In fact, she remembers that most boys fancied Ali and Carla, probably masturbated endlessly while fantasying about them, but both were on a different planet in terms of looks, intelligence, prospects and as it eventually became obvious sexual preference. Alison is pleased to see her. They chatted for a while before she becomes tired and Sophie leaves promising to return.

Arriving at the church, Sophie parks along the street and walks to the incident room to see Indah and give the police the file she had been exercised about.

'You've been avoiding me.'

'Busy Sophie,' Cully explains, finding her in front of him.

'I have to make a statement.'

'Ah, Indah is about, I'll get her to take it.'

'Can't you?'

'No, you know we're too close.'

'Are we still close?'

'Of course Sophie.'

'Good,' she smiles. 'There is something else. It's just that I've been wrestling with ethical issues and I've brought you this.' She produces a thin manila file. 'I've worked with John Carter as his therapist. He's emotionally mutilated poor man.'

'Thank you,' Cully says taking it. 'I'm guessing you've worked with others.'

'Why do you say that?'

'I know about Jamie. Also your advert in the Alumni magazine, it's how I knew to refer Linda to you. What about the others?'

'I can't say, I really can't.'

'Can't I persuade you?'

'You know of course that Indah was in court applying for warrants, but Patrick delayed things.'

'I told her to, we need the files Sophie.'

'If you come to me, tonight, I'll print them off for you. You can have everything Cully,' and she strokes his arm

'Indah, you've come to collect Ms Cairns,' he says, stepping away.

'If she can drag herself away,' Indah glares at Sophie.

'Of course, I can. See you later Cully.'

Sophie follows Indah into the Portacabin.

'Nice perfume Sophie,' says Indah.

'It's from the perfumery in the forest village and from the smell of you, you go there as well, but Indah, might I suggest something with more spice.'

Indah stares away for a moment, but then continues. 'Present are Sophie Cairns and Detective Constable Kasali. Thank you for coming.'

'Happy to help.'

'Firstly, I need to ask you about Davis and the night he raped you and crashed the car.'

'I've already told you about my rape and it's in my book.'

'For the tape please, everything you remember,' Indah says firmly. 'Please.'

Sophie talks for half an hour, in detail, as if it is something she has previously repeated over and over, possibly in her head. 'I suppose I was lucky to survive.'

'Do you know the name of the person that got you out of the car?'

'Isn't it obvious?'

'Please for the tape.'

'It was Cully.'

'Why was he there?'

'He chased after us.' Sophie explains they had all been at the "off to university party". 'Someone drugged me and Davis forced me to go with him.'

'Wait a minute, you and Davis were from different gangs, weren't you?'

'At school, yes, but things were less rigid afterwards.'

'Who else was there?'

'It was a long time ago.'

'You remember every detail don't you.'

'Everyone, Sean O'Leary, Miranda Pegg and Michael Bradman, Tash Brown with some bloke she'd picked up, Ali Grey and Felicity Taylor and so on.'

‘You dislike Jenny, don’t you?’

‘Dislike is a strong word.’

‘You blame her for what happened to you?’

‘Blame is also a strong word, DC Kasali. You were asking about Cully. He drove up as we crashed into the field.’

‘Saved your life.’

‘He did. He came to see me in hospital, but I didn’t want him.’

‘Why?’

‘Because I was ashamed, I was dirty damaged goods.’

‘You don’t feel like that now do you Sophie? You’re not a victim anymore, not prey, not a survivor are you? So, what are you Sophie?’

‘I’m a rescuer, I suppose.’ She sighs. ‘Fuck! Why do things stay with us for so long?’

‘You’re the therapist.’

‘Touché!’

‘Did you buy the flash bangs from Turner?’

‘Yes, to scare off pigeons from Rachel’s vegetable patch.’

‘How did you know about them?’

‘The Internet.’

‘Did they work, did they scare away the birds?’

‘For a few hours. It was stupid of me.’

‘Interview terminated,’ and Indah records the time.

‘Good, I need to get home to cook. Cully’s agreed to come to dinner tonight. I’ve told him he can have anything he wants. Goodbye DC Kasali.’

++++

There are two enquiries now running. His, and IA’s. The Chief Constable has organised an IA task force to look into the armed officers and the flashbangs, what happened Tuesday night at the rental house, Kerry’s death and Tom’s shooting. Her argument is that they are connected, but also because of staff shortages across the region. Cully understood they needed to keep things totally separate.

In the incident room, Lisa has added another suspect with motive, if you can call the forest-dwellers a suspect, but there is a clear, if unsubstantiated, link. Ballard’s death resulted in the collapse of the proposed oil drilling and with the injunction the forest village is safe for now. At the centre of the board is a picture of John Carter. Around him were pictures of Sophie, Vicar Mandy, Alison Grey, Judge Le Strange and the forest village all of whom had motives. Cully knew he should add a picture of Jamie, but could not bring himself to do so. Had they conspired in some way to persuade Carter to kill the others? Far-fetched, but it is now obvious this has nothing to do with drug dealing.

Moving outside Cully stands at the entrance to the church hall staring at the Portacabin aware the two women are in there. He knows these attacks were personal and targeted against the Nasty Gang. There is a chance they might be dealing with a conspiracy and, as Indah thinks, Sophie is at the centre of it. So, Cully has instructed Indah to extend the warrants beyond Sophie's files, e mails, and telephone records to include communications sent and received by the others. Indah has arranged for the applications to be in front of an independent judge on the mainland on Monday. It is a delay, but it would avoid further conflicts of interest.

Cully watches as the two women emerge from the Portacabin, Sophie heading away and Indah coming towards him, her face knotted and he wonders what she is about to say. 'Do I smell good to you?' He is not expecting that. 'My perfume, does it need more spice?'

'No, "Forest Glade" suits you perfectly.'

'You know the name?' she brightens. 'Really?'

'I recognised it the first time I was close to you,' he lies, thanking Linda, although he'd realised she and Mary fortuitously wore the same fragrance. 'It's perfect on you. What's up?'

'Are you seeing Sophie tonight?'

'Of course not, I'm seeing you. Is that what she told you?'

'It doesn't matter, sorry Cully,' she smiles weakly. 'I'm being stupid,' and she hurries passed him into the incident room.

'Did you speak to her about Jenny?'

'No.'

'Why not?'

'So far, we've got nothing to link Sophie to Jenny's death.' Indah picks up an envelope, tears it open. It's the written response as to why the warrants were turned down. 'Shit!.'

'What?'

‘Nothing. Please Cully give me some space,’ and watches him walk away. ‘Sorry.’

‘I’m here when you’re ready,’ he smiles.

Sitting at her desk, Indah makes telephone calls and pushes paper about, but her mind is elsewhere. How foolish to believe anything Sophie says about Cully. Are she and Sophie really in competition for his attention and affection? Worse, the signature on the feedback from the warrants application is that of Crystal Smalls. ‘Shit!’

Why did she lie to Sophie about Cully wanting to see Jenny? What if Sophie, angered, had gone to see Jenny because of what she had said to her? What if she killed her? Indah pulls a sheet of paper towards her. ‘Shit!’ She hadn’t noticed the coffee cup and it tips over, spilling over stuff she’d already done. ‘Shit!’ Chalky is quickly there with paper towels. ‘Thanks.’

‘What’s up?’

‘Regretting some things I’ve said, things I shouldn’t have said.’

‘We’ve all done that.’

‘But consequences, what about them Chalky?’

++++

DCI Mount from Internal Affairs has been put in charge of the task force, but already knows she will need more help to manage the various investigations the Island is producing. Instead of staying on the Island after inspecting the forest site she returned to the mainland. At Headquarters that morning, she interviewed Peter Grimes with Linda Cully present and now turns her attention to Tizard.

‘You could have seen me yesterday. It’s a waste of time dragging me over here, when I should be on duty at the church.’

‘Sergeant Tizard, might I remind you that as of today you are under investigation on a number of serious matters and you won’t be on duty anywhere until we’ve finished.’

‘This is rubbish.’

Tizard’s union advocate leans forward and repeats the same.

‘Noted, however we’re here now so let’s get on with it. I’d like to begin by asking you about the flashbangs you bought from Turner. We have statements from your own officers and from Turner confirming what you did.’

‘And Ted is dead, I should be with his family, not here.’

'Yes, the death is a tragedy, as is the fact Sergeant Tom Whitworth is critical. What went wrong?'

'Nothing from my team, but the dogs didn't pick up Carter's scent.'

'You don't like taking responsibility for things do you?'

'What's that supposed to mean?'

'Later. Let's get back to the flashbangs.'

'What about them?'

'You knew they were illegal?'

'If Headquarters fail to provide us with enough equipment for training, I have to improvise.'

'By breaking the law?'

'Come off it. Firework legislation, nothing else.'

'The law is the law Sergeant.'

'Sergeant Tizard will accept a note on his file,' says the advocate.

'He'll accept what he's given.' Mount is tired and glancing at her sergeant her sitting next wonders *'if there is any chance of seeing the children over the weekend?'* 'Let's move on to the custody suit shooting.'

'What's that got to do with anything?' Tizard demands.

'We weren't warned about this,' says the advocate. 'We should have been warned and can I remind you Sergeant Tizard was exonerated.'

'We now know the Glock 17 used in the custody suit shooting is the same one used in the school hall and rental house shootings.' She pauses, letting these facts sink in. 'We think that's more than a coincidence.'

'No idea what you mean.'

'The gun and you link the three incidents.'

'So does Cully and Joe Dabell.'

'Superintendent Cully was shot twice, fell to the ground bleeding heavily and was in fear for his daughter. You on the other hand, chased the shooter out of the station and down the road. You shot and killed the shooter.'

'The investigation said the shooting was justified,' states the advocate.

'It does mean the shooter can't tell us what happened to the gun. Convenient, don't you think?' Silence. 'The Glock was never found. Did you pick it up?'

'No.'

'Officers have re-examined the files and revisited the scene.'

'Which officers?'

'DCI Amelia Fox has prepared a statement.'

'This is a stitch up, Cully used to fuck her.'

'We know the history, but that does not change the facts.' '*Amelia is a lucky bitch, how long is it since I and my husband have found time to fuck, or has he lost interest in me? There is the woman at his office and another at the tennis club he played doubles with.*' 'We know from Mary's, your wife's statement…'

'What statement?'

'We did a Teams link this morning from the Island.'

'I'm sure that's not legal,' interjects the union advocate.

'It is,' states Mount. 'She believes you found the gun in the street and took it home.'

'She thinks, she thinks too much.'

'She's your wife Tizard. Mary says that six months ago you were in financial trouble. You couldn't pay the mortgage; credit cards were maxed out and one of the children needed urgent dental work. The bank refused a further loan. She claims you got a phone call one night and you were suddenly excited, but nervous. You spent time in your workshop and the next day went off to the mainland. She always knew you had a secret account to pay for hobbies and your women. Suddenly, there was plenty of money and everything was paid for. Explain please.'

'I did lots of overtime and worked as security at several clubs.'

'Against regulations. We've seen the account.'

'You've done what?'

'We obtained warrants for your bank accounts and telephone records. We've also got a warrant to search your shed which my colleague will do over the weekend, won't you, Sergeant?' '*Because I'm having at least Sunday off, seeing the kids and confronting my husband*'. 'Yes Sergeant?'

'Yes Ma'am.'

'I want to see the warrants,' begins the advocate, 'and we need time to consult a lawyer.'

'Fine, interview suspended until tomorrow morning. Sergeant Tizard, there's a room booked for you in staff quarters. Don't return to the Island and don't contact witnesses.'

++++

Phone rings.

'Dad?'

'Linda. How's it going with Pete?'

'Fine, IA didn't push too hard, they are much more interested in Tizard. I think Pete will get a note on his file, a recommendation for counselling and a referral to retake the firearms course, but nothing else. We're on our way back to you. I'll drop him off and then go to Adam's to finish an essay that's due in Monday. You don't mind if I miss the memorial service?'

'No, I wish I could and you make a great advocate.'

'Pete told me about the army interview,' continues Linda. 'Carter is a skilled, efficient fighter and responds to orders. He'd be obedient don't you think?'

'You should never have done that profiling course,' he laughs.

'You know as well as I do, despite the stuff of fiction, profiling is useless until you know the perpetrator and then you can build the picture around him or her.' She pauses in thought. 'You have got your vest with you, haven't you, Dad?'

'I have, but I'm sure he's not coming our way.'

'Even so, be careful. One other thing Dad, that journalist Peppermint something, has been in touch again. I'd love to do it. It would be great fun. Please?'

'You know I can't say no to you.' Linda squeals with delight. 'Let's do it.'

'Love you and speak soon.'

Cully likes and appreciates solitude. Apart from the Vicar's ladies coming in with coffee, sandwiches and cakes he is left alone for several blissful hours, then he hears the incident room door open and close. He looks up.

'So, this is where you hide out.'

'I'm busy. What do you want?'

'I've been looking for you.'

'Flattering. You feeling better?'

'Much. I went up to see Alison before I left hospital. She's better and gave me an interview. You two used to walk home together. I've already sold it to one of the daily newspapers.'

'Good for you Peppermint.'

'Peppermint?'

'A family joke. What do you want with me ?'

'Do I get my tablet computer back?' She sits in front of him, crossing her legs. Her skirt is short and she's wearing stockings like Indah. 'Well?'

'Linda and I will do your interview if you still want us?'

'Fantastic, but don't change the subject. My tablet?'

Phone rings.

'Excuse me while I take this. Cully.' It is a call from the Coast Guard. 'Thanks. Shit!.'

'What is it?' Minty asks, leaning forward, her interest pricked. 'Come on Cully, give me something to work with, please?'

'Come to the memorial service and I'll give you something afterwards.'

++++

The four o'clock briefing goes ahead with everyone there apart from Pete, still on his way back from the mainland with Linda. Cully is able to tell them that Tom is still critical. As far as Carter is concerned the Coast Guard has found the boat stolen from the mainland in a west Island inlet and Amber and her team are there now trying to establish if he'd been on board. 'She's found blood, an empty box of painkillers and used dressings. We therefore have to assume he was.'

'Why come back?'

'Only he knows that.'

'We've had a report of a car being stolen from near where the boat was found,' adds Lisa. 'We've got patrols out looking for it.'

'He may be heading here for the memorial service,' Cully concludes. 'I've established an outer ring round the church with uniform and armed officers from the Island. The new armed officers from the mainland will position themselves in and around the church. We've also been sent communications gear, ear pieces and mic's, so please wear them at all times and keep them switched on. I want an open network. Monica will remain here in the incident room to co-ordinate communication. Monica?'

'Remember there will be echo in the church so keep things simple when talking please. No chit chat. I may ask you to repeat. We will all be able to hear each other.'

'Lisa,' continues Cully, 'we've secured the church so there is only one entrance, you will be there checking people as they come in. You've got the invite list, relatives, survivors and Alumni Association members, school and NHS staff, local dignitaries and immediate neighbours.'

'It's a long list, Gov.'

'I know, but it could have been longer. Vicar Mandy and the Reverend Skeets will conduct the service. It should last no more than one hour. Chalky, Indah and Becky in the church please, keep your eyes peeled for anything odd. Captain Nadine and the dogs will do a sweep through before we let people in just in case. You've all got a copy of the photo of Carter his wife gave Pete, not the best, but the blond hair is distinctive. Also remember he's wounded and bandaged up. Hurting and psychologically unpredictable is not a good combination. If you see him, do not approach, communicate and we will let our armed officers do their job. I don't want heroes, understood?' People nod. 'Everyone to wear vests please.'

'Might he try a sniper shot?'

'We will have officers on high points, but I doubt it. He seems to prefer close contact.'

'Comforting. What if we scare him off?' asks Indah. She'd tied her hair back in a ponytail, accentuating her high cheek bones and large eyes and he is struck once again as to how beautiful she is. 'This is like a honey trap isn't it? In one sense we want him to come so we can capture him.'

'Yes,' Cully nods. 'So, we have to be careful we don't get caught in our trap.'

'True, but if he sees us, he might run and attack elsewhere.'

'It's a possibility Indah,' Cully nods. They weren't new question, certainly not to him. He'd thought through several scenarios all of which contained significant risk. 'Let's assume he's losing blood, is weakening.'

'But still strong enough to manage a boat and steal a car, Gov,' says Chalky.

'True, but he's running out of options, isn't he?'

'What if there is a target here on the Island we don't know about?' Indah suggests.

'There is, or at least I believe there is, John Sutton's brother Michael. As of this afternoon he's the only surviving member of the Nasty Gang. Philip Andrews is expected to die today. Michael was a bully and his main victim was John.'

'He's come willingly?'

'He feels guilty, wants to make amends. He will be wearing a vest and Chalky will be his bodyguard. That said there are lots of unknowns. We can only prepare for what we know. Sorry, that sounds like crap.'

'No it doesn't, Gov, it's true,' says Lisa. 'It's sort of what you said to me that first night, that there are lots of things we don't know and it's those that should scare us.'

'And they do. Look, he's a soldier and has a particular skill set and therefore is a dangerous predator, even wounded.'

Phone rings.

'Gov,' Chalky starts. 'John Carter's brother has arrived.'

'Chalky, escort him into the church, please.'

Phone rings again and Lisa answers and listens.

'Listen up everyone,' she begins. 'A woman has just rung the help line. She came on a bus from west Island. A man got on and sat next to her. He was odd, didn't speak, but when he got off there was a pool of blood on the seat.'

'Where did he get off?'

'Here at the ferry terminal.'

'Clever bastard, coming by bus. How long ago?'

'Half an hour.'

'Chalky, you and me down there now. Becky, bring Michael Carter in here. Lisa, we need urgent backup.'

++++

The police car slides into the bus station, just missing a double decker bus pulling out and comes to a halt tight against the ticket office wall. 'You've done the police driving course Chalky?'

'Been meaning to, Gov.'

'Out.' Chalky obeys and Cully following scrambles across the driver's seat where he catches his foot in the seat belt. 'Shit!' Tangled, he closes his eyes, catches a memory from a burning car, panic, takes a deep breath and releases his foot.

'Gov?'

'I'm here.'

Crouching, guns in hand, they pause behind the car as Chalky waves people away. 'We should wait,' he says, 'but we're not going to are we, Gov?'

'I'll go right, you left.'

Reaching the narrow entrance to the toilet block, they hesitate for moments before going in. The stench of urine is powerful. 'Get out,' Chalky shouts at a man standing at the urinal. 'Go.'

'I've not finished,' he complains before seeing the guns. 'Fuck!' Swinging round he sprays across the floor, runs between the police officers, and leaves. Outside a woman screams.

Inside Cully kicks open the first cubicle, nothing, then the second and still nothing, but the third door doesn't give so easily. He kicks it again, it shudders inwards and a young boy, about eight, trousers round his ankles, sits there. 'I'm only doing a poo,' he says.

'We're police,' Cully mumbles. 'Hurry up and finish.'

'I can't with you staring at me,' he complains.

'Christian,' a woman's voice calls. 'Where are you?'

'In here, mum. Some blokes are watching me.'

'Bloody perverts, I'm getting the police.'

'We are the police,' Cully shouts, closing the cubicle door on the kid. 'Finish doing your poo.'

An armed officer appears at the entrance.

'Shall we let this woman in Sir?'

'Might as well.'

'What do you need guns for, you'll terrify him. Aw, this place stinks. Men are so disgusting. Christian?'

'Finished mum.'

'Have you wiped?'

'Yes, mum.'

'Then come out and wash your hands like a good boy.'

He emerges smirking, this will be a story told over and over again at school and elsewhere and no doubt embroidered to his benefit. He goes to the sink. 'I'm guessing you want the guy.'

'What guy?'

'The guy that was washing his hair when I came in. Over there at the other sink.'

'Thanks, now go your mum's waiting.'

'Don't I get a reward?'

'Yeah, he should get something,' she agrees, glaring at Cully.

A thick ear Cully thinks, remembering grandmother used to threaten it, but never did it or any other physical stuff. One of her looks was enough. Reaching inside his jacket Cully hands over a fiver. 'Now get out both of you, this is a crime scene.'

'No need to take that tone. Come on Christian, you can buy us both an ice cream.'

'Aw mum.'

'There are discarded bloody dressings under the sink,' calls Chalky. 'A morphine file, battlefield kit. This guy is equipped for war.'

'That's what I'm afraid of. He's dyed his hair,' says Cully, standing at the blackened sink. 'There's a lot of blood. He must be weakening.'

'Let's hope so, but why come back to the Island? He was clear and away.'

'I'm guessing, unfinished business.'

++++

Cully stares at the table plan, up at the chart Tom had put together and then the long photograph. Something is wrong, but he's too tired to think and he needs fresh air.

Walking out of the incident room, across the car park he goes down the school drive towards the hall, still surrounded by blue and white police tape, flapping in the breeze. He keeps walking until he reaches one of the benches overlooking the cricket field where the white H Chalky painted is still visible. He sits, trying to clear his head. Has it only been a week?

Eventually, standing Cully walks back towards the church as people begin to arrive for the service. He can see the armed officers from the mainland in various positions on the ground and above on roof tops. He sees Patrick Le Strange and waves. 'How are you?'

'I'm fine Cully, you?'

'I'll be glad when this is over.'

'Of course. I see you're doing a reading,' and lifts his copy of the order of service. 'I remember the girls used to get you to do their readings at assembly. You could never refuse. Cash in the bank I'm guessing?'

'Patrick?'

'A favour for a favour,' but sees Cully's face, 'sorry I'm being frivolous.'

'Sorry, I'm exhausted. Patrick, what people were already on your table when you arrived Friday night?'

'Quite a few.'

'The place cards were already out?'

'Yes,' he nods, but hesitates. 'I've just remembered Sean was changing them, or at least swapping over two.' He laughs, smiling. 'He's never forgiven you for stealing Rachel from him.'

'She'd already dumped him.'

'Is that what she told you?'

'It was thirty years ago,' Cully sighs.

'Sean's not done well, at least in his eyes, and that can make one bitter. Talk of the devil, here he comes, with Sophie another he missed out on because of you. See you later.'

Cully can hear Sean talking to Sophie about the art exhibition, asking her if she would like to come. She's not sure, explaining she has to get back to the mainland, but before he can say anything else, Sophie calls out. 'Cully, there you are.' Her voice is suddenly playful and by the look on his face Sean registers the change. 'How is your officer, Tom is that his name?'

'He's critical.' How often had he said that in the last twenty-four hours. 'He should recover.'

'You go ahead Sean, I'll catch you up,' Sophie encourages. 'Go on.' Sean moves away without a backward glance. 'He's getting tedious,' Sophie complains. 'He keeps being there.'

'He's obsessed. Sean moved the place cards to be next to you Friday night and put me next to Jenny.'

'He did that, the horrible little man.'

'You'd done the table plan to put us together.'

'You've found me out,' she giggles.

'I've been reading your book. Is all that stuff in the first chapter true, the drug abuse?'

'Come to dinner tonight and I'll reveal all my secrets to you.' She brushes his cheek with the back of her hand. 'You need a shave. I remember when your face was so soft. Just teasing. See you later,' she kisses him before heading into the church.

‘Just in time, Pete.’ Cully looks at him. Unshaven, his eyes dark-ringed, his hair needing a wash. He wore a black suit, shirt, but no tie. ‘I should send you back to the hotel to get cleaned-up.’

‘I’m not in a good place. Sorry Gov.’

‘No need to be sorry, I’m not much better and you’ve had a rough couple of days and you’re my best man for this if you can stay awake. What did IA say?’

‘That they’ll be in touch, but Linda is excellent. She wants to take you and Adam out to dinner tomorrow evening and you should bring Indah.’ Pete smiles, pleased the message is delivered. ‘How is it here?’

‘Tense.’ Cully explains about the boat and what they’d found in the toilets. ‘He’s here somewhere. We’ve got the place locked down as best we can. The Chief Constable sent over extra armed officers. Every entrance is covered and we’ve even got snipers on high buildings. Pick your position.’

‘Lisa, start letting people in.’

++++

‘Indah, why aren’t you wearing a vest?’

‘There were none left.’

‘Here, take this one,’ and he starts to take his off.

‘Cully, you’ll need it.’

‘I’m not intending to get shot again, now take it please,’ and he watches her walk away with it, desperate for this to be over and to be with her.

‘What a lovely man you are, protecting your chicks, or is it about getting into her knickers?’

‘Vicar!’

‘Ah, I sense you’re already in them, but neither the Gods nor luck will save you from a bullet Cully. You should find another vest.’

‘You’re not wearing one Mandy.’

‘My collar is my vest,’ she laughs. ‘But as a non-believer you can’t rely on God Cully. Have you practised your reading?’

‘Once,’ he admits.

‘I’m sure it will be fine.’

The church is gradually filling. Cully could see Sophie and then Minty. Indah is patrolling the aisle, moving towards the alter, speaking to people here and there. ‘If anyone wants me, I’m going to get some fresh air,’ Cully says, but stops, looking over to where Indah is talking to a man next to a woman in black wearing a cloche hat. 'Who is he?'

'Excuse me sir, you can't sit there,' Indah says.

'Why not?'

'It's reserved.'

'For whom exactly?'

'Family members. If you'd like to move back a few rows, that would be good.'

'I'm not moving anywhere.'

'Sir, please.'

'Sit down next to me.'

'Sir?'

'Or I will kill you.' He holds the gun in his lap. 'Sit.' She obeys. 'That's better.'

'You're bleeding,' she says.

'I used to bleed from my bum after they fucked me.'

'You need medical help.'

'We used to be brought in here you know, paraded across the road from the school. The Reverend Poulson buggered me there behind the alter.'

'Indah?' Chalky asks in her ear, 'is something wrong?'

'I'm fine,' she mumbles.

'Who are you speaking to?'

'I'm sorry,' she stutters.

'What does sorry mean and what do you know about it? Ever been fucked up the bum against your will?'

'No.'

'Indah, I'm coming now,' says Chalky.

'You wouldn't like it.'

'I'm sure I wouldn't.'

'The cunt is made for fucking, not the bum.'

'Right, you're right John.'

'Clever bitch,' he hisses, pushing the muzzle of the pistol into her side. 'No more chat. Where's my brother?'

On the other side of the church, Pete is scanning people as they enter. He recognises one or two he has spoken with at the hospital. One of them nods to him and he nods back. 'Gov?'

'Gov, Indah's in trouble,' says Monica in his ear.

'Pete, who is Indah talking to?'

'Where?'

'Near the front, the dark headed guy.'

'Shit! It's him. How the fuck did he get in? Lisa?'

'I don't know, Gov. I'm useless.'

Cully does not disagree.

'What do we do?' Pete asks. 'I've no gun.'

'Clear the church,' says Cully. 'Chalky?'

'I'm here, coming down the aisle.'

'Get up, snaps Carter. 'Do as you're told.' Indah obeys and he pushes her towards the alter. He holds her wrist tightly in his free hand, the muzzle of the Glock 17 pressing into her ribs. 'Stop!' He fires into the roof. 'No one moves.' Some scream, but stay where they are. 'Stay seated all of you.'

Cully walks slowly down the aisle alongside Chalky. He knows Pete is moving along the left and Lisa down the right.

'John,' Cully begins.

'What?'

'I'm Superintendent Cully, Cully remember? We were at school together. Remember?'

'Should I?'

'Think. We were in the same year at school.'

'Were we? Where's my brother? He's the last one I've to kill.'

'I'm putting my gun on the ground,' says Cully and does so.

'Don't come any closer. I'll shoot the girl.'

'Her names Indah,' Cully says, edging closer, 'and why would you want to hurt her?'

'I'm military remember, I know how it works, you try building rapport.'

'Of course, you do, but she's done you no harm.'

'I want my brother here now.'

'That's not going to happen. Killing the others, isn't that enough?'

Cully stands three metres away. 'Well?'

'Don't come any closer.'

There is eye contact between Cully and Indah. She's beautiful, her eyes wide and alluring, but she's scared, terrified and he can't stand the thought of her getting hurt. Cully nods and she elbows Carter in the ribs, but it's not hard enough and he doesn't let go. Cully gets in between them. 'Indah, get out of the way.' Cully pushes her to the side. She stumbles and falls, screaming as Carter swings round and fires. The shots thunder through the church, echoing back and forth from floor to high ceiling and back again. Four shots in succession. The first bullet ricochets up off the tiled floor of the aisle, hitting Chalky in the arm as he runs forward. The second hits Cully in the chest. He stumbles backwards when the next hits, he falls, catching his head on the corner of the alter and there is blood, lots of blood. The fourth hits Carter in the chest, fired as the others advance on him. Then another throwing Carter back against the alter where he slides to the ground beside Cully. He twitches and Pete fires again, again and again.

++++

'Don't waste your time, he's a cullender. Send him down to Gerry.' The consultant moves across the space. 'What about him?' she asks a colleague.

'Not good. Shot twice. There's nothing much to do.'

'I'll leave him to you.'

'Stand clear. Shocking.'

'Still nothing. I think we should stop. What do people think?'

'Agreed.'

'Any objections?'

'Time of death?' Someone answers. 'Nice try everyone. Family?'

'There's a daughter.'

'Someone needs to contact her, we can't let her see this on the news. Now the other one.' The consultant moves across the room. 'Where are we?'

'No output.'

'How long have you been trying?'

'A good while.'

'Still nothing.'

'Continue compressions Staff.' Mary stands next to the bed, places her hands, one on top of the other, and begins.

'One, two…'

'Stop.' Mary does. 'Still nothing. We should stop,' but Mary ignores him. 'Mary, leave it.' She doesn't. 'Mary, I said stop.'

'No.'

'Mary.'

'No.'

'We've got an output.'

'I love you Mary Tizard, you bloody stubborn woman. I want him in the scanner. Take him staff, you're his angel. Go.'

'Now, what else have we got?'

'Incoming.'

'Move,' a paramedic shouts and Pete steps out the way. 'One coming in now.' Paramedics wheel a stretcher through the door and into a bay. 'Mary what's happening?' She passes him pushing the trolley. 'Mary?'

'I can't stop.'

'What happening?'

'He died.' She pushes the trolley into a lift. 'Bloody men!'

'Simpson?'

'Dead,' she calls as the doors begin to close. 'His daughter needs telling.'

Pete goes to the drinks machine, finds a few coins in his pocket and inserts them. A plastic cup drops and fills with thin black coffee. Picking it up he sips, finds a seat in the waiting area and watches the clock. Dozes, wakes suddenly and finds himself between two women. 'Are you twins?' he asks sleepily.

'No,' says Linda, 'go and get some rest. I'm here for Dad now, but IA want to see you again. What the fuck happened, Pete?'

'Lisa froze and I grabbed her gun.'

'But you emptied the clip, Pete. IA are furious, they wanted him alive to question him. I'm not sure I can get you out of this one.'

'I know.' He stands wearily. 'You'll keep us updated?'

'Of course,' and she watches him walk away.

'Two dead, two hanging on,' says Mary. 'Alison Grey, walking out of the hospital the other day hasn't helped her and she's got no fight.'

'You saved Dad, I saw through the glass.'

'I was doing my job Linda, being hit twice is no picnic, but unlike Alison he's got plenty of fight.'

In a cubicle, Chalky is resting on a bed, his arm bandaged.

'How are you feeling?' asks Pete.

'I've had worse. We're both ex-military, you know how things happen.'

'I fucked up yesterday Chalky. I should have put him down, killed him.'

'Pete, I get it, but mustn't blame yourself. Things happen really fast, like today. I should have shot the bastard in the church before he shot Cully.'

'Now you are being silly. I should have been with Tom.'

'Tizard said it was safe.'

'The last person I should have trusted.'

'Should have, could have.' Chalky starts. 'I'm coming back to work.'

'Don't be silly.'

'How's Indah, she'll need help. The assault and then this.'

'I reckon we'll all need help after this. You should go home Chalky, at least overnight.'

'He's right,' says Lisa, appearing through the gap in the curtains. 'Go home Chalky.'

'No Ma'am, I'm coming in.'

'Pete, IA are in reception, go out the back. God knows what got into you, but let's keep you away from them as long as possible,' Lisa sighs. 'I'm going down to see Gerry.'

'We'll wait for you.'

Leaving them Lisa takes the lift down.

'Go away.'

'Gerry, it's me.'

'Piss off. I've had enough of you lot and the bodies you bring.' He sweeps the room with his arm where two corpses lay under sheets. 'You see what you do?'

'It's Carter, not us.'

'But what made him do it, can you answer that?'

'Hate, anger, revenge you name it.'

'Well, Lisa, I've had enough.'

'Gerry you're drunk.'

'Not yet, but I'm getting there. Do you want one?' She shakes her head. 'I'm having another one,' and pours more into his glass. 'Pete Grimes made a bloody mess of this one.'

'My fault I froze and after what happened with Tom, Pete just lost it.'

'The second shot killed him, two were enough, Lisa. Overkill I'd say, but understandable after Cully was shot. Sure you don't want a drink?'

'Pour me a large one Gerry, please.'

‘It’ll be a pleasure. When Internal Affairs come sniffing round, I’ll tell them Pete had to shoot him a dozen times because he kept twitching.’

‘Bastard,’ she laughs. ‘I don’t care what happens next. Tell the truth.’

‘But you’re in charge now,’ he says pouring several fingers for Lisa and more into his own glass. He hands her the drink. ‘Fuck the bastards.’

‘Fuck the bastards,’ she repeats and drinks.

Saturday

Linda stands at the entrance to the hospital with her arms folded staring into the darkness. In the distance, a clock strikes midnight and a dog barks in response, and then another and another until it feels she is surrounded by noise. Shivering she turns to go back in, meeting Lisa, Pete and Chalky emerge from a side entrance. Linda laughs, reassuring them that the IA team have gone to the canteen, but advising them to prepare statements, especially you, Pete. 'You can't keep ducking these people.' She watches them go.

'Linda, there you are.'

'What do you want?'

'Sorry, I…'

'What?'

'I'm sorry about Cully, your dad and I'm not here looking for a story, promise,' Minty sighs, looking forlorn. 'I expected more press here.'

'There is nothing here for them to feed on so they've gone to the school.'

'I've decided I don't like real journalism,' Minty admits. 'I'm sticking to social candy floss in future.'

'Linda, we need you inside.'

'Mary, what's happened?'

'It's your dad, come quickly.'

Meanwhile, Pete drives Lisa and Chalky along dark deserted roads towards the incident room in silence. Then suddenly, turning a corner, the road is full of people and light. A media scrum crowds the space between school and church and turn on the car like hyenas with the scent of fresh prey. Edging through, Pete resists the temptation to mow them down. Uniformed officers block the entrance to the car park and after letting the car through turn back to keep the pack at bay. Parking next to the portacabin and ignoring shouted questions they enter the incident room where they find Monica, Becky and Amber silently working.

'How long have they been out there?' Pete asks.

'Hours,' Amber complains.

'Where's Indah?' Lisa asks.

'Not seen her,' Monica calls back.

'No idea,' adds Becky.

'We need to find her. She's in a bad way. Someone please.'

'I'll go,' Becky volunteers, pleased to get out of the incident room to clear her head which is swimming. 'We've completed the church statements.'

'The team are nearly finished sweeping the church,' Amber announces. 'We think the gun has gone under the alter, wedged there. We can't get it until tomorrow, but we'll need lifting gear. I'm waiting on the bullets from the autopsies. Gerry said you had them, Lisa.' There is silence. 'Sorry, but…'

'You're doing your job,' says Lisa, handing over plastic evidence bags. 'I know it's late, but let's try and keep going. Becky, please find Indah.'

Taking the back entrance Becky slips through the community garden and skirting the media pack enters the lower quad through the side gate. The buildings are in darkness. She stops suddenly wondering where she is? 'What am I meant to be doing?' she mutters. She feels faint, weak and leans against a wall. Her mouth is dry. 'Move.' She obeys, continuing she recognises the steps to the sixth form block and goes in. Why not locked? What if Carter had an accomplice? What if? Then she sees a strip of light under a door, one she recognises, and going in hears voices and there, sitting on the stage of the mummery are two women. Indah, knees pulled up to her chest, arms hugging them, rocking backward and forward and crouching next to her is Vicar Mandy. 'How did you know where we were?'

'The only place with a light on,' explains Becky.

'Well spotted,' says Mandy, trying a smile. 'You'll make a good detective.'

'We've been looking for you Indah,' says Becky exchanging glances with Mandy. 'Indah, you've had a terrible experience, maybe you should go home.'

'There's no one there.'

'Cully wouldn't want you feeling sorry for yourself, he'd want you home or doing your job.'

'How do you know what Cully wants?'

'Sorry, I was…'

'Becky is here to help,' Mandy says softly. 'You've all had a terrible nightmare week.'

‘Tom and now Cully and that woman Jenny Sykes,’ Becky begins. ‘When I saw her on the beach, I wanted to run away. So much death Vicar. How do you keep going?’

‘I don’t,’ and she beckons for Becky to sit beside her, which she does and passes over her flask. ‘This helps. This week has tested every part of me,’ she sighs, placing her arms round the shoulders of the young women sitting either side of her. ‘I’ve even started preying again.’

‘Cully gave me his vest,’ Indah mumbles.

‘This is all my fault,’ admits Mandy. ‘I shouldn’t have insisted we have the memorial service. Cully was in two minds, but I pushed. So much for a service to start the healing process. Fuck!’

‘Vicar,’ warns Becky and takes a second swig from the flask, coughs and passes it back.

‘Fuck!’ Mandy repeats. ‘Fuck everything.’

‘It’s not your fault,’ Becky says. ‘The only person responsible is Carter.’

The three women sit close together staring ahead at the rows of empty chairs.

‘I’m going to the hospital,’ declares Indah, struggling up.

‘There’s nothing you can do there,’ says Becky, standing.

‘I don’t care, I’m going.’

‘You can’t, we’ve got a briefing. The Chief Constable wants to speak to all of us. Lisa needs us there. Indah, we have to support the DI.’

Outside Becky takes Indah’s hand in hers and they walk hand-in-hand to the incident room where they drop hands before going in.

++++

‘DI Lynn.’

‘Chief Constable?’

‘I’d come across myself, if it wasn’t for the fog, but I know you’ll cope.’

‘Thank you, Ma’am.’

‘Can you see me?’

‘Yes, there’s a good picture this end. Can you see us?’

‘Yes, hello everyone. Sorry to meet under these circumstances. We know it’s only John Carter involved, don’t we?’

‘It looks that way.’

'Looks? Don't over complicate this DI Lynn. This is a big opportunity for you. I know there are a number of loose ends, but keep your eye on the shootings and Carter. The Simpson connection and Eva what's-her-name will be handled by City. As far as Kerry is concerned leave it to DCI Mount and the IA team, but from what I'm reading it is definitely suicide, poor kid. DCI Mount will also deal with Tizard's failings and what happened at the house and in the forest. He's on gardening leave for now. Understood?'

'Yes Ma'am.'

'Lisa have IA collected your weapon?'

'Yes,' Lisa nods.

'You've all been made aware you'll have to make statements?' They all nod. 'Good. Pete Grimes?'

'Ma'am, I'm here.'

'What the hell got into you? Don't answer that. I've no choice, you're suspended as of now and stop playing fast and loose with IA,' she sighs. 'You shouldn't even be there,' she tells him. 'Back to Carter. He had motive, means and opportunity to kill these people didn't he?'

'Motive, means certainly, but as for opportunity there are gaps, but we are working to fill those,' Lisa explains. 'We now know he attended the school open days. We can't prove he stole Simpson's hand from the morgue.'

'There isn't going to be a trial, we don't have to prove every detail beyond reasonable doubt do we?'

'Also, we talk about means,' Lisa continues, not giving-up, 'yes weapons were found and he was a soldier, but did he have the ability to plan and carry out these attacks, especially the second one on the rental house? The pizza guy ruse was the mark of a cool professional.'

'DI Lynn,' Sylvia says coldly. 'Listen to me please.'

'Ma'am?'

'Close it and if it reassures you, I'll get a senior officer from headquarters to go over the case files and I will sign them off myself. I'll do the media briefing later today and Sunday.'

'Thank you, Ma'am.'

'In the circumstances, the very difficult circumstances, you've all done an excellent job. As for Cully, I've known him longer than any of you and if anything he's a fighter. Keep me informed,' and the screen goes blank.

They return to their seats

'Gov?'

'What? I'm not Gov, I'm Lisa,' she snaps. 'Sorry Monica, sorry everyone, I've never been involved in anything like this before and I'm feeling awful.'

'It's all arranged,' Pete announces, loudly, coming off his phone.

'What is?'

'Food and drinks at the pub.'

'You know it's gone midnight?'

'Only just,' says Monica. 'You're bloody well suspended, Pete. You heard the Chief, you shouldn't even be here.'

'I wanted to do something,' he groans.

'Don't care what time it is,' admits Becky, 'I need something, a wine or two and food sound exactly right.'

'Not tonight,' Lisa states, feeling slightly hungover from the session with Gerry. 'It's not right. Tomorrow maybe.'

'I need a drink because all this is my fault,' Pete moans.

'Of course it's not.'

'If I wasn't a clumsy old git, not tripped then Carter would have been dead in the forest and Cully and Chalky wouldn't have been shot for Christs sake! My fault, Lisa.'

'No Pete. I froze in the church and, you heard what the chief said, it was Carter. His responsibility and his alone.'

'And Cully? I owe that man everything. I was in a hole so deep when he came to MIU, I wasn't climbing out, but he offered me a hand and pulled me up. I'm here because of him and I've let him down. I'm going.'

'Me to,' says Chalky

'I need you here,' but knows she's lost them and not for the first time wonders what she is even doing there. 'Chalky please.'

'I'm going,' and he walks out, the door slamming behind him.

'Chalky,' begins Monica. 'Sorry Ma'am, I'll talk to him and following him out finds him sitting forlornly on the portacabin front step. The media throng have left and all is quiet. As she sits down Pete walks by and away into the darkness. 'Come back in,' she says gently to Chalky. 'You're feeling sorry for yourself and let's face it we all fucked up, but I don't think any of us could have done better. You've been so strong for us all, mister dependable Chalky White. Come in, apologise to Lisa and let's go for a drink.' She helps him up and they go back in. 'We're back,' she announces cheerily.

'Sorry Ma'am.'

'It's alright Chalky, we're all stressed out.'

'Ma'am,' Monica begins, 'I know it's not my place, but I think it's a good idea for all of us to get out of here.'

'I guess you're right. Go on, all of you.'

'Anyone joining us?' Monica asks.

'I'm in,' says Amber.

'I should be at the hospital,' Indah mumbles, but hardly able to bare what might be waiting for her. 'I'm going there.'

'I'll take you,' says Becky, briefly touching Indah's hand. 'We'll go together.'

'Ma'am?' Monica looks towards Lisa. 'Ma'am?'

'Go all of you.'

'Come with us,' Monica urges.

'Internal Affairs want to interview me in the morning.'

'Always better with a few drinks inside you.'

'I've had a lot already.'

'Then food and coffee will do you good. Come on.'

'Ma'am,' calls Chalky cheerfully from where he is standing in the doorway, 'your sisters here and she's brought some guests.'

++++

Monica is proud of her Roma heritage, dark looks and deep eyes of a fortune teller. Although she would never let on to her colleagues, she believes in the powers the Healer has and will visit her in the Great Forest when she gets a chance. Life growing up in Transylvania had been hard, but as a child riding in the back of her father's horse drawn wagon there was determination to do well and she knew even then that to fulfil her ambition she had to leave Romania. An intuitive detective she is objective and thorough when it comes to evidence and building a case and things about Sophie have been bothering her from the moment Cully and Indah started mentioning the woman. In Cully's case, his objectivity is blurred by his history with Sophie while Indah has been drawn into a distorted *ménage a trois*.

Monica sits alone in the church office. Lisa is with IA, a rather sulky Becky has gone to be with Jenny Sykes' daughters while they identify the body of their mother, there is no sign of Indah and Chalky is on the phone in the incident room. She has taken Sophie's book from Indah's desk and is thoughtfully reading the first chapter for the second time. The computer in front of her beeps and placing the book aside opens the email. Occasionally being Romanian is useful, especially when the records clerk at the hospital is also Romanian and is open to persuasion. 'But it's against the rules and the law,' he objected.

'I'm a police officer and I'm giving you permission.'

'It's confidential material.'

'Only I will see it,' Monica reassured him. 'Please, this is really important and you will be helping me.'

Sophie Cairns medical records from thirty years before are on the screen. They, alongside the traffic officers report of the crash which Monica eventually found misfiled, confirm the suspicions Monica has been struggling with. The problem is, how is she going to tell Cully the truth without devastating him?

++++

Phone rings somewhere in the room and sleepily Indah reaches out and takes it from the side table. 'Mmm?'

'Cully?'

'Wake up,' Indah hisses, holding the phone against her naked breast. 'Wake up,' she hits out.

'That hurt. I'm bruised remember,' he grumbles, pushing himself up. 'Bloody vest.'

'Saved your life and I didn't think you had one.' She hits him again. 'I was terrified. Bastard!'

'That really hurts. I always keep a spare in the car.'

'I thought you were dead. Now take the phone, it's Chalky.'

'Hello?'

'I didn't mean to disturb you, Gov. Sounds like you're hurting.'

'Like blazes, but painkillers help.'

'All sorts of things help,' Chalky chuckles, but quickly continues. 'I'm on duty here at the incident room. I've just had a call from your DCI at MIU.'

'Amelia Fox?'

'She's been trying to get hold of you.'

'Shit!' Cully scrolls down and there are several missed calls. 'What time is it?'

'Ten o'clock.'

'In the morning?'

'In the morning, Gov,' Chalky assures him.

'Why do you sound so chipper Chalky.'

'Navy, I'm hardened,' he laughs. 'I know I was down for a bit last night, but I'm fine now.'

'What does Amelia want?'

'A woman walked into HQ, off the street early this morning and said she's responsible for Jenny Sykes' death.'

'Seriously?'

'I don't think she'd joke about it.'

'No, of course not, sorry Chalky, I've not had much sleep.'

'Really, Gov?' Pauses for a moment. 'DCI Fox put her in a car and is sending her back to us. It's our case.'

'I suppose,' Cully nods. 'Name of the woman?'

'Sophie Cairns.'

'Shit.' He thinks. 'Ok, I'm going to ring Amelia, then Monica and then Indah.'

'You need to ring Indah, I thought…'

'The case belongs to Monica and Indah,' says Cully, ignoring the innuendo. 'I'll let Lisa know what's happening.'

Cully cuts Chalky off and rings Amelia.

'Sorry, I missed your calls. I'm full of pain killers.'

'You got hit twice?'

'I had a vest on.'

'Even so, bloody painful Cully. I remember. You know this Cairns woman?'

'Yes.'

'She just turned up. She said she'd returned to the mainland yesterday evening after Carter was shot and once she'd made certain you were alive. How well do you know her?'

'We went to school together.'

'She holds a flaming torch for you? People become obsessed and I'd say she's disturbed. She thought things through overnight and decided to come in. She said she wanted to do the right thing. Were they arguing over you Cully?'

'I doubt it Amelia, what did she say she did?'

'She didn't. To be honest I didn't give her a chance. It's an Island case.'

Cully rings Monica and asks her to liaise with the escort bringing Sophie over and interview her. 'I know you and Becky dealt with Jenny's death and Indah knows Sophie, but this needs very experienced handling. Lisa is with IA. Can you and Chalky take it?'

'Of course.'

'I'll ring Indah and explain.'

'You need to ring Indah, Gov?'

'Speak to you later Monica.'

'Wait, there is something important I need to speak to you about.'

'I'll be in later,' and hangs up.

After ringing Lisa and leaving a message, Cully leans back, wincing at the pains in his chest, thinking things through and gradually recalling the night before.

Insisting he needed to leave, the hospital reluctantly released him and Mary drove Linda and him to the incident room, picking up Adam on the way. Greeted warmly by the team, although Indah is surprisingly cool, they go on to the pub. Later, a glass raised to his lips, he watches Becky and Indah giggling together.

'They're both attractive, aren't they?'

'I'm old enough to be their dad, Lisa.'

'So?'

'You're a bad influence.'

'No, I'm jealous,' she grins.

'How do I choose between them?'

'Maybe you don't,' Lisa smiles.

'What is it?' asks Indah, easing herself up into a sitting position, long dark hair falling around brown shoulders. She pulls back the duvet to look at the livid blue, black and red bruises that cover his chest. 'You poor darling, it must hurt a lot.'

'It does. I'll get the Healer to rub some green stuff on them.'

'Bastard,' but doesn't hit him again. 'One thing I don't understand, you died and I was so worried. Then you turn up like nothing has happened. You could have let me know, I thought we had something?'

'We do. I only died for moments and Mary didn't give up. Second bit of luck, I wasn't going to get a vest, until Vicar Mandy reminded me not to rely on luck or Gods. Sorry, I didn't ring, but I was coming to you and yes we have something very special.'

'I forgive you.' She lowers her head to kiss his bruises, hair brushing over his skin. 'What's going on with work?' she asks, lifting her head, finding his eyes with hers.

'Sophie has handed herself in. She's said she was involved in Jenny's death. No idea how yet. I've allocated Monica and Chalky to interview her, I don't think you should be involved, sorry. Be warned the gossip has started.'

'Don't worry,' and she kisses him, 'I won't say a word.'

'Can you make coffee, black?'

'Of course my liege.' She leans forward and kisses him again. He feels himself responding as her breasts brush his chest, but pushes the feeling away.

Watching her go, he cannot help, but smile. 'Wake up,' he gently kicks the body on his other side. 'Wake up.'

'What is it?' she sighs sleepily, turning over, to look up at him.

'You're needed.'

'I know,' and he feels her hand finding him. 'Anything you want darling.'

'I need pain killers.'

'Poor baby.'

'You're a nurse, I'm sure you keep some in your bag, don't you Mary?'

++++

Patrick Le Strange takes the call on his mobile as Becky drives them towards the ferry. Finishing he half turns in his seat. 'That was Andrew,' he grins. 'He's feeling much better, the surgeon is pleased with how he's progressing and he's looking forward to seeing me.'

'Good news.'

'It is and this is good of you. There was no need, I could have got a taxi.'

'I wanted to.'

'But Becky you're not so happy with things?'

'I'm fine.'

'I'm a judge remember and will have you sent to the cells for perjury unless you tell the truth.'

'I think driving people is all I'm cut out for.'

'You don't like driving me?'

‘No, that’s not it. I enjoy talking to you.’

‘Good and I enjoy your company. I’m glad I no longer need armed protection, although Pete was good company as well. Where is he today?’

‘He’s been suspended because of shooting Carter. He went too far .’

‘Poor Pete, but I’m sure Cully will find a way to get him off.’

‘Then I had to take Jenny Sykes’ daughters to identify her body which was upsetting for all three of us. I didn’t know what to say.’

‘That would have been really hard Becky.’

‘I keep putting my foot in it, ever since that first night, I was gushy with Cully.’

‘But he still brought you into the team?’ She nods. ‘And he hasn’t sent you packing?’

‘No.’ Becky considers this. ‘I’ve been lucky to have the experience.’

‘Which has been bloody to say the least.’

‘I’m being selfish, you knew most of them.’

‘In truth, I’ll only mourn Jenny.’

‘I can’t get the sight of her body out of my head and I attended the autopsy yesterday morning and nearly fainted.’

‘Horrible for you Becky. You’ll get used to it and death is such a taboo subject. I’ll mourn James when he goes.’

‘James?’

‘Ah, sorry, a friend in the hospice. How is your detective?’

‘Still critical’

‘And Cully?’

‘He died.’

‘What?’ Alarmed, Patrick sits back. ‘I thought…’

‘Sorry, he died for a minute. There I go again opening my mouth without thinking. I don’t know if I can do this job anymore.’

‘Once you get through this terrible week, you’ll make a good police officer Becky,’ he tells her. ‘If ever you need a reference, let me know.’

‘Thanks,’ she smiles.

‘I’m sorry about the officer that was killed.’

‘So many dead,’ she sighs. ‘Then there’s Kerry.’

‘The suicide, I’m not tuned in am I?’ Patrick is thoughtful. ‘All because of what happened thirty years ago, frightening. John Carter was a bully, but with hindsight I can understand him better and feel sad about the things that made him the way he was.'

'Things?'

'Abuse, I'm sure of it. Working in court you get to know the most horrendous things, witness what harm people can do to each other.' He goes silent. 'Becky, pull in here will you?'

'But what about your ferry?'

'There will be another ferry.'

The ice cream parlour is open and entering the bell above the door tinkles. 'Have a double, triple scoop.' They are the only customers and stare into the glass fronted counter. 'This place has been here for decades. Italians do make the best ice cream. Now, it's my treat. What are your favourite flavours?'

'Strawberry and pistachio,' she says. 'I can't risk a third,' and pats her stomach.

'Silly girl,' he laughs. 'Very nice, pistachio is Andrew's favourite. We used to come here after school, just the two of us. I'm having chocolate and vanilla, very conventional and it's what I always used to have.' Patrick orders. They find a table and the waitress brings over fluted glass dishes with the ice creams to which she has added several cigar shaped wafers. 'Wonderful,' he grins.

Eating, Becky dabs away cream from her chin.

'Becky, there is something else troubling you,' he says, crunching on a wafer.

'You'll laugh.'

'No I won't.'

'Cully is over twice my age, right?' Patrick nods. 'But there's something about him, charisma I suppose. He's been good to me, tolerated my stupidity. Then I was scared he was really hurt. When he turned up at the pub, he gave me a big hug and I thought…'

'You'd end up in bed together?'

'Anyway,' Becky continues without acknowledgment, 'I'm chatting to Indah and she says she has to go to the loo, but doesn't come back and suddenly Cully has gone as well.'

'You're pissed at Indah.'

'Judge language, but yes.'

'Thirty years ago Jenny poisoned Sophie and Cully's relationship and that night, after we walked away from the beach party, Jenny and Cully vanished from the pub. I don't think Sophie ever got over it and then what happened to her left her with very deep scars. Thirty years later the feelings rumble on.'

'What do I do?'

'Don't let this thing with Indah hurt you for longer than a day or two, but if you want Cully then get after him.'

'It's not Cully I want.'

++++

'Now, where were we?' DCI Mount is feeling much better after getting home the night before, finding her husband had sent the kids to their grandparents, prepared a scented bath surrounded by candles, a meal and taken her to bed for surprisingly creative sex. She wonders, *'where he'd learned the thing with his tongue and her arse hole, but didn't care because it was everything she needed for then.'* 'Ah, yes we were talking about your finances.'

'My client,' begins the solicitor, Tizard now sits between the solicitor and his advocate, 'wishes to challenge the validity of the warrants.'

'That's for court not here. According to the statements from your secret bank account.'

'Not secret Chief Inspector.'

'Mary Tizard, your wife, never saw it.'

'We all keep secrets from our wives,' states the solicitor.

'Do you?' *'Her husband was obviously feeling guilty,'* she tells herself, *'otherwise why go to so much trouble? It has to be his doubles partner. The thing with his tongue was something the slut would have taught him. Did he have secret accounts?'* 'There are lots of payments in.'

'I've done several jobs on the side, we all do on the Island.'

'Against regulations.'

'I leave money stuff to my accountant.'

'You have an accountant?'

'Yes, James, he's done well by me. I suppose maybe it's income from investments.'

'So much, he must be a very good accountant?'

'He is.'

'We need to speak to him.'

'He's ill, dying in the Island hospice.'

'Convenient.'

'Not for him.'

'But for you. Moving on. We believe you supplied the Glock 17 used in the custody suit shooting eighteen months ago, then at the school hall, the rental house and finally the church.'

'This is bullshit.'

'You think so?'

'I've done nothing wrong.'

'Buying illegal flashbangs, being absent from your command, working on other jobs, having an affair with a junior officer who died mysteriously.'

'There's no mystery, she committed suicide.'

'Did she?' DCI Mount pauses, smiling. 'My Sergeant is currently searching the shed.'

'He won't find anything.'

'He won't in your shed, as we discovered yesterday, nor your house.'

'You had no right to search my house without a warrant.'

'Your wife gave us permission. Wives and women generally are allowed to part own or own property nowadays you know,' she states staring at the solicitor. *'My home is in both our names. I'll get to stay there and keep the children. He could go and live with the whore from the tennis club.'* 'We've been searching Kerry's shed.' Tizard glances from his advocate to his solicitor. 'So far, we've found tools, oils and parts required to maintain firearms. Also a shotgun, high powered hunting rifle and pistol.'

'I've got licenses.'

'DCI Mount,' begins the solicitor smiling like a crocodile, 'I believe your team are questioning another person about the Glock?'

'Moving on, let's talk about the raid on the rental house where the two women were killed, where your officers failed to protect them.'

'They made the mistakes, not me,' but Tizard is looking uncomfortable.

'You were very late getting there. Your wife tells us you weren't at home, where were you?'

'Out. I went for a ride on my bike to relax.'

'All evening?' No reply. 'You'd had an argument with Kerry Harris?'

'I don't remember.'

'You were seen arguing with her at about three that afternoon.'

'Who saw us?'

‘It doesn’t matter at this time. What was it about?’

‘Her and me.’

‘Be more specific?’

‘She wanted us to get back together.’

‘You didn’t want to?’

‘No.’

‘She was junior to you. You took advantage of her?’

‘You didn’t know Kerry.’

‘So, you’ve no alibi for the night Kerry died,’ she states. ‘Let’s move on to what happened in the forest.’

‘No more, I think we’ve gone far enough Chief Inspector. My client won’t be answering anymore questions.’

The door to the interview room swings open.

‘I’ve heard enough,’ the Chief Constable states stepping into the room. ‘Thank you Detective Chief Inspector for all your efforts. Sergeant Tizard, stand up please.’

‘Ma’am.’ He obeys. ‘What is it?’

‘As of now I am suspending you from duty. Human resources will be writing to you with a list of offences.’

‘Alleged offences,’ the solicitor interjects. ‘This is totally out of order Chief Constable. You have no right to treat my client like this.’

‘I’ll decide what I have a right to do. This man’s behaviour has disgraced the force and led to the deaths of at least two people. A tribunal will be convened to decide on professional breaches while the Chief Inspector here will discuss criminal charges with the Crown Prosecution Service, including the suspicious death of DC Kerry Harris.’

++++

Indah slides a handwritten note across her desk to Cully. It reads: ‘Mary says she is free tonight if we want to party?’

Cully considers the invitation before writing on it. ‘Nice, but I’d rather spend the night alone with you.’

‘Right answer, Gov,’ she says, grinning. ‘I’ll make coffee. Who wants coffee?’ she asks loudly standing. ‘I make that five,’ and she heads for the kitchen.

Phone rings.

'Patrick, good to hear from you.' Cully listens. 'Thanks for letting me know and I'm glad Andrew is better. In fact, she's just come into the incident room. Speak to you soon.'

Becky is carrying a plastic bag. Placing it on a desk she lifts out three large tubs, a box of wafers and a scoop. 'Anyone for ice cream?'

'Fantastic,' beams Chalky.

'Becky,' Cully smiles. 'You are a life saver, ice cream from the Italian, fantastic.'

'I just thought…'

'A perfect and timely lift for us all.'

'I expect you want me to make coffee for everyone?'

'No Becky, Indah is goffering today. I need to ask you a couple of things.'

'You do?'

'Before I speak to your sergeant, are you willing to stay with the team for another week?'

'Yes, I'd love, I mean that would be good.' She brightens. 'There is something else?'

'I need your view. Could you take the reports on the people that bought flashbangs from Turner, Mandy, Sophie, Alison and the paintball people and anyone else and give me your opinion on what should happen to them.'

'My view?'

'Yes, you've a good common sense approach. Then you can talk them through with Lisa or me and then the CPS.'

'I'll get right on to it and thank you.'

'Have your ice cream first.'

'I'm guessing you prefer chocolate, Gov?' shouts Chalky.

'A scoop of chocolate and vanilla together please,' he calls back.

In the kitchen, Indah waits for the machine to finish producing coffee when the door opens and closes behind her.

'Hi Becky.'

'Can I help?'

'Sure.'

'Missed you last night. You slipped away.'

‘Should have said something, but Lisa’s sister offered the Gov and me a lift and to be honest I was bushed. It’s good with you,’ Indah says, ‘we should go out.’

‘We should?’

‘Definitely.’

‘I know you are flying on to greater things, but can we still be mates?’

‘Only mates?’ Indah pulls Becky to her and kisses her firmly on the lips. ‘That’s for starters, but not tonight sweety, ok?’

Back in the incident room Chalky is chasing ice cream down the side of his cone with his tongue.

‘Pete, where have you been?’ Monica gets up and goes to where the detective has entered. ‘I’ve been worried about you.’

‘I’m fine. I’ve just come in to say hi and clear my desk.’

‘What are AI saying?’

‘They are talking about a manslaughter charge.’

‘Jesus no,’ complains Becky. ‘They can’t.’

‘They can, but Linda is already putting up a defence. One that might work thanks to the Gov,’ and Pete looks up. ‘Thanks, Gov, you didn’t have to. So glad you’re ok.’

‘What have you done Cully?’ asks Indah going over to him as Pete starts telling everyone about the crazy night he spent in the woods. ‘I’m taking her out tonight.’

‘On a date?’ Chalky asks.

‘Yes.’

‘Then I really do need to get you to M & S today, don’t I?’

‘Please Monica, I want to do this right.’

‘Where do you take a forest-dwelling healer on a date?’ Becky asks.

‘Her Jane him Tarzan,’ Chalky laughs.

‘Perfect,’ announces Cully, ‘“Jungle Book” is on at the cinema in town.’

‘Funny,’ Pete moans.

‘A pity it’s not “Forrest Gump”,’ declares Lisa.

‘“Forrest Grump”,’ Cully adds, or “Wicker Man?”’

‘Fuck off, all of you,’ Pete complains, grinning. ‘Is there any ice cream left?’

‘Some,’ says Becky. ‘Chocolate?’

‘We all like chocolate, don’t we?’ Indah smiles. ‘Don’t you?’

‘I think I love chocolate,’ Becky admits.

'Don't get carried away,' Indah warns softly, before going back to Cully, standing close, bodies touching. 'You've not said what you've done for Pete?'

'I did a report this morning arguing that I and IA, when they interviewed him yesterday, should have recognised he was suffering from PTSD and he should not have been allowed to work. Linda reckons that at worse he'll get disciplined for excessive force and offered early retirement. He can live with the Healer in the forest.'

'What about you?'

'A reprimand and promotion, according to Sylvia. Now, we must get on and,' he whispers, 'can't wait to see you later.' He steps away from her. 'Ok people, I know school is nearly out and I'm aware you had a briefing from the Chief Constable last night and she has her mind made up about Carter. I agree with her, but we have to bring it together. She wants it done and dusted as soon as possible. Just to update you on what I can, Tizard has been suspended and is facing a professional conduct panel and maybe criminal charges.'

'About time,' Lisa mutters.

'While that's all sorted out, armed response need a sergeant and someone with the experience and ability to sort them out. Good luck Monica.'

Applause all round.

'Chalky, Bethany?'

'Her aunt arrived early this morning. A really nice woman. Bethany is staying with us and the aunt is in a hotel while she sorts the Simpson's affairs out.'

'Good and Chalky, you need a couple of days out to prepare for next Friday and your Sergeant's exam.'

Phone rings and Chalky answers.

'Gov, the car with Sophie Cairns has arrived.'

++++

Cully stands in the narrow portacabin corridor watching the interview on a monitor. Squeezing shut his eyes he wonders what, if anything, he misses in all this? Probably plenty, he tells himself.

'Can I call you Sophie?' asks Monica. Cully chose her to do the interview because she is the best interrogator out of any of the team and she's not personally involved. She and Chalky sit one side of the table with Sophie alone on the other. 'Can I?'

'Yes.' Sophie looks small, curly light brown hair dishevelled and there is a slight tremor in her voice when she speaks. 'Of course you can.' Cully has got to a point where he wonders if it's an act. 'Just ask your questions.'

'This isn't a formal interview, we're not recording it, but that might change depending on what you say. You voluntarily came into police headquarters this morning and announced that you were responsible for Jenny Sykes death?'

'I'm afraid I might be.'

'DCI Fox sent you back to us.' Sophie nods. 'We want to know what you did to Jenny?'

'We argued on the cliff path?'

'Was the meeting arranged?'

'No, I needed to speak to her. I sat next to Tash at the event. I had Sean O'Leary on my other side and he is such a prat it was better to talk to Tash. Anyway, she said Jenny walks her dog there twice a day.'

'So you took her by surprise. Why did you want to see her?'

'To talk about Cully. At school, we both went out with him, but I did first, during and after the play.'

'Play?'

'"Abelard and Heloise" by Roland Millar. He was Abelard and I was Heloise. Jenny stole him from me. She ruined my life.'

'This all happened thirty years ago,' says Chalky.

'He was, is attractive. DC Kasali understands about Cully.'

'How's that?'

'Jenny and I competed for him then and now she and I compete for him.'

'Let's get back to the cliff path,' says Monica firmly, aware they need to keep focussed. 'You argued about school days?'

'Yes. We'd never had it out and I wanted to make certain she didn't mess things up for us again. We've always been together, not actually, I'm not crazy, but in our hearts.'

'You hated Jenny?' Chalky asks.

'Too strong and I don't hate Indah either for wanting him,' says Sophie. 'I know what she's up to and she lied to me about Jenny leaving a message for him.'

'Is that why you assaulted her at the court building?' Chalky asks.

'I didn't.'

'After the hearing, you argued and then attacked her.'

'I didn't.'

'You argued with Jenny,' Monica intervenes. 'Did you threaten her, physically, assault her?'

'I told her to stay away from Cully or else.'

'Else what?'

'It was just words.'

'Did you touch her?'

'I slapped her.'

'So, as you admit to assaulting her we will need the clothes you were wearing. Will you give us a DNA sample?' Sophie nods. 'Thank you for that.'

'When I left her, she was alive.'

'Then why do you think you're responsible?'

'I accused her of something terrible,' Sophie admits. 'The guilt of it made her jump.'

'You think she committed suicide?'

'Didn't she?' Sophie grimaces. 'Someone drugged me when I was raped.'

'Jenny?' asks Monica, aware having read Indah's notes.

'I'm sure.'

'How do you know?'

'Davis told me as he penetrated me.'

'In which case you had a motive to kill Davis and Jenny.'

'I did, but I didn't.'

'Reading your book,' continues Monica, 'I get the impression you're intolerant of people that allow themselves to become victimised?'

'I'm not.'

'Because you allowed yourself to become victimised?'

'I'm not a victim. I help victimised people to assert themselves.'

'The introduction is all about you. You allege in it that you were raped, burned in the car crash, developed a drug problem and sold yourself for sex. Is all that true?'

'Yes.'

'You entered rehab, but it's clear it still affects you thirty years later?'

'I've worked through it. I was prey then, but now I'm…'

'A predator?'

'I was arguing with Jenny about the here and now.'

'You can repress the memories as long as you want, but they always find a way to express themselves don't they Sophie?'

'So, now you're a therapist Sergeant?'

'I'm a woman, I'm a victim,' Monica answers. 'Everyone is in some way. Sophie Cairns, we're going to pause now and reconvene in one hour when we will interview you on the record. You should get a solicitor.'

++++

'I had the experience, but missed the meaning,' Cully mutters and walks out of the portacabin, into the incident room and goes over to Indah's desk where he finds a copy of Sophie's book. Sitting he starts to read the introduction again when the main door opens and closes. 'Dad, your phone has been off and I wanted to make certain you were ok. You shouldn't be working, you died.'

'For a few moments,' he reassures her. 'Come and sit down. I probably should have remained in hospital, but needed to see the team and you enjoyed the party didn't you?'

'I did. So did Adam. He was chuffed to be there. You slipped away without a word,' Linda scolds him. 'With Indah?'

'Mary gave us a lift. She got my heart racing again.'

'I bet,' Linda grins. 'Becky wasn't happy when she couldn't find Indah, she sulked and left.'

'Not surprised. She is more interested in Indah than she is in me. Lisa told me the other night.'

'And Indah?'

'I've discovered is bi.'

'How do you know that?' Linda shakes her head. 'Don't say, I don't want to know. Jesus, your love life's complicated.'

'At least, I've got one at last. It's what you wanted Linda.'

'With one woman, not a stable full dad.'

Cully thanks her for what she's doing for Pete and then tells her about the interview he's just watched. 'Not sure if Sophie's a little crazy or acting a part. I used to like her a lot, but she's changed.'

'Not surprising after thirty years.'

'I didn't know half the stuff about her, especially the drug addiction. It's an amazing piece of writing,' he admits. 'Incredible that she survived, but I reckon that's what changed her.'

'It would have changed anyone,' Linda admits. 'Are you in love with Indah?'

'Not yet. I'm "Drowning in the Sea of Love"' he smiles

'Fleetwood Mac?'

'Your mother and I…'

'I know,' Linda squeals, 'made love to it, the night I was conceived. I miss mum.'

'So do I and feel guilty having feelings for another woman.'

'Women,' Linda corrects, grinning. 'Before mum went, she said you had to find someone else and it's been ten years. We should take flowers to the graves,' and they agree to go the next day. 'What happens now with Sophie?'

'They will interview her on tape later. She's admitted common assault, but forensics may come up with something more. Whatever, she needs help.'

'Because she's obsessed with you.'

'Right, she's got to be mad.'

'And Indah?'

'I'm flattered, enjoying it,' he smiles, 'but know when I'm being used. She's ambitious and deserves to be. I'm useful to her. She's talented and will go far. I'm a stupid old man.'

'You're not old,' Linda laughs. 'Enjoy it, you deserve some fun.'

'What about the law and your ambitions?'

'You've noticed? Of course you have, you're the great detective. Do you mind?'

'No. I can't wait to appear in court with my daughter the barrister.'

'I must go, Angus's in the car and I promised him a walk on the beach.'

Watching her walk away he marvels again at how like her mother she is, tall, long limbed and at last getting back to being effortless in her movements. Smiling, but the smile fades. He was there when the bullying and the abuse took place, hated the Nasty Gang, was involved with these women, but didn't see what was happening. He pulls himself together. It is pointless indulging in regrets and dwelling on lost opportunities from schooldays, but he couldn't let go of one thing however hard he tries.

++++

'You were born in Serbia, in eighty-five,' states DCI Mount. 'Your father was a low level member of *Groupa Europa*. You did well at school especially in science and English. The gang began to take an interest in you Sarafina, your real name, and arranged…'

'This is absurd. I've heard of *Groupa Europa* and my father was a runner for them, but that's all. As for my name I changed it to make things easier for me in England. I came with my family to do my degree.'

IA had invited Amber in for an interview and she'd assumed it was about the shootings. They had still not been able to get church permission to bring in lifting gear to lift the alter and retrieve the Glock used by Carter. She is frustrated, but now is feeling ambushed and angry.

'You got a first, did an MA in forensic science and applied for a job with the Forensic Science Service. They grabbed you, of course they did, and you were exactly where *Groupa Europa* wanted you, the inside girl able to tamper with evidence.'

'This is rubbish, I've never done anything wrong,' she grimaces. 'You can check all my cases.'

'The government disbanded FSS and you went private with Biotech Laboratories. You've risen to director, but are never far from the action.'

'All true.'

'Ten years ago,' continues Mount, 'the gang ordered you to find out where the Cully family were being hidden. They asked you because they guessed they were in a safe house somewhere in the south, probably on the Island and you were already here with Biotech, a junior, but nevertheless useful.'

'This is crazy. Do I need a lawyer?'

'That's up to you,' Mount smiles. 'You seduced Tizard and while you were swallowing his cock he told you where they were. You're attractive, sexy and use your body to gain trust, allocation to certain cases and promotions,' Mount's smile widens, rather enjoying the subject matter. 'Men are stupid when it comes to you. You got yourself into the team that went to the White House after the shooting and removed the Glock 17.'

'Madness. Why should I do any of this?'

'Loyalty to the gang, money and ultimately fear because *Groupa* would kill your family if you didn't cooperate.'

'No, just because I was,' she emphasises, 'Serbian, is that what this is about? You're fucking racists.'

‘We have evidence to suggest you are an armourer leasing out the Glock, either working for *Groupa* or yourself.’

‘If this is true, then why did I share my findings with Cully, connecting the custody suit and school shootings. I would have hidden the link and why am I sweating myself silly trying to get the gun out from under that bloody alter?

++++

It starts to rain, but the art centre is not far from the church and Cully believes he can out run the rain. Thirty years since the events he’s having to relive, but so much success since and Indah is so special. The investigation is more or less over and he’d survived another shooting, he should be walking on air. Perhaps, people were right he’d never dealt with all the deaths that surround him. It is as if all the pent up emotion, the responsibility, the frustration, the fear is poised to explode within him.

The rain grows heavier.

The mobile library is parked outside, an old single decker bus with posters on the windows and about it an air of sad desperation. Leaning against the cooling rain helps bring his emotional temperature down.

At the door of the centre is a poster advertising “The Tragedy of Abelard and Heloise on canvas by the artist Sean O’Leary”. Striding in, the door slamming behind him, he ignores the startled woman on reception. Beyond is the entrance to the gallery and entering, he looks around, but sees no one. There is a table, covered with art materials, standing on a large paint splattered dust sheet. There is also a tool kit for assembling frames from the lengths of wood piled on the floor. Against the table lean a number of canvasses and Cully starts sorting through them recognising scenes from the play. Sophie is in everyone as Heloise and in several Sean has portrayed himself as Abelard. They are good, Cully admits to himself, but the obsession is obvious. ‘Poor bastard,’ he mutters, feeling his anger abate and some sympathy for short arse take its place.

‘We’re not ready I’m afraid,’ announces a woman, coming into the room. In her thirties, tall with black hair and wearing a paint smeared smock. ‘They’re good aren’t they? You know Sean?’

‘I used to,’ he nods, lifting one of the paintings. ‘You must be Cordelia.’

‘And you are, don’t tell me,’ she smiles as recognition lights up her dark eyes. ‘Oh my God, it’s you isn’t it, the policeman on television, the one that got shot saving the woman in the church.’

‘How much is this one?’ Cully asks about the painting he holds. Sophie stands alone early in the play before she falls in love with Abelard. Sean has captured the innocence in her face, especially in the eyes, that have now become so cold and alien. ‘How much?’

‘We’ve not priced them yet, but we can reserve it. It’s good to have pictures up on the wall with sold stickers, encourages people to buy.’

Suddenly there is a man’s small voice, or is it a small man’s voice? He is quoting lines from the play. ‘That’s your madness. Bury yourself alive if you must, don’t bury her too’

‘She’s willing,’ says Cordelia.

‘Of course she’s willing! She’d go through hell if you asked her,’ calls Sean.

‘I know she would,’ shouts Cully, replacing the painting. ‘Isn’t that what infuriates you Sean, that she’d go through hell if I asked and still would?’ No answer. ‘You are talented, I’ll give you that.’

Sean appears, staring in surprise at Cully. ‘What do you want?’

‘He wants to buy one of your paintings Sean, your first sale,’ says Cordelia, but senses the mood and is uncertain what to do. ‘Shall I make tea?’

‘That would be nice,’ says Cully. ‘Sean and I have some things to discuss,’ he adds watching Cordelia retreat from the room. ‘Well little man?’

‘Don’t call me that.’ Sean moves out of the shadows to stand on the other side of the table. ‘I don’t understand.’

‘Why did you lie to Jenny about Rachel and me?’

‘It was thirty years ago.’

‘That doesn’t answer my question,’ Cully states, stepping closer.

‘You took Rachel off me. It was always easy for you, they lined up. What about Sara before Rachel?’

‘What?’ Cully stares at him in disbelief. ‘All I did was snog her once at a party at Philip Simpson’s.’

‘I planned to ask her out.’

‘Strikes me Sean, you’ve spent your whole life planning and never doing.’

‘Rachel was special.’

‘If you call being easy, special. The rumour you made up to poison me and Sophie was in fact true. Rachel had tasty tits and a tight cunt, what more could a teenage boy want to feast on?’

‘I don’t believe you,’ Sean sobs. ‘She was under age.’

‘By a few months and it made it better, doing her against the law.’

‘Sophie didn’t want my rugby shirt to play netball in, said it was too small. She took yours instead. I saw the two of you at the disco and everyone talked about how good you were together in the play. I couldn’t believe how Sophie looked at you.’

‘You jealous bastard, you thought that if you broke us up Sophie would come to you, poor little short arse.’

‘Stop it!’ Sean is trembling. ‘It’s my curse Cully, I love a woman that doesn’t want me, doesn’t even like me.’

‘What about at the party before we all went off to university? You left university early, failed exams, couldn’t hack it and then there’s your drug problem.’

‘How do you know about that?’

‘I’m a cop. Tell me about the party.’

‘You just waltzed in with Sophie. It’s Cully they shouted as if you were a pop star, but the two of you’d been arguing and I enjoyed you being unhappy.’

‘What did you put in Sophie’s drink, RHB? You didn’t have the courage to even try to have sex with her yourself. Cock too small Sean?’

‘Fuck off!’

‘I’m guessing you set Davis up, told him Sophie was gagging for it. It was you who told me Sophie had gone off with him, that he was drunk.’

‘You’re mad Cully, there was nothing like that. Sophie was furious with you. She went off with Cameron to spite you, but the crash even worked in your favour. She’s fooled you. You can’t believe anything she says or has written in that bloody book,’ he scoffs. ‘There’s nothing to suggest she ever had a drug problem or prostituted herself. She’s a fantasist. There was even a rumour she was pregnant a few months after the crash. Was she so badly injured? Have you actually seen her scars?’

‘Boys! What is going on? You sound like kids.’

‘We went to school together,’ Cully explains and takes a mug of tea from the tray she has brought in. ‘We’re sorting out some old stuff,’ he smiles at her. ‘I was in the play at school.’

'I bet you were Abelard.'

'I was.'

'How fabulous. I could be Heloise.'

'How do you see me?'

'A man in his prime,' she responds, smiling.

'And you, you are at the spring time.'

'You remember the lines.' She is excited. 'Do you hear that Sean, he remembers the lines?'

Cully takes a sip of tea, pretending to savour it, but keeps his eyes on Sean who is fiddling distractedly with tools on the table.

'I'd love to know more about police work,' she says and steps closer to him. 'You must be terribly busy.'

'I'm here for another week.' Cully is grinning, looking over her shoulder at Sean. 'Let me take you to dinner?'

'I'd love that. Sean, give me a brush,' but he doesn't move. 'What's wrong? Be like that,' she rebukes him, 'I'll get my own,' and picking one up from the table, dabs it in a pot and writes on Cully's proffered palm. 'There.'

'Where shall I paint my number?' he asks.

'Anywhere you like,' she giggles.

'Instead, I've got a card,' and hands it over.

'Spoil sport, you won't forget, will you?'

'Absolutely not. I'll ring you.'

'I must go.' She kisses Cully on the cheek. 'I'll tell everyone I've got a date with super cop. Sean, I'm going shopping and might treat myself to a new dress,' and winks at Cully. 'I'll be back in a few hours.'

Watching her go Cully turns to a scowling Sean.

'She's a bit tall for you, but don't worry I'll let you know what she's like afterwards.' He then notices Sean is holding a Stanley knife, flicking the blade in and out. 'Come on Sean do it, you know you want to.'

++++

The wooden stairs are stained and not a little rickety. They creak as Cully climbs and memories flood back. He stops, glancing out of a small round window cut into the stone wall, the whole school laid out beneath him, telling himself things had not been so bad. Pushing open the narrow door the mustiness assails him, but there through the flecks of dust caught in the rays of light spilling through low windows she sits and he is transported back. 'What was it you said that time?' she asks.

'That you were an angel. That every time I was with you I was in heaven.'

'We were Abelard and Heloise until torn apart'

'It was the best of times,' he admits.

'Dickens,' she remembers, 'a set book on our English Lit' course.'

The old library is small and dimly lit, but the big table is still there at the centre and the shelves are packed with dusty books. He goes to the narrow window, looks out across middle quad to where the new glass and steel learning centre glints in the sunshine. He doubts there were many books there, but plenty of computer terminals.

'What are you thinking?' Sophie asks.

'That times have changed.' He sits down across from her, reaching into his inside pocket, pulling out a crumpled copy of the play. 'Remember this?'

'You've kept it.' She takes it, turns faded pages, reading lines and annotations she had written there. 'My copy, I gave it to you,' she remembers, excitedly.

'You wrote S.W.A.L.K on the back cover,' he reminds her.

'So I did,' she smiles. 'I meant it.'

'We had a party the last night.'

'Had too much to drink and you walked me home. We should have done it, but you were chivalrous, although I felt your desire against me. You were a gentleman, said we were too drunk.'

'I must be better than I think.'

She looks at him slyly. 'Oh, I think you know how good you are Cully. We are who we are Cully. We can't escape our nature. You're a good man. There's something I need to tell you, even if it is thirty years too late,' she says looking down. Then lifting her head, holds his eyes with hers. 'I should never have believed Jenny.'

'It wasn't her.'

'What?'

'I'll explain later. You were saying.'

'That day, that special day when we met in the High Street and later made love at your place, our first time and the weeks that followed.'

‘There should have been many more times. We shouldn’t have gone to the party.’

‘The “off to university party”,’ Sophie remembers. ‘I talked you into it, I wanted to show everyone we were back together.’

‘We argued,’ he remembers, ‘because I wouldn’t let you drive.’

‘You flirted with Rachel and Jenny.’

‘And you with Cameron. You vanished with him.’

‘It’s a blur. I must have passed out.’

‘You were drugged?’

‘That’s what that horrible policeman said, that if my story was true then it was my fault.’

‘It wasn’t your fault, none of it.’

‘I remember…’

‘You don’t have to.’

‘I do. I remember Davis on top of me. The stench of his horrible breath. It was so painful and then driving away scarily fast and you chased after me. You saved my life.’

‘But you wouldn’t see me, Sophie.’

‘I was damaged goods.’

‘I could have been there for you.’

‘I know that now Cully, but you found happiness with Caitland and Linda is so beautiful.’

‘But what about you?’

‘I didn’t matter, I was dead inside. ‘I can’t go on, I must go on.’

‘Becket?’

‘Another set book. I climbed out of that dark hole and made good use of my life, didn’t I, helping people?’

‘You did. The team are looking for you, ready for your formal interview. You’ll tell the truth won’t you?’

‘Of course.’

‘The whole truth Sophie, everything.’

Door swings open with a crash. ‘There you are. Sorry Gov,’ begins Becky.

‘Not now.’

‘Sorry, but…’

‘What is it?’

‘We’ve been looking all over for Ms Cairns, they are ready to start the interview. The duty solicitor is here and I’ve got the recommendations on the flashbangs for you to look at.’

++++

The rest of the day the team use to prepare and complete the files that will be sent to Headquarters for signing off. Vehicles arrive to remove the portacabin to the cheers of the team. Cully is completely taken by surprise when Rachel turns up to find out what is happening with her sister. The teenager that started so much of this has grown up, tall yet slight, long blonde hair pulled back in a severe pony tail and wearing jodhpurs, knee length boots and carrying a crop she taps distractedly against her thigh. Cully had forgotten horse riding is her obsession and the strangely sexy smell of saddle soap that surrounds her. The team, especially Indah, stare agog as Rachel follows him into the glass-fronted inner office. He closes the door and they talk, even laugh for a while before she emerges smiling and leaves without a backward glance.

‘Just to update you,’ begins Cully following, ‘Amber is taking some leave, she’s exhausted bless her.’

‘And?’ Indah demands a little too sharply. ‘What about Rachel?’

‘She’s offered to meet any bail conditions on Sophie, money, accommodation and so on. Now, I’ve got a visit to make and I suggest you all get off and we’ll wrap things up tomorrow.’

An hour later Cully emerges from the hospice into the dusk, walking towards his car he’s aware that there are voice mails and several texts waiting on his phone. Getting in he takes a deep breath before listening to the first from the Chief Constable. ‘Glad you’re ok Cully. I’ve got a job for you. There is a promotion with it. Speak soon.’

The second: ‘Fuck Cully!’ Shouts a drunken Gerry. ‘How many more bloody bodies are you sending me? Suicide is catching. I’ve had it with you.’

Texts next.

Dad, all well here. Adam and I are playing Scrabble and drinking expensive wine. Table rebooked for four, for dinner tomorrow night. Don’t expect to see you tonight! Enjoy whomever you are with. Love you.

Next from Mary. *Thought you'd like to know Alison Grey has agreed to see the shrink. Don't you dare be a stranger.*

Abelard. Help me please, from Sophie which he ignores.

There is a text from Indah, wanting to know if he is on his way. He rings back. 'Hi, leaving the hospice now. Jamie has not got long left, a few weeks if he's lucky, or unlucky depending on how you look at it. He wants to see you. He's asked me to kill him again which I won't. What about you?'

'Hurry up and get here lover, I'm in my riding gear.'

Cully rings Chalky.

'Anything I should know about?'

'A suspected suicide at the arts centre. A male. Monica is dealing and the body has already gone to Gerry.'

On his way to Indah's, Cully drives to the centre and parking next to the mobile library sees Monica emerging. She waves, briefly speaks to the uniformed officer guarding the door before coming over and climbing in beside him. 'Glad you're here, Gov. As far as the suicide is concerned, slit his wrists with a Stanley knife. Cut all the faces out of his pictures, poor sod.'

'You'll notify the father?'

'Yes,' she confirms. 'I've been digging into things. Not the suicide, it's about Sophie. What do you remember about the night of the car crash?'

'I know about Sophie.' Cully sighs and starts talking, beginning a few weeks before the crash. He'd split from Jenny after "A" levels. Sophie and he avoided each other and then the exam results came out. She got straight A's and he sent her congratulatory red roses and they worked. Getting back together they were hardly out of each other's company for weeks until the "off to university party". 'Sophie was in a mood because I wouldn't let her drive my car,' he continues. 'I'd only started teaching her and she was bloody dangerous. Everyone was there. There was plenty of drink and some drugs. Much later I found out Sean O'Leary was dealing. Sophie drank and smoked dope. I drank, but I've never smoked anything. Jenny was there and came over to me. She was always touchy feely and that pissed Sophie off even more. She started flirting with the boys, ignoring me. The more she flirted the more I did and then Rachel turns up with Cameron Davis. She was high on something, came over to me.'

'And your teenage brain started thinking threesome?'

'I suppose. The next thing Sophie and Cameron vanish.'

'What did you do?'

'I remember, being tempted to stay with the girls, but sensed something wasn't right. I asked Sean where they'd gone and he laughed. "Cameron's gone to give her one", is what he said and I ran outside in time to see Cameron's car speeding away. I followed. The driving ahead of me was fast and erratic, swerving this way and that and then the car went off the road, rolled over and caught fire. I pulled-up, ran across the field towards it and carried Sophie clear. It was only then I saw Davis, sitting on the bank.'

'I pulled the local paper front page,' explains Monica. '"Hero Teenager Saves Girl's Life". The article says you undid her seatbelt and dragged her free, carried her to a horse trough to cool her burns, then held her until the paramedics arrived.'

'I didn't want any publicity, but Sophie contacted the press. She got some details wrong.'

'Gov, from which side of the car did you lift Sophie?'

'It was dark, I'd been drinking.'

'Gov?'

'Driver's side I think, but she could have been thrown there.'

'So, Sophie could have been driving?'

'Yes, and I didn't drop her in the horse trough, I simply used the water to splash on her.'

'According to hospital records she only had minor burns down the left, not the right side of her body, did not need plastic surgery and was released after only five days. She was driving, not Davis.'

'I think I knew, but I traded on it. The following week I had the interview board for the police undergraduate scheme. Sophie's Dad did an amazing reference and the board loved the fact I was already a hero. I was a shoo in. I met Caitland on the programme and our lives moved on together.'

'Davis was charged with drink driving and reckless endangerment,' explains Monica. 'In his statement, he said he couldn't remember, it was all a blur. In her statement, Sophie blames him, but did not mention any rape. I've checked records. Sophie told Indah that she spoke to a sergeant called Harris about the rape, but she couldn't have done. He was in hospital in traction. Gov…' Monica hesitates.

'She wasn't raped by Davis,' Cully sighs, understanding he'd been taken in. 'Why make it all up?'

'Have you read any of the reviews of her book?' He shakes his head. 'They all say how inspiring it is that a victim shows such strength to overcome and want to help other victims. The book is good, but it's success is based on her personal story in the introduction. It's all made up, the burns, the rape, the drug dependency. Gov, I'm sorry, Sophie Cairns is a total fraud.'

'What did she say in the interview?'

'Nothing. It was no comment all the way through, but we've charged her with the assault on Jenny. SOCO have found evidence of a struggle at the top of the cliff and CPS are pushing for a more serious charge. Sorry Gov.'

'No need. Do what you have to do Monica.'

Eight Weeks Later

Standing before the full-length mirror, she looks herself up and down. The uniform suits her as do the stripes on the shoulder. Her black hair is tied back in a tight pigtail. While her mum struggles to understand about the promotion, let alone who she is, Indah wishes her father were alive to see her.

'You look wonderful.' Standing behind her he places hands on her shoulders. 'You look incredibly sexy in uniform.' He kisses the nape of her neck, smells the wild flowers in her hair. 'Indah.'

'Stop it, we can't. Not now, Cully.' She swings around to face him. 'Look at you, in your uniform, handsome man.' She brushes fluff from his collar. 'I love a man in uniform.'

'You've done so well,' he says, resisting asking the obvious question.

'It's all thanks to you.'

'Rubbish, it's totally down to you, Indah, you've worked hard for this.'

'The DVHC Unit is not exactly my first choice. Is it because I'm black, I'm going there?'

'Possibly, or because you are going to make an excellent sergeant. You will you know and the DVHC is better than traffic. That's where they sent me. Do a year and you can apply to CID or go back to MIU. Amelia wants you back.'

'I told the staff I'd look in on mum, let her see the uniform, not that she'll understand, but I'll try. They are good to her. I couldn't do it on my own.' She knew it was a relationship of mutual dependency. 'Thank you.'

'Thank Sylvia and the relatives fund.'

'Why haven't you asked?'

'What about?'

'I lied to Sophie. Why haven't you ever asked?' she repeats.

'I suppose it wasn't important in the scale of things. Sophie mentioned it during the interview. Did you lie?'

'Yes.'

'On tape?'

'No.'

'She can't prove it, your word against hers. What did you tell her?'

'That Jenny left a message wanting to see you. I just wanted to hurt her. What if believing that she went to see Jenny and killed her?'

'If Sophie killed her, it goes deeper than what you said, it goes back thirty years and is as much my fault as anyone's.'

'Did she kill Jenny?'

'I don't know, but I don't believe they'll make the manslaughter charge stick. She assaulted her, but that's all they've got.'

'I've taken advantage of you, haven't I?' she says.

'I think that works both ways doesn't it?' He grins. 'We've both enjoyed the ride.'

'You're a bad man, Detective Chief,' with emphasis, 'Superintendent Cully.'

'I'm going to miss you.'

'I'll be back over most weekends and you can look after my little house for me,' she says and kisses him on the mouth. 'Sharing your mainland home with Linda will be fun.'

'I dread to think what the two of you will get up to.'

'You could find a place with Sophie over here, if she gets bail,' she teases. 'Maybe she was right, I'm here for the sprint, but she's there for the marathon.'

'She's in prison and is that what she said?' Indah smiles thinly and nods. 'I must admit you exhaust me, but can't I have you both?'

'No, the thing with Mary was a one-off,' but suddenly alarmed. 'You've not seen her again, have you?'

'Sophie or Mary?'

'Either you bastard.'

'Neither, but what about you and Becky?'

'You know it never got going. I realised I just wanted…'

'Yes?'

'To be here with you. Anyway,' she breathes, ignoring him, not quite believing the feelings of jealousy she is experiencing. The last few weeks living there with him had been blissful. Linda visited, accepted them as a couple and there had been no tension with Amelia during the weeks at MIU before the promotion came through.

'Indah?'

‘Sorry, miles away. I can’t be here if and when Minty turns up to do her article, imagine what she’d do with that,’ she laughs. ‘I need time to sort mum out, but I’ll be there up on the hill later.’ She kisses him lightly, but then again. ‘God, this is too much.’

‘We’ve got hours yet,’ and he takes her hand.

‘My uniform,’ she grins.

‘I’ll iron out the creases,’ he offers leading her.

‘What are you going to do about Tom?’

‘Talk to him.’

‘And if he won’t listen?’

They kiss and collapse on the bed laughing.

++++

Kissing Indah goodbye, Cully leaves the house and drives to the police station. The uniform chaffs and he cannot get used to junior officers saluting. Even Monica does, then laughs and hugs him. Lisa simply smiles and congratulates him. ‘Congratulations to you as well, Lisa, you’ve earned it.’

‘I’m not sure I have, but thank you. When do you come over officially?’

‘Next week.’ They are sitting in her office. Cully has put his cap and gloves under the seat. ‘I’m staying at Indah’s for the duration.’

‘I’m sure you…’ but stops herself.

‘You sent me an e mail about the Alumni Magazine?’

‘After we got the court order, you asked Monica and I to go through Sophie’s files, note books, professional diary, and tapes, but it’s taken us ages, because of day to day Island crime which I have to say has been a relief after,’ she hesitates, ‘well you know.’

‘I do. I was looking at the crime figures, pretty routine stuff by the look of it, but still takes time.’

‘We finished last week and want to know what to do with our findings. We know about her advert in the magazine and Sophie is contacted by several people wanting help and she puts the group together. In her diary, she calls it the Island group. Linda’s name is also in there, but as a one to one client.’

‘I suggested she contact Sophie after I saw the advert, but Linda doesn’t fit.’

‘Sophie saw you through Linda,’ Lisa states, smiling.

‘You’ve become a psychologist, Lisa?’

'Maybe, Gov,' she hesitates, 'it was also a subconscious way for you to get back in touch with Sophie.' No reply. 'In her diary, Sophie writes that she's in conflict with organising the group, she should have excused herself, but she convinces herself to run the sessions because she understands the people. I really don't think Sophie had a plan beyond wanting to help, but the group dynamic took over. She tape records group sessions and keeps written records of one to ones. She's very thorough. The key tapes are of twelve sessions. Don't get me wrong Sophie is really good and a group of victims do help each other through the process. James Brady, Vicar Mandy, Judge Le Strange, John Carter and Alison Grey made up the group with Sophie leading. We know the trauma each person suffered and we know they were all victims of the Nasty Gang.'

'In James Brady's file, recording the one to ones, he tells Sophie that he liked you, that he blamed himself for you getting the slipper from Poulson. Apparently he made a mistake in the work you copied so Poulson knew you'd cheated and where you got it from. He got the slipper and more from Poulson. He regretted dropping you in it.'

'I'm far too close to all this.'

'You've kept boundaries, Gov, right from the start,' Lisa reassures him. 'We found no evidence of the group conspiring, but that doesn't mean they didn't. I think Carter listened to everyone else, was surprised how the others welcomed and supported him and decided to be their avenging angel. In particular, James Brady. It's clear Carter and Brady developed a bond. Carter admits to abusing Brady, he apologises and Brady forgives him. After that Carter is like,' and she pauses, 'like a puppy dog in awe of Brady. During group sessions Carter talks about his interest in green issues. Sophie feeds it, encourages it. Sophie and Brady could have got Carter to do anything they wanted.'

'Go on, Lisa,' Cully encourages her.

'We know from Sophie's records Jamie was badly abused at school. He got a first in mathematics from Oxford. He did an MA in accountancy and by all accounts he's the best accountant you'll find. He's expensive, but worth every penny. As an Alumni and the accountant to many of the dead he knew all about them, understood them. I'm never getting an accountant, they come to know everything about you. Brady advertised in the Alumni Magazine and they all went to him. He knew every detail of their lives and if we get a forensic accountant involved I'm sure we'd find he eased the Simpsons into bankruptcy and maybe syphoned off from the others as well.'

‘Carla Scutari was in financial trouble as was Cameron Davis, but why take the money?’

‘Punishment. What if Brady used the money to finance the campaign to save the forest village, keeping Carter on side?’

‘Clever Jamie,’ Cully smiles. ‘So, if anyone worked with Carter it was Brady, and there’s no evidence to support what Tom is suggesting, a wider conspiracy.’

‘Exactly, but Tom won’t let go of the conspiracy theory, that the group planned it together with Sophie at the centre of the web.’

‘I’ll speak to him.’

‘Good luck, something’s wrong with him, but I don’t know what it is, being shot or a suspect in Kerry’s death, or baby brain.’

++++

‘Tom, your wife said to come through to your sanctum.’

‘Gov, I didn’t expect…’

‘No, just a welfare visit. Perhaps I should have rung ahead,’ Cully accepts. ‘I’m afraid I couldn’t resist looking behind the curtain and discovered this.’ He sits in the middle of the room looking at the wall covered with photographs and written notes. ‘Impressive stuff.’

‘I’ve had plenty of time.’

‘You’ve got Sophie at the centre of your web.’

‘Well she is isn’t she?’ Tom pulls a chair to sit next to Cully. ‘Never seen you in uniform before, Gov?’

‘I hate it, bloody uncomfortable, but I’ve an appointment. You look well Tom. How do you feel?’

‘Good, but it’s been tedious at home.’

‘I like that, the same picture we had in the incident room.’ Cully points to the long school photograph at the top of the wall. Strands of wool link young people in the photograph to the adult photographs below. ‘Past links the present.’

‘Not the same one though, Gov.’

‘Of course not Tom, you of all people wouldn’t remove case material.’

‘Congratulations on the promotion, Gov, it’s fantastic to have you in charge on the Island.’

‘Thanks. You’ve kept up with the changes?’

'Lisa up to DCI, Indah over to DVHC and Chalky promoted to sergeant and taking over armed response permanently. What about Becky?'

'She is too new to come into CID right away, but once she completes her second year, I've received assurances she can join us. Monica is seconded to us until you've settled back in and Pete is being allowed to retire without criminal charges over shooting Carter. He's getting married to the Healer. We're all invited to a forest wedding.'

'I'm not sure I'm ready for that, after what happened to me there,' Tom says softly. 'Gov, I need to talk to you.'

'I've got an appointment in an hour I can't miss, but I'm listening.'

'I've had so much time and…'

'I've heard you were sneaking around.'

'Not sneaking, Gov, researching. I don't think Carter acted alone. I'm not only thinking about Sophie.'

'Vicar Mandy?'

'Not sure.'

'Alison Grey?' Tom shrugs. 'Judge Le Strange, the forest-dwellers.'

'Forget the forest-dwellers, but the others all attended Sophie's group with Carter and could have planned it together.'

'A possibility, but unlikely. What about me Tom, do you think I'm the puppet master?'

'No of course not.'

'What about Linda, she was one of Sophie's clients?'

'Now you're making fun and she wasn't in the group.'

'Sorry.' Cully puts up his hands in surrender. 'You know the DCI and Monica have looked at Sophie as a possible nexus. They went through everything we got under court order from Sophie's therapeutic practise. They read the files and listened to all the tapes. They found nothing to make a case, but Sophie's on remand on Jenny Sykes' murder although I don't think there is a case to answer.'

'You wouldn't.'

'What do you mean by that Tom?'

'She's your Heloise.'

'Was Tom. Refusing her bail is crazy, but I agree with the need for a psychiatric assessment. She does seem rather obsessed and needs help.'

'Tizard may be involved. What's happening with him?'

‘It’s complicated, but they won’t make a murder charge stick in respect to Kerry.’

‘Because of me?’

‘Partly you and Mary as you both provide an alternative theory. MIU interviewed you?’ Tom nods. ‘To be honest Tom the evidence against the two of you is nearly as compelling as that against Tizard.’

‘I know,’ Tom agrees with a downward glance.

‘But maybe it was murder. Gerry argues that Kerry had drunk a large amount of alcohol in a short time. She hadn’t eaten a bite. If not unconscious, she would have been delirious, weak. It seems unlikely she could have hung herself, let alone stand, tie the noose to the beam, stand on a chair and kick it away. It seems more likely someone strung her up. However, Kerry could have planned her suicide, prepared the noose, got drunk and had enough strength to climb on the chair herself. We may never know.’

‘Tizard gets away with it?’

‘If he did it, but he’s not getting away with anything else. He’s off the force and has already pleaded guilty to the flashbang offences and got a fine. He denies having anything to do with supplying the Glock to Carter despite some evidence to the contrary. I think they’ll make a deal. You’ve had counselling?’

‘No.’

‘You were shot. Headquarters will take a poor view, if you don’t. The counsellor will have to sign you fit to work. Your wife says you’ve been feeling low, reluctant to go out. I’m concerned Tom, that’s all. We can discuss this again, but I’ve to get to my appointment. Come with me, we can talk in the car. Congratulations by the way.’

‘What about?’

‘Trudi’s pregnant. With two kids, you’ll need extra money. We need to get you through your inspectors legal exam and board. The Chief Constable is mumbling something about a disciplinary hearing after you contaminated the scene at Kerry’s, but I think I can persuade her otherwise.’

++++

‘Let’s talk about Kerry,’ begins the DCI from Serious Crime.

DCI Mount sits next to him. She rather likes him and now her husband has gone off with the bitch from the tennis club, she thinks: *'I could do with some company. He's wearing a wedding ring, but that doesn't mean a thing anymore.'*

'Tell me about her.'

'We've done this.'

'My client has co-operated.'

'Even so, you told us before she came after you?' he nods. 'How long did the affair last?'

'Nearly a year.'

'Kerry was home sick the day she died. She texted you at five. "I love you. Please come round". According to your phone you didn't look at that until six thirty. You didn't answer?'

'No, I deleted it.'

'And you deleted the next four messages, each getting more pleading, even desperate.'

'I figured she was drunk.'

'Did she drink a lot?'

'She could do.'

'At seven, she sent you another and then at seven thirty she sent you yet another which read; "You can't treat me like this. I'm going to tell everyone the truth". But you didn't read that one until nine. Why not?'

'I was with a friend.'

'Ah yes, your alibi. She says she doesn't know you.'

'She's a liar.'

'Can't blame her if she is. She's married to a local villain you once arrested. He's a violent offender. If he found out about this alleged—'

'It's true,' Tizard corrects, interrupting.

'If he found out about this alleged relationship, he'd probably kill her and you. True or not she's not going to say anything. You're screwed,' he smiles.

'My wife could have killed her. Kerry told me Mary threatened her and drugged her. She's strong enough to lift her up to the noose. Goody-two-shoes Tom Whitworth could have…'

'We've interviewed them. Moving on, at nine-ten constable Miller rang you to say there had been an incident at the rental house and you were needed.'

'Why your motorbike? Asks Mount, not wanting to be left out. 'That late at night, wouldn't your car have been quicker?'

'The bike is quicker.'

'Because you go cross country?'

'Sometimes, but not that night, I went by road.'

'I drove by car from your house to the rental house,' begins the DCI from Serious Crime, 'and, keeping to the speed limit, it took me twenty four minutes. If I had put my foot down, especially with empty roads as it would have been at the time of night you left home, I reckon I could have done it in fifteen. My colleague here, loves her motorbikes. Don't you Sergeant?'

'I do Sir,' agreed a woman officer sitting at the back of the room. Mount does not see her as competition for the DCI's affections, having decided the hatchet-faced woman is a lesbian. 'Yesterday, as you know I borrowed your machine. A lovely bike. I took it cross country on the route you suggested to Kerry's cottage and then to the house. How long do you think it took me?'

'I don't know.'

'Twenty minutes without stopping and I'm not used to the route.'

'It would have taken you longer at night.'

'How long did it take you?'

'I went by road.'

'But you often went across to Kerry's at night, didn't you?' No reply. 'You often told your wife you were working or going out for a ride to relax, but were in fact visiting Kerry?'

'Yes.'

'It was easy for you to visit her. You lied to your wife. You committed adultery with Kerry and took advantage of her vulnerability after the suicide of her father. She was a junior officer and you broke regulations by starting an affair with her.'

'We were based in different teams.'

'Did you love her?'

'No.'

'She was madly in love with you. So, it was just for sex?'

'I liked her a lot.'

'Right, but you had no plans to leave your wife and settle down with her?'

'No.'

'Let's go back to the night in question,' begins DCI Mount. 'Did you go to Kerry's cottage on the way to the rental house that night?'

'No.'

'The neighbour heard a motorbike.'

'He's an old man.'

'Old men don't hear right?' She pauses. 'The rope with which she was hung up has your DNA on it, can you explain?'

'We played games.'

'Sex games?'

'Yes, she liked to be tied up.'

DCI Mount wonders if she'd like to be tied up? '*Would it hurt? A little pain, not too much, but some like when her nipples are pulled and twisted.*'

'We've talked to three previous boyfriends and none of them say anything about Kerry enjoying bondage.'

'They were boys, she told me they didn't understand her.'

'But you did, you understood her needs and one of those needs was to be tied up during sex?'

'Yes.'

The interview continues in circles, but as it draws to an end the solicitor nudges Tizard.

'There is something I need to put straight, on which I misspoke.'

'You lied about. Go on.'

'The custody suit shooting. The Albanian starts shooting and then runs. He bumps into Pete who was having a cigarette outside.'

'The Pete Grimes that saved Linda Cully's life. Tied a tourniquet on her leg and kept her awake?'

'Yes, and the same one that's being let off for filling John Carter full of bullets,' Tizard snarls, but the DCI waves it away. 'I followed as Ted shot him and then,' he pauses, 'I shot him, but he didn't have a gun. It was already gone.'

'You shot an unarmed man?'

'Yes, I was scared, but I said he did to cover my back.'

'I was thinking,' the solicitor interrupts, then pauses, 'if we might be able to work out a deal?'

++++

'You know what they say when you arrive on the Island?' begins Cully as he slows behind a horse and cart carrying bales of hay.

'No, what?' admits Tom.

'Turn your watch back fifty years, maybe a hundred.'

'Where are we going, Gov?'

'You're an Islander aren't you, why have you never left?'

'I've never thought about it and when you leave you never come back.'

'Is that such a bad thing?' wonders Cully. 'Tom, I'll support you if you can find evidence to prove your theory beyond a reasonable doubt, but headquarters will not thank you if you're wrong.'

'Are you warning me off?'

'I'm asking you to think about your career,' says Cully swinging into a car park. 'Do you like ice cream Tom?'

'Yes, but you said you had an appointment.'

'I do, but this is connected. Come on, what's your favourite flavour.'

'Vanilla.'

'You should be more adventurous,' Cully tells him. Climbing from the car he leads the way into the ice cream parlour. The bell tinkles and two young women, both brunette with fox faces, look round. 'The girls are here,' he calls happily. 'You know Linda Tom and this is Sabrina, a nurse from the hospice. Do you want more ice cream?'

'Yes please and we've got everything organised for the wake,' Linda tells him.

'In here?' Tom is bemused. 'What's going on?'

'That's what he wanted Tom,' says Cully,' carrying two brimming cones across to a table. While the waitress takes more ice cream across to the young women. 'There you go,' licking his own pistachio. 'Tom, while you were away, the Chief Constable got her deputy and senior officers to go through everything we did and apart from a few procedural criticism, they agreed that Carter was a lone gunman. He was mentally ill and wanted to kill the people because of the abuse he suffered at the school. Case closed as far as they are concerned.'

'I've read the report and I'm not saying he wasn't the shooter. He was an obedient soldier.' Tom produces his note book. 'The Colonel told us that Carter took orders, but couldn't think for himself, but this whole thing is so sophisticated, well beyond him don't you think?'

'Turner identified him as a man he sold flashbangs to.'

'I know, but I believe other people were manipulating him, controlling him.'

'Headquarters are going to love you Tom.'

‘We have to get at the truth. That’s why we need to look deeper at Sophie and her group of alumni, to find the truth. I know it’s them,’ Tom states. ‘If anyone was in the perfect position, it’s them. They hated the Nasty Gang and they could manipulate someone like Carter.’

‘Why did these people wait so long to get help for their trauma and, if you’re right, seek revenge?’ But Cully already had an answer remembering the defence psychiatrist remarking that “aging is a chance to face hidden conflicts”.

‘We’d need to ask them, but eighteen months ago Inskip decides to use the Alumni Association to make money for the school. He didn’t want anything to do with the people who made up the Association, he wanted the brand. He came up with the idea of the glossy magazine and organising money spinning events. This is the first magazine,’ Tom says, pulling it from under his jacket and hands it to Cully. ‘It includes the decision to invite people to fund raising weekends in year groups. Look at the adverts and the names under the heading of “Alumni in the News”.’

‘I’ve seen it, uncle showed it to me when it came out. It didn’t do Inskip any good. A company has bought the school, will bulldoze the place to the ground and build luxury homes.’

‘In the magazine,’ Tom continues, not interested, ‘there are lots of adverts and amongst them is one for the therapeutic services offered by Sophie, another for James Brady’s accountancy business, one for Scutari’s fashion house and a fourth for the Simpson’s wine business. The names in the news include Judge Le Strange, Ballard for some oil deal he’s done and a piece about you. There’s also an article announcing the appointment of Mandy Bannon as vicar. I believe this magazine was the trigger starting everything. There are always consequences. A chain reaction. You said that to me beside the swimming pool in the rental house after we found the women.’

‘Dad,’ Linda appears next to them, ‘I’m heading on up. I’ll see you there.’

‘Sabrina?’

‘She’s staying here to organise things.’

‘See you there sweetheart. Anything else Tom?’

‘The accountant James Brady. We should interview him under caution. ‘The others are involved, Gov, I’m certain, but Sophie is key. Gov, we need to question Brady as a matter of urgency.’

‘You’ll need a psychic or a Ouija board to do that Tom.’

++++

'I thought Brady lived on the mainland?'

'He died here in the hospice and wants to be buried up top on the hill.'

'You knew he was here all the time, Gov?'

'I visited him the day of the school hall shootings.'

'You didn't say.'

'It wasn't immediately relevant and I respected his privacy, but you'll find it in Indah's report on me.'

Tom is silent, looking out of the window as they drive along the narrow winding road towards the top of the cemetery, trying to fit the new information into what he already thought he knew. He watches in silence as hundreds of graves in well drilled ranks pass by. 'How did he know about this place?'

'He came here with me and gran. Jamie was having a torrid time at school,' Cully explains, managing the car round a tight narrow bend. 'He wandered lonely as a child, poor Jamie. Every so often he would come and stay with us. We've always been close mates, do anything for each other.'

Cloud cover is grey and low. A mist is creeping in off the sea, rising from the valley towards them, gradually hiding the countryside and closing in.

'When you saw Brady at the Hospice, did he say anything?'

'I didn't interrogate him if that's what you mean?'

'I didn't mean…'

'He was full of morphine. Here we are.' Cully brings the car to a halt beside a row of metal watering cans hanging on a rail by a water trough. 'I used to fill a can for gran to water the flowers she brought to put on the graves. My wife, mum and grandmother are buried here all in a row. Hurry, we'll be late.'

Cully is gone before Tom moves. Getting out it is strangely quiet as the mist closes and he cannot see Cully. There is movement ahead. Tom shivers, then suddenly enters a clear space where The Reverend Skeets stands at the head of an open grave. To his left is Judge Le Strange. A few feet away Sophie, a uniformed figure standing behind her. At the far end of the grave stands Mandy Bannon. Cully is to the right of Skeets flanked by Indah and Linda. Between them and Mandy is Alison.

'Jesus said, 'I am the Resurrection and the Life; the one who believes in me, though he die, yet shall he live, and whoever lives and believes in me shall never die.' Skeets, head bent, orates the service in soft tones. Ten minutes later each of them throws a handful of soil into the grave, drumming on the coffin, before Skeets completes the committal. 'Grant that our brother James may sleep here in peace until you awaken him to glory.'

They stand in silence, each lost in thought, for several moments.

'I need to go,' declares Alison. 'Standing is still painful.'

'I'll give you a lift,' Linda says from the other side of the grave. 'Let's help you.' She walks round the hole in the ground, slipping her arm round Alison's waist. 'Come on, I know what it's like. I recommend strong painkillers. I keep some in my car. We can share them.'

Mandy throws her collar into the grave. 'I'm done,' and walks away.

'Mandy,' shouts Indah, 'wait for me.' She moves to go by Tom, but pauses. 'I've got my promotion. The Gov has a high opinion of you Tom, but don't do anything crazy. Think about it,' she advices. 'Mandy, I know the way down. I've walked it.' The mist engulfs them. 'Wait!'

'Cully, don't go.'

'Sophie?'

'You can still have me,' she pleads, her slate eyes lifeless. 'Make me feel something please. You know you can. I don't care about Indah, keep her, she's intelligent and beautiful, but please, don't leave me. We were always meant. I had fantasies about you and handcuffs,' she smiles, 'but not like this,' and lifts her hands to show her wrists are secured together. A female prison officer moves from behind her. 'I've got to go,' she says. 'I don't want to miss dinner,' she adds managing a thin smile.

'Sophie, I'm not going anywhere.' He leans forward, kisses her on the cheek and whispers, 'You'll be alright.'

'Sophie.'

'Yes Patrick?'

'I want to offer my services. I'm told I was a good barrister, although my niece thought I worked in a coffee shop,' he chuckles. 'I've dabbled in criminal law. I'd be more than happy to represent you against the forces of law and order. What do you say?'

'Yes please Patrick.'

'I'll walk you back to the van and then visit you on the remand wing tomorrow.'

They vanish into the grey.

'Sergeant Whitworth.'

'Reverend?'

'This is for you,' and Martin passes over a sheaf of paper. 'I and DC Kasali were with Jamie as he lay dying. It's his confession, the last words of a dying man dictated to us.' Skeets hands it over. 'No one else was involved apart from Carter and him. There are even,' and he groans, 'terrible, terrible films. Jamie wanted the truth out there. I'm staying and taking Mandy's place, if you want me,' and he walks away.

'Just us left Tom.' Swirls of mist swim between them. 'Any thoughts?'

'What am I going to do, Gov?'

'Give that statement to Lisa, engage with the counsellor and let your unfounded suspicions go. Then Inspector Whitworth will happen.' Cully steps away into the mist. 'Take care Tom.'

++++

The gate to the White House is open allowing him to drive through and park. He gets out, enjoying the warmth of the sun, walks to the front door, is surprised to find it open and steps inside. 'Gov, you here?' He looks into the front room, but there is no one there. Ten years since he'd been there, forgotten the cherubs climbing up the stairway. 'Gov!'

'Through here,' calls a woman.

Confused, Pete walks deeper into the house, entering the kitchen at the back of the building. He can see the garden through open French windows where there is a colourful display of summer flowers open to the sunshine. Bloated grey pigeons peck at the green lawn and there is bird song spilling from a row of fruit trees.

The woman sits on a stool on one side of the breakfast bar and points with a silenced pistol to the stool on the other. 'Sit.'

'Caitland, but how…'

'Please sit, Pete.'

'You're dead.'

'I'm not, am I?' She smiles. 'Recognise this?' He shrugs. 'It's the Glock 17, Pete.'

'The gun went missing in the church, how did you get it?'

'I was there, sitting in the front row. I look great in black. I took it when Carter dropped it and you executed him so thoroughly, to keep him quiet I presume.'

'Caitland, I...'

'I had to die to protect my family or *Groupa Europa* would have kept coming after us. I even went to my own funeral, saw you there, when they buried a box full of bricks.'

'Why am I here?' although he already knew. He stares, assessing her. Mid-forties, tall, long limbed, fox faced, hardbody under pale blue t-shirt and jeans, with brunette hair tied back. The woman reminded him of Linda, but that's where the similarity stopped, this woman was emotionless. 'Caitland?'

'Why, Pete?' She frowns. 'You've caused so much hurt, it pains me to think about all the terrible things you've done.'

'I doubt you feel hurt.'

'Why, because I'm not showing any emotion in respect to you and why would I?'

'I...' but Pete does not rush to answer, wondering if he can talk his way out. 'I needed the money, I was desperate. Ex-wives, three kids and I gambled, lost a lot, that's how they found me, through my debts.'

'They told you to find out where the Cully family were being hidden. They asked you because they guessed we were in a safe house somewhere in the south, probably on the Island. How much did they pay you to betray us?'

'Ten thousand and they said if I didn't help they'd kill my kids.'

'So it was your kids or my Linda? You could have come to us.'

'They would have killed us all. I had no choice Caitland, for god's sake.'

'Nice try, but taking the Glock after the shooting here at the White House and setting up your own business was your idea. You saw the Glock as an opportunity to make extra cash. You became an armourer for anyone prepared to pay. We believe this gun has killed twenty-five people, gang members, a financier here on the Island and a couple of redundant spouses. Literally a gun for hire. How am I doing?' Pete doesn't answer. 'At ten thousand pounds, a pop you've earned a tidy sum, but we know most of its gone, frittered away.'

'We?'

'Secret police, hidden state, intelligence services whatever name you want to use. You see because I'm dead, a clean skin, a ghost, I'm useful to the state,' Caitland smiles thinly. 'Eighteen months ago *Groupa* contacted you to make certain you were involved with the task force intercepting the Albanian smugglers. *Groupa* wanted it stopped, Serbians hate Albanians and it would eliminate the competition, but they wanted one Albanian to get away as they wished to deal with him personally. You gave him the Glock that nearly killed my daughter and Cully for a second time.'

'I didn't mean them to get hurt I saved Linda's life.'

'True, but it doesn't change what you did.'

'I like Linda a lot and Cully, he's a mate, it went wrong. I had no choice, the gang had me over a barrel. Does Cully know you're alive?'

'Of course and Linda.'

'Do they know what you're doing here and now?'

'No, this down to me and me alone, Pete,' she smiles coldly. 'Moving on. You got the Glock back and a few months ago leased it to John Carter for the school shooting that's why you were desperate to find him and kill him, you didn't want him questioned.'

'I didn't know what he was going to do. I'm ready to do a deal,' Pete says. There is a tremor in his voice now. 'I can give you a list of the people that hired the gun.'

'We've got that. My daughter is the most precious thing in the world to me,' Caitland continues softly. 'She was terrified by your betrayal here and was nearly killed eighteen months ago. You can't begin to imagine what pain she's been in because of you.' She does not take her eyes off him. 'Cully has done so much to support you, yet you so easily betray him and nearly got him killed on three occasions.'

'I'm sorry.'

'But I've found a way out.' Caitland pushes a sheet of typed paper across the worktop. 'Sign this.'

'What is it?'

'Your suicide note. We've included the sort of typos you make and your fingerprints and DNA are on it. My colleagues are thorough. When the police read it, they will hear the voice of a depressed man, suffering from PTSD, explaining he feels guilty about Tom, Cully and John Carter.'

'I'm not signing that.' Pete looks away, considering his options. He could run through the French windows or the front door, fling himself across the worktop or...but there is nothing else and there is something cold and calculating about this woman and he's not fit. Cully is always on at him to get fit. 'I won't.'

'Sign it and your reputation remains intact, your kids will get your death in harness grant and pension and it'll save the police force embarrassment. Take the deal, Pete.'

'No.'

'If you don't, I will shoot you, leave you incapacitated to bleed out and then drive the short distance to slowly kill your new woman in the forest. I will then take a ferry to the mainland and kill your children.'

'You wouldn't.'

'I've even got the route planned on my car navigation system. I'm as cold hearted and ruthless as *Groupa Europa*. They made me, remember? Please believe me, Pete.' She's quick to transfer the Glock to her left hand and produce another in her right which she levels at him. 'I thought it would be fitting for you to shoot yourself with this very Glock,' and she spins the gun across the divide. Only one bullet. The police will think you picked it up at the church, already planning your way out. Your choice entirely, Pete.'